CupidCats

KATIE MacALISTER

CONNIE BROCKWAY

VICKI LEWIS THOMPSON

A SIGNET ECLIPSE BOOK

SIGNET ECLIPSE
Published by New American Library, a division of
Penguin Group (USA) Inc., 375 Hudson Street,
New York, New York 10014, USA
Penguin Group (Canada), 90 Eglinton Avenue East, Suite 700, Toronto,
Ontario M4P 2Y3, Canada (a division of Pearson Penguin Canada Inc.)
Penguin Books Ltd., 80 Strand, London WC2R 0RL, England
Penguin Ireland, 25 St. Stephen's Green, Dublin 2,
Ireland (a division of Penguin Books Ltd.)
Penguin Group (Australia), 250 Camberwell Road, Camberwell, Victoria 3124,
Australia (a division of Pearson Australia Group Pty. Ltd.)
Penguin Books India Pvt. Ltd., 11 Community Centre, Panchsheel Park,
New Delhi - 110 017, India
Penguin Group (NZ), 67 Apollo Drive, Rosedale, North Shore 0632,
New Zealand (a division of Pearson New Zealand Ltd.)
Penguin Books (South Africa) (Pty.) Ltd., 24 Sturdee Avenue,
Rosebank, Johannesburg 2196, South Africa

Penguin Books Ltd., Registered Offices:
80 Strand, London WC2R 0RL, England

First published by Signet Eclipse, an imprint of New American Library,
a division of Penguin Group (USA) Inc.

First Printing, July 2010
10 9 8 7 6 5 4 3 2 1

CUPID CATS SHELTER:
Bring a little magic and love into your life
Adopt a Cat

Unleashed

by Katie MacAlister

Chapter 1

"*T*hey ran right over me, and my head came off. I kid you not, Jas; my head came right off! There I was, lying in the mud without a head, and a herd of oxen stomping all over me. It was surreal! No, more than surreal. Well, it *was* a past-life regression, so I expect a certain amount of surreal is bound to be there, but still, my head! In the mud! And cows all over me! Well! You're not going to believe what happened next!"

"That's hardly surprising, given that I don't believe what you're telling me now," I murmured, squinting at the computer screen.

"Then the woman who ran me over with her ox cart got down and tried to put my head back on, just like in a cartoon or something, but of course that didn't work."

"Of course." I frowned as I scanned the latest memo to come from my supervisor. "Greg can't possibly be serious. The entire department will use his guts for garters if he thinks cutting the release-to-wild program will ease budget concerns."

"So then this guy comes along, and he sees the crazy ox woman with my head and, after all sorts of misadventures, he bites her!" my sister continued, obviously too caught up in the bizarre dream she was telling me about to pay attention to anything else. She picked up a pen and spun it around her fingers.

Shaking my head at my e-mail in-box and sighing, I took my favorite pen from Corazon and went back to deciphering the latest governmental mandate regarding the proposed hatchery and fishery reform policy, listening with half my attention as she yammered on.

"He was kind of cute, although all that blood . . . urgh. I tell you, Jas, it was freaky, downright freaky."

"Dreams often are," I said absently, giving up on the policy. Although it was a bit out of my bailiwick, concerned as I was with the enforcement of the Washington Department of Fish and Wildlife laws, and not policy, it behooved me as an officer of that department to stay current on anything that might affect my job.

"It wasn't a dream!" She whacked me on the arm. "Aren't you listening? It was a past-life regression! It was all real! Well, it was real in the past, but I was reliving it. Anyway, I came a bit unglued at the vampire, so I made Barbara, the hypnotherapist, bring me out of it. And then Patsy told us about her gorgeous neighbor who swims naked, and we went over, only she had to wee, and *he* was the vampire."

That last word caught my attention. I turned to look in astonishment at her. Although she was eighteen months younger than I, we looked enough alike to frequently be confused as twins. Her hair was the exact same shade of amber as mine, although her eyes were a darker brown, mine waffling toward hazel. "You were a vampire in your past life? Do Mom and Dad know?"

"Will you listen to me?" Cora's expression was rife with annoyance. "I wasn't the vampire; he was—Patsy's neighbor."

"Patsy, your friend? She has a neighbor who is a vampire?"

"Yes! At least, she didn't seem to think he was one, but because I had to fly up here first thing this morning, I haven't had a chance to talk to her since she and Terri brought me home last night. But, Jas—vampires! They exist!"

"Nonsense," I scoffed. "You were probably just lit up and imagined all of it."

"Oh, we were drunk all right," she admitted, opening the top drawer of my desk and absently poking through it. "But there's nothing like a vampire to sober you up right away. I didn't imagine either the past-life thingy or Patsy's neighbor. Oh my God, did you kill this bear?"

I took the picture from her and tucked it away in my drawer again. "You know I don't kill animals unless they are severely injured and too far gone to be transported to a vet. That bear was just sedated."

"You have the best job," she said with more than a dollop of envy in her voice. "Beats being a secretary to hell and back again."

Catching sight of a familiar figure in the doorway to the office, I ducked low over my desk, pulling Cora down with me as I prayed Greg wouldn't stroll back to this part of the room. "Hide!"

"Huh?"

"It's Greg. I don't want him to see us."

"Oh, your evil boss?" She hunkered down with me. "Is he still hitting on you?"

"He backed off after I mentioned the phrase 'sexual harassment' to him, but that's not why I'd prefer not seeing him. The latest worm in his brain is to go out in the field with all the officers and evaluate their work. Not for promotion purposes, but because he's kissing up to the lieutenant governor's butt by proposing all sorts of departmental cuts, and he's looking for people to ax."

"Morning, kitty," one of my coworkers said as she strolled past me, carefully setting down a latte cup on the desk of the cubicle next to mine. Still hunched over, I rolled backward in my chair enough to glare at her. She giggled.

"Why did she call you kitty?" Cora asked in an exaggerated whisper. "Oh my God, Jas, you're not undercover, are you? Some sort of animal spy?"

"You are watching way too much of the espionage channel," I told her with a quelling look. "I am a simple wildlife officer, nothing more."

"Hey, kitty." Joe, an officer who worked the graveyard shift in the region next to mine, tossed a manila file folder on my desk. "While you were getting your beauty sleep, we caught the cougar that attacked the kid. Looks like you're off the hook for whispering, eh?"

I tried to punch him, but he deftly sidestepped my attack and laughed as he walked away.

Cora raised a questioning eyebrow at me.

"I'm not undercover. It's just that people here . . ." I

ground my teeth for a moment. "They call me the kitty whisperer."

"The what?"

"Kitty whisperer. Because I work with big cats. It's just a joke, nothing more. A very irritating joke," I said loudly as I glared toward Jane, my coffee-bearing neighbor.

She laughed.

"Your coworkers think you have the psychic ability to talk to cats?" Cora asked with blank incredulity before bursting into a ripple of laughter. "You! Psychic! You're the least psychic person I know!"

"Hush!" I said, pinching her wrist as I carefully poked my head over the cubicle wall to look for Greg. He stood at the door, talking with some poor victim who'd been unwary enough to enter the room without first checking whether the coast was clear. "It's bad enough without your adding to it."

"You don't believe in anything paranormal," Cora said in a quieter tone, although mirth still filled her voice. "I can tell you don't even believe in my vampire."

"That's because they don't exist any more than people can psychically talk to animals. The skills I have in understanding the feline mind come from years of work, not from any woo-woo source. Oh, hell, what now?"

I'd glanced at my computer screen while talking and saw the new e-mail in my in-box. I groaned at the subject line.

"What are you 'oh, hell'ing about?" Cora asked, wiping tears of laughter from her eyes. "Is it something to do with your taking me out into the bush today? Because I have only four days here before my cruise to Alaska starts, and you promised me a day of nature and hiking and all sorts of exciting wildlife."

"I'm taking you out in the field, not the bush." I quickly turned off the e-mail client without reading the e-mail. "And I promised you nothing of the sort. I said you could come along with me while I made my rounds, but if anything dangerous comes up, you'll have to stay in the truck. Before you ask again, no, the e-mail isn't going to cancel our outing. It's just from the owner of a sheep farm complaining yet again about the regional crackpot, Albert Baum."

"Hunter?" she asked, knowing how much grief we in the Fish and Wildlife Department have with irresponsible hunters.

"No, just the opposite—very antihunting. Albert Baum heads up the Leshies, an animal rights collective up in the mountains."

"That sounds like it's right up your alley," Cora said, shifting backward so I could get into the bottom drawer of my desk to pull out my gun and holster.

"Well, I admire their goals of preserving endangered animals, but it's the method they use that gets on my nerves. They go around scaring non-endangered animals away from hunters, which sends the hunters screaming at us to stop them. We've also caught them setting mantraps to injure folks, but that ended after we tossed a couple of Baum's group in jail. The latest bee in Baum's bonnet is the way we release captured animals into the wild. He wants us to release them on his land so he and his group can protect them."

"That doesn't seem too bad," Cora said, watching with interested eyes as I packed my field case with a mini first-aid kit, notebook, tranquilizing gun and darts, and assorted measuring equipment.

"It's a matter of what's legal and what isn't. The Leshies have almost ten thousand acres they call preserves scattered around three states. But neither the preserves nor the group is recognized by the government as being such, so we can't release animals into the Leshies' custody." I peered over the cubicle wall again. "Oh, good, he's gone. Come on—let's make a dash for it."

I snagged my car mug as we skulked out of the office, hustling Cora before me to the latte cart in the lobby of the building. As I was looking for money, my cell phone burbled, indicating I'd received a voice mail.

"Phone," Cora said helpfully. "So, if people think you are a kitty whisperer, does that mean I'm a vampire whisperer?"

I goggled at her as I punched in the code that would bring up my voice mail. "What?"

"Well, you said you can talk to cats because you spent all that time in Africa studying lions and cheetahs and things like that, so maybe I'm a vampire whisperer because I had that past-life thing going on with Patsy's gorgeous bloodsucking neighbor."

"We seriously need to investigate the possibility of getting you some counseling," I told her before holding up my hand so I could listen to the message.

"Pot, kettle, black," she said, digging out money to pay for our lattes.

"Jacintha! Just the person I was looking for."

I groaned to myself as I accepted the travel mug now filled with a latte. "Damn it. He walks as softly as a cat," I muttered to Cora before turning to greet my boss with a polite smile. "Morning, Greg."

"Coming in or going out?" he asked, giving me one of his quasi-leering once-overs before he turned his attention to Cora. "Ah, this must be your sister I've heard so much about."

Cora blinked in surprise at him.

"We're just heading out, and yes, this is Corazon."

Greg shook her hand as he said in what I'm sure he thought was a seductive voice, "Two such pretty sisters. I've always had a fondness for Latina women, you know."

"Have you?" she said with only the faintest hint of a twitch around her mouth. "Whereas I just can't get enough of pasty-assed WASP guys. Not that I'm implying your ass is pale. But you know what I mean."

It was my turn to stifle a smile. I did my best to ignore my outspoken little sister, giving her a shove toward the door. "Sorry, Greg. We're in a bit of a hurry. Just got a call."

"Ah. Excellent. I'll tag along with you, if you don't mind. A morning's hike in the mountains will do me good," he said, holding the door open for us.

Cora shot me a horrified glance.

"Oh, Greg, that is too bad." I summoned up what I hoped passed for an expression of regret. "I wish I could ask you along for the survey, but I just got a call for a pickup of a cat over at the animal shelter, and I know your allergies would make it hell for you to be in the truck with one."

"A cat at an animal shelter?" he asked, squinting slightly. Greg Morrison was tall, blond, handsome, and extremely suave—too suave for my tastes. That he was my boss, I could live with, but there was something about him I didn't trust. He was too handsome, his smile just a bit too charming, his eyes entirely too innocent. Most of the women in the department were in love with him, all but those in my office, who knew he was looking to cut positions in order to plump up the budget. "Surely they don't need an officer for that?"

"This is a big kitty," I said, smiling.

"Lynx?"

"Bigger."

"Not another cougar?" he asked, dismay visible in his clear blue eyes.

"Sounds like it," I said, crossing my fingers against the little white lie.

"Oh." His face fell. I could see him struggling with the desire to spend the day shadowing me, and the unwillingness to put his raging fur allergies on edge. He rubbed his nose as if just thinking about it made him itch. "Perhaps if I took an extra shot—"

"I wouldn't dream of putting you through so much physical discomfort," I said swiftly, edging around him toward the front doors. "I'll have to spend some time with the cat, examining it, taking measurements, trying to locate where it came from, and so on, and I know how even the hint of dander on someone's clothes can make your face swell up."

He took a step back from me as if I were already contaminated by cat. "I suppose you're right. Although it seems a shame to waste such a perfect opportunity for discussing the plans I have for your region—"

"Another time!" I said, giving him a toothy smile as I pushed Cora through the open door and hurried through it.

"Wow. You're right. He is a creep. Likes Latina women, indeed!" Cora huffed as we headed out to the car lot where the state trucks were located. "You should totally be reporting his ass to the HR people for sexual harassment."

"So long as he's not openly hitting on me, I can live with it," I murmured as I signed out a truck.

"Hrmph. So I get to see a cougar up close and personal?" she asked, plopping down into the truck.

"Only from a distance." I scooted in behind the steering wheel and opened my laptop to fire up an incident report, filling in the information from the voice mail. "You can stay in the truck and see the cat from there."

"Aw, Jas!"

"It's too dangerous," I said, typing up a brief summary. "I have no idea what sort of a state the cougar is in. It could be hurt, and very dangerous for someone who doesn't know how to handle one."

"Keep up that tone of superiority, and I'll start calling you kitty, too," she answered, crossing her arms and glaring out the window as I closed the laptop and stared at the truck.

Luckily, Cora had never been one to hold a snit for long. She was silent for all of five minutes. "Right, so you're a cat whisperer. Got that."

"I'm not any such thing."

"And you go out and rescue people who have been attacked by bears and cougars and stuff. Got that, too."

"More like I rescue the animals from people."

"But what I don't get is why they're calling you in for an animal shelter. Yes, it's a cougar, but I mean, can't they just open the door and shoo it out?"

"It's part of my job to deal with any sort of a nuisance animal, be it deer and elk grazing on valuable crops, or the more dangerous beasties that end up in human areas due to encroaching development on the little habitat left to them. So no, they can't just open the door and shoo it. I will have to sedate it, and, after an examination, will take it to a release area deep in the mountains where it will hopefully keep away from further contact with humans."

"Bet that drives your PETA group nuts."

"We don't have PETA here; just the Leshy group, and they're enough, thank you."

"So what other kind of animals do you have to rescue from people?" she asked, opening the case for my digital camera.

"The big four are bears, cougars, lynx, and bobcats. Those are the dangerous ones, and put that back before you drop it. I need to take pictures of the cougar for the incident report."

"What's a cougar doing at an animal shelter, anyway? It didn't, like, break in to eat the other animals, did it?"

"No, of course not. Don't be ridiculous. Cougars normally stay far away from people. But what this one is doing in the shelter is a very good question," I answered, wondering the same thing. Luckily, we didn't have long to wait. Allison, the manager of the Cupid Cats Shelter, was waiting in the back of the building with three other women, all huddled around together and each clutching a paper latte cup.

"Jacintha! I'm so glad you're here!" Allison said, separating from the pack to hurry toward me. "We can't even get in because he's awake. Oh, hello. Are you another ranger?"

"This is my sister, Cora." I clipped the tranquilizing gun to my belt, making sure the cartridge was loaded.

"I'm a secretary, not a wildlife control person," Cora said as she climbed out of the truck. "This is so exciting! I've never seen a cougar up close before. Did it eat any of your animals?"

"Merciful heavens, I hope not," Allison replied, looking horrified. "I never even thought of that. Jo?"

Jo was Allison's partner, a no-nonsense woman who handled all the unpleasantries that came with running a cat shelter, leaving Allison to charm patrons and contributors. She frowned. "Didn't see any signs that he'd eaten anyone."

"You said it was a cougar with melanistic coloring? I don't think I've ever seen a black cougar before. How badly is it hurt?" I asked, glancing at my watch and making a note of the time in my pocket notebook.

"I don't think it's a cougar," Allison answered, her hands fluttering. She was a petite woman, prone to soft, gauzy materials, with a halo of burnished gold curls. Her face bore testimony to having lived at least a handful of decades, but it was unlined, somehow ageless. "He's big, though, and there are markings in his black coat."

"Markings?" I pulled on my leather gloves, the heavy ones I wore to deal with wounded animals. "Like a leopard, you mean?"

"Yes, just like that. Wouldn't you say so, Jo?"

"A leopard!" Cora said in a delighted tone. "Wow! Can I take the pictures? I'd like to get a couple for me to show the ladies at work. They aren't going to believe I came to Washington and saw a leopard."

Jo's face scrunched into a thoughtful expression. "Looked like one of those spotty cats to me. He's a big boy, so you be careful in there with him, Jas."

"You're going to stay out here where it's safe," I told Cora, taking the camera from her and putting it back into the truck. "If the leopard is awake, as Allison says, he is probably very frightened and possibly injured."

"You are such a party pooper," she told me.

I turned to Allison. "You said you found him inside, with the doors locked? No signs of a break-in?"

"None," Jo said. "I came in to check on the medical cases and opened up the office, and there he was, big as life, lying right in the middle of the hallway. Looked drugged to me, not injured, although he lifted his head and growled at me when I came into the room. Almost stepped on him, in fact. Gave me quite a start. Al thought we should wait for you to take care of him rather than try to shift him ourselves."

"That's always a good idea when it comes to wildlife, although if it really is a leopard, it must be from someone's private collection. Someone's *illegal* private collection," I mused. "But how he ended up here . . . Well, perhaps the answer is inside."

"Jas, are you sure I can't just come in and have a peek?"

"No. Stay out here where it's safe."

Allison looked worried as I gathered up my things and headed for the heavy metal door that led to the kennel area of the shelter. "You'll be careful, won't you, Jas? I don't think he knows where he is, and he may be confused enough that he lashes out without thinking."

"Oh, don't worry," I said as I opened the door and paused to toss a smile back to them. "I know my way around a big cat. There's nothing your visitor can do that will take me by surprise."

Chapter 2

"Hello, kitty. Ah, not a leopard, but a jaguar. How very interesting. Where did you come from, I wonder? There's a jaguar colony in Arizona, but you are way out of your territory. What on earth are you doing in Washington State, of all places?"

The big cat lying smack-dab in the middle of the hallway lifted his head and peered groggily at me. Even though he was a rich black, I could see the faint rosette pattern in his coat, and the stockier, heavier frame that, combined with a shorter tail, told me this cat originated in South America, not Africa, as the leopard did.

"Well, well, well. You look healthy, at least," I said, pulling out my mini tape recorder as I slowly approached the cat. "Incident report #3421, Jacintha Ferreira, investigating officer. Location is the Cupid Cats Shelter. Subject is a male melanistic jaguar, approximately one hundred kilograms, about seventy-five centimeters at the shoulder, and length slightly under two meters."

I'm six foot two, actually.

I spun around at the sound of the male voice, but there was no one in the hallway with me. "Hello? Who's there? Cora, is that you?"

Behind me, the cat growled huskily as he scrabbled on the floor with long, wicked claws until he managed to heave himself onto his chest, his heavy head bobbing as he tried to hold it up.

"Cora, damn it, I told you to stay outside!"

Silence filled the building. It had a thick quality to it, the kind you get when you are the only person in the place. "Cora?"

Only the faint sound of a logging truck rumbling down the highway filtered through the dense silence. "That wasn't Cora," I said to myself, keeping one eye on the cat. It was a man. "Whoever you are, please stay back. I don't need the cat frightened," I said in a louder voice, but no one answered me.

"Great. Now I'm imagining voices." I watched the cat warily for a moment, assessing just how drugged he was. Cats coming out of sedation will sometimes strike at a keeper, not in anger, but purely as a protection response. The big cat's head bobbled a bit more until he finally laid it down between his paws, his big blue eyes unfocused.

"Blue eyes?" I said aloud, dropping to my haunches in order to appear less dominating to the cat. "I've never seen a jaguar with blue eyes." I flipped my voice recorder back on. "Subject appears to have been sedated and is aware of his surroundings, but mostly unable to control primary motor functions. Subject also exhibits unusual coloring of the irises."

I get my eyes from my mother.

"Please, whoever you are, this is no place for frivolity!" I glared over my shoulder down the hallway behind me, making sure to keep my voice level and calm, lest the cat pick up on my anger. "I must insist that you leave right now."

All right, but I think you're going to have to help me up off the floor. I should never have had that last drink. It's given me a hell of a hangover.

"Look, here, Mr. Smart-Ass," I said, my voice tightening as I got to my feet. The cat's tail twitched irritably. I made an effort to move slowly and speak with a placidity that was belied by my words. "I am an officer of the fish and wildlife department. If you do not leave the premises, I will arrest you for interfering with the duty of a peace officer. Got that? Good. Now scram."

Oh, man. My head is killing me. I mean seriously killing me. It's like someone is pounding right here.

The jaguar growled and rubbed one paw over its face.

"That's it. No more nice guy," I said, gritting my teeth slightly as I edged my way down the hall.

A tendril of cold air wrapped around me. "Jas? You okay in there? You've been awfully quiet. Aren't you supposed to let us know you're all right?"

Cora's head poked around the doorjamb.

"Do you see anyone back there?" I demanded.

"Where? Here?" She slid into the room and turned three hundred sixty degrees. "Nope, just me. Why?"

"Because a man keeps talking, and I don't know where he is."

"Want me to look—oh, wow! Is that him? He's black!"

I am?

"He's not a leopard; he's a jaguar—and what are you doing in here?" I asked, worry about the unknown stranger in the building having driven out concern for my sister. "Go back outside where it's safe."

"Stop hogging all the fun. He doesn't look like he could hurt a fly, let alone attack two grown women."

Appearances are deceiving. I'm quite dangerous when I want to be. Rawr.

"Look, whoever you are, just get the hell out of here!" I said, spinning around to throw open the door to the front area of the shelter.

"Who are you talking to?"

"The man! Didn't you just hear him? He's boasting about being dangerous."

I never boast.

"There! He just did it again!"

Well, almost never.

Cora pursed her lips. "Um . . . okay. I didn't hear anyone, Jas."

"Don't you play games with me, missy," I told her in my most obnoxious older-sister voice. "Of course you heard him. He spoke just as clearly as anything."

"Uh-uh. I don't hear anyone talking but you."

I gritted my teeth, determined to find the jokester. Cora followed me as I stormed through the reception area, Allison's office, Jo's office, and the small hospital area before returning to the corridor leading to the cattery.

"Well?"

"This is ridiculous. I could hear him. I know someone else is here."

"I don't think so, Jas, not unless he's disappeared into thin air. We've looked everywhere. Unless you really are a cat talker, and you're hearing Midnight, there," Cora said, waving at the groggy jaguar.

Christ, I didn't think it was possible to have a hangover this bad.

I looked with animosity at my sister. "I suppose you're going to tell me you didn't hear that?"

"Hear what?"

I felt like banging my head on the wall I leaned against, but that wouldn't help the drugged jaguar. "It's only a little after ten in the morning, and already I'm tired of this day."

You and me both. Would you mind helping me up off the floor . . . er . . . What did you say your name was? Jacintha? Pretty. I seem to be a bit out of it.

The jaguar grumbled and tried to get to his feet, heaving himself up until his four legs were splayed out, barely supporting him as he weaved back and forth. He looked down at his feet for a moment, then up at me, his eyes wide with shock.

What the hell?

"Wow, he's really pretty, isn't he? Can I pet him?"

I stared at the cat, my flesh crawling.

What the hell?

"Do you think he'd bite me if I got close enough for you to get a picture of us together? I'd love a shot of us so I could put it up on my Facebook page."

Two things struck me at that moment—the first was that no one else was in the building other than Cora, and the second was that it was the cat who was talking.

"Holy Mary and all the little saints," I swore, star-

ing at the cat as goose bumps trotted up and down my
arms and legs.

"No? Damn. That'd be a picture to end all pictures,"
Cora said, looking from the jaguar to me. "What's
wrong? Why do you have such a weird look on your
face?"

"Did you just . . . uh . . . talk?"

I'm a panther?

"Of course I just talked. I've been talking the whole
time." She squinted at me. "You're not having some
sort of a nervous breakdown or something, are you?"

"Not you. The . . . er . . . cat."

A panther?

The cat's voice sounded wild with horror and shock
and surprise, which pretty much mirrored my own
feelings. It was then I realized he was speaking without moving his lips.

"Holy shit! You really can cat whisper? How cool
is that!" Cora exclaimed, looking utterly delighted.
"What's he saying?"

"He appears to be upset he's a jaguar," I said slowly,
narrowing my gaze on the cat, looking for a radio trans-
mitter. "How are you doing that? Are you some sort of
ventriloquist? Oh God, what am I saying? He's a cat,
Jas. He's not a ventriloquist. He's not talking. Someone
else is. You must have a radio on you somewhere, kitty,
although I'll be damned if I know where."

*Avery. My name is Avery, Avery Scott, and how the hell
did I get changed into a black panther? What did you do to
me?*

"So it's the cat who's been talking to you all along?
This is *so cool*!"

"I didn't do anything to you," I told the cat slowly. "Cora, this is . . . this is really strange. You don't think my mind has snapped, do you? You don't think I'm really insane? Holy Mary! I'm an insane cat whisperer. Make it stop, Cora! I don't want to be crazy!"

Well, I don't want to be a black panther, either, the voice in my head answered, in a somewhat surly tone that irritated me. *Of the two of us, I think I have more grounds for complaint.*

"I don't think you're crazy," Cora said, eyeing me closely. "I think you can just talk to cats." She glanced at the wobbly jaguar. "Really big cats. Is he talking now? What's he talking about? Does he have a Spanish accent?"

"No, he has an English accent."

Scottish.

"Correction, Scottish."

"You're talking to a Scottish jaguar?" Cora's incredulity was great, but it was nothing on what I was feeling.

What the hell did you do to turn me into a panther?

"Look," I told the cat, my hands on my hips, distracted by his ignorance. "You're a melanistic jaguar, not a black panther. There is no such thing as a black panther. So stop calling yourself that, and lie back down before you fall over and hurt yourself. Now, let me think. . . . When did I go insane? I was fine this morning. . . ."

"Weren't the black panthers some sort of radical rights group?" Cora asked, taking a step back as the jaguar weaved toward her. "You're talking to an extremist, politically agendaed Scottish jaguar? Man! I've heard about some of those South American political groups. They kidnap people."

"I don't think he's a Scottish jaguar," I said softly, unnerved by the look in the strange blue eyes.

For the love of all that's holy, woman, I'm not a jaguar! No Moravian has ever been a shape-shifter, and I don't intend to start a new trend.

"Moravian? Isn't that somewhere in Russia? I thought you said you had a Scottish accent?"

"He's Russian? Russian Mafia?" Cora asked, looking confused. "You know, Jas, this is odd. Really odd. I think you have even my past-life regression beat."

Moravian Dark One is the technical term. And before you ask, yes, I have my soul.

"What a bizarre thing to say."

"What is?" Cora asked, watching the jaguar closely.

"He told me he is from Russia, and he has his soul."

"Hmm. It must be important, though. I mean, why would a strange jaguar march up and tell you he has a soul if it wasn't important? Hey, why is he banging his head on the wall?"

"I don't know. I'll ask him. Avery—"

"Huh?"

"He said that's his name. Avery, why are you banging your head on the wall?"

You and your sister are driving me daft, woman! I told you I have my soul because of what I am. Dark Ones don't have souls. I have one; hence the fact I'm what is normally referred to as a Moravian. My parents were Joined before I was born, you see.

"Uh . . ."

"What's he saying?" Cora asked in a whisper, pluck-ing at my sleeve.

Now, my brother Paen, he didn't have a soul, not until he met Sam. She got it back for him, which is a long story I won't go into now. Will you please change me back so I can return to being a perfectly normal Moravian?

"He's talking about some people called Dark Ones who don't have souls. Maybe I'm not the insane one after all," I said, considering the cat. "Maybe he is."

I'm not insane, although I'm about to get very, very pissed, and you don't want me to go there.

"Oh?" I tipped my head and looked the wobbly cat up and down. "Why? What will you do?"

For a moment, my mind was filled with erotic im-ages, those involving a handsome blond, blue-eyed man doing the most amazing things to me, things that set my body humming with desire and passion. "Holy Mary!"

There's more, but I don't think you're ready to hear about it, the cat said in a sage voice, squinting at me. *Now, whatever it is you did to me, make it stop.*

"I didn't do anything to you."

Cora looked from the cat to me. "He thinks you did something to him? Did what?"

"Turned him into a jaguar, evidently."

Do I look like I was born yesterday? His eyes narrowed even more as he eyed me up and down. *Are you nursing a grudge against me? Did I love you and leave you? I don't recall doing so, but the events of last night are a bit fuzzy. Still, you don't look like the kind of woman I'd get tired of quickly.*

"You are really offensive, you know that?" I told

him. "If you were a man and you said that to me, I'd deck you."

"Now you've lost me."

"It doesn't matter. He's just being cranky."

I am not cranky! I do not get cranky! And I am a man. Well, I'm male, since Moravians aren't strictly human. Change me back!

"How many times do I have to tell you that I didn't do anything to you! I'm an officer of the fish and wildlife department. I'm not a . . ." My hands waved around in a vague gesture as I turned to my sister. "What sort of person turns other people into jaguars?"

"Oh, mercy. I don't know." She bit her lower lip. "A witch, maybe?"

"I think Wiccan is the politically correct term these days, and I'm not sure they can change people into things," I answered, turning back to the cat. "Well, I don't know what sort of person would change someone into a jaguar. I mean, that's impossible to begin with, but I'm not very well versed on folklore, so I don't know what that would be, but whatever it is, I'm not one."

Folklore, he said slowly, as a speculative look came into his unnaturally blue eyes. *The Leshies!*

Now that was a word I was familiar with. "Leshies? Did you say Leshies?"

Yes. Danielle's family, to be specific. Oh Christ, that I do remember. She wanted me to marry her.

"The animal whackos?" Cora asked.

The cat looked consideringly at her. *You know them?*

"I do, a little. Cora doesn't."

"I don't what?"

"Know the Leshies. I've dealt with them a few times," I said cautiously.

You're not part of them, are you?

"No. I told you, I work for the state. But what does a group of animal rights activists have to do with you?" It was becoming easier and easier to believe that the cat wasn't what he seemed, although my brain had a hard time wrapping itself around the thought that the jaguar before me was really a man.

I just told you. Danielle wanted me to marry her. But I refused. Somehow, one of the Leshies changed me into a panther.

"Jaguar," I said automatically.

I wonder who changed me? It was probably her father, the wicked old sod. She said he wouldn't let the matter lie when I turned her down.

"You're talking about Albert Baum, aren't you? I've never met his daughter, I'm afraid."

That's the bastard. He did this to me! Well, if he thinks that's the end of the matter, he can bloody well think again. No one messes with a Moravian.

"What's he saying?" Cora hissed.

I gave her a brief rundown before turning back to the cat. "I'm sorry. I'm still confused. You keep saying you're from Moravia, but you're also Scottish?"

Moravians are commonly referred to in mortal terms as vampires, he said absently. I could feel him thinking furiously, creating and discarding any number of plans of revenge.

"Vampires?" I gasped, the word reverberating in my brain.

"What?" Cora reeled back.

"Avery the cat says he's . . . a vampire," I said, feeling my eyes bug out a little.

"Oh my God, not another one!" Cora wailed, scooting away from him. "They're everywhere!"

I'd prefer it if you would use the term Moravian. Vampire is so Twilight.

"The kind of vampire who sucks blood?" I asked, feeling it important to make that point clear.

Moravian. Yes. Do you have some sort of problem grasping that concept?

"A Dracula sort of vampire, with stakes, and children of the night?"

"They're following me!" Cora yelled as she turned and ran down the hallway toward the large metal back door. "Everywhere I go, they're there! First Patsy's neighbor, now a vampire cat—what next?"

The cat sighed into my mind and bumped my knee with his nose. *M-o-r . . . Oh, to hell with it. Call me whatever you want; it doesn't matter. I have to get back to the Leshy compound and make Albert Baum change me back.*

"Back into a vampire."

You seem to be stuck on that point.

"Well, you have to admit, you don't run into vampires every day," I pointed out.

Actually, I do. My brothers are Moravians, as well, as I believe I just mentioned. He wobbled over to the door that led to the area where the cats lived and banged his head on the doorknob.

I rubbed the back of my neck, feeling the faintest twinges of a tension headache. "Now, wait—that doesn't make sense. I've seen movies. What you're saying is that you're a werewolf vampire, and you know, that's completely against all the rules."

Werepanther, I believe, would be the technical term. And who says there's a rule that Moravians can't be shape-shifters? Just because I don't know of any doesn't mean there haven't been some. Damn it. Come open this door for me.

"Werejaguar."

Avery, werejaguar vampire cat, shot me a look filled with undiluted irritation. *Panther sounds more manly.*

"It's a misnomer, however. You wouldn't want to go around telling people you're a panther when you're not, now, would you?"

Lovely. I get the anal-retentive cat whisperer, he answered, trying to turn the doorknob by getting a grip on it with his teeth.

"I am not anal retentive! And stop that—you're getting slobber all over the handle. All right. For the sake of time, my sanity, and to keep my sister from having a nervous breakdown—Cora! Stop yelling. You're upsetting the cats in the back! Go outside to the truck and get the camera for me if you're upset. I'm just going to move past the whole impossibility of the situation. Just show me you are what you say you are, and I'll help you. How, I don't know, but I'll try my best."

Show you?

"Yes, show me."

Two furry black dots that were his eyebrows rose. *Is that a proposition? Because if it is, I'm going to be obliged to you if you could wait until I'm back in human form to take you up on it.*

"I meant show me that you're a werejaguar vampire. Change."

Change?

My hands did a fluttery thing. "What are you, a werejaguar vampire parrot now? Change. All the movies I've seen and books I've read say that were-whatevers can change their forms themselves. They don't need their girlfriend's father to do it for them."

I am not a whatever. I am a Moravian werejaguar, and a damned nice specimen of one, if this handsome black coat is anything to go by. And Danielle wasn't my girlfriend. I don't have a girlfriend, thus making me able to take you up on your proposition later. She was just a means to an end.

"Thus thinketh many men," I said, the vision of Greg rising briefly in my mind. "Very few actually come right out and say it, though. I may award you bonus points for that. So are you going to change or not?"

You might be on to something there, he answered thoughtfully. *Let me see . . . hmm. How do you suppose you go about changing your form?*

I shrugged. "I don't know; I'm not a werejaguar. I imagine concentrating might do the job. Maybe like meditation—clear your mind of everything but the image of you as a vampire, and see if that does the trick."

His pretty blue eyes squinted at nothing as he focused his attention, one lip curling up as an odd, abstracted expression formed on his face.

"You look constipated."

He stopped squinting to glare at me. *Flatterer.*

"I meant that you're trying too hard. Haven't you ever done yoga or meditated? You need to relax, allow yourself to become one with the universe, let your mind wander. While, of course, holding the shape-shifting thought."

When I get back to the Baum compound, there's going to be hell to pay, he swore as he slumped down onto the ground, his big head between his paws. *I can't relax. I'm too stressed.*

"For heaven's sake . . ." I plopped down onto the ground next to him, and scratched behind one of the rounded furry ears, gently moving across his neck to the other ear.

A low, thick, rough purr of delight answered the quasi massage. His eyes, which had been shut tight, popped open in surprise. *I can purr!*

"All cats can, in some form or another. Yours is particularly . . ."

Masculine?

"Rough. Close your eyes again, let your thoughts go, and when you feel at peace, try to shift back into your normal form," I said helpfully, waiting to see if he was speaking the truth. The idea of there really being vampires trotting around the earth was more than enough to raise my skeptical objections, but the thought of one who had been changed into a jaguar? That was beyond bizarre.

I kept stroking his head until the purr eventually trailed off, his breathing deep and slow. I was just about to nudge his shoulder in case he had drifted off to sleep when my vision went wonky, shimmering and blurring for a few seconds before the cat's body elongated, the mass of it stretching and changing until I sat gazing down with absolute astonishment at the man's blond head that lay under my stroking fingers.

He turned his head to the side to consider my hand, pressing a kiss to my palm before I could snatch it back.

"You're . . . human."

"Not quite, but close enough to make no difference to you."

"You're human. And . . . naked." I couldn't help but notice that. I'd have to have been blind not to notice the thick curve of muscles on his bare shoulder and arm.

"Am I? So I am," he said, pushing himself off the ground into a sitting position.

I tried not to look, I really did, but I would defy any woman to find herself sitting next to a naked man and not look. Especially when he was as easy on the eyes as this one was.

"Holy—"

"Mary and all the little saints. Yes, I know. You were right," he said, smiling lazily at me. "All I had to do was relax. Thanks for petting me. Are you going to stare at my cock for long? I don't mind, but this floor is cold when you're not covered in fur."

Blushing, I dragged my eyes up from his genitals to stare at his chest, my mouth slightly ajar, my brain refusing to understand what it was seeing. He leaned forward, gently placing a finger under my chin and closing my mouth, his gaze fastened on my lips. "Oh, what the hell," he said, using his thumb to prod my chin down a smidgen. Then before I could ask him what on earth he was doing, he leaned forward and kissed me.

At least that was what it started out as, his lips moving across mine in a salute of gratitude, but the second his tongue slid between my lips, a sense of hunger rose in him, a primal, animalistic need to take from me, and what shocked me to my toenails was my desire to give him what he wanted.

"All right, I have the camera, and I insist that you come away from that fur-covered, bloodsucking Nosferatu this instant—good Lord! He's attacking you!"

There was a whoosh of air and a metallic clang, followed almost immediately by the sound of a ripe melon being smacked with a blunt object.

"Get away from her, you fiend!" Cora yelled. I blinked at the sight of Avery laid out flat on his back, blood dripping slowly from a cut over his eye.

"What—"

"Come on! We have to run before he comes around!" Cora dropped the fire extinguisher and grabbed my arm, trying to haul me to my feet.

"He wasn't attacking me, you idiot! He was kissing me! What on earth have you done to the poor man?" I pushed Cora away to examine the bloody lump on Avery's head. He moaned as I gently pressed my fingers around the lump. "Thank God, I don't think you broke anything."

"Jas!" Cora slapped her hands on her legs in frustration. "He's not a poor man; he's a vampire!"

"So? That's no reason to go braining him with a fire extinguisher. Avery? Can you hear me?"

"He's a *bloodsucker*! A naked bloodsucker! Everyone knows those are the worst kind!"

"Don't be ridiculous." I pushed a lock of his hair away from the blood. Avery moaned again, turning his face into my leg as he swore softly.

"Don't you understand, Jas? He drinks people's blood!"

"You were absolutely fine with him when you thought he was a werejaguar," I pointed out.

"That's different!"

"Oh really? How?"

She blinked at me. "He's . . . deadly."

"I'm deadly in any form," Avery said, touching his wound and wincing. "Bloody hell, woman. What did you hit me with?"

"You don't want to know," I told him, helping him sit up. I had to admit I didn't at all mind the silky sensation of his naked back against my hands. "How do you feel?"

"That's it. I give up. He's clearly got you under his sway, or lure, or whatever it is vampires do. There's no hope for you now," Cora said, slumping down the wall to sit on the floor. "Next you'll be eating bugs and calling him master."

"It's called a thrall, and we don't do that," Avery told her, squinting at the blood on his fingers.

"You don't?" she asked.

"No." He gave me a long look; then one side of his mouth quirked up. "Although you *can* call me master if you like."

Chapter 3

"*I* still don't think this is a good idea."

"I know you don't, Cora. But if you can think of another way to explain to Allison and Jo and the other ladies why the jaguar they all saw has disappeared, leaving Avery in its place, then I'm all ears. Because frankly, I barely believe what happened myself—speaking of which, I think we deserve extra bonus points for not running around screaming with our hands waving in the air—and I just don't think I'm up to the explanations needed that would convince five other people of what really happened."

"Hrmph." She glared at the tall figure of a man as he emerged from the small room that served as a hospital for the cats in residence. Luckily, the vet who came by twice a week was male, and if he was heavier and shorter than Avery, at least his emergency clothing fit well enough for Avery to leave the building. "I don't trust him, not one little bit."

"Life's a bitch," I said absently as I tucked my tranquilizing gun back into its holster.

"Jas!"

I paused with my hand on the knob of the back door, surprised by the vehemence in her voice. "What?"

"He's a *vampire!*" she hissed, glancing over her shoulder at Avery as he walked toward us. Somehow, he'd acquired a baseball cap and a beat-up leather jacket that had clearly seen better days.

"So?"

"Just a little bit ago you were telling me they didn't exist."

"Clearly I was wrong. I mean, you can't deny the evidence, Cora. What we have here is a shape-shifting vampire, which I gather is fairly rare."

"What's rare?" Avery asked as he stopped next to us. He slipped into the coat and pulled the brim of the hat low on his forehead.

"You are."

He looked thoughtful for a moment. "I guess I am. I can't think of any other Moravian who's also a therion."

"A what, now?" I asked, glaring at my sister as she glared at Avery.

"Therion." He gave me an odd look. "Someone who can change their shape at will to that of an animal."

"Is there such a thing as a non-therion?" I couldn't help but ask. "Other than the obvious, I mean?"

"Someone who shifts but isn't in control of it?" he asked.

I nodded.

"Yes. Weres."

"Whats?"

"No, weres."

"If you say who's on first, I'm going to deck you," my sister told me with a warning glint in her eye.

I smiled at her. "I think he means weres as in werewolves."

"Werewolves are a fallacy," Avery said, gesturing toward the door. "Mortal lore says they can shift back to human form, but true weres can't. May we leave? I have an old man to gullet."

"Sure. But . . . is the sunlight thing a fallacy, too?"

"Sunlight? Oh—only somewhat. Moravians can go out in the sun if we have protection against prolonged exposure. Hence the jacket and hat."

"Gotcha. Just let me check to make sure the coast is clear." I opened the door a few inches and peered out. Five pairs of eyes turned en masse to look back at me. "Um. Hi. Er . . ." I opened the door more fully. "Sorry to keep you all waiting so long."

"Is everything all right?" Allison asked as Jo craned her head to look beyond me into the darkened hallway. "We were beginning to get worried. Is the cat injured badly?"

"No, not at all. He's fine, in . . . er . . . remarkably good shape. It took me a while to examine him, and then of course, I wanted to speak to his owner when he came to pick up the cat."

"His owner?" The five ladies wore identical expressions of surprise as I stepped out, followed by Cora and Avery.

"This is Avery Scott. He . . . er . . . owns the cat who was left by mistake at your shelter. Evidently the cat was ill and Avery asked someone to take it to a specialist vet while he was off on a business trip, and it was brought here instead," I said quickly, trotting out the admittedly weak story we had hurriedly concocted.

The five pairs of eyes turned to look at Avery, standing in the shadow of the building. He smiled. "I'm so sorry for any trouble that my extremely handsome panther—"

"Jaguar."

"Might have caused you ladies, but I assure you that you will not be forced to endure such inconvenience again."

"But . . ." Allison faltered, and looked helplessly at Jo.

"Where's he gone?" Jo asked in her usual blunt manner. "We didn't see anyone."

"Gone? The cat?" I glanced at Avery. We were so rushed that we had forgotten to come up with an explanation of to where exactly the cat had been spirited away.

"My friend picked him up at the front door," Avery said without batting so much as an eyelash. "I have a special car for him. The cat, not the friend."

"We didn't hear anyone pull up front, either," Jo said, her brows pulling together as she eyed Avery.

I moved in front of him to block her view, lest she recognize the vet's spare clothes. "It was one of those new hybrid cars, very quiet. All's clear in your shelter now, though, so you can feel free to go inside and take care of all those hungry kitties. Avery, I'll give you a lift since your friend took your cat away."

"That was the lamest, most unbelievable story I've ever heard," Cora grumbled as we hurried toward the truck. "A friend came to pick up the cat in a hybrid car! Honestly, Jas, couldn't you have thought of something a little more realistic?"

"Shush, they'll hear you," I warned, glancing back. The three workers had gone inside. Jo stood at the door, holding it for Allison, who was watching us, an odd expression on her face. As Avery and Cora slid into the truck, she smiled, and I could have sworn winked at me.

"So here we are, trapped in a small truck with a man-eating vampire therion jaguar," Cora said, digging her elbow into me as she made herself comfortable.

"Actually, I prefer women as my dinner companions, and do I sense a subtle hostility regarding my origins?" Avery asked politely, pulling down the visor and angling it toward the side of the window where the morning sun was spilling sunlight into the truck.

"You do, you murderous fiend. It was a vampire who bit the lady who decapitated me with her ox cart. The same vampire who lives next door to my best friend, except now she can't remember anything because he did some weird brain thing to her, so she won't believe me when I tell her what happened that night, and what's more, she refuses to move. Luckily, she has retained enough wits to also refuse to give him my name and address, so he can't hunt me down and kill me as he did the ox lady."

Avery's expression of disbelief was priceless. He transferred his gaze of stark confusion from Cora to me. "Your sister was decapitated?"

"It was a past-life regression," I said, waving at Jo as she and Allison entered the shelter. "I assume we can drop you off somewhere?"

He named a rural mountain town about half an hour away. "Since I seem to be without a vehicle, hybrid or otherwise, I would appreciate a ride."

"No problem," I said, pulling out onto the highway.

"So, how is it that a Scottish vampire is in the Pacific Northwest?"

"Will you stop that?" Cora demanded, pinching my wrist.

"Stop what?" I asked, surprised once again by her rudeness.

"You're chitchatting with him!"

"So?"

"He's a vampire! He just wants one thing from you."

"Brains?" I asked, feeling my lips twitch with the effort not to smile.

Avery's lips, I couldn't help but notice from a glance that way, did the same.

"No, you idiot, that's zombies."

"Blood, then. Do you want to drink my blood, Avery?" I asked over her head.

"I'm not particularly hungry at this moment, but if you were offering, I certainly wouldn't turn you down," he said with a devilish twinkle in those clear blue eyes.

Warning sirens went off in my brain, but I ignored them. Oh, I could tell he was a ladies' man, that he was quite comfortable with who he was, and that he could probably charm the spots off a cheetah, but that didn't mean I couldn't appreciate him for the eye candy he was.

"Your pants," Cora announced, nodding when both Avery and I glanced at her in surprise. "That's what he wants. Or rather, that's what he wants to get into. Don't look at me like that, Jas—I've read all sorts of vampire books, and they all have one thing in common."

"Sparkles?"

She shot me a look of scorn. "No. Vampires are always oversexed stud muffins who just want to get into women's pants. And the way this one was sucking your face, it's obvious he wants into yours. If I hadn't come along when I did, he probably would have been boinking you in the hallway of the cat shelter."

We stopped at a red light, giving me an opportunity to assess Avery. "Would you have boinked me in the hallway?"

"No," he said, his lips curving into a slow, sensuous smile that suddenly had me warm all over.

"I think you owe Avery an apology," I told my sister, clearing my throat and wondering if anyone would notice if I turned on the air-conditioning.

She pursed her lips at him and waited.

His smile changed into a grin. "The floor in the hallway was too cold, Jacintha. Now, the room beyond had a lovely rug. I would have boinked you there."

I couldn't help myself; I laughed, Avery joining in with me. Only Cora didn't see the humor, muttering darkly to herself as we drove.

"You didn't answer my question earlier," I reminded Avery.

"I did. I meant it, too. That rug in the other room—"

"The question of why you're here in the first place," I interrupted, wondering for just a moment if he really was serious.

Quite serious.

I almost ran the truck into the side of a small bait and ammo shop at the sound of his voice in my head.

The truck fishtailed on the thankfully empty gravel parking area as I slammed on the brakes, bringing us to a shuddering halt.

"What the hell?" Cora asked as I turned a shocked face at Avery. His eyes were wide with surprise, as well.

"You talked to me!"

"Yes."

"In my head, you talked to me like you did when you were a jaguar. But you're not a cat now. The cat whispering was one thing, but this—this is different."

"I know." His expression froze for a moment. "You can't be."

"I can't be what?" I asked, confused and jittery from the blast of adrenaline that roared through me when we spun into the parking lot. Shakily, I turned off the engine, feeling I needed a couple of minutes to gather my wits again.

"A Beloved?"

"Huh?"

"You're coming on to my sister, aren't you?" Cora demanded, giving him a dirty look.

"No, I'm not," he answered in an abstracted tone, his gaze flicking over me as if he were making an inventory of my person. "The word Beloved to a Dark One has a different meaning than the term of affection, although it is based on that. It is a term we use for a soul mate, the one woman who can redeem a Dark One's soul, returning it to him."

"And to think when I woke up this morning I figured it was going to be just another mundane Friday, the kind that doesn't involve shape-shifting vampires who don't have souls. Wait a second—you told me at the shelter you had your soul. Is this Beloved thing what you were talking about?"

"Yes." He continued to look thoughtfully at me. "And I do have my soul—I don't need it redeemed, but I seem to have marked you."

Cora snorted indignantly.

"I beg your pardon!" I was somewhat outraged at the idea of this marking. Why, I didn't quite know, since it was obvious he hadn't harmed me in any way.

"In this case, the marking is the ability to speak directly to each other without using words," he explained, a slight frown pulling his dark blond brows together.

"Which means, what? That I'm this soul-redeemer you don't need?"

"Why not?" he said, shrugging, as if he had been arguing with himself. "Other Moravians have them. Why shouldn't I? It's just that I didn't expect it." His slow smile caused my stomach to tighten as he reached across Cora and pulled me toward him. "Kiss me."

"What?"

"Hey!" Cora objected as she was smashed into the back of the seat. "Get off me, you bloodthirsty ghoul!"

"Kiss me. Suck my tongue," Avery demanded, trying to haul me across Cora. The seat belt wouldn't allow him to do more than cause my back to wrench painfully.

"Oh my God, I knew it! He's trying to get into your pants, right here in front of me!" Cora shrieked, slapping at his arms.

"Be quiet, woman!" Avery thundered, impatiently

unhooking his seat belt, then doing the same for Cora. Before she could do more than squawk, he hoisted her onto his lap.

"If you think copping a grope on my sister is going to encourage me to French kiss you, you need to think again," I told him sternly. "I do not share my men."

He rolled his eyes, scooted over to where Cora had been sitting, then summarily dumped her into his spot, next to the passenger door. "Kiss me. It's the third step."

"Third step of what?"

"Joining. Kiss me, damn it!"

"Why?" I asked, suspicious all of a sudden, although more than a little overwhelmed with both his demands, and the sudden nearness of him, pressed up next to me, all hard lines and muscles and body heat that made me feel very feminine, even in my work uniform.

"Confirmation," he said, a moment before his lips descended on mine.

"Where the hell is a fire extinguisher when you need one?" I heard Cora yell, but dimly, as if she were at a distance away. Every ounce of my attention was focused on Avery: Avery and his tongue, Avery and the hard, warm chest I was pulled up against, Avery and the little tremors of heat that seemed to come from his fingers as they stroked the back of my neck. But most of all, I focused on the strange presence in my mind that I recognized as being him. I was flooded with all sorts of emotions that weren't mine, everything from arousal (which I was somewhat disconcerted to realize matched my own), to surprise, to a deep, burning hunger that burst into being with a strength that rocked me.

But it was his pleasure in tasting me that amazed me and heightened the enjoyment I was feeling. It was as if our individual emotions were feeding each other, ping-ponging back and forth in a spiraling twist of arousal, need, and unadulterated sensuality.

I thought you said you weren't hungry.

I wasn't then. I am now.

So you are . . . Hey! That's not hunger, I answered, my mind filled with the most erotic thoughts it had ever been my (extreme) pleasure to entertain. *Good Lord, man, that last one has to be illegal.*

It isn't. But it should be, he said with languid sensuality.

I squirmed and moaned into his mouth as one of his hands continued to stroke the back of my neck, a suddenly highly erogenous zone, while the other slid down my arm to my rib cage, his fingers spreading to cup my left breast.

This is unbelievable.

I know. I had no idea this is what men felt when they kissed me. What happens if I do this?

I laid my hand on his thigh, gently kneading the heavy muscles. A jolt of electricity shot through him, pushing his arousal—and subsequently mine—to new peaks.

Dear God, don't do that, he groaned in my mind. I moved my hand off his leg, pausing when he asked, *What are you doing?*

Moving my hand. You asked me to.

*Don't listen to me! I'm clearly too caught up in amaze-
ment to know what I'm saying.*

I didn't know it was possible to laugh in someone's
head, but that was what I did as I replaced my hand
on his thigh, massaging the muscle there as he thoroughly examined every part of my mouth. *I'm caught
up in amazement as well. You really do know how to kiss.*

*That's not what I meant—oh, hell, I'll just have to show
you. Do you mind feeding me?*

I was turning that thought over in my mind, weigh-
ing the building desire that was claiming his sole attention with my own reticence to become someone's
snack, when his mouth moved off mine, and he said
something in a language I didn't understand, his lips
burning a path down my chin, to my neck.

*This is a bit cliché, but I doubt if you would appreciate my
doing it anywhere else in front of your sister. . . .* His words
were still echoing in my head when a sharp, hot pain
flared to life and was instantly gone, replaced by the
most incredible sensation I'd ever felt.

*Oh my God, you're doing it, aren't you? You're drinking
my blood!*

He moaned into my brain again. *Christ, yes.*

I was simultaneously shocked and thrilled. That he
was feeding off me was a concept that should have
been repugnant, but it was so far from that, my head
spun. *This is wild! I can feel you drinking it. I can feel it
sliding down your throat. I can feel . . . oh, my. You, too,
huh?*

I just wanted to see if it was true.

If what was true? I asked.

He ignored my question, his arousal and mine so tangled together, I knew we were both close to burning up with desire. *We have to stop. If I go on . . .*

Yeah, I know. I'm really close, as well. Avery, don't.

Don't?

Don't stop. . . .

Just as I was about to throw self-control to the wind and rip off his clothes to have my carnal way with him, a familiar noise pierced the dense cloud of sex that seemed to hold us in its velvet grip. It was a sharp noise, one that tickled the fringes of my awareness, re-minding me of something. I was just about to examine it closer when Avery stiffened in my arms and pulled his mouth off my neck. I caught a flash of his startled blue eyes before they rolled up and he fell forward across my lap, smacking his forehead loudly on the window.

Cora sat at the other side of the truck, my tranquil-izing gun still leveled at Avery, a smile on her lips.

"Got him," she said with grim satisfaction, her gaze rising to meet mine. "No evil undead bloodsucker makes *my* sister dinner!"

"Oh, Cora," I said, my entire body quivering on the edge of an orgasm. "You have the worst timing of any-one I know."

Chapter 4

"So now what do we do?" Cora asked, prodding the bed with the toe of her boot. "How long is Vlad going to stay that way?"

"I don't know, and most likely about four hours." I frowned down at the man who lay on the bed of the cheap motel just outside the town to which Avery had asked to be taken. "I'm not sure because I've never used the tranquilizer on a person. And you shouldn't have—it's dangerous, since the dose for animals is much different than for people. You might have killed him."

"Yeah, right. He's the evil undead, remember?"

"Oh, he is not," I snapped, tired of the way Cora constantly harped on the fact that Avery just happened to be a vampire—one that could turn into a melanistic jaguar.

Dear God, what had I gotten myself involved in?

"You've fallen for all that Beloved talk, haven't you? Don't deny it—I can tell you have."

"I haven't done any such thing," I objected.

"I know you, Jas. You're the most romantic person I know, constantly watching those sappy old romance movies, mooning about wishing you had some guy from the cover of a romance novel, and waiting for a dashing knight to roll up on a white horse and whisk you away."

"You are being obnoxiously rude. Just because you don't have an ounce of romance in your soul doesn't mean I'm some sap waiting for a man to complete her life. I do just fine on my own, thank you."

"Uh-huh." She waved toward the figure on the bed. "So you don't want to jump his bones?"

I opened my mouth to tell her I would never even think anything so crass, but the words refused to come. I let my gaze linger on Avery for a moment, feeling my cheeks heat up as I met her eyes. "Attraction between two consenting adults is not a shameful thing, Miss Prude. Yes, I happen to find Avery . . . interesting. He's different from any other man I've known."

"I'll say he is."

"There's no need to be snide. You know what I mean. I like him. He's fascinating. I mean, think about it, Cora—he's a vampire jaguar! That's just so amazing!"

She rolled her eyes and kicked at the bed again. "You're nuts, that's what you are. I can't imagine finding a bloodsucker sexy. And if you think I'm going to sit around this dump for four hours waiting for Sleeping Beauty there to wake up, you're even nuttier than I think you are." Scorn dripped from every word.

"He wouldn't be asleep if you hadn't tranquilized him," I hastened to point out.

"Yeah, yeah, move past that," she answered, blithely unaware of my sharp glance. "You would have done the same for me."

"No, I wouldn't have."

"I say we—" She paused and shot me a curious look. "You really would not have saved me from a bloodsucker?"

"No. Not if you mean someone like Avery."

"But . . . he's bad!" she said, waving her hand toward the comatose man. "Despite your thinking he's Mr. Sexy Pants, he's evil, Jas! Evil!"

"How do you know that? You don't, do you? No, you don't. But because you had some bizarre past-life experience—the idea of which, I have to admit, I think is totally unrealistic and hard to believe—you're a vampiphobe."

"You don't have any problem with a jaguar-shaped Scottish vampire, but you mock my very frightening and absolutely real past-life regression?" Cora asked, her arms crossed.

I glanced away and cleared my throat. "Point taken. I will accept that you believe you underwent a past-life regression—"

She coughed meaningfully.

"That you experienced a past-life regression wherein you saw a vampire chomp on some woman who lopped off your head with an ox cart, but that doesn't give you any right to assume that all vampires are the chomping sort. Avery seems perfectly nice, perfectly civilized, and, frankly, sexy as hell."

"Keys," Cora said, holding out her hand.

"What?"

"Give me the keys to your truck. Clearly you are under that thrall thing he mentioned, and you're not thinking straight. I need to go find the nearest hardware store to pick up a stake and a shovel and maybe an ax or a chain saw, just in case Drac here gets uppity when he wakes up."

I was about to protest such a ridiculous idea when two things struck me: The first was that there were no hardware stores within an hour's drive, and the second was that I would much rather be alone with Avery than have my somewhat truculent sister present to put a damper on everything.

Just what constituted "everything" was something I wasn't willing to examine at the moment, but I had to admit the idea of a few hours in Avery's company held a great attraction.

"All right, you can borrow the truck for a bit, but just you remember it belongs to the state, and I'm responsible for it, so be careful."

"Call me if he wakes up. And don't let him have any more of your blood. Maybe that's how he maintains control of you." She marched off, shoulders twitching with irritation, her head high with determination.

I waited until I saw her drive off down the highway—in the direction that led deeper into the mountains, and away from populated areas—before turning back to examine Avery's pulse and breathing again.

Judging by the slow, steady pulse, I knew I had nothing but time until he came around. "Time," I mused to myself, tapping my fingers on the cheaply laminated table. "Hmm. What I would really like to do is to go see the Leshies. If you're sure Albert and his group are the ones who turned you into a jaguar, then I need to talk to them. I mean, what's to stop them from doing it again? I can't have the area flooded with exotic cats—there would be no end of trouble explaining that, not even if I knew how to do so. No, Albert has to be made to stop, and he and I have always had a pretty good relationship. Not like his weird sons, but that doesn't really matter, does it?"

Avery snorted in his sleep.

I waffled for a few minutes, but there was really no choice between staying in the dim, mildewy, tacky motel for hours watching him sleep, or taking a brisk hike through the woods to confront the man who may or may not be out changing innocent vampires into exotic cats.

"The question now is whether or not I should tell Cora where I'm going," I said to Avery's back. He snored softly in response. "I agree completely. If I tell her, she'll just insist on turning around and accompanying me, and while Albert knows and trusts me, he doesn't know Cora. And his whole group is rather skittish where people are concerned, so really, the best idea is to just leave a note and go from there. Right? Right. I'm so glad you see things my way."

I scribbled a brief note and taped it to the spotted mirror that grimly reflected images with a sense of futility and hopelessness that was beginning to get on my nerves. I blew a saucy kiss to the blond man snoring gently on the bed, and I escaped the depressing confines of the room.

The motel was made up of twelve little cabins spread out in a drunken line on either side of an equally squalid office, all of which clung to the side of the highway that ran up into the mountains, through to the eastern side of the state. I took stock of my surroundings, pulled up a map on my cell phone, and scurried around be-

hind our cabin to the dense alpine growth. I knew
from times tramping through the region that there was
a narrow dirt road about a mile away used by utility
officials to maintain the large power lines that ran up
and over the mountain pass. If I remembered correctly,
the western edge of Albert Baum's land wasn't more
than another mile east of that track. It wouldn't take
me more than an hour to hike across the Baum land to
Albert's compound, have a quick chat with him, and
be back before Avery woke up.

Twenty minutes later, as I ignored a weathered No
Trespassing—Private Wildlife Preserve sign that hung
from one corner on a listing fence pole to climb a rot-
ting wooden fence (no barbed wire for the animal-
oriented Leshy group), I congratulated myself on my
smart thinking. "I'll have Albert Baum all taken care
of by the time Avery wakes up. Maybe Albert can even
remove whatever it is he did to Avery."

A thought occurred to me in a voice that sounded almost identical to that of my sister. "I'm not compelled
to help him," I argued with what I knew she'd say if
she was with me. "He's a nice man, no matter what
you think. And don't ask me how I know; I just do—I
could see into his mind, and although he's very full
of himself, he's . . ." My voice trailed off as I trudged
across a small open meadow, and I struggled for a
word to define what I felt inside of Avery.

A female Roosevelt elk and her calf, no doubt one of
Albert's transplants from the Olympic National Park,
emerged from the dense growth of trees and watched
me warily as I followed a game trail through the knee-
high grass. I made an abstracted mental note to check

my clothing over carefully for deer ticks before I entered Albert's compound.

"Honorable, that's the word," I said finally as I left the meadow and struggled up a short, sharp incline. "He's honorable."

"Aye, but you're not," a man's voice said from behind me. I spun around, out of sheer instinct my hand on my tranquilizing gun, only to find a tall, lanky man with long brown hair scowling at me.

"Oh, hello. You're Franz Baum, aren't you?"

"Dieter," he corrected me, taking a step toward me that was filled with enough menace to have me scrambling backward up the hill. "Franz is my brother."

"That's right. I don't know if you remember me or not. My name is Jacintha Ferreira and I'm—"

"You're the female from the government. The one who's always after Da." He continued to stalk toward me, lifting his chin to sniff the air. "You're not in heat."

I blinked a couple of times as I crested the hill, glancing quickly behind me. In the distance, about half a mile away, I could see the earth-tone tops of the half dozen durable canvas tents that made up the Leshy compound. "What on earth does that have to do with the price of tea in China?"

"What are you doing here if it's not for breeding?" Dieter asked, sniffing the air again. Suddenly, he froze; then, before I could do so much as take a breath, he growled, "You smell like him!" and leaped toward me.

Time seemed to slow down just like something out of a movie special effect. I watched with open-mouthed astonishment as Dieter's body, in midair, did that same sort of shimmering thing that Avery had done. His clothing fell to the ground as a large, slavering gray wolf slammed into my chest, knocking me backward a good two yards. Instinctively, I put up my hands to keep the wolf from snapping my neck, but before I could so much as rally a single thought, a furious scream ripped through the still afternoon air. It was the scream of a cat, a big cat, and all it took was the flash of black as a large body sailed through the air, landing on the wolf and yanking him to the side, to let me know that Avery had woken up a whole lot earlier than I imagined.

"Holy Mary and all the saints!" I yelled, scrambling out of the way of their bodies as the two predators attacked each other. "Is *everyone* around here a shapeshifter? Knock it off, both of you! Right, that's it. You want to play hardball? I can play hardball. Stop or I'll shoot!"

Avery at least glanced toward me when I took up a shooter's stance and aimed my tranquilizing gun at the twisting, snarling mass of gray and black bodies, but the Dieter-wolf paid absolutely no attention.

"Big mistake," I told him. Narrowing my eyes, my hands following the pair as they fought while I waited for the moment when the wolf's body would be exposed long enough for me to get off a shot.

The gun popped and bucked in my hands as that moment came. Dieter didn't seem to notice it until I yelled at Avery not to kill him. Dieter, who was trying to snap his jaws on Avery's thick, heavily muscled neck, suddenly staggered. Avery would have gone for a killing blow, but I moved forward quickly, saying as I did, "It's okay. I got him. He'll be out in another couple of seconds. Please don't kill him. I have no idea how I'd explain it to his father."

The big cat was breathing heavily, his eyes glittering with a feral desire that I had no trouble identifying.

"Calm down, Avery. It's over. Look—he's asleep now, see?" I gestured toward the wolf as he collapsed onto the ground. "Everything's okay."

"That is not in the least bit true," he answered as the cat's body did the shimmer into his normal human form. There was blood on his neck and shoulder.

"Are you hurt?" I pulled out a couple of tissues, my gut tight as I tried to stop the flow of blood from the deep bites.

"Yes, but not seriously. What are you doing?"

"Dabbing. I don't want to hurt you. What on earth . . . ?"

"I told you it wasn't serious." The blood had already stopped sluggishly pulsing from his wounds, and before my amazed eyes, the puncture marks began to close and heal over.

"That's amazing!"

"Not really. Moravians have tremendous powers of recuperation." He glanced around, then turned on his heel and stalked across the small clearing. No longer concerned about his being injured, I allowed myself to enjoy the view. I made a little effort to keep from ogling his bare butt as he walked away, but it was no good, and I knew it. I gave in and had a good, long look, admiring the length of his legs, the easy stride, the muscled calves that swept with gentle curves up to heavily muscled thighs.

You have the nicest butt I've ever seen, I found myself telling him.

Thank you. It's all the riding we do. My mother says she fell in love with my father because he rode daily.

You have parents? I asked, somewhat surprised as he disappeared into the trees.

Of course I do. Don't you?

Well . . . yes. But I mean, vampires . . . I thought you guys were made? That's what happens in the Anne Rice books, anyway.

Popular mortal fiction is not a representation of reality, was all he said before he emerged from the trees, clad once again in the vet's emergency clothing.

So your parents were vampires?

My father is a Dark One; my mother is his Beloved. She got his soul back for him, but not until my oldest brother was born. He's married now to his own Beloved. In fact, it's because of the two of them that I'm here.

"Oh? They sent you out here to become a what-chamacallit? Therion?"

"No." He looked grim as he marched up to me, his eyes on the prone form of the wolf. "Sam—that's Paen's Beloved—is a private investigator. I do work for them occasionally. They sent me here to discover who was shipping exotic animals to a private reserve in Scotland. Why did you leave me?"

"I didn't leave you," I said, wondering about the reserve. "What sort of exotic animals?"

"I was asleep, assumedly because that blasted sister of yours shot me with that gun, and you weren't there when I woke up. If that's not leaving me, I'd like to know what is."

"I wanted to talk to Albert Baum. Exotic as in animals from the Pacific Northwest? Or something else?"

"Both. What did you do to set Dieter off on you?" he asked, nudging the body of the wolf with his bare foot.

"Nothing. He said I smelled like him, whoever he is."

"Me."

"Huh?"

"You smell like me." Avery gave the prone wolf a sour look.

"I do no such thing," I said, scandalized for no explainable reason. I took a couple of steps back and tried to take a covert whiff of myself to see if I smelled like a man.

His expression morphed into impatience. "You wouldn't be able to smell it. Only therions can. Dieter probably recognized my scent on you, knew you must have been with me, and attacked."

"Oh, really? And why would he do that? What have you done to him?"

"Nothing."

I really enjoyed watching the expressions flit across his face. I've heard it said that some people's thoughts are transparent, but Avery was the first person I'd met whose expressions mirrored every emotion he was feeling. Most men leaned toward somewhat stoic expressions until you got to know them well, but Avery was different. Right now, the chagrin on his face that chased away the impatience told me volumes. I couldn't help but wonder what sort of an expression he'd wear when he was in the throes of sexual ecstasy.

"That will have to wait," he said, frowning at the wolf. "Right now we have to get you out of here so I can deal with Baum and his band of insane tree huggers."

"Excuse me?" I put out a hand to stop him as he came toward me.

"Tree huggers. It means someone who—"

"I know what it means," I interrupted, noting that his expression was now one of grave concern. About what? "What did you mean with that bit about it having to wait? You were reading my mind again, weren't you?"

"Yes," he said without the slightest hint of apology or embarrassment that I had caught him. "Why should I be embarrassed?"

"Stop it!" I shouted, putting my hands over my ears as if that would keep my thoughts in, and him out.

"It's not something I can help any more than you can help being able to read my expression, which I assure you is inscrutable to others."

I had my doubts about that.

"What I meant is that I can't make love to you right now, as you clearly wish me to."

"I wish no such thing!" I said, shocked and, at the same time, strangely titillated at the thought. "I just met you! And you were a panther at the time!"

"Jaguar," he corrected.

"Gargh! You see? You have me so crazy, I don't know what I'm saying!"

He put his hands on my shoulders and gave me a quick, hard kiss that effectively stopped my wailing.

"Yes, we've just met each other. And no, I hadn't anticipated settling down to just one woman now. I'm known all over Scotland for my sexual prowess. I'm a highly desired lover and have been much in demand for almost two hundred years."

"You're about to get a pop in the mouth," I warned, my fingers curling into a fist.

"But that doesn't change the fact that you are clearly my Beloved, and that we will spend the rest of our lives together. And since there isn't a Moravian born who didn't fall madly in love with his Beloved, and vice versa, I anticipate that will be the state of things between us, as well."

I stared at him in astonishment. "You're not trying to say you're in love with me, are you?"

"No," he admitted slowly, a look of discomfort in his eyes. "I'm not one of those fall-in-love-at-first-sight sort of people, Jacintha. In fact, I'm not sure I ever have . . . No. That doesn't matter now."

"If I recall correctly what you told me earlier, and I assure you I have a very good memory for conversations, you told me you had your soul, and only Beloveds could get them back for your fellow vampires. So how can I be one if you have your soul?"

"There are Beloveds, and then there are Beloveds," he said as if that made sense, then grabbed my hand and started pulling me back the way I'd come before I was attacked. "How long will Dieter be out?"

"Normally I'd say about four hours, but you came out of it much faster than that, so who knows?" I dug in my heels and refused to budge. "Look, the potential relationship question aside—"

"There is no potential about it. We are what we are."

"Thank you, Popeye the Vampire Jaguar Man. As I was saying, that aside, what do you think you're doing? I don't want to go back to the motel."

"I don't blame you. It's a repulsive spot. Why did you dump me there?"

"Because I had no idea where you were staying, and it seemed wiser to let you sleep off the tranquilizer in comfort, rather than crammed into the cab of my truck. How did you find me, anyway?" I asked, that question having tickled my brain long enough that I had to ask.

"Your scent," he said, trying to tug me forward.

My eyes widened in horror. "I do not smell! I took a shower just a couple of hours ago!"

"You smell to me."

Mortified, I felt tears spring to my eyes, but before I could tell him just how obnoxious I thought he was, he pulled me into an embrace, holding me tight against his chest, his chin brushing my forehead as he spoke. "You do not stink. You smell wonderful, as a matter of fact. Like . . . like a summer day, full of warm earth and flowers and green leaves and sunshine. But even before that bastard Baum turned me into a panther—"

"Melanistic jaguar," I murmured into his collarbone, allowing myself to sag against him, my hands gently stroking his back even as I breathed in the woodsy, masculine scent of him.

"I would have known your scent. Now that my senses are somewhat heightened, it wasn't difficult for me to follow your trail. And just in time—I'll kill that bastard Dieter for daring to attack you."

"No, you won't," I said, managing to push myself away from him, telling my mind to stop indulging in entirely unseemly fantasies about him.

He grinned.

"I am not responsible for what my mind thinks about you!" I told him primly as I straightened the shirt and jacket of my uniform. "So you can just stop looking smug about that bit with the warmed chocolate and pastry brush."

"All right, but only because I much prefer the one where you're tied spread-eagle—"

I clapped a hand over his mouth and glared at him. His eyes danced with laughter. "You will not kill Dieter because I don't hold with that sort of thing. And stop thinking the phrase 'culling the herd' at me, because it's not applicable here. Besides, his father would be pissed, I'm sure, and he's going to be difficult enough to deal with as is without his finding out you killed his oldest son."

"You aren't going with me to confront Baum," he said in one of those definitive, stern, masculine voices supposed to cow women into agreeing.

"Like hell I'm not."

"It's too dangerous. If he could do this to me, he could do it to you. And besides . . ." His voice and thoughts trailed away uncomfortably.

"Besides what?" I asked, curious about what he was suddenly hiding.

His jaw tightened.

I prodded at his arm, but he said nothing. With eyes narrowed in concentration, I thought hard at him. *Besides what?*

It doesn't matter. You can't go with me.

"You're trying to protect me from something," I said slowly, catching the faintest whisper in his mind. "You feel all paternal about me."

His lips twisted. "Trust me, Jacintha, what I feel for you is anything but paternal."

"You know what I mean—you've gone into protection mode. Why? I've dealt with Albert Baum before, you know. He's not a threat to me. In fact, just the opposite—we get along pretty well, despite our different beliefs. He knows I value animal life as highly as he does, and although we've clashed over his methodology once or twice, our relations have been amicable." I glanced at the still-sleeping wolf. "At least my relationship with *him* is amicable."

Avery's shoulders sagged for a moment. "You're not going to do as I ask, are you?"

"No." I examined his face curiously. "Did you honestly think I would?"

"Not really. I just kind of hoped it would work, but after watching Paen try to deal with Sam—"

"Did I hear my name taken in vain?"

We both turned to see a man and woman striding toward us across the small clearing.

"Oh no," Avery groaned, rubbing a hand over his eyes.

Chapter 5

"*H*ow did you find us?" Avery asked the couple.

The man smiled. He wore a long duster and matching suede fedora. Something about his eyes was familiar. . . . "You've never been able to hide from me. All I had to do was focus on you, and I knew where you were."

"Damn," Avery swore, his lips thinned. "I've always hated that."

Who are they?

"My brother and his Beloved. Hello, Sam, Paen."

Your brother's name is Pain?

Paen. It's a long story.

I bet. What are they doing here?

I have no idea. "What are you doing here?" Avery asked them as the tall, black-haired man stopped in front of us, his handsome gray eyes narrowing first on the wolf at our feet, then at me. He sniffed the air delicately, then, with raised eyebrows, gave his brother an odd look.

"You didn't check in with us last night, and since I had a new lead, I convinced Paen that we should leave the girls with my parents and make sure all was right with you. I see it is. Hi, I'm Samantha Scott, but please call me Sam. This is my husband, Paen."

The woman who held out her hand to me was on the short side, somewhat stockier in build than I, but with warm eyes and a genuine smile.

"Jacintha Ferreira," I said, shaking her hand. "I'm not . . . um . . . with him or anything, if that's what you're thinking," I added, gesturing toward Avery.

"The hell you're not," he said placidly.

"You're not?" Sam asked at the same time, and made an almost imperceptible sniffing noise, just as her husband had done.

"Don't tell me you two are jaguars, too? I swear to the saints, I'm getting a bit paranoid about everyone's smelling me!" I crossed my arms, my hands in my armpits, as if that would help.

"Jaguars?" Sam looked at Avery with confusion.

"It's a long story," Avery said somewhat wearily. He wrapped an arm around my waist and hauled me up against his side, much to my surprise and secret delight. "Yes, your nose doesn't lie—she's my Beloved. The man you sent me to investigate turned me into a therion. How, I don't know yet, but I was about to go find out. Jas here found me in black panther form."

"Beloved? But you're not—oh, the kind that goes with a Moravian, not a Dark One. Avery, I'm so happy for you!" Sam said.

"You were a jaguar," I told the annoying man at my side, digging an elbow into his ribs. "Which you full well know, and if you don't unhand me *right this second*, I'll shoot you. Again."

Paen looked at me with interest as I pushed myself away from Avery. Sam beamed with delight. "You shot him?" Paen asked.

"Not really. My sister did. It was my gun, though." I glared at Avery as he frowned at me. *Stop being possessive. You have nothing to be possessive about.*

Yes, I do. I explained it to you already.

And it doesn't make the slightest difference. Stop pretending we're a couple.

"Jacintha is having some difficulty accepting the situation," Avery told them, which just infuriated me all the more.

"Right. That's more than I can bear." I pulled my tranq gun from the holster and leveled it at him. "Say good night, Gracie."

You wouldn't dare.

Try me, Dracula.

Avery sighed and made a low, sweeping bow to me. "Very well, I will withhold my claim upon you until we have dealt with the situation at hand. Does that satisfy your need for denial?"

My finger twitched on the trigger, and for a moment, I contemplated the peace I'd have if he was laid out beside the wolfish Dieter, but I thought perhaps that wouldn't go over so well with the large vampire standing within biting distance, so I slipped the safety back on and put the gun away.

Paen wouldn't bite you. Once a Dark One has Joined and drunk from his Beloved, all other blood is poison to him.

I glanced at him, startled. *That seems rather extreme. What if we were meant to be together, and I got run over by a bus or something?*

He gave a mental shrug. *Beloveds, both those of Dark Ones and Moravians, are immortal once the Joining is completed. But Moravians can survive if their Beloved is lost to them—only the Dark Ones can't drink others' blood once they are Joined.*

Then I guess it's a good thing you have your soul, I said, feeling somewhat peevish for some bizarre reason.

Extremely so, he agreed with maddening complacency.

I wanted to hit him.

"If you are finished?" Paen asked, glancing from me to his brother, obviously aware we'd been talking to each other. "Perhaps you'd like to explain about the jaguar?"

"I have to admit, I'm rather curious about that, too," Sam said, eyeing the wolf.

"I've never heard of a Moravian being turned into a were," Paen continued, looking over his brother. "But it's obvious the effect wasn't permanent."

"Not a were—a therion," Avery corrected. "As to just how he did it, I don't know. That's what I was going to find out."

"*We* were going to find out, because unlike your irritating brother, I have a very good relationship with Albert."

Sam laughed. "I like you already. I can't tell you how happy I am that you're going to take Avery in hand. He's been much too wild the last few years, flitting from woman to woman, never staying with one for more than a couple of days before he tired of her."

"Oh, really," I said, giving the object of the conversation a raised eyebrow.

Avery looked uncomfortable. "Sam exaggerates."

"No, she doesn't," Paen said cheerfully, smiling broadly at his brother. "I'm surprised you bothered to wear trousers; you had them off so much of the time."

You dawg! I thought at him with unreasonable fury.

Jaguar, not a dog, he corrected me. *Don't listen to them. Paen's just paying me back for the years of teasing he got when he found Sam.*

"None of that is important." Avery waved away the subject of his promiscuous ways. "What is important is that I'm close to getting the proof of the man behind the animal smuggling."

"I think perhaps you'd better wait until you hear what Sam found out, and then we can make plans accordingly."

Avery slid a look toward me.

"Don't even think of excluding me. I may not be a vampire or a jaguar, but I'm involved in this now, and I'm responsible for what Albert does to the wildlife in this area."

"Ah, that's why you're wearing that outfit," Sam said, her gaze drifting over my uniform.

I explained my job and waited while she exchanged a glance with her husband, the air humming strangely.

Can they talk to each other like we can?

Yes. Sam is a half elf, not that it makes any difference in that regard, but she's also a Beloved. He thought for a moment. *And now a Moravian, too.*

Huh?

She was attacked, and Paen had to turn her to save her life. It stripped her of her soul, but he got it back for her.

You guys really can turn people into vampires?

Moravians, yes. It doesn't happen often, because the

Moravian Council frowns heavily on it, but once in a while there is a need to turn someone.

Cold, clammy fingers crawled over my skin at the thought of being changed into a vampire.

Avery put his arm around me again, pulling me against the warmth of his body, and this time, I didn't resist. *Don't worry, love. I won't let anyone turn you.*

"I think perhaps we need to have a little talk," Sam said, obviously having finished her discussion with her husband. She looked at the sleeping wolf. "Somewhere a little less likely to be discovered."

"There's Avery's motel room. It's not too long a walk from here."

"I thought you were staying with the Leshies?" Sam asked Avery.

"I was. Jacintha put me into a squalid little motel when her sister shot me."

"This sounds a lot like a story I want to hear," Sam said, threading her arm through mine as we turned to walk back the way we came. "You can tell me all about it, and I'll tell you about Paen and me, so you don't think you're alone with arrogant, bossy vampires. Let me see, where should I start? We have the two most adorable girls. Jenna is four, and Laurie is just about to turn two, and we live in Paen's castle in Scotland. My cousin Claire is a fairy, and she's married to another brother, Finn. Has Avery told you about all the brothers? And their parents? You'll like them; they're very nice, although they prefer to spend most of the year in the most primitive areas of the world, studying indigenous peoples. . . ."

I glanced back over my shoulder at Avery. *What about Dieter?*

He'll be fine where he is. I took the dart from his shoulder, so even if old man Baum finds him, he'll have no proof of who sedated his maniac son.

It's not his father I'm concerned about. "I'm sorry," I said, coming to a halt. "I can't leave."

"You can't?" Sam's face scrunched up in confusion. "Why not?"

"Dieter is sedated. Look at him. He's completely vulnerable should a bear or cougar come upon him. I just can't leave him unprotected like that."

Avery sighed a heavily martyred sigh. "I never thought I'd regret being born Moravian, but I'm starting to think it may happen."

Paen laughed so hard his wife punched him in the arm. "You have no idea what hell is in store for you," Paen said as the two men hoisted the sedated Dieter.

The walk back to the motel was much longer than the one out. I gathered up Dieter's clothing, which evidently fell off his body when he shifted into wolf form, and trailed behind the two men as they complained their way back to the dingy, dank motel. By the time they deposited Dieter in the bathtub, Avery's expression was black and Paen had adopted a martyred air.

"So, what exactly is this important news that you couldn't relate in a call or text to me?" Avery asked, slumping on the bed with a groan. I was about to take one of the two chairs when he snagged my wrist and pulled me down onto the edge of the bed. I glared at him but figured he was due a little slack since he had just hauled a heavy wolf two miles through the woods.

"We did call you, but you didn't answer. And Sam didn't want to text just in case you were found out and your text messages could be read," Paen answered, gingerly seating himself in one of the two rickety chairs that were at least twenty years older than I.

"Finn was poking around on the Leshy server and found an archived e-mail that leads us to believe someone else is involved with the smuggling," Sam said, glancing at her husband.

"Poking around?" I asked, my eyes narrowing. "You mean your brother-in-law hacked the Leshy Web site?"

Her gaze skittered away from me. "Er . . . something like that. Normally, I wouldn't condone illegal actions, but we felt this situation warranted a little . . . er . . . irregularity concerning privacy laws."

I gawked at her for a minute. "I admit that smuggling animals into another country is not at all good, but honestly, what you're doing is highly illegal, and immoral to boot!"

Sam's gaze swiveled to Avery. "You didn't tell her?"

"Not all of it. Jas," Avery said, suddenly sounding weary. I turned to look at him, lying on the bed, his eyes glittering sapphires in the gloomy light of the room. Hunger rolled off him.

You're hungry again?

I'm afraid so. The shape-shifting and healing are somewhat energy-intensive, he answered, apology in his voice.

Instantly, I was contrite. *I'm sorry, I didn't think. Of course that would wear you out. Er . . . did you wish to dine with the others here?*

Amusement and something warm and smoky entered his eyes. *Decidedly not. We'll wait until we are alone.*

It was clear he was expecting to do more than drink a little blood, and although I had no intention of allowing him to have his wicked way—at least, not without knowing him better—I decided to let that point pass and move on to those issues that were claiming all our attention.

"What is it you're not telling me?" I asked Avery.

He looked surprised for a moment, a vision lovingly held in his mind of our naked selves twined about each other in an act so erotic, my entire body blushed.

"Not that," I snapped. "That's all you've been thinking about for the last ten minutes, and you can just stop because it's not going to happen. And that. I'm allergic to cherries, anyway. Now, that one is just underhanded. Avery! Stop thinking smutty things at me! I can't concentrate when you . . . Hoo, mama! Is that . . . No. I'm not listening to you anymore."

Paen laughed aloud, and Sam looked like she was fighting to keep from joining him.

I poked Avery in the ribs. "What I was trying to ask before you went off to the land of whipped cream and love swings is what you were keeping from me about the Leshies. What haven't you told me?"

He sighed and pulled himself up to a sitting position, leaning against the headboard. "What do you know about the Leshies?"

"Not a whole lot," I admitted. "Albert Baum is the leader. There are five other members in the group for this area, including Albert's two sons and a daughter."

"The nubile Danielle," he said, nodding.

I pinned him back with a long look, but he met it with nothing but patience. "You said she wanted you to marry her—did you seduce her?"

"No." Chagrin flickered in his eyes for a moment.

I prodded him again on the ribs. He took my hand and flattened it on his chest, rubbing my fingers absently. "I didn't seduce her, although I did let her think I was interested in her. I had to have some way to infiltrate the Leshies, and since women like me, that seemed the best route."

"I'm sure it did," I said drily.

"Men!" Sam said under her breath, and I felt an immediate kinship.

"What I know about the Leshy group is that they are devoted to animal welfare. They vigorously defend what they call their wildlife preserves. There are a couple of small compounds where they live in rustic simplicity, so as to be more one with Mother Nature, or so Albert says. They also have a passionate dislike of hunters and hunting, and have been known to make trouble for hunters when they find them out in the woods. There've been a few assault charges, with one or two members of the group receiving jail time, but for the most part, they stay on their own land and take care of the animals that live there. I take it you were staying at one of their compounds?"

Avery's lips twisted. "If you call the motley collection of tents and moth-eaten cots a compound, yes. It's nothing more than a campsite so far as I'm concerned."

"Thus speaks a man for whom the concept of nature in the raw is repulsive," Paen commented.

"Really?" I asked Avery. "You don't like camping?"

He grimaced. "It's uncomfortable, unhygienic, and reminds me far too much of the time I spent in service to the king."

"What king?" I asked, momentarily sidetracked from the subject at hand.

"George." He grinned. "The first time I went to war, I was seventeen."

"I remember that," Paen said thoughtfully. "You had been pestering Father to let you join the mortals' war on the Continent for a couple of years, but he felt you were too headstrong, and wouldn't give his permission."

"You fought against Napoleon?" I asked, having a hard time coming to grips with that idea.

"No, unfortunately. My father wouldn't let me go."

"So instead you waited until he and I were doing another switch, and you ran off to join the cavalry," Paen said with an unreadable look at his brother.

Avery grinned even more, his eyes twinkling. "That was in 1812."

The date resonated in my brain. I've never been a big one for history, but even I recognized the importance of the year. "You fought against the United States?" I whomped him on the arm. "You did, didn't you! You fought against my country! Well, all right, my family didn't leave Mexico until the 1930s, but still! It's my country now! I can't believe you'd kill Americans and then have the balls to come over here and act all innocent!"

"I didn't kill anyone," he said, grabbing my other hand and holding it, too. "My father had me sent home before my unit saw action. So you can stop thinking those thoughts about standing me against a wall and unleashing your sister on me."

Mollified somewhat, I pulled my hands out of his. "Back to the Leshies, please. I've told you what I know about them; now it's your turn. What have you been withholding from me?"

"Your precious animal-loving mates are murdering innocent people," he said simply.

"What?" My jaw sagged as I gawked at him.

"And our furry friend in the bathroom is a part of it."

"Dieter?" I shook my head. "I can't believe it. I mean, he's intense and all, but murdering people? I just can't believe that!"

"It's not quite that simple, but that's the gist of it," Sam agreed. Her face was somber. "What Avery appears to have *not* told you is that the animals are being smuggled to a private reserve in Scotland."

"No, he told me that," I said, more confused than ever. "I don't see—"

"A private hunting reserve," Avery clarified, taking my hand again.

"Oh. They're collecting wildlife here—I assume big game, since that's what hunters like—bears and cougars and such, and smuggling them into this private hunting reserve? That's terrible. It has to stop. Not only is it wrong and illegal, but it's bad for the population here. We in the wildlife department work very hard to keep the animal populations robust and healthy, and if people are capturing them and shipping them off to be hunted elsewhere . . . well, I won't stand for it. I just won't stand for it."

"You don't understand, Jacintha," Sam said softly, giving Avery a look.

He sighed again. "I told you they were smuggling *exotic* animals into Scotland."

"I assume Pacific Northwest wildlife would be considered exotic there."

He watched me closely for a moment. "It's more than that. They also smuggle big cats like lions, tigers, and leopards. And some other game—buffalo, rare deer, even elephants."

"From where?" I asked.

"Here. The Leshy camp."

"How can they do that? None of those animals are native to this area. Where are they getting them from?"

Avery said nothing, just stroked my hand, his mind filled with sadness.

I stared at him in incomprehension for a moment before it sank it. "They're turning people into animals? Like they did you? And then sending them to Scotland where they're . . . My God!" He nodded as my skin crawled with the realization of what Albert and his group were doing. "That's wholesale murder!"

"Yes. And it's why I felt it was so important to infiltrate the Leshies—I needed to see who was in charge and how they were getting their stock." He gave a wry little smile. "Unfortunately, I have all too good an explanation of where they're getting the animals."

"Holy Mary—"

"And all the itty-bitty saints," finished a voice from

the door. "I agree, although what the saints would have to do with the heinous undead is beyond me. Please tell me that Vlad there hasn't turned you into a vampire yet? I bought only one stake."

Cora held up a gardening trowel.

"That's a trowel, not a stake," I felt obliged to point out.

Your sister is not going to live with us.

There is no us, Buster Brown. At least, not in the way you are thinking about, although I have to admit that bit about the bathtub and bath oil is intriguing.

"Trowel, stake, same difference. It'll do the job. Hello." Cora noticed Sam and Paen as she laid a coil of hose, the trowel, and a pair of gardening shears on the tiny table.

"Er . . . hi," Sam said, eyeing the things.

I made a quick introduction, adding at the end, "What in God's name have you bought, Cora?"

"Stuff to take care of the Fanged One over there. I see he's awake. Don't suppose you'd care to let me have your gun again?"

"You've really gone daft, haven't you?" Avery asked, sighing again as he sat up. "You might as well know that Paen is my brother."

"Yeah? So?" We watched her for a moment before it sank in. She spun around, clutching the trowel and giving Paen a wide-eyed look. "Two vampires! My God, you're breeding like bunnies! It's a good thing I bought the extra-long length of hose—they were out of rope, so I figured the hose would do to tie Avery up. Now I'll have enough for both."

"What a very odd woman you are," Sam said, tipping her head on the side to consider my clearly de-ranged sister. "You don't like Dark Ones?"

"Like them!" gasped Cora, horrified.

"Don't get her started," I begged Sam, marching over to Cora to gently pry the trowel from her hands. "There will be no staking and no tying anyone up with a hose, not that I think you could to begin with. Honestly, Cora, a hose?"

"It's all they had," she snapped, her arms crossed as she plopped herself down on a low chest of drawers. "And can I just say that you know how to ruin *any* fun I might have?"

"Hush up, or we won't bring you up to speed with everything that's happened in the last hour and a half."

It took a good fifteen minutes to explain everything. By the time we were done, I was glad to see she was looking at Avery with less hostility. "You saved Jas's life?"

"Of course."

"The mortal belief that Dark Ones are undead and evil is wrong," Paen said. "We are neither. We're simply people like you who happen to be immortal and require ingestion of blood to exist."

Cora shuddered.

"The act of feeding is actually very erotic," Sam added, gazing at her husband with dewy eyes. He winked at her.

"Uh-huh. Right. Well, since Mr. Bitey over there saved my sister from a werewolf—"

"Therion wolf," Avery corrected.

"Then I won't stake you as I planned, although I'm

going to be keeping an eye on you," she finished, giving him a hard look.

"I shudder in my boots," he answered, flashing her a particularly effective grin.

Stop flirting with my sister, I growled at him.

Jealous?

Don't be stupid. I just don't like your flirting with her.

You don't lie very well, do you, love?

And stop calling me that. You already admitted you're not in love with me.

No, but you're beginning to grow on me, he said with an oddly warm rush of emotion.

"Why is everyone so quiet? You're all thinking at one another, aren't you?" Cora stomped her foot. "I hate being left out!"

"You'll have to find your own Dark One, then," Sam told her as she kissed Paen.

The expression on Cora's face was priceless but beside the point. "What is it that your cousin found when she hacked the Leshy server?" I asked Sam.

She stopped making bedroom eyes at her husband and looked, if anything, guilty. "Er . . . I suppose it's okay to tell you. The e-mails Claire and Finn uncovered were between someone at the Leshy group—they weren't signed, and were sent to a generic address, so we assume it was Albert Baum, the leader—and someone in the Washington Department of Fish and Wildlife."

"What?" I shrieked. "Who?"

"A man by the name of Morrison. Gregory Morrison."

Chapter 6

"That's impossible. Greg? Selling animals? But . . . how? Why? He's always been . . ." I paused, unsure of how to go on. It was true that I had never liked Greg, not trusting that smooth demeanor, and the ruthless way he cut jobs and programs in order to pad the budget, but that was a far cry from being a part of a ring that more or less murdered people. Wasn't it?

"A bastard?" Cora offered.

I frowned.

"Oh, come on, every time you've told me about him, you mentioned how much you didn't like him. You said he doesn't give a rat's ass about anyone but himself. That sounds like a man who wouldn't turn a hair about turning people into jaguars and sending them off to be hunted."

"What exactly did the e-mails say?" I asked Sam.

"Most of them just talked about some unnamed plan that they were putting into place, but this one was particularly damning." She pulled a piece of paper out of her purse and handed it to me. Avery and Cora both read over my shoulder.

It was a brief e-mail: *I've taken care of everything, so stop worrying. Why would anyone notice a group of peace-*

able animal lovers? Just keep your nose clean, and no one will bother you.

"*I've taken care of everything,*" I mused, noting the date. "That was right around the time he axed four jobs. We all had the regions we covered doubled to compensate. That bastard. That moneygrubbing, animal-hating, murdering bastard."

"Told you," Cora said smugly, sitting back on the edge of the bed next to me. Avery, on my other side, hmmed softly to himself.

"What?" I asked him.

"Nothing."

"That wasn't a nothing hmm. That was a 'Something has just occurred to me, but I don't want to tell anyone' hmm."

"Sometimes," he said with great dignity, "a hmm is just a hmm."

"Thank you, Dr. Freud," I answered, trying to open myself up to his thoughts. It was an awkward thing, trying to get inside someone else's brain to see what he was thinking, but I managed it, and I was pleased when he allowed me to peer at his thoughts.

"Hmm," I said.

"Oh, for heaven's sake!" Cora said, pinching me.

I offered an apologetic smile to everyone. "Sorry. Just slipped out. Avery feels, and I have to say, it's an intriguing thought, that perhaps this is all just a bit too pat."

"Too pat?" Sam asked, looking at her paper. "How so?"

"The Leshies don't operate that way," Avery said. "They are very close-knit and keep to themselves. In the entire three weeks I've been with them, I've never seen them speak with anyone outside their group. They have cell phones, but they don't use them. When I told them my phone was dead and I needed to send some e-mails, I was informed that the only computer they had was locked up in a seldom-visited warehouse."

"Then why do they have a Web site?" Cora asked, becoming intrigued by the situation despite herself.

"It's a front," I answered.

Avery nodded. "Most likely."

"They want to make everyone believe they're nothing more than a group of people devoted to the welfare of wildlife, so they put up a Web site with a bunch of activist-speak, and no one's the wiser."

"So how does your boss fit into the picture?" Cora asked me.

"Scapegoat? Red herring? Deliberate attempt to involve him? Or perhaps he really is a part of it, and we're falling for a grandiose whitewash. I don't know, but I intend to find out." I glanced at my watch as I stood up. "Time to ask Greg a few questions."

No, you're not.

I stopped at the door, and Cora, who had followed me, bumped into me. *I beg your pardon?*

It's not safe for you to confront him.

"I thought you just said Greg wasn't involved?"

"I think it's very likely he isn't, but until I'm sure, it's not safe for you to confront him on your own."

I looked from him, to Cora, and on to Sam. "Does he really think he can boss me around like that?" I asked the latter.

"Oh, they all do," she answered placidly, patting her

husband on his leg. He glared at her. "They're all into this macho he-man crap that says they can't let their women do things on their own. Because, you know, we're so frail and delicate and don't have a brain among us."

"I've never said you don't have a brain," Paen said quickly. "You are an elf, however. You are delicate because of that."

"As delicate as a two-ton truck," she answered, smiling at his scowl.

"Did he say elf?" Cora asked me in a whisper.

"I think so." We both looked speculatively at Sam until she laughed and gestured toward her ears. "Half elf, really, and my ears have been bobbed. But getting back to the subject at hand—I have to admit, as intriguing as this e-mail is, I'd really like to see the Leshies. I'm a pretty good judge of when people are lying to me, and I bet I could get to the bottom fairly quickly of whether or not Jacintha's boss is involved."

"Well, I don't care what we do—I just want to do something," Cora said, picking up her hose and her trowel. "This sitting around talking is getting us nowhere. Besides, I bought this stuff to use, and by God, someone is going to get tied up, if not staked!"

"When did you become Buffy?" I asked her.

"More important, why does she think she's a part of this?" Avery asked, matching her frown with one of his own.

"Oh, I'm part of it. I'm not going to let Jas walk into a group of weirdos without someone to watch her back, and just you remember that, sparkle boy."

Sam snickered as both Avery and Paen looked offended. "I would never let Jacintha be harmed," Avery told her. "And we do *not* sparkle."

"Whatever. Let's just get this show on the road." Cora pushed past me to stand impatiently at the door.

Avery gave me a long-suffering look.

"I am not responsible for my sister," I told the look, holding up my hands. "So, where to first? Greg or Albert Baum et al?"

"If I told you it was too dangerous for you to go to the Leshy compound—," Avery started to say.

I pulled my gun from the holster. "I'd shoot you and go anyway."

"Atta girl, Jas!" Cora cheered.

"In that case . . ." Avery thought for a few moments. "I am tempted to confront Albert Baum now, but if we were to all arrive at the compound, they would probably attack us."

"And we'd be vulnerable since they must have warning of visitors," I said. "The couple of times I went there, they were waiting for me."

"They have sentries, yes." He looked at me for a moment, then beyond to his brother. "How do you feel about a nighttime assault?"

Paen cracked his knuckles. "A little action would be welcome."

Avery grinned. "I thought you'd like that. Sam?"

"Oh, I'm totally in on this. No way you boys can keep me out of it."

"It might be dangerous," Avery warned.

"Pfft. Like I can't take care of myself?"

Paen made a wordless protest.

"Besides, I have Mr. Big and Bad here, and with the

exception of that time I had my throat slit, he's never let anyone hurt me."

"I didn't let that bastard slit your throat—," Paen started to say, but Sam cut him off with a giggle and a kiss.

Avery turned back to me. "There's no sense in telling you not to come, is there?"

"None whatsoever."

"Me, either," Cora said.

It will be dangerous, you know. Very dangerous. Once the Leshies realize you are with me, they will view you as their enemy, too.

I gave a mental shrug. *I have a feeling I wouldn't be on their good side anyway, once Dieter tells them I shot him.*

There is that. "Very well. Shall we regroup in"—he consulted the battered clock hanging drunkenly on the wall—"six hours?"

"That sounds good. It gives us a chance to find a motel," Sam said, looking around the room with distaste. "Another motel."

"There's a nice one in a town about twenty minutes from here," I told her, and gave her directions.

"What about him?" Cora asked, nodding toward Avery.

"I am not staying here," he said quickly. "This motel makes me itch. It's barbaric."

"How on earth did you last three weeks in the Leshy compound?" I couldn't help but ask him.

He shuddered. "It wasn't easy."

"Well, he can't stay with us," Cora said, giving him a narrow look.

Avery just looked at me.

Do I take it that you'd like to stay with me rather than find a motel?

Only if you want me to.

If I want you to what—do all those wicked things that you've been thinking? Or just have a place to stay until this is wrapped up?

A slow smile curled the outer edges of his lips. *I will leave that decision to you.*

I blushed at the warmth in his voice, and the obvious sexual intent, not addressing that point as I said, "There's no reason he can't stay with us, Cora. He can sleep on the couch."

"Oh, right, the couch. As if I haven't seen the looks you've been slipping him when you think I'm not looking?" Cora sighed and shook her head. "She's thralled good and proper."

"We don't do that," Paen protested.

Cora just clucked her tongue as a thought occurred to me.

"What do we do with Dieter? We can't just leave him here."

"Why not?" Avery asked. "With luck, the roaches might eat him."

I ignored that comment. "The tranquilizer will be wearing off in a few hours. And the first thing I'd do if I were he would be to run right back to Daddy and tell him the big bad wildlife officer shot him."

Avery's lips thinned. I had an almost-overwhelming urge to lick them. "You'll have to sedate him again."

"No."

He slid a curious look at me.

"No," I repeated. "It's one thing to knock him out

because he was a wolf and was attacking us, but these drugs aren't a precise dose, and I'm not a vet. We're either going to have to let him sleep it off and go back to camp to alert everyone, or . . ."

"Or we'll have to take him somewhere he can't quickly return from," Avery finished for me. "That's no problem. We'll just tie him up and toss him in the back of Paen's car, and he and Sam can haul Dieter somewhere remote."

"Like hell you will. I don't want to be stuck with a pissed-off therion," Paen protested.

"No other choice," Avery answered, glancing around the room. He briefly examined the hose Cora had brought, obviously rejecting it. "We need something to tie him."

"Afraid I'm fresh out of rope," Sam said, making a show of patting her pockets.

"Nothing else for it," Avery sighed after a quick search of the room, pulling off his shirt and tearing it to strips.

"You told him to do that, didn't you?" Cora accused me.

I tried very hard to drag my eyes off the sight of Avery's bare chest to look at her, but my brain couldn't seem to get the order through. "Huh?"

"I can tell by the look on your face that you're snatching at any excuse to get him shirtless."

Avery, with a roll of his eyes, finished twisting the strips of shirt and turned to go into the bathroom.

My eyes widened even more at the close-up view of his back. He wasn't bodybuilder muscley, but he was a damned fine sight nonetheless. My brain just kind of shut down as I drank in his naked upper half, wanting to stroke the long planes of his back, to trace out the hills and valleys caused by the silky-smooth skin lying over ropes of muscles that made me feel intensely female, and, more than anything, I wanted to run my tongue along the long line of his spine.

Right, that did it. The stroking I could cope with. The tracing was pushing it. But the tongue up my back was too much. You can't think thoughts like that at me and not expect me to act on them.

Stop eavesdropping! I yelled, mortified and aroused at the same time.

Never. Your place or mine?

Your place is with a bunch of animal-changing maniacs!

True. Your place, then. Just as soon as we can manage.

I didn't answer, not trusting myself to respond reasonably.

By the time Avery and Paen had the still-sleeping Dieter-wolf tied up and deposited in the back of a black sedan, and I had given them directions to a suitable release spot, it was past two in the afternoon.

"I should get the truck turned back in," I said with a glance at my watch. "So I think it's a good idea to head back to the office. Hopefully, Greg will be there, and I'll be able to talk to him."

"*We* will talk to him," Avery said, taking my hand as I started for the truck.

"Are all vampires this pushy?" Cora asked Sam.

"Unfortunately, yes. Your sister had better get used to it. They don't get any better." Sam paused at the look her husband gave her. "What?"

"Don't tell her that. She'll never agree to Join with Avery, and we'll have him on our hands for eternity."

Avery made a rude gesture at his brother that caused him to laugh, but he accepted the shirt Paen handed over from his luggage. Once Avery's distracting chest was covered, we all dispersed to our respective vehicles; Avery, Cora and I to the state truck, and Paen and Sam to their rented wolf-laden car. I sat in the middle, next to Avery, who claimed he preferred to drive.

"Don't tell me you're the sort of man who hates to be driven by a woman," I said, giving him the keys that Cora had grudgingly handed over.

"I don't like being driven by anyone, but that's not pertinent. If you drive, your sister will insist on sitting between us, and my ribs are already bruised from where she's repeatedly dug her elbows into them."

"Cora!" I gave her a scathing look as I scooted over next to Avery, unable to ignore the part of my mind that was making happy noises at being pressed up next to him. His body was warm and hard and so incredibly male it made my mouth water.

"Who, me? I would never do anything so petty." Her face was angelic, but I wasn't in the least fooled.

I focused on keeping my hands to myself and on not touching Avery.

But I'd like you to touch me. Not as much as I'd like to touch you, though.

I kept my mind firmly on what I was going to say to Greg. "I think we're going to have to be straightforward with him. He's never been the sort of guy to pick up on subtle hints."

"Subtle as in, stop hitting on me; I'm not interested in you?" Cora asked.

Avery's thoughts were suddenly filled with violence.

Stop pretending to be jealous.

I'm not pretending.

It's not going to impress me. Greg hasn't done anything to warrant your thinking things like that. Or that. And gelding is definitely out. They have laws against that, you know!

I'm a Moravian, Beloved. I am above such things as mortal laws.

And conceited to boot. You can posture all you like, but it's not going to impress me.

He said nothing, but I caught a shadow of a thought that had me worried he wasn't trying to play he-man just to impress me.

By the time I turned the truck in and made it back to the office, we hadn't come to a consensus on how to deal with Greg.

"If you two would just stay here, I will go see if he's even in the office," I told Avery and Cora as they followed me down the hall to the big room that housed all the officers for the two counties we covered.

"Jacintha!"

"Too late," Cora said softly, watching with bright, interested eyes as Greg emerged from his office at the end of the hall and came barreling toward us.

"Just the woman I hoped to see. Perhaps you can spare me a few minutes to talk about some upcoming plans I have for the department. Your input is invaluable when it comes to making decisions, you know."

He stopped in front of me, giving me his usual oily smile, one that faded slightly when Avery wrapped an arm around my waist and hauled me tight into his side.

"Er . . ." Greg looked askance at Avery. "And this is?"

"Her fiancé," Avery said in a voice that was outwardly pleasant but with a distinct undertone of warning.

Oh, you are not!

You're my Beloved. That is infinitely more binding than a mortal engagement.

"Yeah," Cora said, nodding as her gaze narrowed on Greg when I introduced Avery to him. "They're engaged."

I looked at her in complete surprise. "You don't even like Avery!"

"So? He saved you from that weirdo Dieter. And besides, he's better than the alternatives," she said with a pointed glance at Greg.

"Cora! I'm sorry, Greg; my sister isn't usually so rude."

"Oh, I can be."

Greg waved away the insult. "Engaged, eh? Congratulations. Did you say Dieter? Dieter Baum?"

Next to me, Avery stiffened.

"Yes," I said slowly, trying to read Greg's expression. His eyes, not nearly as clear and pure a blue as Avery's, looked confused. "Dieter caught me on his land earlier today when I was going to see Albert, and he attacked me."

"Good God. Come into my office and tell me about

it," Greg said, ushering us into his office. "Are you all right? Did you call the police?"

"I'm fine, and no, no police. Avery was there and managed to handle the situation," I said quickly.

"I see." He looked at Avery again. "How fortunate he was there at that moment."

"Yes. Greg, perhaps you can help me. I would like to talk to Albert about some issues with wildlife in the area, but naturally, after the attack, I'm hesitant to go onto Leshy lands."

Nice ad-libbing, Avery said with approval.

I'm rather pleased with it, myself.

"Oh, I wouldn't be if I were you," Greg said, waving away my worry. "Albert's all right. Dieter's a bit of a nut ball, but if you stay away from him, you should be fine."

"You know Albert Baum?" Avery asked.

"Met him several years ago. He's harmless enough. I won't say he's not a pain in the ass during hunting season, but the rest of the year he's pretty reasonable. If you don't mind my asking, when did you get engaged, Jacintha?"

Somewhat taken aback by the shift in topic, I hesitated before answering. "Well, to be honest, we're not actually engaged."

"Yes, we are."

"Avery is Scottish, you see, and they do things a little differently in Scotland," I explained, mentally growling at the man in question.

"No, we don't."

"I think I understand," Greg said, his face suddenly inscrutable. "Yes, I think I understand it all."

A chill went through me. "When's the last time you saw any of the Leshies?" I asked.

He shrugged. "It's been some time. Maybe six months. Why?"

Rats. I think he's suspicious, I told Avery.

No. Just shrewd.

Not his natural state, I assure you.

That you know of.

True. "I just wondered if perhaps something had happened that would leave them all a bit skittish around outsiders. Or rather, more skittish than normal. Say . . . some problem with their game."

"Game? Do you think they're raising the animals for slaughter?" Greg pounced on my carefully chosen word, leaving me disconcerted.

"No, nothing like that. It was just a slip of the tongue."

"I see. Well, I haven't heard of anything amiss with Baum and his group, but I don't maintain much contact with them at all. Just the odd e-mail now and again, and of course, I hear about their interactions with hunters during the hunting season."

That tells us nothing, damn it. I can't decide whether he looks innocent and is really guilty, or vice versa, I grumbled.

You didn't expect him to admit anything, did you?

Expect? No. Hope . . . kind of.

Greg turned the subject to matters of state policy, asking my opinion on a number of items, which I answered absently, all the while Avery and I trying to figure out whether we had any other conversational gambit to offer.

We didn't. "Thanks for your time," Greg said some fifteen minutes later, giving Avery an odd look as we left his office. "And nice to meet your . . . er . . . friend."

Cora tugged on my arm as Greg toddled off to attend a meeting. "That was boring beyond human comprehension. So, inquiring minds want to know: What were you guys saying on your mental Instant Messengers?"

Chapter 7

"*H*ow do you know we said anything?" I wondered whether there was some way Cora knew when Avery and I were doing the mental thing.

"'Cause you snickered under your breath a couple of times, and I fail to see how policy regarding wild salmon is enough to tickle anyone's funny bone. What did you guys say?"

"Is she always this nosy?" Avery asked as I made a decision and headed toward the entrance of the building.

"Hey! It's called sisterly concern. And you'd better get used to it, bucko, because I'm not going to leave Jas alone so you can brainwash her."

Avery's expression was one of weary resignation. "I'm beginning to see the charm of remaining unentangled."

"If you're referring to me, you're more than welcome to be as footloose and fancy-free as you like," I said with much dignity. "The last thing I want to do is entangle someone against his wishes."

Oh, really? So that thought about tying me down and licking various sticky substances off me wasn't yours?

I blushed remembering it.

"So, what now? We just go home and wait?" Cora asked as I gave Avery directions to my apartment.

"Yes." I glanced at Avery, once again telling my mind to stop flinging itself around in wild abandon at being pressed up against his side. "We should probably stop at a store to get you some clothes that fit, unless you want to keep wearing those borrowed things. There's an outlet mall about half an hour from here. And then . . ."

"Then what?" Cora frowned at Avery when he casually dropped his hand onto my leg.

You need to eat, don't you? I can feel that you're getting more and more hungry. How do you normally handle that?

Feeding? I find someone isolated, feed, and give them a little mind push to forget that fact.

I see. It sounds rather cold and impersonal.

It can be, although usually it's the opposite.

I glanced at him in surprise. *Feeding is stimulating?*

Arousing. Sometimes. Depends on the person.

Irritation prickled along my skin at the thought of Avery's drinking another woman's blood, his body all warm and sensual and so sexy it made my stomach hurt.

It doesn't have to be that way, Beloved.

You can control your horn-dawg ways?

Not in that sense. I meant that if you fed me, there would be no reason for you to feel so jealous.

I am not feeling jealous. I have nothing to be jealous about, despite your claim I'm some sort of quasi soul saver.

There's nothing quasi about you, love.

I dropped the conversation, murmuring something

innocuous to Cora as we drove to the outlet mall. An hour later we arrived at my apartment.

I pointed Avery to the small bathroom attached to my bedroom so he could shower and change.

"I don't suppose it would do any good for me to warn you about the dangers of sex with a vampire?" Cora tossed the question at me as I went into my room to change my clothes.

"None whatsoever," I answered, closing the door behind me.

"Fine, but when you come crying to me about being enslaved to a tomcat vampire, I get to say I told you so!" she bellowed before she headed to the other bedroom to unpack her things.

I am not a tomcat. I am a therion. There is a difference.

You're eavesdropping again.

I can't help it. He thought of licking a line up my spine, making me suddenly stand up very straight. *Now who's eavesdropping?*

I grumbled to myself as I pulled off my uniform, hurrying into the oversized spa robe before he emerged from the bathroom. Steam curled around him through the open door. His hair was several shades darker, wet, and slicked back from his forehead. He wore a pair of jeans he'd purchased, but nothing more. At the sight of me, his eyebrows rose. "I would have been happy to wait for you had I known you wished to shower, as well."

"Thank you, but I prefer to take showers by myself."

His smile, as I passed him to enter the warm, steamy bathroom, was full of promise, but he said nothing.

He wasn't stark naked and in my bed when I came out of the bathroom, as I half expected. Instead, he stood at the window, having angled the blinds carefully so the sunlight wouldn't strike him.

"You really are opposed to our Joining, aren't you?" he said without looking at me.

"I'm not sure I understand exactly what that is," I answered, fingering the thick cotton lapel on my robe.

"For a Dark One, there are seven steps. But for me, there are only six."

"And what are they?"

"A marking, protection, fluids exchange, trust, a second exchange, and overcoming darkness. Dark Ones have a final step: an exchange of blood."

"Fluids exchange?" I asked, creeped out.

His lips quirked. "Saliva counts."

"Oh, that kind of fluids," I said, thinking about the steamy kisses we'd shared. "It seems to me that we've done most of those."

"We have. All but one."

I waited, sure he would tell me.

"Darkness." His eyes glittered in the relative dimness of my room. "You must overcome the darkness that lives within me, the same darkness that resides in all Moravians, for us to be Joined."

"And what happens then? We're . . . married?" I asked, my emotions torn. I had tried to figure out in the shower what I wanted to do about Avery. Part of me wanted to keep him. He was interesting, fascinating, really, so different from other men, and yet there was something about him that resonated within me, as if he were a missing part of my being. My saner self, however, pointed out the obvious: I'd just met him, knew nothing about him, and oh yes, he was a blood-drinking, shape-shifting jaguar.

"Marriage is a mortal custom. It can be broken. Joining is for all time. You would become my Beloved, and we would be bound together for the rest of our lives, which will no doubt be for many centuries."

"Centuries!"

"Beloveds, both those of Dark Ones and Moravians, are immortal." He moved toward me, and my inner self almost drooled while admiring the way his muscles moved together. He took my hands, his thumbs stroking gently over my fingers. "You have seen my thoughts, so you know this is not something I had sought."

"Oh, I'm quite aware that you were very happy seducing every woman who came within ten feet of you."

"Not *every* woman," he said with a devilish grin that melted my heart.

"Do you seriously think I want to spend the rest of my life, spend *centuries* bound to a man with a roving eye and worse? No," I said, shaking my head. "Call me selfish, but no. I told you earlier that I don't share."

"And that is why I never thought I'd want to find a Beloved." His lips curled into a half smile. "It just seemed so limiting. But now I see why Paen and Finn have embraced it. The idea of being bound to you isn't just enticing; it's necessary." He leaned close to me, his breath brushing my lips. "*You're* necessary."

"Avery, what you're asking—"

"I know. We've just met. You feel you don't know me. You're not ready for a commitment like this."

"On the nose," I said, leaning forward to rub my nose against his. "But surely you must feel the same way."

His eyes smiled down at me. "If I said no, would you think I was lying?"

Hesitantly, I let my mind merge with his. His emotions were right there for me to examine, shining with a strength that took my breath away. "You said you weren't in love with me."

"I wasn't. *Then.*"

"How can you fall in love with someone in just an hour?" I asked.

He made a face. "My father once told me it was something bred into Moravians, the way we are engineered. He said he fell in love with my mother two minutes after he met her, and that we're predisposed to be happy with the one person who was born to be our mate."

"Two minutes, huh?" I looked at the clock radio next to my bed. "It took you seven hours. Slacker."

He laughed and let his lips linger on mine, his arms sliding around me to pull my hips against his. He was still clad in only a pair of jeans, and I would be lying if I said I didn't enjoy spreading my fingers across the hair of his chest, my fingertips tingling at the sensation of the heavy muscles beneath the warm, silken skin. "I will obviously have to make it up to you."

"What about the women?" I asked, nibbling on his lower lip a little. "Was your mother as quick to fall in love with your father?"

"No. Beloveds tend to put up some resistance. Dad

said it has more to do with their being women than Beloveds."

I pinched his side. He pulled me tighter, his tongue teasing my lips.

"I'm going to be starkly honest with you, Avery, because you've been the same with me. Right now, I don't know what, exactly, I want for there to be between us. But I think you need me, and that appeals to me. I feel like I have something to offer you, so if you're content to let me have a little space while I make some decisions, maybe we can find out just how things could be."

"You can have all the time you need to work things out, love," he murmured, kissing a steamy path over to my ear. I squirmed in delight, my fingers tightening on his shoulders. "But you're correct that I need you."

"I knew you were hungry," I answered, half gasping when he found a sensitive spot behind my ear.

If you feed me now, I won't be able to control myself, he warned, kissing the line of my throat down to my breastbone.

I've never, ever jumped into bed with a man I just met. I'm not at all that type of person.

His eyes were like molten sapphires, so hot I swear I could feel his gaze scorching me.

Oh, to hell with it. There's always a first time. I pulled him toward the bed.

That was all the encouragement he needed. Before I could even blink, he had his pants and my bathrobe off, and we were lying in a tangled, erogenous heap on my bed.

His kiss was hotter than sin, the taste and feel of him sending my consciousness spiraling into a land of erotic pleasure that amazed and thrilled me. "Go ahead," I whispered, gently biting the corded tendons on the side of his neck. "Feed."

He reared back for a moment, his eyes wide with surprise, delight, and passion; then I was straddling his chest, my breasts at his mouth level. The sharp pain that burned my breast melted into a shock of rapture that swept through my body, pushed higher by the sensations Avery shared with me.

You like it when I touch you, I mused, sweeping my hands upward along his ribs.

God, yes. He pulled my hips over so I straddled his groin, his penis lying hard between us.

I wiggled, and he groaned in my mind, his tongue swirling on my neck. I smiled down at him as I sat up, my back arching and my eyes crossing as his hands took possession of my breasts, the pads of his thumbs gently brushing my very sensitive nipples. *And you like it when I touch you.*

That is clearly obvious. What do you feel if I do this? I shifted so I could take him in my hands, allowing my fingers to dance down the long length of him.

He swore in Latin, his hips thrusting upward.

That good, huh?

His eyes, which had been rolled back in ecstasy, narrowed on me in a way that bespoke retribution. Before I could move, he had me on my back, his hands spreading my thighs, his breath hot on the very center of me. *That sounded very much like mocking, my love. And two can play that game.*

I writhed with anticipation, prepared to enjoy my-self thoroughly, but an odd tickling sensation on my inner thighs had me looking down in concern.

The blue eyes of a black-coated jaguar stared back at me in consternation.

"Um . . . Avery?"

I know. It just happened.

"I'm sorry. I don't want you to take this as a rejec-tion, but I'm not into bestiality."

His jaguar lips thinned. *Neither am I. I didn't intend for this to happen. It just did.*

"Hmm. I wonder why. What were you thinking just before you shifted?"

He looked down at my private parts.

"Oh. You know, as enticing as it sounds to say that my genitalia turn men into animals, it's not nearly as exciting in reality."

His body rippled, elongated, and returned to the form that had me quivering with delight. "Nor for me. I believe it has something to do with strong emotions. When I saw Dieter attacking you earlier, I didn't con-sciously decide to shift—it just happened. And you had me on the verge with the pleasure you were feed-ing me."

My eyes widened. "Oh my God. Are you saying we can't have sex without you turning into a jaguar?"

His head dipped as he swirled his tongue through sensitive parts. I clutched the sheets and bucked up-ward, the sensation almost pushing me over the edge. "Good Lord, Avery!"

He chuckled a breathy, hot chuckle into my groin, then suddenly moved up, wrapped my legs around his hips, and thrust into my body. *It's just a matter of focusing, I believe.*

I tightened all my muscles around him and was rewarded with a groan of the most exquisite pleasure . . . and watched with amazement as black fur rippled up the arms braced on either side of my chest. *Oh no!*

Don't worry—I have it under control, he said, his eyes crossing in concentration as the black fur slowly dissipated. *But if you do that again, I won't be responsible for what happens.*

I pulled him down onto me, nuzzling his neck and wrapping my legs around him, angling my hips upward to better meet his thrusts, my body moving in perfect accord with his.

It sounds trite, but I had no idea that this is what my brothers experience.

I moaned nonstop, dragging my fingernails gently up his spine.

The ability to feel what you feel is incredibly sensual. I had no idea women felt things this way.

I couldn't even think of words to answer him, so plunged into the ecstasy was I. My body was on the brink of an orgasm that I knew was going to outdo any previous one, my mind was filled with the sensations that Avery was experiencing as well as coping with my own, and my soul positively sang with happiness. Just as I was about to fall into a red well of rapture, Avery bit me, his teeth piercing flesh and tissue, a white-hot pain melting instantly to a profound sense of rightness that had me pouring into him more than just life, but every ounce of lightness I possessed to fill the black shadows I sensed within him.

Avery shouted something, but I was too busy becoming a supernova of sexual completion to know just what it was. He reared back a second time, staring at me with wild eyes. "Do you know what you just did?"

"Had an orgasm to end all orgasms," I panted, my entire body quivering with delightful little aftershocks. "I see why the French call it the little death. I think I came very close to passing out. My God, Avery—that was . . . Words fail me. I can only say I hope it's not like this every time, or I really will die."

He stared at me for a moment, his body trembling as well. I stroked my hands up the damp lines of his back as he said, "I don't think that's going to be an issue now."

"Hmm?"

He opened his mouth to say something but shook his head, rolling us over so he was on his back. "I think later is better in this case."

"I have no idea what you're talking about, but since all conscious thought stopped with that orgasm, it's not surprising. I'll get back to you in a few hours, when I can brain again."

He laughed, arranged my boneless limbs across his body, and tucked my head under his chin. "It was a hell of an experience, wasn't it?"

"Oh, yes." I snuggled into him, my hand on his chest, where his heart still beat wildly.

Chapter 8

"Will you stop that?" I whispered to Cora.

"Stop what? I'm not doing anything."

"Like hell you're not. Stop staring at me as if I were a ticking time bomb."

"Well, pardon me for having a little sisterly concern for you. And you can just take that look and shove it, because I've been good. I haven't once mentioned the fact that you and Nosferatu were doing exactly what it's obvious you were doing," she answered with a self-righteous sniff.

"I should hope not. I am an adult, and it's none of your business what I do with Nosf—Avery."

"You just remember you said that when the villagers with the torches come after you."

"That was Frankenstein, not Dracula, you twit," I scolded.

"If the pair of you aren't quieter, we'll have the entire Leshy collective down on us, complete with torches," Avery warned, crawling back to where we were hunkered down behind a wild rhododendron bush.

"What are they doing?" I asked him, squatting next to where he was bent over my cell phone.

"Nothing sinister that I could see. The shift is about

to change, which means we'll have to watch for the new patrol. I didn't see any sign of Baum, though."

"Where are Sam and your brother?"

"Car trouble."

"An accident?" Cora asked.

"They were driving over the mountain pass to the park you told them would be a good place to leave Dieter, when Sam insisted they stop for dinner."

"Did someone hit the car while they were eating?" I asked.

"No, someone left a therion unattended in the car. He came to, managed to get the car started, and left Paen and Sam high and dry."

"Crap," I said, wondering how long it would take Dieter to drive back over the pass.

"My thoughts exactly. Looks like it's just we three, ladies."

I smiled at him, my body thrumming softly to itself whenever he was near.

Thrum. That's a good word to describe it. I begin to see why all the Moravians are searching for their Beloveds. Thrumming is good. I could get used to it.

Even if it means giving up the legions of women you have slept with?

There weren't that many, he said with a mental frown.

Good.

Half a legion. Three-quarters at most.

You are so going to be left to thrum to yourself, I told him, wanting to laugh and punch him at the same time.

I've done that, too, love. You're much better.

I have no idea why you think it's flattering to be told

you're better than jerking off, but that discussion is probably best left for another time.

"You're doing it again, aren't you? I can see you trying not to smile," Cora accused. "What are you saying?"

"I was telling Avery that the discussion about masturbation is best left for another time," I said complacently.

She gawked at me for a second.

"Serves you right for asking. Now, Avery, since we're down two people, do you think we should modify the plan to get Albert alone so we can talk to him?"

"No. I can handle him."

"Like you handled him when he turned you into a puma?" Cora asked.

"Panther," he corrected.

"Jaguar! Honest to God, doesn't anyone pay attention?"

"I wasn't expecting to be turned into a jaguar," Avery continued. "This time I'm ready for him. His tent is the big one, over there. We'll give the patrol time to swing around to the other side of the camp, then make our move."

"How come you're not just flying in there with your bat friends, and flashing fang and claws and stuff and taking them out?" Cora asked in a whisper as we moved as quietly as possible to a clump of laurel that ringed one part of the camp.

"I'm from Scotland, not Hollywood," Avery said grimly. "We don't do those things."

"Boy, that's lame."

Your sister is a big—

You don't need to finish that thought. I am in agreement, although I would like to point out that she's motivated by affection for me. She honestly is worried that you have me under some sort of hypnotic trance.

Did you tell her it was just incredibly hot sex? he asked with male smugness.

No. I told her you were lost and alone, and needed someone to repeatedly explain to you the difference between a panther and a jaguar.

He held up a hand to stop us, gesturing toward a shadowy figure moving silently ahead of us.

Patrol. We'll have to be on guard.

I grabbed Cora's arm and pointed at the shadow, then put my finger across my lips. She nodded her understanding.

The patrol moved off, making almost no noise, just a few whispers from the branches and leaves as he brushed past. We waited a few minutes to make sure he wasn't doubling back, then crept slowly forward until we were behind a stack of wooden crates sitting next to a big old-fashioned canvas tent. A faint glow of light showed within it.

Avery pulled out of his black pullover sweater a small leather case containing, amongst other things, a heavy pair of shears. Quickly he set to work, and in less than a minute had a slit up the back corner of the tent. He peeled back a tiny bit and peered in, Cora and I pressed up close behind him.

What the—

He slipped into the tent without finishing the

thought. I exchanged glances with my sister, then shrugged and sidled through the opening after him, Cora on my heels.

The tent was one that could hold several people, and did in fact have three cots, one of which was occupied—by a figure who was bound and gagged.

"Albert!" I whispered, hurrying over to him. Avery cut off the old man's gag before turning his attention to the hemp rope binding his hands and feet.

"Are you all right?" I asked, keeping a wary eye on the opening of the tent. Although the flap was down, the night breeze made it flap now and again, giving us glimpses of a fire pit in the center of the compound, around which two people sat, talking in subdued voices. "Are you hurt?"

He squinted at me in the dim light. "You're the Mexican girl, aren't you?"

"The politically correct term—" Cora started to say.

"Another time, Cora. Yes, I'm Jacintha from the wildlife department. That's my sister, and Avery I'm sure you know."

"Thought you would never get here, boy."

I stared at the man and blinked a couple of times. "Wait a minute. You expected Avery to come back after what you did to him?"

"Course I did. Why'd you think I dumped him somewhere he'd be safe?"

"It was you who put me in the shelter?" Avery asked, freeing Albert's hands. "Why?"

"To keep you from being killed by my cub, of course."

"Dieter?" I asked.

"Franz?" Avery asked at the same time.

"Danielle," Albert answered. "When I saw that she turned you, I knew she'd be sending you to the farm."

"The hunting reserve," Avery said, answering the question on the tip of my tongue.

"She didn't know you'd turn therion instead of were, though," Albert continued, thoughtfully eyeing Avery. "She didn't ken what you really are."

"And you did?" I asked.

"Aye. Not much slips past me." He winced as Avery severed the ropes on his feet. "Except when my own cubs turn on me. The she-bitch caught me leaving you off, boy, and told me my time was at an end. Lucky for you, folks started showing up at that shelter, so she couldn't get you back."

"Lucky indeed," I mused, looking with warmth at Avery. My blood ran cold at the idea of him, helpless and drugged, in the clutches of a woman who would so abuse her own father.

Avery and I helped him to his feet. The old guy was unusually tall, probably close to seven feet, thin as a sapling, with long salt-and-pepper hair, and a wiry beard that would have been at home in a Tolkien story.

"What about your sons?" Avery asked quietly as he steadied Albert, who seemed a bit wobbly. "Do they know that Danielle is doing this?"

"Not Franz. Boy's as thick as a stump. Dieter, now, he's—"

"Missing."

We all whirled around at the sound of the female voice. Two people stood with the tent flap pulled wide, a petite woman with a gorgeous mane of blue-black raven hair (a color I've always coveted), and a man whose smile left my stomach feeling as if I had been eating lead.

"Greg. I might have known."

"Hello, Jacintha. Yes, you might have, but I've been very careful that you haven't, not even when you came sniffing around my office asking so many obvious questions. Danielle, my dear, it looks like we have three more pets to ship. I hope there is still room on the plane."

Danielle Baum was staring at Avery in a calculating way. Before any of us could move, she whirled around and knocked her father backward with a blow to the face. "You stupid old man. You just had to change him back, didn't you? I told you what would happen if you interfered with my plans again."

Change you back? She thinks Albert changed you back?

She doesn't know I'm a Moravian, he answered. *She doesn't know that's why I'm a therion, not a were.*

"Hey!" Cora said, kneeling next to the prone Albert, who was sputtering in a language I didn't understand. "He's old! You could have broken his hip or something. You okay, old-timer?"

Albert continued to speak, chant really, his eyes closed as his lips moved almost silently.

Danielle laughed and nodded at Greg as she moved over to a canvas duffel bag sitting on a camp stool. "Take them outside. I'll tie up Daddy dearest again."

Greg, who had produced a gun and pointed it at me, frowned at Albert. "Did he hit his head or something?"

"No, he's just babbling to himself," Danielle answered, pulling out a length of rope and moving toward her father. "Summoning the spirits of the woods. Don't worry—they don't answer to him anymore. Do they, old man?"

Her voice held a note of taunting that had my hand itching to slap her.

"This way," Greg said, evidently reassured by her statement. He waved the gun toward the center of the camp. "You first, Jacintha. And just in case your boyfriend gets any ideas, I won't hesitate to shoot you."

Albert's daughter and Greg—what an unholy alliance.

That's what she must have meant about needing a consort, and why she wanted so badly to marry me, Avery mused as we stumbled out of the tent to the center of the compound. The others had disappeared, leaving us four alone next to a large fire. *She was planning on usurping Baum and taking over his position as lord of the forest.*

And she wanted you at her side?

He gave me a mental smile. *I told you I am quite popular with the ladies.*

Were quite popular. Were is the key word there, isn't that right?

I don't know—it's rather enjoyable seeing you jealous.

Retribution for such sentiments aside, what are we going to do?

Stop them, he said simply.

Before I could ask how, Danielle emerged from the tent. "Right, that's done. Now let's take care of these troublemakers before the others come back from meeting Dieter. Once they return, we'll tell them we have a couple extra for the shipment."

"Sorry, Jacintha," Greg said with mock sorrow. "I would say it's too bad the way things ended, but I always knew the day would come when you'd stumble across our business."

"The business of murdering people?" I asked.

He blinked for a moment.

"Didn't Danielle tell you that's what happens to the people who are changed into animals and sent to Scotland?"

He frowned and turned to look at her. "I thought you said they were sent to zoos?"

"Does it matter what happens to them?" she snapped, taking up a stand next to the fire. "They bring us money; that's all that should concern you. Now be quiet and let me concentrate."

Get ready to grab your sister and get the hell out of here, Avery warned me.

What? What do you—

Before I could finish that thought, Avery's body shimmered, shortened, and changed into a sleek black cat.

Danielle stood at the fire, her eyes closed, her hands held out blindly as she started a chant that sounded similar to the one Albert was mumbling.

"What the—" Greg stepped backward as Avery leaped across the fire toward him, knocking him backward onto his ass.

Run!

No! I'm not going to leave . . . leaf . . . love . . . The world around me swam in a dizzying swirl, my head spinning, leaving me with the feeling I was going to pass out, or vomit.

I heard Cora calling my name, but it seemed to come from a very long way away. My entire body felt hot, as if I had a great fever; then suddenly my vision cleared.

The leaves rustled in the trees around us, a wind whipping across the compound and bringing with it the sound and scent of a half dozen animals nearby.

"Oh my God!" Cora yelled, staring at me with huge, disbelieving eyes.

Greg screamed as Avery bit down on his hand, forcing the man to drop the gun.

"Jas! What . . . *Jas!*"

"Excellent," Danielle said, opening her eyes to smile at me. That was when I realized I wasn't looking at her properly. I was several feet lower, as if I'd fallen onto my hands and knees. . . . I looked down and saw two furry feet, and in an instant knew what had happened.

Holy Mary and every single little saint that ever was and ever will be! I'm an animal! A whatchamacallit—one of those weres!

No, you're not. You're my Beloved. You're immortal now.

But you said we hadn't done the Joining thing! How can I be immortal?

We did the last step two hours ago when you took my darkness into yourself, giving me light in return.

I what?

You love me, Jas. You gave me your heart, and that was the final step for us. You're mine now. Forever.

But . . . but . . . I'm . . . this!

Yes, well, I hesitate to guess what this is going to mean for our children, he answered as he head-butted Greg. *It will be hard enough explaining that their father is a jaguar, but when we tell them their mother is a lion . . . I just don't know how they're going to take it.*

Don't kill him! I said, twisting around to look at myself. Even with the strangeness of the situation, I could not help but admire my lovely tawny coat, and the power coiled inside me. I felt as if I could run for miles and miles without even breathing hard. I wanted to hunt, to pounce on things, to corner prey. They were strange, alien feelings and, at the same time, as familiar as the beat of my heart.

Why shouldn't I kill him?

He didn't know Danielle was murdering people by sending them to be hunted. Just disable him somehow.

He grumbled to himself but head-butted Greg again, harder this time, knocking the man out.

We turned to face Danielle, who was looking at me with satisfaction. When she caught sight of Avery coming around the large fire, she stared at him with obvious astonishment. "You . . . you're . . ."

He shifted back to human form, quickly slipping on his jeans, but not before Cora and Danielle both got an eyeful.

"Moravian is, I think, the word you're searching for. And when you try to turn a Moravian into a were, we become therions. Didn't know that, did you?"

Her eyes narrowed on him. "It doesn't matter. Not really. We'll just have one less animal to ship."

For peace-loving animal rights people, they sure do carry a lot of guns, I complained, padding my way over to Avery. I rubbed my face on his leg before turning my attention back to Danielle, wondering if I leaped on her, whether I could knock from her hand the gun she was pointing at Avery.

Don't even try. There's no need.

Huh?

Can't you hear them? Others are coming.

More Leshies?

No. Open yourself to the night.

I did so, instantly becoming aware of the animals on the edge of the compound. *Cougars. Bears.*

Yes. That must have been what Albert was doing— summoning the beasts. Looks like Danielle underestimated her father.

Danielle heard the animals a second after they crossed into the compound. She whirled around, shifting into the form of a white wolf, her lips pulled back in a snarl.

Go, Avery ordered as he ran for Albert's tent. "Cora, follow your sister."

"She's a *lion*!" Cora yelled after him.

"Just follow her."

But . . .

Just get out of here. Albert has summoned the animals to do what has to be done, and I'd really rather you weren't here to see it.

I took one look at the scene in front of us—Danielle poised to leap on a cautious cougar as it approached her—and turned in the opposite direction.

Where are you? I asked as I ran down the dirt path leading to the compound.

Right behind you. I had to get Baum. Danielle will try

to turn the animals on him in order to cement her place as
lord of the Leshies, and I don't know if he has the power to
combat that.

Smart, sexy, and honorable—I guess I'm going to have
to keep you.

I know I'm keeping you—if for no other reason than black
and gold look good together.

You're assuming I can get out of this shape. We don't
know that. We don't know that . . . Ooh, bunny!

Stop chasing prey and get yourself and your sister out of
there. And don't try to shift until I get there.

Why not? I asked, curious and more than a little
worried.

A scream rose high in the night, half animal, half
human. It was wordless, but it carried impotent fury
that made my hackles stand on end.

You don't have any clothes.

Ten minutes later, I sat on the backseat of my car
and looked at Albert Baum. He looked back at me, his
bonds once again removed.

"You're sure?" Cora asked Avery for the third time
as we bounced down the track, heading for a paved
road and civilization.

"Yes. She's my Beloved. She's immortal. She'll be a
therion just like me."

"Guess you really will be a cat whisperer now."
Cora had a little quirk to her smile as she turned to talk
to me.

I tried to growl at her, but it came out a purr.

"Aww, isn't that sweet? Big kitty is purring at me,"
my obnoxious sister said, patting my head.

I thought about biting her hand for a good minute, but, in the end, decided that I'd wait to get my revenge.

"This is the strangest vacation I've ever had," Cora said to me three days later, as we stood with her at the cruise line's dock. "Vampires, werekitties, and a lion for a sister . . . Man. I just don't know how I'm going to top that next year."

I smiled and hugged her. "We'll have to worry about that then."

"Yeah, right." She gave me a wary smile, then turned to the man at my side, giving him a long, considering look. "You'd better take care of her."

"I will," he answered gravely, bowing over her hand in a courtly, old-fashioned way that made my heart beat faster.

"And if she gets turned into anything else—"

"She won't."

She bit her lip for a moment. "I get to come see you guys in Scotland."

"Our home will be yours," Avery said with that same polished courtliness.

You know she's going to hold you to that, I warned him.

He laughed. *I know. But I mean what I say—your family will be welcome at any time. I know it's going to be difficult for you to adjust to living in another country.*

Hey, I thought we agreed to split time between yours and mine?

I believe that's still under debate. . . .

"Let me know if I'm needed to testify," Cora said, interrupting his thoughts.

"I don't think Greg is going to stand trial for anything, let alone the murder of Danielle. For one thing, she was mauled, not shot, and for another, he's absolutely bonkers. Marge from my office went to see him at the hospital, and they wouldn't even let her into the ward. He thinks he's a wolf."

She stared at me with startled eyes. "That crazy lady didn't, you know—" She waggled her fingers in the air. "Magic him, too, did she?"

"No, just me. He's just gone nuts, which, given what happened, is pretty much justice. With Danielle receiving the justice of the forest, Albert regaining his health after months of abuse at her hands, and the Leshies in jail for illegal animal smuggling, it's better for everyone concerned."

"I guess so." She gave me a questioning look, then hugged me again, whispering, "If you ever need me, just yell, and I'll be there with a stake and my hose."

I laughed, kissed her on the cheek, and waved goodbye as she was swallowed up by the crowds heading for the cruise liner.

I turned to Avery, wrapping my arms around his waist, kissing his chin, and marveling to myself that such a handsome man was mine.

"All yours, Jacintha. How long will it take you to finish things here? I'm anxious to take you home. You'll like the castle. It's big, and old, and drafty, and filled with Paen's and Finn's kids racing up and down the halls."

"Sounds like heaven," I said, letting the love in his eyes warm me to my toes.

"But best of all, there are two hundred acres of land around it."

I cocked my head in question.

"Perfect for running," he explained.

"Oh. Well, I've never been one for jogging," I started to say, when I realized what was behind the mischievous grin. I had a vision of us running over hill and dale, his sleek black form contrasting with my tawny elegance as we bounded after rabbits. "Dibs on the first bunny!"

"My bloodthirsty little panther girl," he said with a laugh, turning and escorting me toward the parking lot.

"For the love of the saints, Avery! Don't you ever listen? Lion girl, not panther! I swear you have panthers on the brain."

"Panthers are cool."

"There is no such thing as a panther! It's all just a misnomer. Now, listen, we'll go over it again. . . . The jaguar is a member of the *Panthera* genus. Panthera is a Greek word meaning leopard, so as you see, there really is no panther at all. The lion is also in the same genus, but we're *Panthera leo*, whereas you are *Panthera onca*. . . ."

Catscratch Fever

by Connie Brockway

Chapter 1

She was an old cat—a very old cat—but she still purred.

She purred now as the dark-haired little girl with a seemingly innate understanding of how tender old bodies could be scratched her gently under the chin. Taking the purr as an invitation to have a seat, the child plopped down cross-legged in the Cupid Cats Shelter's Meet and Greet room, where the woman at the front desk had directed them. With the arthritic grace of an aged ballerina, the tiny ginger cat minced her way over and climbed into the little girl's lap, turned once, and then nestled into a tidy ball. Closing her eyes, she purred even louder.

And with that, five-year-old Chloe Curran fell madly in love. She turned her wide blue eyes up into the lean face of the tall man standing over her.

"It's Pixie, Daddy," she whispered excitedly. "It's *Mommy's* Pixie!"

"It *does* look like Steph's cat, Jim," Melissa said. Melissa was the eldest of the Curran siblings, a dominatrix of the hearth who, after Steph had died, assigned herself the role of head surrogate mother, not only to Chloe but to Jim himself.

She was here under duress, having *strongly* advised Jim against adopting a cat from an unknown shelter with irregular operating hours. She hovered in the doorway leading from the reception room, clearly trying to gauge how he took this reference to his deceased wife.

He took it fine. Stephanie had died almost six years ago. You'd think by now his family would have stopped tiptoeing around the mention of her. He and Steph had shared something wonderful and unique, but he wasn't that sensitive or, well, the word *pitiful* came to mind. "All ginger-colored cats look pretty much alike, don't they?" he asked.

"No," said Melissa.

He accepted her words as given. What did he know? There hadn't been a cat in his life since Pixie had run away on the day Chloe had been born—the day his wife had died. In the rush to get Stephanie to the hospital, Pixie had slipped out the front door. There hadn't been time to hunt for her. Steph had been in labor and, besides, Jim hadn't expected to be gone for a week. By the time he and Chloe had returned to their brownstone—but not Steph, never again Steph— the cat had disappeared.

"It's Pixie," Chloe avowed with a five-year-old's certainty.

"I don't think so, Chloe," he said, gently ruffling his daughter's dark curls. "Pixie was already an old cat when you were born, and cats just don't live that long."

"It's Pixie. I know it is. She looks just like the kitty in Mommy's picture," she said, citing the picture of Steph that graced the top of Chloe's dresser. In it, Steph was putting what Jim had always laughingly called the Death Grip-o-Love on the cat.

Jim hunkered down beside his daughter and petted the cat's delicate little wedge-shaped head. She moved into his touch, her eyes opening into milky jade green slits before closing again. She had cataracts; she was a *very* old cat. "Look, kiddo, even if Pixie was still alive, this couldn't be her. We lost her in New York just after you were born and we moved to Chicago—too far for an old cat to walk."

"Someone coulda drove her."

It was times like this that Chloe most reminded him of Steph. Just as there'd been no arguing with Steph once her mind was made up, once Chloe seized on an idea, she'd no sooner let it go than a dog would give up a juicy bone.

"Can we take her home, Daddy?"

"Jim . . ." Melissa laid a cautionary hand on his arm.

He felt a tinge of irritation. He wasn't an idiot. Chloe had been bugging him for a kitten since she could talk; he wasn't about to make her dreams come true by getting her a cat that looked like it might not make it through the summer, let alone the rest of her childhood.

He'd originally planned to give Chloe a kitten on her birthday next month. A month ago they'd moved here from out of the old neighborhood where his sisters and their families still lived and where they'd been within shouting distance of her aunts and uncles and cousins. The move had been hard on Chloe. She missed the attention, she missed the constant flow of family in and out, and she missed being the youngest cousin amidst a dozen teenagers.

She'd been after him for weeks now to "just look at the kitties" at the shelter they'd discovered around the corner from their new home—the only bright light in this move as far as Chloe was concerned. He'd managed to resist until this morning, when Melissa had "dropped in to see if everything was going all right," a habit she shared with his three other sisters. He'd planned to spend the hot afternoon teaching Chloe to ride her two-wheeler, but as soon as Melissa appeared, he had put the idea on hold, perhaps selfishly not wanting to the share the experience. So he'd opted for plan B, hoping to curtail her visit.

Melissa was not overly fond of cats.

After all these years he should have known better. And so here the three of them were, Melissa giving him the evil eye.

"The lady at the front desk said they've got some really cute kittens, Chloe, and you haven't even seen them yet," Jim said enticingly. What little girl wouldn't prefer a kitten to a scrawny old cat?

"I don't want to look at the kitties," Chloe said. "I want Pixie."

Apparently his. "I don't know if that's such a good idea, Chlo-Schmo," he said, preparing for battle. Chloe was generous, funny, and lively, and she also had the willpower of a master yogi and the determination to go along with it. *And* a temper. It was the temper he was most concerned about. "We might have to think about it some."

As the realization that she might not be walking out of the shelter with Pixie dawned on Chloe, storm clouds gathered in her eyes. "I don't *want* to think about it!" she said on a rising note. The little cat's eyes popped open, startled, and Chloe lowered her voice. "I. Want. *Pixie*."

Melissa bustled forward, her face pleated with sympathy; so much for her misgivings. If Chloe "wanted" something, Melissa automatically transferred that condition into "needing" it. Jim braced for an argument.

"Now, darling," Melissa crooned," if you *really* want, er, Pixie—"

"Ishy." The female voice coming out of nowhere cut through the rising tension as neatly as a diamond cut glass. John turned around to face the newcomer, and Chloe leaned forward, trying to peek around Jim's legs.

A woman, bent over, was backing out of what looked like a cleaning supply room and was pulling a bucket on casters. Her loose T-shirt draped over a nicely rounded bottom, the uneven hem of a pair of baggy, over-long shorts flirting with the backs of slender thighs and shapely calves that led down to a pair of dingy running shoes.

Chagrin followed an undeniable stab of heated attraction. Man, if a cleaning lady's tush could set his pulse racing, he really needed to start dating again.

"Excuse me?" he asked.

"Ishy," she repeated, still bent to her task. "The cat's name is Ishy."

She cleared the door to the maintenance room, kicked it shut, and turned.

She was unkempt and dusty. She'd hauled most of her hair into a lopsided ponytail, but one loop had caught in the rubber band and stuck out now like a wicket on a croquet field. There was something weirdly cute about her dishevelment, a sort of unconscious sexiness about her loose T-shirt and long, well-toned legs.

Jim stared but not because she was weirdly sexy. He stared because of all the people Jim might have expected to find scrubbing floors in a nonprofit cat shelter, Dr. Edith Handelman—research department head of the company where nine months ago he'd hired on as chief visionary officer—was dead last. Edith was empirical and rational, her life defined by order, cleanliness, and reason. Until this minute he'd have bet a living wage that her only interaction with animals was with her lab rats.

He smiled, surprised by his pleasure. Along with her plain brown hair, she had plain brown eyes and, he'd always assumed, a plain figure; yet even when she was wearing a lab coat and hair net, he'd never been able to dismiss her as, well, *plain*. In fact, he hadn't been able to dismiss her at all. There was just something about Dr. Handelman that *got* to Jim. She was such an odd little mouse, and apparently he had a hidden thing for mice.

Once, when he'd been taking a shortcut through the research department, he'd heard her laughing. A little investigation had discovered her and some of her colleagues bending over a slide. When he'd asked what was so funny, she'd jolted upright, spied him, and flushed, and the mask came slamming down. It was one of her coworkers who finally answered, "Nuthin', boss. Lab humor."

Ever since, he'd wanted to hear her laugh again, see her smile—not the professionally donned smile she did so poorly, but the feature-lighting mirth that transformed her.

For the briefest of seconds, she checked, and he thought he detected a hint of surprise in her caramel-colored eyes, but he couldn't say for certain because she always kept her expression carefully neutral. Now, calmly snapping on a pair of oversized rubber gloves, she simply said, "Hello, Mr. Curran," as if she saw him at cat shelters every day.

"Hi, Edith."

"That's a mean name!" Chloe's indignant voice turned Edith's attention to his daughter.

"On the contrary," Edith replied. "It's a fond diminutive and feminization of the name Ishmael, from *Moby-Dick*, about a sailor who lives through many adventures."

Chloe frowned. "What's a dimmy—dimmytive?"

"Diminutive," Edith corrected in the manner of one used to correcting others, which she was. "It means small."

"Do you know this person, Jim?" Melissa asked, her tone chill. She'd been halted in mid-capitulation to her only niece, doubtless anticipating little arms flung in gratitude around her neck, and she didn't like being thwarted.

"Yes. She's a coworker of mine. Dr. Handelman, this is Melissa Bandetti, my sister."

But Edith wasn't paying attention. She'd already bent over to open a bottle riding piggyback on the bucket and dump some of its contents into the water.

The sting of ammonia immediately filled the small space. Melissa waved her hand in front of her nose, and Chloe scooted away from the offending odor.

"Ishy is still a *mean* name, and it's not hers," Chloe insisted.

"Oh?" Edith asked, taking the mop from the bucket and slapping it on the linoleum, splashing Jim's trousers. He backed away.

"My kitty's name is—"

"Excuse me," Edith said to Jim, interrupting Chloe. His daughter blinked, stunned. Chloe was unused to being interrupted, let alone ignored.

"You should move," Edith said. "All of you. Little girl, pick up Ishy and go to the other side of the room there," she ordered his daughter. When Chloe just stared at her, she added, "Or put her down. Either way, please hurry up. I have three more rooms to mop before I leave."

Melissa made a soft, indignant sound and glared at Jim as though he should put a stop right this minute to anyone's telling Chloe to do anything she didn't want to do—except for Melissa, of course, and sometimes, but only occasionally, Jim.

Chloe, on the other hand, seemed more fascinated than offended. Carefully setting the cat on her feet, she got up and then just as carefully gathered the old cat back up again before heading dutifully to the far side of the tiny enclosure and sitting back down.

Edith turned her intelligent, candid gaze on Jim. Her lashes were dark and spiky, and she had the sort of complexion he imagined Irish lasses living on the moist coast of a green island to have—creamy, dewy, and radiant. Or it could be that she was sweating. It was hot in here.

"If you're her father," she said, "you ought to keep her from sitting on the floor at animal shelters. Fecal matter carries all sorts of potentially harmful bacteria as well as parasi—"

"Oh, for the love of God, Jim!" Melissa said, whooshing forward, clasping Chloe by the arm, and hauling her to her feet.

The cat leaped with weightless grace to the floor as Chloe, always attuned to something new and taboo, demanded, "What's fecal?"

Edith considered a second before her face cleared. "Crap."

Chloe gasped. Saying "crap" was definitely taboo.

"Listen," Melissa said. "Doctor or not, coworker or not, you shouldn't use words like that in front of children—especially other people's children."

Edith cocked her head. "Why? I assumed from her ignorance of the word 'diminutive' that she wouldn't have understood the word 'extreca.' Was I wrong? Some of my colleagues use the term 'crap' interchangeably with—"

"No. You weren't wrong," Melissa interjected forcibly. "But *that* word is a no-no word in our family."

"What term would you have preferred I use?" Edith didn't wait for an answer but wrung out the mop in the squeeze bar, got it soapy again, and once more slapped the mop on the floor with enough force to spray the tips of Melissa's leather Manolos. Melissa leaped back with a gasp.

Edith looked up. "I told you to move."

"This is ridiculous." Melissa spun toward Jim. "Someone ought to know there's a person back here driving off potential clientele."

"Settle down, Melissa," Jim said in a low voice, taking her arm and pulling her off to the side. "Look, she didn't mean anything by it. Edith just doesn't have many social skills."

"Many?" Melissa repeated. "Try any."

"That's just the way she is. The day we met, she asked me why Global Genetics needed a talking head."

Melissa gasped. "Did she *want* to get fired?"

Jim smiled, glancing at where Edith and Chloe stood regarding each other like alien species from different planets. Neither was paying any attention to them. "First, I couldn't fire her. She doesn't report to me. Second, she didn't mean to be insulting. She just heard someone call me that and used the term without understanding the subtext. She's a little different. She doesn't do idle chitchat. That's probably why she's been assigned cleanup duty."

"You sound like you like her." She sounded accusing.

He shrugged. He did like her, despite her social awkwardness. He'd spent enough time with her to realize she didn't have a mean or spiteful bone in her body. Edith was a genius with the girl-next-door's face, and the social acumen of Sheba the Wolf Girl. "I think she's unique."

Melissa shook her head. "So are these shoes. I waited for these Manolos to go on clearance for months, and this is only the third time I've worn them." Clearly, a line had been crossed when Edith had water-spotted her new shoes. "She should be reprimanded. I'm going to talk to that old bat out front. She's probably the director." That said, she was gone.

Jim looked at Edith. She was listening. "I told her to move," she said faintly.

Jim's heart went out to her. It wasn't Edith's fault she was one hot mess. Her file said she'd graduated high school at age fourteen, finished college by fifteen, and received her *second* doctorate by twenty. Now only twenty-eight, she'd already been head of Global Genetics' research department for three years. Those who worked in her department loved her. Those who didn't wrote her off as too frank, too gauche, and too odd, but one helluva research head.

"I didn't realize you liked cats, Edith," he said.

She blinked at him. "Yes. I find the combination of domesticity and independence interesting."

She spoke as though she felt she needed an excuse to like cats. He smiled. "Have you worked here long?"

"I've been a volunteer here for just over four years."

"I didn't know that." But then, he didn't know much about Edith's life outside of Global Genetics. She was a very private woman.

"Why would you?" she asked, sounding puzzled.

Because I'm interested in what makes you tick? he thought, but instead answered, "It's just the sort of thing I would have expected to come up in casual conversation."

"Oh," Edith said, and returned to her mopping.

Chloe had edged around the parameter of the room, carefully avoiding the wet parts of the floor, until she

stood beside Edith, frowning in consternation. Jim
looked on in amusement. Chloe had finally run into
a woman who wasn't charmed into helpless servitude
on first sight of her curly dark hair and wide blue eyes,
and apparently it shook her child-sized world.

"This kitty's name isn't Ishy," she said pleasantly.
"It's Pixie. And we're going to adopt her."

"No, you're not," Edith replied, wiping a loose strand
of hair out of her eyes with the wrist of one blue-gloved
hand. "Ishy is the shelter's cat. This is her home."

That pretty much put paid to that. Jim knelt down
by Chloe. "Sorry, kiddo."

"But she's my *mommy's* cat!" Chloe insisted. "We
can't leave her here."

Jim raked his hair back with his fingers. He loved
that Chloe believed anything and everything was possible, and it seemed needlessly cruel to insist she give
up her belief in this little piece of magic she'd conjured
for herself. She was still so little. But how was he to
convince her the old cat was better off here, without
destroying her illusion that the cat was Pixie? Added
to which, he didn't want Chloe thinking he would
abandon Steph's cat.

Apparently deciding that the major obstacle standing between her and the cat was Edith, Chloe brought
out the big guns. She turned her big blues on the good
doctor and said in a small, heartrending voice, "My
mommy's dead."

Jim winced. It was a ploy Chloe had been using lately
and always to great effect. And he hated it. Somewhere
during the last year his poppet, sweet as pie and twice
as cute, had become a master manipulator.

He waited for Edith to drop her mop and scoop his little motherless girl up in her arms, promising Chloe that she not only could have the cat, but any ten cats she wanted and not only that, but that Edith would come over every day and clean the litter box.

"Mine is, too," Edith replied. "What has that to do with your adopting Ishy?"

Chloe's mouth fell open and she stared, stunned into gape-mouthed silence. Jim burst out laughing and at once, consumed with guilt, turned it into a cough. Dead mommies were no laughing matter.

Melissa reappeared in the doorway, wearing a decidedly unhappy expression as Chloe just stood there, little and defenseless, cradling the old ginger cat. The cat *did* look like Pixie. And he *had* promised Chloe any cat she wanted. And guilt over his mistimed laugh was having its way with him.

Before he could stop himself, he heard himself asking, "Can't the shelter get another cat?"

Edith opened her mouth to reply, but before she could speak, Melissa broke in. "Look, the cat will have a much happier life with Chloe," she said in the manner of a woman about to whip out her checkbook and say, "Name your price." "She'll have a great home, great food, toys galore, and the run of the neighborhood."

"You would give her open access to the out-of-doors?" Edith asked.

"Of course," Melissa said. "Cats need to be free."

"No, they don't," Edith said. "That's a myth, as damaging as the notion that neutering an animal destroys its spirit. The average life span of indoor cats is about fourteen years whereas cats allowed to roam have an average life expectancy of four. Not only are outdoor cats more than likely to become infected with parasites and diseases and have high incidents of injury by car or in altercations with other animals, but scientists list cats as the second-most serious threat to bird populations worldwide. Based on the proportion of cats bringing home at least one prey item, a 1997 British study of nonferal cats' impact on wildlife estimated that their nation's population of approximately nine million cats would have brought home twenty-five to twenty-nine million birds over a six-month period. Given these facts, one of the stipulations for adopting a cat from this shelter is for the prospective owner to sign a contract promising to keep the cat indoors."

"Twenty-five million birds? That's ridiculous. I don't believe it. It's just propaganda," Melissa declared. "Cats hate being kept in prison in a house. It's unnatural."

Edith looked at Jim, her brow furrowing. "Clearly, any discussion is pointless. This woman is one of those people for whom data and evidence have no meaning. So, what should I say to her now?"

During the year since he'd been hired by Global Genetics, Jim had taken on the part-time task of mentoring Edith in learning more sophisticated social skills.

Growing red-faced, Melissa stared at her, "*Excuse me?* One of *those* people?"

Edith nodded, happy to elucidate. "It's quite common. Many people form emotional attachments to opinions that exist irrespective of the facts of the matter. Researchers have shown that for these people overwhelming evidence has no impact on beliefs."

"*This* woman," Melissa announced in a tight voice, "will be waiting for you in the car, Jim. *Don't* be long." She whirled around and stomped out the door.

Chloe regarded him with a trembling lower lip, Edith looked confused, and the cat kept purring.

"Daddy, please can I have Pixie?" Chloe whispered.

Jim met Edith's gaze. "Look, Edith, I promise not to let the old girl out. Can't the shelter get another cat?"

Edith didn't answer him. She answered Chloe. She squatted down so she was eye level with his three-foot-tall daughter and said, "It's not the shelter's say; it's Ishy's. Other people have tried to adopt her and only a few have even managed to get her out as far as the street. The two people who did finally get her to their homes ended up bringing her back because she yowled nonstop from the moment they took her until the moment they brought her back. I'm not going to put her through that again. She's old. She wants to stay here."

Edith peered up at him. "It's really a rather fascinating example of locale fixation in a domesticated species. What makes it interesting is how she imprinted on this area so late in her life. I wish I knew her history. The answer may be as simple as early cognitive familiarity."

Jim smiled weakly. For a moment there, Edith had almost seemed like a real girl.

He put a hand on his daughter's shoulder. "The kitty likes it here, Chloe."

Chloe shook her head. "She wouldn't go with anyone else 'cause she didn't belong to them. She was waiting for us."

Edith straightened and stepped over to the door

marked EMERGENCY EXIT. She took out a set of keys, disconnected the fire alarm system, and pushed open the door. "Go ahead. Try to take her through."

Not a shred of doubt appeared on Chloe's face as she marched for the door carrying the cat. The ginger cat began to squirm. Then wriggle. Then yowl. Jim started forward, concerned lest the cat scratch Chloe, but at the same instant the cat broke free and launched herself from Chloe's arms onto the floor, scuttling away.

Chloe stared after her, betrayal and hurt filling her little face. She turned her gaze up at Jim. "Why'd she do that, Daddy? I thought she liked me."

"She does like you, Chloe," Jim answered. And, indeed, the cat was already back, rubbing lightly against Chloe's legs and purring gently. "She just wants to stay here, Chloe. She's not Pixie."

"She is," his daughter whispered, reaching down to pet the ginger cat's little wedge-shaped head. She sighed, and Jim's heart turned in his chest; this was her first real experience with rejection.

"Maybe she's just not ready yet," Chloe said. "If she wanted to go with me, would you let her go?"

"If Ishy ever went willingly with someone, we certainly wouldn't stop her," Edith said, sounding a little gruff.

"Really?" Chloe asked.

"Really," Edith answered.

"Come on, Chloe," Jim said. "Let's go look at the other kitties, shall we?"

"No," his daughter said simply, straightening and slipping her hand into his. "I don't want another kitty. I think I just want to go home now."

"Okay, cookie," Jim said, drawing her toward the door. "We'll go look at another shelter tomorrow."

At this, Chloe stopped sharply, tightly squeezing his hand.

He looked down. "What?"

"No, Daddy!" Chloe said. "Pixie just doesn't know me yet. As soon as she does, she'll come home with us. You'll see."

Damn. "Chloe—"

"We'll come tomorrow and the next day and the next until she knows me real well, and then she won't be scared to leave with us," Chloe said. "It's like when we moved here and I was kinda scared, and you said once I got used to it I'd like it. Pixie's the same. She just has to get used to me. She never met *me* before, you know," she finished reasonably.

Helplessly, Jim raised his gaze to Edith. Why he should look to her for help was a mystery, but apparently he'd underestimated her.

"You can come anytime you like," she said. "It will be interesting to see if your theory can be substantiated." Her words were uncomplicated, direct. They offered no promises, no assurances. Edith merely gave simple permission for Chloe to try her experiment, one scientist to another.

"Daddy? Can we come back again? Tomorrow?"

"We're open only in the evenings on weekdays," Edith said, "and on the weekends from eleven a.m. until four p.m."

What harm could it do? Jim thought. Chloe was only five. It wouldn't take too long before she got tired of trying to coax an antique cat through a door. And in the meantime it would give her the opportunity to see and fall in love with a more suitable companion.

And he could explore this new aspect of Global Genetics' strangely attractive research head.

Melissa was waiting for them in the car when they walked out of the brick storefront, having insisted on driving them in her Saab the marathon one and a half blocks over here. She reached across and unlocked the door, not so subtly reminding Jim that when he'd moved out of Highwood, he'd left behind the safety of the neighborhood where he'd grown up and where his sisters still lived with their families. Not that Parkwood Knolls was exactly the crime capital of world; in fact, it had even fewer police incident reports per week than Highwood. But according to his sisters, if you weren't on a first-name basis with everyone within a ten-block radius, you couldn't really feel secure.

Jim opened the door, and Chloe scooted into the backseat and buckled herself in. Then he got in, sliding behind the steering wheel.

"I wish you hadn't taken off like that," he said to his sister. "It really wasn't worth bit—"—he abruptly chose a different word when he caught sight of Chloe, and finished—"stirring up trouble for Edith."

"A hundred bucks may not be much to you, but to me it's worth bit—*fussing* about," Melissa said sarcastically, and then, shooting an irritated glance at him, added, "Oh, don't look so pi—angry. Carol—that's the woman out front—isn't the director of Cupids Cats. It turns out Dr. Handelman runs the da—darn good place."

Chapter 2

$\mathcal{E}$dith saw Jim Curran at Global Genetics the following day. He was heading for the elevator bank that would carry him to the corporate offices high above the research floors. She wasn't surprised he didn't see her. In her lab coat with her hair once more neatly drawn back, she would be interchangeable with most of the females in the department. For a second, she considered saying hello—she even half lifted her hand—but decided against making such an overture. He might think she was using their chance encounter at Cupid Cats as an excuse to presume a social friendship.

Besides, she was still trying to figure out what she'd said that had made his sister so antagonistic. She hadn't made any value judgment about Melissa's inability to process information in a logical manner. She'd simply pointed it out. She sighed. Her interactions with the general population typically were fraught with misunderstandings and tensions she was at a loss to explain. She did better with empirical rather than speculative thinkers. She would do well to remember that.

She began walking briskly in the opposite direction. Objectively, there was no reason for her and Jim to talk at all except on those days he insisted she come along to help "impress" prospective investors. If anyone else had said such a thing to her, she would have been inclined to think they were being sarcastic; she was well aware of her lack of social acumen. But Jim Curran was not like that—although her willingness to make so unsubstantiated a judgment was a little unnerving. Making evaluations based on intuitions went against a lifetime of habit.

Besides, if they were to talk in an extended and purely social manner, what would they say? She was a scientist. He was a professional charmer. Oh, she understood it took more than charm to graduate with honors from the Carlson School of Business, but in the end, he was about sociology whereas she was about hard science. She was a geneticist, a genius, a geek. The combination tended to either intimidate people—especially men—or put them off.

It did neither to Jim Curran; it seemed to challenge him. Over the last year, he appeared to have made it his personal mission to turn her into an asset during his presentations. He did so by insisting she join him in various social milieus to practice her "people skills."

"A smile now and then, Edith, just to let folks know the fumes in the lab haven't frozen your face," he'd advised her. Another recommendation was, "Fewer syllables and more accessibility." Well, she'd tried using slang yesterday with his daughter. Apparently, one could be too accessible.

Yet he'd made all his suggestions with good humor. She appreciated that. He never treated her as if she were a geek or as if she had Asperger syndrome—there had never been a clinical diagnosis—but rather as if she were simply inexperienced.

She was. She'd never had much of a social life. From the time she could read at age two, she'd been accelerated through every institute of learning she'd encountered, heading at breakneck speed through high school, college and graduate school, fellowships and more graduate schools. Consequently, she'd never spent much time learning those skills others took for granted. Even more debilitating, whenever she was nervous or uneasy, she automatically retreated behind her vocabulary and her IQ, causing her expression to grow immobile with tension. Ultimately she'd spent more and more of her life focusing on her work.

She liked her work. She *loved* her work. But there hadn't been much else in her life. No sleepovers, band trips, proms, and not many dates. There had been her ill-considered engagement, but that had been a short-lived situation. She didn't have any family nearby, and though she had a few friends, they were, to be blunt, just as awkward as she.

Until she'd wandered into Cupid Cats one day.

It had been soon after she'd been hired by Global Genetics four years ago. She'd gone with the idea of adopting a cat to help ease the loneliness of moving to a new city. The shelter had been about to close up, the director moving to another state. She hadn't intended to take over. She knew nothing about nonprofit organizations, but she did know about cats. She'd had one since she was a little girl, and the thought of all those unwanted cats that day had struck a chord in her she could not ignore. Before she knew it, she'd inherited a small group of volunteers and the lease on the building that housed the shelter. But being director of a cat shelter didn't exactly promote social adroitness. She understood full well that she was hardly Jim Curran's "type."

But if she was being honest—and Edith Handelman was always honest—she would admit she liked the time she spent with Jim Curran. She liked his smiling Irish eyes and his tousled dark hair, the way his smile carved a dimple in one lean cheek, and his ex–all conference swimmer's physique; however, she understood all of this was simply animal attraction based on her genetic predisposition, pheromones, and cultural conditioning. She was objective in this. Such attraction did not ask permission; it just was.

"Edith!"

She turned. Jim Curran was trotting down the corridor toward her. Her shoulders dropped in a swoon of appreciation. He was *so* gorgeous.

"A minute, Edith?"

He looked troubled. "I didn't actually call that board member a Neanderthal," she declared. "I only implied it."

He stopped beside her, his expression confused. "What?"

He wasn't chastising her? "Nothing," Edith said. "Is there something I can do for you, Mr. Curran?"

"No. I wanted to thank you for being so nice to Chloe. I know I tend to overindulge, but she really does think that old cat is the same one Steph and I had."

Steph. That was the dead wife. She hadn't been above eavesdropping when Jim Curran's name was brought up around the water cooler, and with a man as handsome and charming as Jim, that was regularly.

"I don't think it will take too many visits before Chloe gets over the idea that she's supposed to adopt your cat," he said.

"She's not mine," Edith said automatically. "She just showed up a while ago, over five years now. And she refuses to leave." His blue shirt made his eyes appear like sapphires, and he'd taken off his jacket and rolled up the sleeves. He had well-muscled forearms and strong-looking hands—very healthy and tanned. She hoped he used a good sunscreen.

He smiled. "That's rather begging the point, isn't it, since she lives in a shelter you own and you've assumed responsibility for her care?"

She could almost hear a brogue in his voice, which was absolutely ridiculous since his employee file said he'd been born and raised right here in Chicago. She knew because she had peeked into his files. She cleared her throat. "The shelter's not mine, either. It's a nonprofit entity. But I understand the point you were trying to make."

His eyes widened in mock surprise. "What? You're not going to debate the issue into the ground? Lord, Edith, you keep this up and I'll think you're loosening up. Someone might even dare tease you, at this rate."

He was already teasing her, and he knew she knew it. She blushed, uncomfortable but perversely flattered, and so sounded gruffer than she'd intended when she answered. "You've thanked me. Was there something else you wanted?"

He didn't take offense; his grin just broadened. "Nope. That's it."

She was relieved. She hadn't wanted to offend him. Sometime over the past months she'd developed a full-blown crush on Jim Curran, a crush with all the immature, girly, insipid callowness the term implied. How lowering. How common. How . . . *enervating*.

Even now, her nerve endings were flooding with chemicals that heightened her tactile responses. She imagined she could actually *feel* her pupils dilating and—she leaned closer and very discreetly took a sniff—yes, *yes*. Her sense of smell was definitely more pronounced, and the scent she was gathering from Jim Curran was wholly individual, wholly masculine, and wholly attractive to her.

An appealing scent was not simply a sign of sexual approval; it was far more individualized than that. Unlike the general population's appreciation of symmetrically proportionate faces and breeding-ready physiques, this attraction was specific to her and Jim. *He* smelled good to *her*—not just good, wonderful, thrilling, erotic, yes, but also comforting because his genetic makeup complemented her own.

Research had proven that women could smell subtle differences in the sequences of a system of genes known as the major histocompatibility complex, and women reacted most positively to those men who were immunologically dissimilar, but not too dissimilar, to themselves, thus helping to ensure healthy progeny. Not that Edith was anticipating having a child with Jim Curran. But there were other proven ramifications to scent compatibility, one of which was increased arousal and amplified sexual satisfaction. Immature her crush might be, but solid science was behind it, and that comforted her.

"You look funny, Edith. What's up?" Jim asked, cocking his head to the side.

As gauche as Jim thought her, she wasn't about to blurt out, "You smell good," so she said, "I was thinking of genetic hardwiring."

"Oh. Interesting." He didn't look interested—he looked amused. "What time does the shelter close?"

"Generally at nine p.m." She didn't see any point in telling him she often stayed until ten or so just for the company the cats provided. It made her sound pathetic.

"Good. Then I can walk Chloe over before dinner tonight. We live only a half block down and around the corner from the shelter. We moved there a little more than a month ago."

She didn't know how to respond. It was a piece of personal information she hadn't asked for, and she wasn't sure why he'd offered it or what it meant. Logic said he was trying to make small talk with her because, well, because he was a charmer and charmers made small talk with people. The thought depressed her. "Oh."

"So I guess I'll see you tonight? About six thirty?"

"Yes."

His brow furrowed for a brief second, but all he said was a light, "Have a nice day, Edith." Then he turned, once more heading for the elevator bank and leaving her discreetly testing the air where he'd been.

Chapter 3

Jim arrived with Chloe at half past six, but as soon as he and his little girl entered the reception area, his iPhone chirruped. He glanced at the screen and scowled, his fingers flicking over the shiny surface. He grimaced and looked up, giving Chloe an apologetic smile. "Sorry, toots, but we'll have to go. I have to look up some figures on the home computer and send them to this guy. He needs them now."

"Dad-dy! No!" Chloe protested, her lower lip thrusting out like the prow of a very small ship.

"Can't be helped. We'll come tomorrow." He glanced up at Edith. "If you're open."

She nodded.

"But we haven't even *seen* Pixie," she wailed. "Can't we just *see* her? You *promised*."

"Chloe—"

"Chloe can stay here with me while you attend to business," Edith offered.

Both Jim and Chloe turned to stare at her, Jim with obvious surprise segueing immediately into doubt, and Chloe with criticism.

"I am perfectly competent to watch over a five-year-old," Edith said a trifle defensively. True, she'd never actually supervised a child. Babysitting had not been part of her adolescent experience. She'd been studying at Stanford when the rest of her chronological peers had been earning five dollars an hour babysitting their next-door neighbors' offspring. But she was confident in her ability to oversee Chloe for, what? Half an hour? Besides, she liked children. Their thoughts were like mold, deceptively simple, yet wildly proliferative.

"I don't doubt that, Edith," Jim said. "I just don't have the right to ask you."

"You didn't," Edith replied. "I offered."

"Please, Daddy. I'll stay with the lady, er, Miss . . ." Chloe looked askance at Edith.

"Doctor. Dr. Edith Handelman," Edith supplied.

Without missing a beat, Chloe turned her big blue eyes on her father and said, quite solemnly, "Edie said I could stay."

"*Edie?*" Edith's eyes rounded. No one had *ever* called her Edie.

"It's a fond *dimmytive*," Chloe explained patiently.

Edith felt herself flushing with pleasure even though the child's words were clearly designed to mollify her father by introducing an emotional connection that did not exist. She noticed Jim watching her with an odd expression and cleared her throat. "Diminutive."

Chloe ignored her. "Please, Daddy. I'll be good, I promise."

Jim studied his daughter doubtfully. "Well," he said slowly, "if you're sure she won't be a problem?"

"I'm not sure of that at all," Edith replied, "but she demonstrates unexpected sophistication in her manip-ulation of others that suggests she is intelligent enough to take basic directions. And I *am* sure that should she prove a problem, I am up to the task of keeping her safe from the consequence of her misbehavior."

Jim eyed her. "Yeah, well, if she's naughty, give her a time-out."

"I won't be naughty," Chloe promised.

Jim ruffled her hair. "You'd better not be, or Edith— Edie won't let us back in."

Edie. Flustered, Edith kept her gaze fixed determinedly on Chloe, saying with mock severity, "That's right. I will revoke your visitation rights."

Jim laughed. Edith liked the sound. She liked that she had aroused it. It gave her a weird sense of pride, as though she'd achieved something important, such as sequencing a specific strand of DNA. She always felt disappointed that people outside her immediate milieu always seemed to take her so seriously.

"What's that mean?" Chloe asked.

"It means you won't be welcome here," she explained.

Chloe blew out her cheeks. "You sure use a lot of big words. Couldn't you use words I understand?"

"I tried that, but your aunt scolded me."

"That's 'cause you said a naughty word."

"Crap isn't a naughty word. Its etymology is—"

"It's an inappropriate word for children to use, Edie," Jim said. "It's a cultural thing."

"Ah!" she said, unenlightened but distracted by his casual use of the name his daughter had given her.

He left shortly thereafter, and Edith escorted Chloe back to the vestibule where Ishy generally hung out, but the cat was not there.

"Will you look for her with me?" Chloe asked.

Edith nodded, oddly touched to be included in the search.

"Come on," Chloe said, inserting her small hand in Edith's. It was warm and slightly sticky, and after making a mental note to inform Jim that his child's post-dining hygienics were lacking, Edith allowed the child to tug her along in her small wake as she looked for Ishy.

Chloe chatted nonstop as they went on their search. Within a few minutes Edith had learned Chloe was five and was starting kindergarten this coming fall; she had three aunts, two uncles and one "part-time uncle," six boy cousins and two girl cousins, all older than she; her daddy and she had moved into a house with a swing set but no microwave; and Chloe liked Polly Pockets, Bratz, and Hannah Montana. Unfortunately, Edith had no idea who these last three were, though she did have a vague recollection of a female character named Montana in a Kurt Vonnegut novel and so assumed this must be to whom Chloe was referring. She found that fascinating. Even to Edith, Kurt Vonnegut seemed advanced for a five-year-old. But then, she realized she found much about Chloe fascinating.

Though she knew the desire to be based on a biological imperative, she'd always wanted a child. But with the end of her engagement five years ago, she'd put all thoughts of motherhood on hiatus. She had not precisely given up on the idea of being a mother— adoption and single parenthood being viable options— it just made no sense to waste time ruminating over something not in her foreseeable future. But being with Chloe awakened those dormant urges.

The shelter was not very big, as most of the animals were fostered, so it didn't take long before they found Ishy in the Meet and Greet room, a small room in the back of the shelter outfitted with a sofa, a cat tree, and a window box where potential adopters could meet the cat they were interested in without the distraction presented by the other animals.

The old cat was roosting in the center of the raggedy orange and gold tweed sofa. Without a word, Chloe climbed into one corner and sat down cross-legged, swiveling to face the cat while Edith took a place on the other end, Ishy splitting the distance between them. She was staring unblinkingly at a blank wall. Occasionally, the very last two inches of her tail would twitch and she would make an odd sound deep in her throat.

"What's she looking at?" Chloe asked after a few minutes, her voice hushed so as not to disturb the cat's Zen-like focus.

"I have no idea," Edith admitted.

"I think she's looking at something only she can see," Chloe said, glancing at Edith.

"The possibility has some merit," Edith agreed. "Especially in dim light. Cats' eyes have a structure called the tapetum lucidum, which reflects light back into the eye, enabling it to see motion in near darkness much better than humans can."

Chloe sighed. "What's that mean?"

Edith frowned. What did it mean to a five-year-old? "It means if there's a bug on the wall, she can see it when we can't."

"Oh," Chloe said, her face clearing, then added, "I don't think she's looking at a bug. I think she sees something only cats can see, like a fairy. Or a unicorn. Or a *ghost*."

Oh, dear. Edith understood that fantastical thinking was considered a normal part of a child's psychological development, though she herself had been a more concrete thinker. She also recognized that people were very sensitive about when and how their children's fantasies were dispelled. Take, for example, the Santa Claus debacle of her fourth year. Who could anticipate Gary Knutson's mother would take such umbrage at her son's being informed that Santa Claus was not real? Gary had been six if he'd been a day.

So now, Edith considered her options. She did not want to be responsible for destroying yet another child's illusions.

"I think she sees a ghost," Chloe whispered.

Edith mumbled noncommittally.

"Don't you?" The little girl turned her gaze up at Edith. Her eyes were the same bright blue as her father's.

She didn't believe in lying, even to children, so she avoided the issue altogether. "Hey. You know what?"

"What?"

"I think it's really most admirable that you want to adopt an older animal."

As a distractive ploy it worked, although Chloe's reaction was not what Edith expected. She expected Chloe to say thank you. Instead, the little girl scowled, concentrating, then asked, "Why?"

"Why?"

"Yeah," Chloe said seriously. "Why is that so great?"

Edith shrugged. "Most people don't want old cats. In fact, many shelters consider them unadoptable."

"What's unadoptable?"

"It means something about the cat makes it unlikely anyone will want it."

"Like what?"

Edith appreciated Chloe's interrogation. She would not be satisfied until she had an answer that made sense to her. She reminded Edith of herself—and not just at five.

"Oh, for example, if a cat is malformed. That means there's something different about how it looks or how it acts. For instance, it might have one leg shorter than the rest or it might be blind or it might not be able to meow. Or it might be morbidly ob—" She cut herself off. *Small words*. "It might be really, really fat. Or it might not be well socialized."

"What's that mean?"

"It isn't used to being around people. And sometimes cats not used to being around people are so scared and nervous around them that they might bite or scratch."

"Ow."

"Yes. So you can see why someone might not want them."

"But when they get used to being around people, they won't bite," Chloe asserted hopefully.

"Perhaps," Edith allowed. "But even if these unsocialized cats don't actually bite, they may never become as cuddly as most people want their pets to be."

Chloe had nothing to say to this because, Edith supposed, she was one of those who preferred cuddly.

"And sometimes," Edith continued, "people don't think a cat is adoptable if it's too old. They want a young, playful cat or at least one that will be with them for a long, long time."

"Oh." Chloe fell silent a long minute, studying Ishy. Then, with the ability to commit that only the very young enjoy, she said, "I don't care. I still want Pixie."

Edith didn't even bother correcting her this time. Chloe's ability to believe what she wanted to believe was a wondrous and formidable thing.

They continued sitting on the sofa in companionable silence for a while longer before Chloe said, apropos of nothing Edith could discern, "My daddy likes you."

Edith didn't know how to respond, so taking her usual course, she didn't. But Chloe seemed as unconscious of social delicacy as Edith. "Do you like my daddy?"

"He's very nice."

"Do you like him?"

"Yes."

"A lot?"

"How much is a lot?"

"More than you like Pixie."

"What makes you think I like Pix—Ishy?"

"Because you let her live here."

"That might only mean I don't know what else to do with her."

Chloe gave her an exasperated look. "Well, do you like Pixie?"

"Yes."

"A lot?"

"How much is a lot?"

For a second, Chloe stared at Edith, her brows dipping toward each other in obvious confusion. Then, suddenly, abruptly, her expression cleared, and she laughed, a sweet, chuckling roll of a laugh. "As much as you like my daddy."

Edith grinned, charmed. "What makes you think I like your daddy?"

"Because you let us come here."

"That might only mean I don't know how to get rid of you."

Chloe burst into louder giggles, and Edith joined in just as Jim Curran appeared in the doorway. "Hey. What's up?"

Chloe popped off the sofa and dove at her father, wrapping her arms around his legs and peering up at him, her face shining. "Edie doesn't know how to get rid of us!" she crowed as if this were the best thing in the world.

Jim, hands resting lightly on Chloe's shoulders, looked over her at Edith. Heat climbed into her face. "It's not as it sounds. We were . . ." She sought an appropriate term.

"Being silly!" Chloe supplied.

"Yes," Edith said. "We were just being silly."

"Ahuh. Apparently." Jim nodded and swung his daughter up in his arms. "Sorry I took so long."

Edith shook her head. "There's no need to apologize. I enjoyed it."

Jim smiled at her, right into her eyes, and her heartbeat fluttered unevenly in response. His smile didn't mean anything personal. Of course he'd smile, she chided herself. She'd just complimented his progeny. People liked having their offspring approved of; it reflected on their mentoring and breeding abilities.

"We'd better get going, Chloe," Jim said. "Dinner's going to be way late as it is."

Dinner. She'd forgotten about dinner.

"Can we take Pixie with us?"

Jim glanced at Edith.

"You can try," she said. "But you mustn't be disappointed if she doesn't go."

Chloe nodded, her dark curls bobbing as she let go of her father's legs and skipped back to the old couch. Carefully, she collected Ishy in her arms and then, very slowly, walked out of the Meet and Greet room and down the narrow corridor toward the lobby. The cat purred, nuzzling her head up under the little girl's chin. Edith and Jim trailed after her.

They made it all the way to the front door of the shelter before Ishy started struggling. For a second, Chloe clutched her tighter, her face betraying frustration and hurt, but then she bent over with a gusty little sigh and released the old cat. Ishy didn't run away. She only sauntered off a few feet, sat down, and began patiently grooming a shoulder.

"She almost got through the door with me," Chloe said. "I think she really wanted to, but she got scared."

"Possibly."

Chloe gave a little sigh. "I can come back tomorrow, can't I?"

"Of course you can," Edith said, trying to hide her eagerness.

" 'Fraid not, Chlo-Schmo" Jim said.

"Why not?" Chloe demanded, echoing Edith's own thought.

"Tomorrow's Tuesday. Spaghetti night at your aunt Susie's."

Chloe's brow furrowed over a mutinous expression. "But I wanna see Pixie tomorrow!"

"Family first," Jim said, a note of iron creeping into his matter-of-fact tone.

"Ishy's not going anywhere," Edith said, trying to forestall the tantrum she saw threatening in Chloe's mulish expression. "She'll be here the next time you visit."

"Pixie!" Chloe glared at her, tears starting in her eyes. "Her name is *Pixie*!"

She stomped her foot in frustration.

"I'm sorry," Jim told Edith, taking a firm hold of Chloe's hand.

"Why?" Edith asked, ignoring Chloe's thunderous expression. She'd begun trying to yank her hand free. "Emotionally, children are primitive creatures, reactive rather than proactive. While not incapable of delaying gratification, they are still extremely resentful of having such a necessity imposed upon them. Chloe is simply acting like a five-year-old." When she'd thought she would be a parent in the near future, she'd done some research into child psychology—just light reading.

"Almost six!" Chloe shouted.

"A five-year-old," Edith said, pleased Chloe had been listening.

"Five or six, she's not coming tomorrow. She may

not be coming the next day, either, if she keeps this up," Jim added.

Chloe, looking from Edith to her father, decided he meant it. With a gruff little sigh of capitulation, she stopped yanking at his hand and contented herself with staring accusingly at Edith as if she had been somehow responsible for Tuesday-night spaghetti suppers. "Promise she'll be here?" she demanded.

"I promise."

"Next time I bet she comes home with me."

"We can only wait and see. In the meantime, I have a litter of kittens coming in tomorrow evening. Perhaps you'd like to see them? Not as a replacement for Pixie, but to help me name them."

Chloe's face lightened up. "Can I?"

"I'd appreciate it. I never seem to come up with very good kitten names," Edith said. "Every kitten people adopt from me ends up with a different name from the one I give it."

For some reason this seemed to amuse Jim. He grinned broadly. "You mean people *don't* want cats named Ishmael?"

"No. Or Ovid. Or Damocles. Or Macbeth."

"Imagine." His blue eyes were sparkling, and the long dimple in his lean cheek had deepened. For a second she felt a little light-headed. Pheromones weren't supposed to cause light-headedness. At least, she didn't think they were. She'd have to do some research.

"Come on, Chloe. Let's get some grub," Jim said, swinging his daughter up into his arms. All was apparently forgiven, for Chloe wrapped her arms around

Jim's neck with a confident familiarity that sent a ping of yearning through Edith. What would it be like to embrace someone so publically and without the slightest hesitation because you *knew* you wouldn't be rejected?

"Hey, Edie, have you had dinner?" Jim suddenly asked.

"Ah, no."

"Why don't you come and have dinner with us?" He bounced Chloe in his arms, and she giggled.

"Oh. No. I mean, no, thank you. I—I have to clean up here." Dinner? With Jim Curran and his Chloe. The idea confounded her.

"We could go home, get things ready, and you can come over when you're done here. We took up your evening. The least we can do is make you dinner. It won't be anything fancy, but . . . ," he said, trailing off enticingly.

She wanted to. Lord knew she wanted to, but . . . but . . . "No. I . . . No," she finished, hoping he wouldn't press her, yet hoping he would.

He looked openly disappointed, but he did not press her. *Damn.* "Okay, but you'll be missing out on some spectacular ground turkey glop."

She unlocked the front door, holding it open and standing aside so they could pass through. As they walked away, Chloe looked over her father's shoulder and waved.

Behind her, Ishy-Pixie yowled plaintively. Stupid cat. She wouldn't go with them, so what right did she have to complain?

Chapter 4

"You're kidding! You're *that* Jim Curran? The captain of the soccer team and homecoming king?" asked the pretty, curvy blonde sitting across from Jim. She leaned forward, eyes sparkling.

"Ah, yeah." Jim shifted in his chair and wished the waiter would show up and take their order. High school was a long time gone. Candice—Connor? Or was her last name Connell?—was laughing, her corn silk blond bob swinging lightly against her rounded cheeks, her adorable dimples deepening. Melissa, who'd set up this blind double date, beamed approvingly while her husband, Phil, grinned, clearly enjoying Jim's discomfort.

"My sister-in-law was your homecoming queen!" Candice crowed. "Darry Jurovich."

Jim looked up, his earlier discomfort forgotten. "Really?"

"Yeah!" Candice nodded excitedly.

"Candice went to Hamilton High, too," Melissa put in.

"Sure did," Candice acknowledged. "I was three years behind you. Still"—her eyes fell modestly to the white linen tablecloth—"I'm sure you saw me even if you don't remember me. I captained the Pantherettes dance line."

He didn't recall her, but it would be rude to say so. "Sure, I do," he said, and was gratified to see her pink up with pleasure. She was a nice woman, pretty in a Nordic goddess sort of way—tall and buxom, with a broad smile and an easy laugh.

"Well, even if you're lying, I'm going to pretend you're not. And let me say," she declared with an impish smile, "that despite having packed on some, er, more curves over the last ten years, I can still do a mean high kick."

"Really?" Phil said.

"Really. But I'm not going to give any demonstrations, so don't ask."

Phil shrugged. "Talk's cheap."

"No, you don't," Candice said, waving a finger under Phil's nose. "Last time I decided to show off, my shoe flew off and hit some poor innocent bystander in the forehead!"

They all laughed at the image, Phil saying, "Ah, come on, Candy. Maybe just once in the parking lot after dinner?"

"Nope." She shook her head. "Can't afford another lawsuit."

They were laughing again when Melissa abruptly said, "Candice also pitched for the girls' fast pitch softball. And still does."

Most women would have been embarrassed by Melissa's all-too-obvious listing of credentials, but Jim had to give Candice credit; she handled it with aplomb, being neither too self-effacing nor too boastful.

"Just a city team, but we're good. Took second place last year." Candice smiled. "I love being part of a team, you know? I just . . . I like people." Once again, her gaze dipped a little shyly, but becomingly so. She reminded him of someone. He couldn't place who, but . . .

The waiter appeared to take their orders. Candice barely glanced at the menu before smiling up at the middle-aged waiter and saying, "You have a T-bone? Back in the kitchen? Good. Medium well and, yeah, I know, it's disgusting, but bring some ketchup. And some sort of potato. I like au gratin."

The waiter made an effort to maintain a neutral expression. So did Jim. She intended to desecrate a steak with ketchup? May the food gods forgive her.

"I'm sorry, ma'am, but we have only baked or smashed with horseradish."

She pulled a face. "I love that they call mashed potatoes smashed now. Love it. But why do you have to mess up a perfectly lovely potato with horseradish?"

Jim admired the waiter's restraint. The same might be asked about steak and ketchup.

"Couldn't you do something about it? Please? I know I'm a heathen, but I just don't have a very adventurous palate. Come on. Take pity on me." She said this so winningly and with such good humor, Jim could actually see the waiter's stiff stance relax.

"Of course," he said.

"You are a doll," Candice said, and once again, Jim had a sense of déjà vu. He wondered if perhaps he did remember her after all.

The waiter took the rest of their orders and left, and the conversation flowed on at an easy pace. They traded anecdotes and names, moving gradually away from the past to the present. Candice was comfortable to be with, natural, funny, and engaging.

He learned she was an occupational therapist, working primarily with kids, and it didn't surprise him. Kids would love her. She'd never been married and dismissed her unattached state with a casual wave of her hand, saying she was "waiting for Prince Charming, but the bastard refuses to show up!" She liked many of the same things he did and held many of the same views. She even came from a family as tightly knit as his.

But there was something . . . missing—some indefinable spark of attraction. At the same time, there was something reassuringly familiar about her. He didn't realize why until they'd reached dessert and she was stealing the maraschino cherry off Melissa's hot fudge mini-sundae: She reminded him of Stephanie. She even looked something like Steph, with her curves, blond hair, and her wide blue eyes.

She finished the cherry and dabbed at her mouth, tossing the linen napkin lightly to the table. "You'll have to excuse me," she said, pushing back from the table.

Melissa started to get up to follow, but Candice waved her down. "Stay put, Mel," she said. "This isn't a group effort." She headed out of the dining room.

At once, Melissa's head swiveled toward Jim. "Well?"

"Well what?"

"What do you think of her?"

Jim fidgeted, noting Phil's sympathetic glance. "She's really nice."

"Isn't she?" Melissa enthused. "She's just about the nicest woman I know. Everyone loves her. And"—she hesitated—"well, did you . . . did you notice how much she resembles Stephanie?"

"Yeah," Jim answered, "I did." But she wasn't Stephanie. She could never be Stephanie.

"So, are you going to ask her out again?" Melissa asked.

Jim squirmed. Was he? "Come on, Mel. I dunno. Maybe. Maybe . . . not. I—I dunno."

"Mel, it's not really your business," Phil said gently.

She rolled her eyes and made a dismissive sound. "Anything I'm interested in is my business, and I'm interested in seeing that Jim isn't lonely the rest of his life." Her laserlike gaze swung to him. "This is the third blind date I've set you up on this year, and no one's good enough. What exactly are you looking for, Jim?"

He shrugged. What was he looking for? Melissa was right. Every one of the women she'd set him up with had been perfectly nice, smart, and pretty.

" 'Cause apparently you aren't interested in smart, pretty, nice women. I know." She snapped her fingers and intoned in a voice full of sarcasm, "How about someone like that weirdo at the cat shelt—" She stopped, abruptly having read something in his face. "Jesus," she breathed. "You can't really consider her dating material."

"No, no," Jim denied. "Of course not. We're just co-workers. But that doesn't mean I don't like her, and she's not weird—she's just different."

"So is a black hole . . . much like her personality."

"Really nice, Mel," Jim said, surprised by his anger.

Mel must have heard the warning edge in his voice, because the sneer fell from her face, leaving only concern and exasperation. "Look, Jimmy," she said, reaching over the table and covering his hand with hers. "I know you loved Steph—we all loved Steph—but I can assure you, she would not want you to spend the rest of your life pining for her. It's time to move on."

"I'm not pining," Jim said, still irritated. "Just because I'm not sure I want to ask Quasi Steph out on a date doesn't mean I'm pining."

"*Quasi* Steph?" Mel intoned, shocked.

"Yeah."

"That's really . . . low."

"It's true. I'm thinking of all the women you've set me up with over the last few years, and I just realized something. They're all Steph knockoffs."

Melissa threw up her hands in obvious despair. "So what?" she asked. "You loved Steph. It only stands to reason that the things you found attractive about her would be the same things you found attractive in other women!"

She was right, of course. It only made sense. The anger drained away, leaving him feeling unsettled and unsatisfied. Candice returned to the table, but even her effervescent personality couldn't quite return the group to their former good humor. She knew something was up, and when he walked her up to her door after taking her home, she looked up into his face and said, "Knowing Melissa, I'm guessing she's all ready to send out our first kid's birth announcement."

Jim laughed, relaxing.

"Look," Candice said, "I know she means well, but I hope she didn't push me down your throat. I mean . . . I think you're a nice guy and, well . . . we could have fun together."

"I'm sure we could."

Putting her hands on his chest, she moved in closer and kissed him. He responded, wrapping his arms around her, liking the substantial feel of her, the softness and sheer physical presence. Their kiss deepened, becoming more ardent. "Do you want to come in?" she murmured against his mouth, sounding a little breathless.

Did he? Yeah. But only because he missed a woman's body next to his. "Better not. My niece is sitting and her mother will skin me if she gets home too late."

"Oh," Candice said, disappointed. "Okay. Maybe . . . another time." She just kept it from being a question and though he started to reassure her, something kept him quiet. He had her number. He could call. She could call, for that matter. She didn't strike him as the type of woman who would stand on ceremony.

"Thanks, Candice. I had a great time," he said.

Again, disappointment flashed across her open countenance, but she didn't push. "I did, too. Good night, Jim."

He drove home feeling vaguely unsettled until at a stoplight he realized why. He was trying to determine if Melissa's accusation had merit. He didn't feel like he was pining for Steph. He missed her, but he didn't still grieve for her. He didn't think he had lived through his one and only shot at love and romance and companionship.

So why am I still single? Come on, Jim. Married? You haven't even dated anyone seriously. The most interest you've shown in a woman is in Edith Handelman, and that's purely friendship. Well, maybe not purely. There are those intermittent pings of potent attraction.

Perverse pings they were, too, since she'd told him the day they'd met she didn't know why Global Genetics needed a "talking head." Though that should have set the stage for an antagonistic relationship, it hadn't because at the same time he'd been reeling from her comment, he'd realized she hadn't meant it as an attack at all; she'd simply been relating the charge she'd overheard, unaware that it was an insult.

So, instead of walking away, he'd stayed and explained Global Gen needed *his* talking head to attract investors. *Then* he'd walked away and straight to his computer where he'd opened her file. Nope. No mention of Asperger's. But there were a lot of other interesting facts that shed some light on her social liabilities. Her parents, both army, had moved often when she was a kid—she listed eight addresses before she went to college at age twelve. She had no siblings and no close relatives, her parents now being deceased. Her education had been wildly accelerated, entailing frequent moves to various states for different fellowships. She'd never learned the social lessons—some good, most cruel—that middle and high school imparted. She'd never had much opportunity to practice purely social skills. He'd closed the file, intrigued and oddly touched—and maybe a little challenged.

A horn honked behind him, and he realized he'd been sitting at a green light for who knew how long. He lifted a hand in apology at the driver behind and drove on, frowning. He wasn't supposed to be thinking about Edith. He was supposed to be thinking about Candice and whether or not he wanted to go out with her again, and whether there was a future there. There was attraction, certainly. And she had a good sense of humor. And she was caring.

Ah, hell. He was overthinking this way too much. Of course he should ask her—

A small shadow dashed across the street and dove right beneath his tires. Jim wrenched the steering wheel hard to the right, and the tires squealed in protest. He slammed on the brakes, and the BMW fishtailed wildly as he turned into the skid, finally bringing the car to a standstill. His hands frozen on the steering wheel, he peered out at the roadway lit by the car's headlights, searching for the animal he was certain he must have hit. Nothing. He looked up into the rearview mirror, expecting to see a flattened squirrel in the road, but the pools cast by the red brake lights revealed nothing. . . .

Wait.

A little cat stood on the edge of the road, its eyes glowing eerily. It looked . . . It looked like a ginger cat, though it was hard to tell in this light. Jim frowned. It couldn't be Edith's cat. Could it? Edith said the cat never left the premises, and there must be a thousand ginger-striped cats in this part of Chicago. As he thought these things, the cat moved back into the street. It moved daintily but arthritically. *Geez*. It was the shelter cat. What was she doing out? Had someone else convinced Edith to let them adopt her, but now having escaped, she was on her way back?

She stopped in the middle of the road, lit by the headlights, and looked full at him. He could swear she saw him behind the windshield. He hesitated. If she'd lived all her life inside that building, she wouldn't know her way home. She might get lost. She might get hit by a car. He opened the car door and leaned out. "Here, kitty-kitty. Come here, kit. You can come home with me for the evening. The street isn't any place for a girl to be out by herself."

The cat looked at him. He got out, intending to go fetch her, but the little cat leaped away, arching her back and sidestepping. Clearly she did not want to be picked up. He got back into the car and watched as she began hobbling away down the street.

"Ah, come on, cat. At least get off the freaking road."

The cat ignored him, heading away into the night, angling back into the main traffic thoroughfare.

"Shit," Jim grumbled, and slammed the door shut. He pushed the car into gear, muttering under his breath. At least the cat, if it was Ishy, was heading in the right direction. He could follow behind her the few blocks to the shelter and make sure no one came cruising up on her. And if she left the street and popped off into the darkness, he could rest with an easy conscience. If she didn't, he'd figure something out when they reached the shelter. He could always call Edith at home. . . .

It didn't take long. Sure enough, the cat followed the road all the way to the intersection where she unerringly took a left turn onto the street where the shelter was located. Five minutes later, as Jim pulled to the curb in front of the shelter, she disappeared into the alley behind it. Even though it was past eleven, there were lights on inside, illuminating the small lobby.

He frowned. There was nothing in the shelter worth stealing, which meant anyone in there could only be up to no good. He got out of the car, reaching back for his cell phone and preparing to call the cops before he did a little investigation by himself. If anyone was hurting those animals—

He stopped as a figure walked in front of the lobby window. It was Edith. She was cradling a mottled white and caramel cat in her arms, her usual cool expression gone, replaced by one of tender amusement as the cat she held batted lightly at her chin. He watched, entranced, as she dropped a kiss on the cat's head. He realized he was smiling.

He went up to the front door and knocked, calling out at the same time, "Edith? It's Jim Curran."

A few seconds later the door opened and Edith peeked out. "Jim?" She sounded confused. Her hair was held back in some sort of clip, and the harsh overhead lighting sculpted shadows beneath her cheekbones and in the delicate hollows of her temples. She looked naked, vulnerable. . . . She was holding a Taser.

As soon as she saw it really was him, she tucked it back into the pocket of her smock.

"Geez. I didn't realize you considered me threatening," he said, a little unnerved. "Listen, I swear there're no current restraining orders out against me," he said, trying to make light of it.

"Current?" she echoed, a fleeting smile turning up one corner of her mouth.

He liked teasing out these sneak peeks of her humor, the slow unfolding of the mystery that was Edith. "Current."

She gave a sound that sounded suspiciously like a snort. "I didn't hear the name clearly," she explained laconically. "And I certainly have no reason to expect you to be banging on the shelter door at"—she glanced at her wristwatch—"eleven twelve at night."

"Hi, Edith. I know this sounds weird, but I was driving home from a date when I swear that old ginger cat of yours almost made himself roadkill under my tires."

Rather than alarmed, she only looked more confused.

"The old ginger cat?" Jim said. "You must have let someone try to adopt her. Well, she's not having it. If you look in the back alley, you'll find her. I followed her all the way from Forty-fifth Street to here."

"Ishy?"

"Yeah. Ishy."

"No one tried to adopt Ishy," she said.

"Well then, she must be leading a secretly much more adventurous life than you give her credit for, because she's been out, well, catting around. She must have slipped through a door when you weren't looking."

"No."

"Edith, if you'll just look in the alley."

"I don't have to look in the alley. Ishy's in the Meet and Greet room, asleep on the couch where she's been all night. I was just with her ten minutes ago."

She stepped aside and motioned him in. "See for yourself."

His brow furrowed, but he accepted the invitation, moving past her and heading through the door she indicated, then entering a small hallway. "It's the door at the end," she said.

He strode to the door and opened it. It was dark inside, only the streetlight in the alley offering any illumination. He made out the dark silhouette of an armchair and an old couch. He didn't see a cat. Edith reached past him and flipped on the light switch.

Light blazed on from overhead. Dazzled, he squinted against the sudden brilliance. For a second he thought he saw a sort of shimmering cloud hovering above the couch cushions, but it faded quickly, revealing only a small, roosting ginger cat, blinking myopically at them.

Impossible. There couldn't be two antique ginger cats with an attachment to this place.

He swiveled around, facing her. "Where's the door to the alley?"

She pointed at a door in the far wall, and he headed toward it, flinging it open and stepping down into the poorly lit alley. He turned slowly, scanning the alleyway, searching for the tiny semicrippled cat. "Pixie? Ishy?" he called.

Nothing.

"It's very kind of you to curtail your date by attempting to rescue a stray cat, even if it's not the cat you assumed it to be," Edith said from behind him.

"Oh, it wasn't curtailed. I'd already dropped her off."

"Oh."

"And I could have sworn it was your cat."

"The cat's not mi—"

He turned around, smiling at her. "Yeah. I know. Technically she is the responsibility of the shelter. Have a problem with owning things, Edith?" he teased lightly.

"Yes," she answered bluntly, surprising him. "I find the very notion of owning another sentient being presumptuous."

So concrete, she was; so exacting. Conversation with her was always interesting, unexpected, thought provoking.

"How about saying she belongs to you, then?" he said. "As in, she is attached to you by virtue of your having accepted responsibility for her and her dependence on you for those things she requires. Like a child belongs to its mother, or friends belong to one another, or other sorts of interconnected people."

She gave his suggestion serious consideration, tipping her head as she commenced some inner debate. She caught his eye and asked for elucidation. "The requirements in the cited relationship differing, but the dependence on each other to fulfill those requirements forming the bond?"

"Yes." Had Edith ever belonged to someone?

"Like lovers?" she asked, startling him.

"Excuse me?"

"I suppose, then, that lovers could be said to belong to each other," she explained, clearly trying to work out whether she could agree with his semantics.

"Many poets seem to think so."

"I wouldn't know too much about that. My romantic involvements were never . . . very romantic."

No, he supposed not. And it saddened him.

"And do you consider that you belong to the person whom you dated this evening?" she asked, so quizzically he could not mistake it for personal interest. She was simply collecting data.

"No," he said. "No. It isn't that sort of relationship."

And never would be, he realized, looking into Edith's lovely clear brown eyes. He didn't want to date Candice Connor. He just wasn't interested. He just might, he realized, want to date Edith Handelman. He was definitely interested.

"Oh," she said, and then began to fidget, most uncharacteristically. Did he make her uncomfortable? In what way? He wouldn't be opposed to making Edith Handelman uncomfortable. "Well, now you've seen that Ishy is safely within and apparently the cat you followed is nowhere to be found."

It was obviously a hint for him to take off. Not subtle, but then, this was Edith, and in the Edith-verse something as understated as a hint came damned near to being Machiavellian.

Uncomfortable he might want to make her but not unpleasantly so. "I'd better go. Sorry to bother you," he said.

"Not at all. Your motives were commendable," she said.

He headed back toward the front of the building. She followed him, turning off lights. At the front door he stopped and turned, noting as he did so that Ishy had followed them and was standing behind Edith, her milky green eyes fixed on him with unblinking concentration. Without thinking, Edith bent down and scooped her up into her arms.

"Good night, Edith," he said.

"Good night."

There was nothing more to say. He pushed open the front door and headed outside for his car. She held the door open, watching him leave.

He turned. "What are you doing here so late, anyway?" he asked.

She didn't answer at once; instead her long elegant fingers played lightly over Ishy's small triangular face. A smile flickered briefly across her soft lips. "I belong here. Good night, Jim."

She closed the door.

Chapter 5

"**L**ook! Look! Look!" Chloe announced two weeks later as she burst through the front door of the Cupid Cats Shelter.

Edie was standing by the reception desk talking to Carol, the same middle-aged woman who'd been manning the front desk the first day Jim and Chloe had come to Cupid Cats. She looked around, and Jim noticed at once that her hair was loose, falling in thick waves that framed her face and looking ridiculously silky. A few tendrils curled against her temple, inviting someone to tuck them back. Not someone. *Him*.

She wore a drab T-shirt, the only virtue of which was the scoop neck that exposed her delicate clavicle and the very topmost swells of her breasts. His gaze fell to her long legs, covered by capris that looked as if she'd bought them from a geriatric cruisewear catalogue. And still the sight of her galvanized him.

"Look!" Chloe was bouncing up and down in front of Edie, holding up the doll that her cousin Mandy, away at state college, had sent as an early birthday present.

Edith recoiled. "What *is* it?" she whispered.

"It's KidZ DivaZ's Chloe!" Chloe screeched in jubi-

lation. "*Chloe!* Like me!" She thrust the plastic doll into
Edie's hand.

Reluctantly, Edith turned it over in her hand. She
cleared her throat. "How laudable of the toymakers of
America to model empathy for the less fortunate by
producing dolls with birth defects," she said, smiling.
"And how laudable of you, Chloe, to so wholeheart-
edly embrace your 'special' dolly."

"What's she talking about?" Chloe asked her father.

"I'm not sure."

Edie turned to Jim and Carol. "With what is the
doll supposed to be afflicted? Macrocephaly? Hydro-
cephalus?"

Dear God. She thought the doll was some sort of
politically correct empathy doll. Not a bad guess, he
admitted, looking at the sticklike little plastic body
mounted by a gargantuan head with bulging eyes and
overinflated lips.

"That's it," Carol tch'd, scooping up her cell phone
and dumping it in her purse. "That's it. I'm getting
you a subscription to *People* magazine. You gotta know
what a KidZ DivaZ doll is. Every little girl in America
has one or wants one."

"Why?" Edie asked, sounding lost.

"I don't have time to explain. I gotta get to my son's
house. I have babysitting duty tonight."

Edie's amber-shot brown eyes swung toward him
inquiringly.

"It's not supposed to have anything wrong with it,
Edie. It's just supposed to be cute. At least the sub-ten
set seems to think so."

Edie stared. "You're teasing me. This doll is seriously

malformed—" She caught Chloe's eye and made the unexpectedly politic gesture of dropping the subject.

No one Jim knew was more out of touch with popular culture than Edie. She didn't own a television, she didn't read tabloids or magazines, and she didn't go to movies. Until a few days ago he'd assumed she didn't have any interests outside of her work and the shelter. But that was before he'd discovered that his prim, starchy little scientist was a closet epicurean and total foodnetwork.com junkie.

For two weeks he'd been trying to lure her into having dinner with him and Chloe. She always refused, so last week he'd stopped by a Greek restaurant that was getting rave reviews in the local press and picked up some food. The sensuous appreciation on Edie's face when the smell of braised lamb in lemon had hit her nose had made the price tag worth it. And when she'd licked her lips, the tip of her tongue slickering the plump bow of her lower one, he'd gone weak in the knees. He caught the sound of her inhaling, and her eyelids slipped half shut as she'd sighed with pleasure.

Nope. No two ways about it. It might be well hidden, but beneath that well-controlled, cool, and collected exterior lurked the heart of a sensualist.

Edith Handelman was driving him crazy, and she didn't even know it. She was driving him crazy with her spiky lashes and her dewy complexion, her trim ankles and elegant fingers, the way she screwed up her brow in concentration, the way she laughed, abruptly and loud, and then looked surprised by it. She was driving him crazy with her vulnerability, her deadpan wit, and tender heart. But most of all she was driving him crazy with her total failure to recognize that she was driving him crazy. She had no idea she set his blood afire, that thoughts of her had begun creeping into every hour of his waking day and plaguing his nights.

Every other weekday he took Chloe by the hand and went calling on Edie at Cupid Cats. "Calling," quaint and old-fashioned a term as it might be, was the only one that fit the bill for what he was doing. He was sure his mother would have been vastly amused, but he wasn't. He was frustrated, exasperated, and physically damned uncomfortable. He wanted to grab her and *do* things to her, with her, for her. He hadn't even held her hand yet.

"That's okay, Edie," Chloe was saying. She took back her doll and gave Edie a comforting pat on the hand. Chloe was growing used to Edie's lack of familiarity with all sorts of important things such as Web-kinz and SpongeBob SquarePants. "Didn't you ever have a doll?" she asked curiously.

"Good question," Carol muttered, rummaging in her purse for her keys.

"Yes," Edie answered. "When I was ten my parents ordered me Anatomy Jane, which, as its name implies, was an anatomica—" She caught Jim's eye. "Yes. I had a doll. Just not as . . . interesting as this one."

This seemed to satisfy Chloe. "Can I go see the kittens?"

"Yes. As long as it's fine with your father."

"Yes, Chloe, go ahead."

She bolted, leaving Jim with Edie and Carol. Edie looked at Jim, opened her mouth, and shut it again;

then she spun on her heels, leaving him standing behind and watching her in bemusement.

Carol glanced up and smirked. "Man, she really likes you."

"Yeah. She could barely drag herself away," Jim replied drily. Last week he'd contrived a meeting with a potential investor just so he could insist Edith come along. Rather than growing more comfortable with him, she seemed to have taken a giant step backward. Oh, here at Cupid Cats she might be eager and inquisitive and unexpectedly droll, but as soon as she stepped outside, she reverted to the stiff, gauche brainiac.

The only breech in her armor was her blushes. She blushed gorgeously, ravishingly, a delicate apricot stain that sifted like the finest powder across the pale porcelain perfection of her skin . . . and she blushed every time she saw him, which meant he was finding all sorts of lame excuses to visit the research floor.

He was flat-out smitten, but something was going to have to give. He'd hit a wall, and he didn't like it.

"Ha!" Carol's hand dove into the bottom of her monstrous tote and returned triumphant with a set of keys. "Look, I've worked with Edith for years now, and I'd say I know her about as well as anyone without a PhD in this town. I just want you to know that she's not as strange as she seems. Don't get me wrong— she's plenty strange, but most of that comes from lack of experience."

"Listen, you don't have to tell me—"

"Yeah, I do. She really does like you and, well, you're not that hard to read."

He didn't deny it. "So, what am I supposed to do

about it?" Jim asked, leaning over the counter separating them. "I've asked her to dinner and she won't go."

"Have you ever asked her why?"

"Yeah. She says she wouldn't feel comfortable with a social relationship, seeing as how we're coworkers. I told her there was no company policy against coworkers fraternizing, but she—"

"Hold everything, sport," Carol interrupted, holding her hand up. "You didn't actually say *fraternizing*?"

"Well, yeah. I thought she'd appreciate it if I put it in the same terms she would use."

She stared at him a second, then muttered, "If that isn't a male way of thinking, I don't know what is." Shaking her head, she brushed by him on her way out the door, pausing only to say, "If anyone comes in to see about a cat, tell them to come back tomorrow," and with that she was gone.

Meow.

He looked down. Pixie-Ishy, or Ishy-Pixie as Edie now called her with a straight face but a sparkle in her eyes, looked up at him from slowly twining her way around his legs. He bent down and carefully scooped her up.

"Hello, old sweetheart," he murmured, chucking her gently under the chin. The old cat climbed her front legs up around his shoulder and rubbed her face against his jaw. Her purr sounded rattley, and she felt as light and insubstantial as a November oak leaf. "There's nothing to you, is there, little girl?"

She sighed and it felt as if she might simply fade away in his arms. He stroked her gently. She did look a lot like Pixie. How Steph had adored that cat. His chance encounter with a kid and a box full of seven-week-old kittens had resulted in a last-minute replacement for the bouquet of flowers he'd been on his way to pick out for their first anniversary. He hadn't taken the kitten; he'd taken the mother. Steph had showered all the love of a very loving heart on the little beast.

She'd been one of those people who drew others to her like a magnet, the first to be there with a congratulatory bottle of champagne, the last to leave if someone needed comforting. She laughed often and effortlessly, sang out loud even though she was tone-deaf, and never wore shoes if she could help it. Even in the winter she had to be barefoot. She was a bon vivant and a clown. She'd loved him as much as he loved her, and he would never, ever find her like again. In spite of the Herculean efforts of his sisters.

The ginger cat batted his face with one paw, seeking attention. He looked down into her milky jade eyes.

"Have you been waiting for someone to come back for you, too?" he asked softly, though he knew it was nonsense. Like Edie said, the cat had just fixated on this locale. She wasn't holding out, waiting for some beloved former owner to come claim her. And had she been, how terribly sad that would be, to think of all the fruitless waiting while the other potential owners came and went. On the other hand, maybe she just didn't have it in her to love another person.

His brow furrowed thoughtfully. He wasn't certain if he ought to feel a little guilty that he had fallen for a woman who was about as dissimilar from his wife as he could imagine—except they both were smart, had

generous natures, and—he rubbed the cat's silky little
ear tabs—loved cats. But he didn't feel guilty.

"Daddy, one of the new kittens is an *albino*. That
means it's all white but has pink eyes like a rabbit!"
Chloe's excited voice preceded her arrival. Edie followed her, cradling a softball-sized bundle of white
fur. She looked relaxed, and the smile hovering at the
corners of her mouth was soft.

Chloe skidded to a stop when she saw whom he
was holding. She approached them slowly, as Edie had
taught her, and reached up and scratched the ginger
cat between the ears.

"Hello, Ishy-Pixie," she said with a giggle. She found
the cat's new moniker hilarious.

The cat peered over Jim's arms at Chloe and purred.
Chloe secured Jim's free hand and tugged him toward
the doorway, where Edie stood watching him. He was
beginning to be able to read her expressions, surprised
he'd ever thought her face empty of emotion. Hers was
simply a more subtle countenance. It took study to be
able to read it. She was Sanskrit, not graffiti.

"Look, Daddy. Pink eyes!" Chloe said, jumping up
and down in front of Edie.

The sudden movement startled the kitten. With a
tiny hiss, it scrambled loose of Edie's clasp and tore
up her T-shirt, disappearing over her shoulder beneath
her cloud of hair.

"Ouch!" Edie reached back to pull the kitten free,
but the little spitball hissed again, tangling further in
the thick, wavy tresses.

"Wait," he said, handing Ishy-Pixie to Chloe. "It's
all tangled up. Let me work it free."

He stepped behind her and filtered his hand beneath the heavy curtain of hair, lifting it away from the nape of her neck. It was just as silky and fine as he'd imagined it would be. His mouth went dry. Edie froze. The kitten dove toward her far shoulder, yowling as a hind leg got snared. Jim looped one arm in front of her and plucked it off by the scruff of its neck. It gave a piteous bleat and went limp.

"Don't hurt it!" Chloe exclaimed.

"He's not hurting it," Edie said. She sounded a little breathless.

With his other hand, he reached over her shoulder and began untwining her hair from around it.

"Scruffing is used by mother animals to pick up her progeny," Edie went on in her high, professorial voice. He'd noticed that the more flustered Edie was, the more wordy she got. "You may have noticed, Chloe, that as your father dislodged the kitten from my person, it automatically went limp and is currently quite immobilized. This is an involuntary reflex in neonatal animals that helps facilitate the transporting process. As the animal ages, its weight will disallow such action as the strain of its increased weight on its skin would be painful, but right now the kitten is quite comfortable."

The longer his hands were on her, the more syllables she used. By God, she'd probably spew out the formula for time travel if they ever actually kissed. He grinned behind her back as his fingers continued to unravel her tresses from around the kitten.

"I didn't understand any of that, Edie," Chloe said patiently. "Can you tell me again later, using words I know?"

"Oh! Oh, I'm sorry," Edie exclaimed, taking a step away.

Jim gave her hair a gentle tug, stopping her. "Stand still and be quiet," he murmured. "I'm concentrating."

Chloe retreated to the counter and set Ishy-Pixie down, then flopped cross-legged on the floor. She propped her elbows on her knees and balanced her chin in her fists, regarding them impassively.

Edie didn't make any further protest. For several minutes he worked on getting her hair untangled in silence, all too aware of the heat of her skin where his knuckles grazed her collarbone, the fresh scent of her shampoo rising from the silky coils of hair near his lips, the size of her, the shape, the aura. . . .

Twice he heard her draw in deep breaths and thought maybe he made her nervous. She was making him a lot more than nervous.

He finished untwining the last bit of hair and brushed it away from Edie's cheek, his right arm still looped in front of her in a parody of a lover's embrace. All he'd need to do was turn her and tilt her head up and—

"Is this going to take much longer?" Chloe's plaintive voice brought him back to earth with a crash.

His arm dropped away. "Nope. Done."

Edie turned around. Her eyes looked huge, the pupils dark and unfathomable.

Damn, but how had he ever thought she was plain? She was elegant and sparse and . . . sexy as all hell. And he had to get out of here before he grabbed her in front of his daughter. He thrust the kitten at her. She took it, clearly startled, and clasped it to her chest.

"Come on, kiddo," Jim said to Chloe. "Time to go."

"What?" Chloe bolted to her feet. "We just *got* here!"

"We didn't just get here. We've been here twenty minutes." Storm clouds gathered in his daughter's face. "Look, I'll come home early Friday and we'll stay twice as long, okay?"

Chloe weighed the options.

"I'm not really asking, Chloe," he said evenly.

Chloe sighed. "Okay." She popped over to where Edie still stood and reached up, scuffling the kitten's head and smiling up at Edie. "I didn't fill the water bowls, and I didn't play with the kittens, so you're going to have to do it," she confided.

"Okay," Edie said.

"And don't forget to give Pippin a hug." Pippin was Chloe's favorite kitten, a thin little mouse-colored cat with blue eyes.

Edie looked somewhat taken aback by this directive but simply nodded.

"And me, too," Chloe added abruptly, and wrapped her arms around Edie's hips, squeezing tightly.

Over her head, Edie met Jim's eyes. Her eyes went wide, startled and amazed and . . . something profoundly more. She released one hand from the kitten and reached down, spreading her hand wide on Chloe's narrow back and pressing her tightly against her.

For a good thirty seconds no one moved; then Chloe let go of Edie and turned around, casually collecting Jim's hand in hers and leading him out the door. He left, taking heart in being pretty sure Edie was as reluctant for them to leave as he was and plotting a foray to Giorgio's for eggplant rotini that would send her into a swoon. On Thursdays they also made a buttermilk panna cotta—Thursday. Today was Wednesday.

He'd been so distracted by the closest thing he'd had to physical contact with Edie—and how pitiful was that?—he'd forgotten Melissa was coming over. He glanced at his wristwatch.

"What, Daddy?" Chloe asked.

"I forgot today's Wednesday," Jim said, starting up the block toward their home. "It's a good thing we left when we did, because you're aunt Melissa will be here in fifteen minutes to pick you up for your sleepover."

"I don't want to go to Aunt Melissa's tonight. I want to stay home."

Jim looked in surprise at his daughter. This was the first time since they'd moved to their new house three months ago that Chloe had expressed a desire to stay home rather than to spend the night at the home of one of her aunts. She'd always looked forward to sleepover Wednesdays with a fervor that cut at Jim's heart and made him wonder if he'd done the right thing in moving them out of the old neighborhood, the only home she'd ever known until now.

Grieving and ill-prepared for the life of a single parent, after Steph's death he'd returned to Chicago with his infant daughter. His family had become their mainstay. They'd shared meals, vacations, Sunday afternoons, and Friday nights. His family had loved Steph, and they transferred all that love to Chloe, wanting only the best for her. But over the past year, Jim had found himself questioning whether their indulgent, doting care was, well, healthy for Chloe.

Chloe's calculated remark to Edie about her mother's being dead had been becoming typical of her recent behavior. The tantrums were more frequent, her assumption of entitlement more obvious. He'd broached his concerns to his family, but as one they dismissed them, reminding him that they had raised children and whatever behavioral problems he imagined Chloe had were normal. Then they promised to be stricter with her. But within a week they'd all slid back into the old patterns—including Jim. He wasn't proud of it, but there it was.

So last spring he'd moved them closer to the magnet school Chloe would be attending in the fall. The transition hadn't been easy. Chloe had resisted, his sisters had resisted, and his brothers-in-law had resisted. There had been more temperamental behavior, disturbed sleep, and obvious anxiety.

And Chloe hadn't been too happy, either, he thought with a self-effacing grin. So he was delighted to hear Chloe opt for home over sleepover.

"I'd like you to stay, too, Chloe," he said, giving her hand a squeeze. "But your cousins are looking forward to seeing you and Aunt Melissa is already on her way to pick you up. But next Wednesday you and I can stay home and rent a DVD and watch a movie." Movies were a special treat. In the new regime of Chloe-raising, television viewing was limited to a few hours a week.

"Can Edie come over and watch with us?"

"We can sure ask her."

"Yeah!"

Edie. The reminder of her brought back a surge of longing that turned his smile wry. Their weeks at Cupid Cats had been good for Chloe. Since Edie didn't know any five-year-olds, she didn't have any preconceived ideas of Chloe's limitations. She expected her to behave in a certain way and treated her accordingly. And Chloe responded. The few times she'd actually lit into a tantrum on the shelter's premises—and there had unfortunately been a few—Edie's shocked expression had done more to mitigate the scene than anything Jim or his sisters had done. Instead of arguing, fretting, or cajoling his daughter, Edie simply removed herself from the area.

Chloe was not stupid. A temper tantrum without an audience was a wasted effort. For the most part, the temper tantrums had ended.

They reached the steps leading up from the sidewalk to their front lawn. It was overgrown. Since Chloe would be gone tonight, he should mow it, and while he was at it, he should take out the old metal clothesline pole in the backyard.

A horn beeped from behind them. They turned around to see Melissa getting out of her sedan. "Hey, baby brother. Hi there, princess," she said, coming up the steps. "Ready to roll?"

"Hi, Aunt 'Lissa." Chloe gave her aunt a big hug, then hopped back. "I gotta get my Dora the Explorer backpack."

"You're not ready?" Melissa asked in surprise. Usually Chloe was sitting on the top step of the porch when Melissa arrived, her backpack on.

"No. We were at Edie's," Chloe explained as she disappeared into the house.

Melissa gave Jim a look. "Honestly, Jim, I don't know why you insist on dragging Chloe over to that shelter. There are plenty of others around where the directors aren't opinionated control freaks."

"We go because it's really close and a nice walk, plus Chloe thinks that old ginger cat is Pixie, and, well . . . she likes Edie." He almost added, "and so do I," but figured why fan the fires.

"Huh. And I'm sure Edie likes Chloe, too. Free labor. Why, the poor lamb told me that woman had her filling water and food bowls."

At the thought of Edie as a sort of nonprofit Fagin, cynically using kittens to lure kiddies in to fill water bowls for her, Jim burst out laughing.

"It's not funny," Melissa said with a disgruntled snort. Melissa had not forgiven Edie for insisting that cats belonged indoors. More to the point, she'd not forgiven her for having the science with which to back that position up and, worst of all, for doing it in front of Chloe. Melissa took her role as queen of Chloe's heart seriously. In Edie, she sensed a challenger to the throne.

"Chloe likes helping Edie," he said in answer to Melissa's disgruntled snort. "She likes the responsibility, and more important, it's good for her."

"I wish you'd just pick a kitten and be done with this nonsense. It's not fair to keep letting Chloe think that old bag of cat bones is going to come live with you. Even if you could get that feline head case out the front door, it wouldn't be right to adopt a cat that old for a little girl."

"She might come someday," said a small voice from the front door.

Melissa spun around, her expression melting into self-reproach. "Oh, honey. I didn't mean she wouldn't want to come with you. I just wish you'd fallen in love with a kitty. Someone you can grow up with."

Chloe opened the screen door and slipped out, dragging her Dora the Explorer backpack by the strap. Her little face was sober. "Ishy-Pixie's going to come home with us someday, isn't she?" she asked Jim.

"I don't know," he answered.

She was trying very hard to be brave. He could see it, but her lower lip did shiver just a second.

"She was someone's cat, Chloe," he said gently. "Someone took good care of her and loved her, and maybe she's waiting for that person."

"She's *Mommy's* cat," Chloe insisted. "And Mommy *can't* come and get her."

"Well, Ishy-Pixie doesn't know that," Jim said, then added, "But maybe she's *not* Mommy's cat. Maybe she just really, really looks like Pixie."

Chloe sighed, her narrow little shoulders sagging. "Maybe." She looked up at him. "Daddy, I don't wanna stop going to see her. Even if she's not Pixie. I don't want another kitty." She hesitated a second. "Not yet. I love Cupid Cats. I love Edie."

"We don't have to stop going, Chlo-Schmo," Jim said, catching Melissa's eye. "There's no hurry. Now, you'd better take off."

He put her in the front seat, watched as she buckled herself tightly in, and waved as they drove away. Melissa's face was taut with disapproval.

Chloe's words had struck him hard. "I love Edie," she had said.

Of course, Chloe *loved* Polly Pockets, Lite-Brites, and corn dogs, too. Her love was widespread and undiscriminating. But his wasn't, and damn—that made two Currans under the good doctor's spell.

Chapter 6

$\mathcal{E}$dith locked the door behind Jim and Chloe and sagged against it, his gentle touch branded like fiery kisses along her collarbone and the nape of her neck. Why had he looked so strange, and why had he left so abruptly? She was having a hard time maintaining objectivity. He'd touched her and she'd shivered. But . . . she thought he'd shivered, too. So why had he left?

If only she could be more like Chloe, who acted without doubt or hesitation. Tonight, when Chloe had asked her for a hug and squeezed her so tightly, the world felt as if it had dropped away from beneath Edie's feet while at the same time something swelled in her chest until it ached. Edie closed her eyes, savoring the memory of the small body squeezing into her. It had felt so good, so perfectly natural, so easy. And emotional things had never been easy for Edie.

"Maybe I should just forget it—all of it," she said. "Grand, Edith; now you're talking to yourself. There ought to at least be a cat around."

Her mouth twisted in a self-mocking smile. Strange or not, too many cats or not, she loved running the shelter. The knowledge that she was needed by something living, that she could benefit another creature, produce happiness, or contentment, or just a feeling of security—somehow it fulfilled a part of her as nothing else had.

She loved her cats, each one of them. Initially she'd abjured herself for using a term like "love" in reference to her relationship with these stray and lost animals, but she'd long ago gotten over it. Love existed. One could not quantify it or examine it; the proof of its existence relied solely on anecdotal material. And yet she did not doubt for an instant that it existed. She loved her parents, her friends, Chloe, and . . .

She pushed herself upright and as she did so, she thought she heard a soft voice coming from the back of the shelter, where the Meet and Greet room was located. Had Carol come back and entered through the alley?

She went to investigate, her tennis shoes padding softly on the linoleum as she headed down the corridor and stopped, her hand on the doorknob. The voice was gone now, the only sound the soft sibilation of the antique air conditioner struggling to keep the facility cool. She cracked open the door and peered inside. Ishy-Pixie was moving in a tight little circle in the middle of the room, her back arched as though she were rubbing against something, purring loudly.

There was no one else in the room.

"What are you doing in here?" Edie asked. She could have sworn Ishy-Pixie was still in the front lobby where Chloe had left her. And how did she get in here when the door was closed?

The cat opened her milky green eyes and came

toward her, her gait a little uneven, her tail high. Edie
lifted her gently. She weighed no more than a paper-
back book. The old darling would not live much longer. She spent more and more time sleeping the days
and nights away. Food held little interest for her. Only
she and Chloe and Jim awoke what was left of her desire to be with people.

Edie lowered her head, rubbing her cheek gently
across the small head. "Oh, darling. You never are
going to leave the shelter, are you?" The idea filled her
with melancholy. The cat wriggled a little in her arms,
and Edie took her over to the old beat-up sofa, setting
her gingerly on the cushion. It was her favorite place
nowadays. At once, she tucked her little paws underneath her and closed her eyes.

With a final scratch behind Ishy's ear, Edie left her
and headed toward the Cat Room. She might as well
do her final rounds and leave. She did a head count
of the five resident cats in two banks of stacked stain-
less steel kennels, making sure everyone was safe for
the night: Rasputin . . . Morgan Le Fay . . . Dido . . .
Caravaggio . . . Nemo. . . .

Her eye caught sight of something lurking in the
back of the bottom lower-right kennel. She frowned.
No animal had been assigned to that kennel. She bent
down to peer in.

"Geez!" She jumped back.

Catching her hand to her chest, she cautiously leaned
back over again. Chloe's deformed pouty-lipped, giant-
headed doll's abnormally bulging eyes stared back at
her. She reached in and grabbed it, feeling a thrill of
distaste. Chloe must have been playing some sort of

game with it—prison doll?—and in her father's haste to leave left it behind.

Whatever she did or did not do about Jim Curran and the uncomfortable, exciting, frightening, physical yearning he engendered in her had no bearing on her relationship with Chloe. In so many ways, Chloe was direct and trusting and took things at face value. It made her vulnerable. She could not stand to have Chloe thinking she didn't care about her. Her life would be a great deal emptier without Chloe.

Of course, they couldn't all go on like this indefinitely. As Jim had said in the beginning, it wouldn't be long before Chloe realized Ishy-Pixie wasn't her mother's and gave up trying to take her out of the shelter. It had already gone on longer than anyone, save perhaps Chloe, expected. The last few visits, Chloe hadn't spent as much time with Ishy-Pixie, occupied as she was with her "job" of filling water bowls and "exercising" the kittens and cats. Before long, she'd give up, and even if she didn't, Ishy-Pixie . . . Well, she had only a few weeks left, maybe a month. Then what? How could she tell Chloe that the old cat—

A tear welled up in her eye, and she dashed it away angrily with the back of her hand.

She didn't know what to do, and it scared the hell out of her. She hated not knowing. She hated being ignorant. She'd spent her life collecting information as a way of making sense of things, of being able to anticipate things, of controlling things. But this she couldn't control.

Damn, damn, damn. She thought too much! She always had. But rather than free her from making mis-

takes and giving her an advantage in her dealings with
people, it had only backed her into this tight little corner from which she was afraid to move—except with
the cats. Her shoulders sagged. She'd become a weird
old cat lady, and she wasn't even thirty.

She didn't want to be a strange cat lady. She wanted
Jim—and Chloe.

Chloe . . .

Her gaze fell on the Big Head doll.

Chloe would either miss the doll terribly or not realize it was gone. Edith could not assume the latter. She
would take the doll back to Chloe. She didn't see she
had a choice. She stuck the Big Head into her oversized
tote, checked the shelter's voice mailbox to see if any
cats needed immediate rescuing, and then stepped out
into the Chicago summer night, locking the door behind her.

It had been close to ninety degrees earlier in the day,
and the evening didn't promise much relief. She set
off at a brisk pace, rehearsing what she would say if
Jim asked her in. And he would ask her in, because he
was a very polite man. Over the course of the last few
weeks, he'd talked her into going out to lunch several
times, but she drew the line at dinner. That would have
made it too much like a date.

At first, she'd thought he did so out of gratitude for
letting Chloe come to the shelter, and she didn't want to
be thanked for something she did as much for herself as
for the child, so she'd refused. But then he'd explained
that he wanted her to get more involved with the cli-
ents and wished to "brief" her on how they ought to
approach possible investors. That she could agree to.

But if he invited her into his house when she brought the doll tonight, she would decline, of course. One didn't appear on the doorstep and expect to be welcomed in. She was simply returning his daughter's toy—of course.

She turned the corner, admiring the neighborhood. She'd always liked Parkwood Knolls. It was a typical turn-of-the-century enclave, each house set amidst small, neat front yards with their respective detached garages lining back alleys. Every house had steps leading up from well-maintained sidewalks to the flower-bordered front walks of a nice mixture of bungalows, arts and crafts, and prairie-style homes.

A block and a half up the street she found Jim's address, an olive drab–colored stucco bungalow with deep eaves overhanging a front porch painted white. An empty swing hung from the horizontal limb of a giant basswood tree. The grass needed mowing.

She pulled the doll from her purse and climbed onto the porch. The front door was open behind the screen door, the hushed stillness of an empty house waiting beyond. She peered through a short vestibule that opened into a living room. Books, magazines, and toys were haphazardly piled on a hammered-brass coffee table while a variety of stuffed toys had been heaped on a cherry-colored sofa and a matching pair of brown and red patterned armchairs. A floor lamp improbably fringed in copper-colored silk cast a warm amber pool of light on a threadbare Persian rug. In the far wall, an arched doorway opened into what looked like a hall, also cluttered with toys. No one was in sight.

Edith took a deep breath and knocked. She waited.

Nothing. She knocked again, louder this time, and strained to hear. Obviously someone was home; the door was open. Maybe they were eating dinner in some back kitchen area.

"Hello?" she called. "Anyone here?"

No answer. She supposed she could put the doll just inside the door and leave. . . . She opened the screen door, then bent the creepy Big Head doll's stick legs out at a forty-five degree angle and set it on the floor. She straightened and studied the doll. It looked somehow sinister sitting in the center of the tiny vestibule, pouty lips curved in an empty smile, its disturbingly big eyes fixed on nothing. She frowned. She sure wouldn't want to walk into her house and find that doll staring at her. Maybe . . . maybe she should just stick it on the coffee table with the other toys where it wouldn't look so ominous.

She'd be in and out in a matter of seconds.

She slipped into the house and made her way light-footed across the old carpet, floorboards creaking loudly beneath her feet. She grimaced and hurriedly tossed the doll on the table.

"You know, breaking and entering is illegal."

She wheeled around.

Jim Curran stood in the archway, wearing nothing but a lopsided smile and a pair of jeans that molded to his long thighs like velvet to antlers. He was idly rubbing his hair with a towel, the black ringlets shimmering with water droplets. He looked like one of the male underwear models she'd seen in some of the magazines at the dentist's office, only better because he wasn't a smooth boy but a hard, muscular man with a thick furring of dark hair across his chest that thinned as it narrowed over corrugated abdominal muscles and then thickened again as it disappeared under his jeans' low-hanging waistband. Her mouth went dry.

"Hey! I'm sorry," he said, flipping the towel over a broad shoulder and coming toward her, his smile turning into a look of concern. "I didn't mean to startle you. Geez. You look scared to death. Come on in."

She'd frozen in place, riveted by the sight of his arm and chest muscles flexing with the smallest movement. She'd had no idea that all that was going on under his crisp white dress shirts. *Oh my*.

"No, n-no," she stuttered. "I, ah, I just came to return Chloe's doll. I knocked, but no one answered, so I just . . . It looked weird sitting in the entry," she finished lamely.

"It looks weird sitting anywhere," Jim said, stopping a few feet away. He was still smiling, seemingly delighted that she was there. He'd probably look just as pleased if she were the cable installation guy, because she couldn't imagine he'd developed a . . . partiality for her. It would be akin to the high school quarterback falling for the math team captain. Not that she knew any of this firsthand—she'd skipped high school—but she'd picked up the reference from college students.

"Sorry I didn't hear you drive up. I just finished pulling up an old clothesline pole out back." He jabbed his thumb over his shoulder behind him. "So I was in the shower."

In the shower. That explained the wet hair and bare feet. How could she consider a man's feet sexy? But she did. His were long and clean and . . . "I didn't drive. I walked."

"Really? Hey. Let me get you a glass of . . . lemonade? How about a beer? Water?" He looked so eager. Good manners. She'd done him a favor. He needed to express gratitude. "Come on, Edie. It's bloody hot outside."

She was being ridiculous. Worse, she was being weird. Why shouldn't she accept a glass of lemonade? "Yes. Thank you. Lemonade would be nice."

"Great." His grin turned even more dazzling. "I'll be right back. Have a seat." He glanced at the toys piled on all the furniture. "Just dump some of that stuff on the floor."

"I thought Chloe was an only child."

Jim gave her a confused look, probably impressed with her powers of deduction, although her deduction hadn't taken any unusual astuteness. Obviously this kind of clutter could only be generated by a crowd of children. "I divined the fact from the presence of this superfluity of toys," she explained.

He actually blushed. "Chloe is an only child."

"With all these toys?" she asked, surprised.

"She's a little spoiled," Jim said.

"Oh," Chloe said, then frowned. "Of course, you are in a better position to make such an evaluation, but in my short acquaintance with your daughter she has not seemed spoiled, but simply imbued with a child's natural narcissism."

"Ah, thanks, I think."

"It wasn't a compliment. It was an evaluation."

"You sure seem to know a great deal about children for someone not involved with them either professionally or personally."

Heat rose up her throat and into her cheeks. "I always assumed I would have children, so I started studying the subject when I was an undergraduate. I . . ." She hesitated, unwilling to divulge too much but torn by an unusual desire to share something of herself with him. He was smiling at her, looking amused. "I like children."

"That's obvious," he said, moving past her and sweeping some of the toys on the sofa onto the floor. "It might not look it, but the place is clean, just crammed full of Chloe-spore."

"It looks very nice," she murmured, but he'd already disappeared into the back hallway. She looked around and decided the sofa had the least clutter on it. She stacked the toys on top of the coffee table and took a seat.

"Sorry about how hot it is in here," Jim called from somewhere in the back. "The AC is on the fritz."

"On the fritz?" she replied.

"Temporarily not operational."

He appeared in the hallway carrying two glasses— one lemonade and one that looked like water. Or gin. Or vodka. What did she know about Jim Curran's private habits? He had also put on a T-shirt. *Good . . . Damn.* He came over and handed her a glass, setting his on the coffee table before nonchalantly sweeping the rest of the toys piled on the sofa onto the floor. He sat down next to her, angling toward her.

"Thanks for bringing that doll over. I expect Chloe doesn't even realize it was gone or I would have gotten a phone call by now."

"Phone call?"

"Yeah. Chloe's spending the night over at her aunt Melissa's."

Chloe was not there. Edie's disappointment was followed by a shiver of realization; she and Jim were alone. She cleared her throat to cover her sudden bout of nerves. "Melissa is your sister. The one who doesn't like me."

He didn't deny it, but it didn't seem to bother him, either. "Yeah. One of three," he said.

"I know. Chloe told me," she said. "Melissa is the oldest one, the woman with the romantic and indefensible notion that cats must be allowed to roam freely in order to experience true feline fulfillment." She spoke drily but without any expectation that he would hear that. Not many people picked up on her attempts at irony.

But Jim laughed. "Ouch!" he said.

She blushed. "I didn't mean—"

"Sure you did," he interrupted casually. "Don't worry about it. You're probably right, anyway."

"I am right," she said.

He looked up at her, his blue eyes sparkling. "It must be an awful burden, knowing all the answers while the world blunders on in ignorance."

She knew he was baiting her, but she answered anyway. "It is."

"Ever wrong?"

"No," she replied, then amended, "At least, rarely. I may revise my views upon the introduction of new data, but generally speaking I eschew forming an opinion until after a lengthy examination of the facts."

"I see." He took a drink from his glass, and she

found her eyes fixed on the way his throat worked as he swallowed. He hadn't shaved since this morning and a nascent blue-black shadow was forming over the hard, lean angles of his jaw. He glanced at her. "And what's your opinion of me?"

"You?" she squeaked. Squeaked! She would *die* of mortification—no, no, no. That wasn't like her. She wasn't the sort who thought ridiculous things such as "die of mortification"! Not only was it scientifically impossible, but such overt drama was alien to her character.

Jim was grinning at her again. "Yeah. Me."

She picked up her glass of lemonade and took a swallow, giving herself a chance to think. It went down the wrong side of her throat and she choked.

He was beside her in a second, arm around her shoulder, leaning her forward and rapping her on the back. "You okay?" he asked.

She nodded, still coughing.

"Right," he said drily. "Here. Drink this."

She couldn't stop sputtering. He grabbed his glass with one hand, gently easing her upright with the other. She regarded him through swimming eyes, feeling like an idiot.

He kept his arm around her and nudged his glass against her lips. "Drink. Just a sip."

She obeyed, taking a small sip and swallowing. It was water—just water. But as ridiculous as she knew it to be, the fact that her lips were touching the same area Jim's had, sent girlish frissons racing over her skin. She was so pathetic—so absurd.

"Another." He tipped the glass against her mouth

again, and she complied. He leaned forward, setting the glass on the coffee table, and then straightened, his hand coming to tilt her chin up. "Better?"

She couldn't think what to say. She couldn't think, period. His scent—that gorgeous, masculine, warm, vital scent—surrounded her. His arm felt sure and strong around her shoulders. His thigh pressed against her was warm and hard. She managed a nod.

He smiled, his blue eyes looking straight into hers, warm and inquiring. He held her chin gently between thumb and forefinger as slowly, incrementally, his mouth descended toward her, giving her every chance to pull away. She didn't. Her heart thundered in her chest, her hands in her lap clutched convulsively into a hard little ball—waiting.

And then his lips touched hers.

She melted. There was no other word for it. Her hands unclenched and flowed up to his broad shoulders, clinging tightly as her body went lax in his arms and her lips softened beneath his. His arm dropped from around her and he lifted his hands, cupping her face between his big palms. He covered her mouth with his in a long, lingering kiss, gently brushing the seam of her lips with his tongue, warm and urgent.

Her head fell back into the lee of his neck and shoulder, and her fingers stabbed up through his thick damp curls. His scalp was warm beneath her fingertips. Her mouth opened, and her tongue flickered shyly into his. He tasted of wintergreen.

His hands fell from her face, flowing down her neck to her shoulders to her arms and then looping around her back. His mouth still locked to hers, he pulled her around, easing her down onto the cushions and beneath him. He braced himself above her on shuddering forearms, finally releasing her mouth and scattering kisses along her jaw, her throat, and collarbone. She arched into them, wanting more, her head swimming with the sumptuous sensory overload, her hips shifting restlessly.

His hand stole low on her waist and slipped beneath the hem of her T-shirt, gliding up the shallow channel marking her spine in a long, sweet stroke. The sensation had her trembling with desire, needing to explore his body as he was hers. She tugged at his T-shirt, and he lifted himself off her just enough so she could bunch the material high on his chest, the movement dragging her own T-shirt up over her bra. Hungrily, she wrapped her arms around his wide chest and pulled him back down over her, gasping at the erotic sensation of heated flesh against her skin. He looped an arm around her, crushing her to him, his naked chest branding her breasts and belly, hot and heavy with muscle.

She wanted more. The evidence that he wanted more, too, was the heavy, thick pulse of his erection pressed to her outer thigh, and that was the most potent of aphrodisiacs. A sound of yearning rose in her throat. At the sound he broke off their kiss and lifted his head, staring down at her, breathing heavily.

"Edie." His voice held a low question. His eyes glittered like sapphires under a jeweler's light.

"Yes." She nodded eagerly. "Oh, yes. Yes and yes and—"

"Daddy! Where's DivaZ Chloe?" Chloe's loud, fretful voice carried up from the front yard. "Daddy!"

Jim groaned.

Edie pushed him away, her panicked gaze pleading with him. With a rough sound, he jerked back, pulling her upright into a sitting position next to him and pulling down her shirt. He surged to his feet, yanking his own shirt back down just as Chloe burst through the screen door. Heat rushed in a scalding wave up Edie's throat and into her cheeks.

"Daddy! I forgot DivaZ Chloe—hey!" She skittered to a stop. "Edie!" she exclaimed. "What are you doing here?" She bounced over to where Edie sat and plopped down next to her.

"What, indeed," came a woman's overly silken voice as Chloe's aunt Melissa came through the door. Her gaze flitted between Jim and her, finally coming to rest on Edie's red cheeks. "Hi, Dr. Handelman. Hot in here, isn't it?"

"Yeah," Jim said before Edie could answer. "It is." He turned to Chloe. "You left your doll at the shelter, and Edie brought it over because she didn't want you to miss it." He gestured to the doll, lying on its side on the coffee table.

"Wow. That *was* thoughtful," Melissa said, her brows rising.

"Yeah," Jim repeated, leveling his sister with a hard glare. "It was very nice. Don't you have something to say to Edie, Chloe?"

"Thanks, Edie," Chloe said.

"You're welcome."

Melissa sauntered into the room and casually took a seat on the arm of one of the overstuffed chairs. She crossed her legs, nonchalantly swinging the top one. "Get that pole of yours pulled, Jim?" she asked sweetly.

Jim's face went a dusky red hue. "Don't, Melissa."

"Don't what?" she asked. Whatever his sister was doing—and Edie wasn't exactly sure what it was—was making him angry. "I was just wondering if you managed to get that old clothesline pole yanked out of the ground. What did you think I meant?"

Jim ignored her, but his expression was tight and angry. "Here's your doll, Chloe." Jim swept the doll up off the table and handed it to his daughter. "You and Melissa had better skedaddle before you miss whatever your cousins have planned."

"Oh, we're in no hurry," Melissa said. "We're just going to build a fire in the backyard and make s'mores."

She was going to light a fire? With Chloe present? Fires were dangerous. "Do you have a permit?" Edie asked. "You know, you need a permit to . . ." At the look with which Melissa stabbed her, her voice trailed off. "Ah . . . I have to go." She stood up.

At once, Jim was beside her. "You haven't finished your lemonade."

"I've had enough." It was a lie. She was thirsty but not for lemonade. But she was growing more uncomfortable by the second under Melissa's knowing gaze and Chloe's growing look of confusion. "Thank you."

She brushed by Jim, too aware of the thrill of electricity that raced through her with just that slight contact, and fled.

Chapter 7

Jim arrived at work the next day as nervous as he'd been the first time he'd asked a girl to the prom. Last night, Melissa had wisely hightailed out of the house as soon as Edie left, Chloe at her side. He'd spent the evening trying to decide if he should call Edie or not. He distrusted the phone. He had learned to read the delicate nuances of her expression. He needed to see her to know what to say.

So he waited—and recalled the feel of her mouth opening beneath his, her arms clutching him tightly, her body arching into his.

He hadn't slept much.

He didn't bother going to his office but headed straight for the research floor, moving briskly down the hall, through the double set of doors into the lab area and toward her office. What if she wasn't in? What if she just shut him down? Shut him out?

"You'll have to resubmit the data."

It was Edie's voice. He rounded the bank of cubicles and spotted her figure behind the open slats of the miniblinds covering her office window. She was standing by her desk, leaning over a computer monitor. She was in her ubiquitous lab coat, the pocket protector with its array of pens sprouting above the name tag she never forgot to put on, as if she thought people might forget her name.

She looked up and caught sight of him. He raised his hand in greeting. She looked behind her, making sure he wasn't waving at someone else and then, phone still between her ear and shoulder, slowly lifted her hand in a weak reply. Her door was open, so he rapped lightly on the door frame, realizing as he did so that he'd never seen her door closed.

Along with everyone else at Global Gen, he'd always assumed the reason her department had the highest job satisfaction scores in the company was because it was peopled entirely by geeks giddily immersed in high-level geekdom and that the department's phenomenal retention rate could be traced to the same source. But suddenly he realized it was because of her. Her open door and calm disposition, her ability to cut through the bullshit, her respect for not only what her people did but who they were as individuals—all of those things must draw her people to her as surely as they drew him.

She finished her call and set the phone in its cradle, cocking an eyebrow inquiringly. "May I help you?" She was so formal.

"Yup," he said. "I've come to ask you out on a date."

"Oh."

He waited for her refusal, eager to make the rebuttal points he'd been rehearsing since last night. She'd like such clearheaded objectivity.

"When?" she said.

Ah-ha! She was asking for a specific date so she could manufacture a prior commitment. He'd expected that. *No go, Doctor*. "Whenever you can go. Tonight. Tomorrow. This weekend. Next week. You name it."

A small smile turned the corners of her mouth. One of her researchers ambled over, sucking on a Tootsie Roll Pop, and stopped short when he heard Jim. He didn't move discreetly off, either, instead waving over a pair of his coworkers.

"The CVO is asking Edith out on a date," he said loudly.

Jim looked at Edith, fully expecting her cheeks to be flushed with that fascinating shade of pink apricot. They weren't. She didn't look in the least nonplussed. He, on the other hand, was: ill at ease, awkward, and self-conscious. A light blinked on in his head. He got it. This was her turf. This floor and Cupid Cats were the *only* places she considered her turf. The rest of the world was his. But he wanted the world with her, to make it hers as much as this department.

"Well?" he asked.

"Sure."

He blinked, uncertain he'd heard right. She was smiling at him, a bright, open, sunny smile that made him want to step inside, snap down the blinds, and kiss her as he had last night.

"Ah, when?" *Smooth, Curran.*

"Tonight's fine. I can see if Carol will close up the shelter and if not, we can just go somewhere after I finish up. Unless that will be too late for Chloe to be up?"

"Chloe's not coming."

"Oh." Okay, this brought a hint of color to her creamy complexion as well as a flash of disappointment to her burned caramel eyes. Good Lord. With all the women who considered a small daughter added baggage, he'd fallen for the one who thought of him as the auxiliary tagalong.

"Well, then, tonight is fine."

"Is she going?" someone called from the back banks of tables.

The guy with the Tootsie Roll Pop planted in his cheek hollered back, "Yeah!"

"Wow!"

"Why are you going?" asked a stout middle-aged woman who'd wandered over. "Sleeping your way to the top? You're already at the top."

The remark didn't faze Edie in the least. "I'm going because I like him and he likes me," she answered. "Now, is there anything else I can do for you, Mr. Curran?"

"Jim."

"Excuse me?"

"Please, call me Jim."

Again she gave him that startled, pleased smile. "Jim, is there anything else I can do for you?"

"Tell me where I can pick you up."

He picked her up outside a plain, small duplex a couple miles north of where he and Chloe lived. She was waiting for him on the sidewalk outside, and she looked ravishing. Of course, had he seen any other woman wearing a pair of unremarkable tan slacks and a white eyelet blouse with the tails untucked, he wouldn't have given her a second glance. But on Edie it spoke volumes about her willingness to be casual and trusting with him. The implications ravished him anew.

He figured her for a Thai cuisine lover. There'd be something about the juxtaposition of sweet, salty, silky heat and cool crunch that would call to the closet sensualist in her, so he took them to Pho Bay Tau. He didn't make reservations—the popular storefront restaurant in the upper east end of the loop didn't take them—but on a Thursday they wouldn't have to wait long for a table.

He was right. Edie did like Thai and particularly pho. The noodle-laden soup based on a richly spice-infused broth had a hundred variations, and Pho Bay Tau carried most of them, from chicken feet to stewed tripe to crispy pork slices. Edie studied the menu like Chloe did the Kids "R" Us Christmas catalogue, her eyes alight with a beautiful sort of greediness.

They decided to share plates, and he insisted she choose. She ordered pho tai gau, a dish of noodles with tender slices of beef and brisket and bun ga nuong, a cold vermicelli salad with chicken, to which he added an appetizer of fried yams and shrimp. She finished by ordering bubble tea. He made a face.

"You don't like bubble tea?" she asked.

"It's a textural thing," he said.

"I understand." She nodded. "It does feel like a clump of muc—"

"Hey! How about them White Sox?" he broke in.

"White socks?" She blinked, confused.

"They're one of the Chicago baseball teams."

"Oh. What about—" Enlightenment dawned in her

eyes. "Oh! I see. You were trying to prevent me from drawing a correlation between my bubble tea and mucus!" She looked so damned pleased with herself.

"*Futilely* trying," he said.

She burst out laughing with that shotgun blast of humor, spontaneous, unrefined, and completely bewitching. "I'm sorry. I really do have better manners than that. I know I give the impression of having been raised by apes, but my parents really were quite normal. I just speak before I consider whether my comments are appropriate to the situation."

"Why is that?" he asked curiously, eager to know anything and everything about her.

She gave a delicate shrug. "I haven't had much experience in the usual social situations. I was in college by the time I was twelve. Not many college kids are asking their twelve-year-old lab partners to hang out with them after class, so I lived outside of the normal college context. My graduate and post-graduate work all depended on precision, detached observation, and accuracy." She gave him an unexpected grin. "Thus my telling you that bubble tea feels very like—"

"Don't say it!" he begged, holding up his hand just as the waiter returned with her bubble tea.

With a gleam in her eye, she unwrapped the straw, stuck it into the tall, frosty glass, and sipped. Then she sat back, resting her hands, palms down, on the table. "Ah."

He shook his head. "You continue to surprise me," he said.

She tipped her head. "Continue?"

"Yes. I didn't think you'd agree to go out with me.

At least not without a lot more persuasion." He leaned over the table and confided, "I had a whole list of arguments drawn up that I didn't get to use."

She smiled. "I'd hate for you to have to waste perfectly good arguments, and I admit to being curious as to what they are. Please, persuade me."

"Well, I know the best ethnic joints in town and without me to guide you, you'd be doomed to wander around in a culinary desert."

"I admit that's persuasive. Have any more reasons?"

He sat back in his chair, eyeing her. "Yes. I was going to tell you that you need more practice in becoming a convincing Global Gen cheerleader and I am willing to be practiced upon."

"We're going to discuss Global Genetics?"

"No."

"Then that's an invalid argument."

"I didn't say my reasons were valid, just persuasive."

She looked a little scandalized and a lot intrigued.

"And if all else failed, I was going to dangle the possibility of my bringing Chloe along with us."

"Would that be so awful?" she asked.

"No," he answered, then added seriously, "But Chloe doesn't like Thai food."

She laughed once more, charming him all over again. Then she said, just a trifle hesitantly, as if uncertain she had the right, "Where is Chloe?"

"At home with her favorite cousin gorging on pizza and playing Candyland." Once again he leaned over the table, holding her gaze in his. "But you know what the best reason I had for why you ought to come out with me was?"

She shook her head.

"The one you gave, the best reason and the truest: I like you. More than like you."

Her gaze dipped to her bubble tea, and a soft wash of pink rolled up her throat into her cheeks.

He cleared his throat, worried he had said too much and she'd think he was going too fast. "Tell me about Cupid Cats. I—maybe I'm wrong, but Cupid Cats doesn't seem like something you'd name a shelter."

"Oh?" She looked up. Her brown eyes were warm and sparkling. "And what would that be? 'Commit to the Care of an Abandoned or Rescued Cat Who May or May Not Have Emotional and/or Physical Issues for Anywhere from a Few Years to Two Decades?'" She cocked a brow.

"Yeah," he said, and grinned.

"Oh, all right. It isn't my name. It came with the place. After I took the job with Global Genetics, I was looking for a cat to adopt. I always wanted a cat of my own. We had them when I was growing up, but after I went to school, it didn't seem fair to get a pet when I wouldn't be able to spend much time with it. After I joined Global Genetics, I had the time and I knew I wanted to adopt a shelter cat, so I went looking and chanced upon Cupid Cats. It was shutting down, the old director was moving out of state, and she didn't have anyone to take over.

"I went back to my apartment sans cat, but I couldn't stop thinking about the place. The more I thought about it, the more sense it seemed to make for me to just take

over the place and the care of a dozen cats—and we
have about three dozen in foster homes—rather than
taking only one and relegating it to hours of being
alone."

Jim listened, nodding and slowly becoming aware
that something was different about her speech patterns.
She sounded natural, unaffected, and relaxed, her five-
buck words all but disappearing. She was comfortable
with him, he realized. It made him feel as though he'd
won the lottery.

The waiter brought the batter-fried shrimp and
yams; she took one, chomping into the greasy little
morsel and sinking back in her chair, her eyes rolling
up in ecstasy. "Oh . . . my . . . word," she murmured
around a mouthful of fritter. "Even if I didn't like you,
I'd go out with you if you kept taking me to places like
this."

"I'll keep that in mind."

She finished the fritter and polished off another two
in quick succession. He watched her, enjoying her enjoying the food. Finally she wiped her fingers on one
of the paper napkins and pushed herself back from the
table. "Speaking of cats, do you think Chloe's about
ready to give up trying to persuade Ishy-Pixie through
the front door?"

"I don't know. Is she becoming a bother to you?"

"No!" Edie hurriedly denied. "Not at all. I like
Chloe. She's . . . I'm really fond of her. I just don't want
to see her disappointed, and I really don't think Ishy-
Pixie is going anywhere." She glanced up, meeting his
eyes. "She's a very old cat."

He understood. "Yes."

"But Chloe still seems convinced that Ishy-Pixie is the same cat you and your wife owned."

Jim laughed. "There's no way she could be. I don't even know how old Pixie was when we got her. I got her for Steph on our first anniversary. I was thinking of a kitten, but there was something about the mother cat that just . . . I knew Steph would love her. She was scrawny and malnourished but definitely mature. The vet's best guess was that she was six or seven, and then we were married eight years before we got pregnant with Chloe. So if that was Pixie, she'd be more than twenty years old and have had to have traveled fifteen hundred miles."

"And you don't believe that could happen."

"Do you?"

She surprised him. "In science, we're always looking for explanations for things that seem impossible." She lifted her shoulders. "Sometimes we find them. Sometime we don't. Whether or not we know the processes by which something occurs does not negate the fact of something. It doesn't matter what I believe is possible. What is, is."

"You know, Steph might have said something like that." As soon as he spoke the words, he regretted them. The last thing a woman on a date wanted was to hear about the dead wife. But once again, Edie surprised him.

"Really? She was a pragmatist, then?" she asked as a waiter slipped the bowls of pho in front of them.

He laughed. "Not at all. She was a complete romantic. She loved old-fashioned gardens, the sort with more weeds than flowers, and lace curtains and piano music. And cats."

"She sounds . . . lovely," Edie said, but she said it sincerely. It wasn't a throwaway conversation ender, a sort of "Yeah, yeah, your dead wife was a peach. Now let's talk about me."

"Tell me about her," Edie said, her elbow on the table, her chin resting in her palm.

Tell her about Steph? He hadn't spoken about his wife, not at any length, in years. His sisters avoided mentioning her as though the very name "Steph" was hurtful. It wasn't. Nothing about his memories of her caused pain or regret. They were simply wonderful memories that made him grateful for the years they'd shared.

"She had this gift with people, this ability to not only listen, but hear. Do you know what I mean?" he asked after a moment. "She understood people even if she didn't agree with them. I think that's rare. Most people want to be understood."

"Yes," Edie said, nodding. "Did she have a career?"

Jim smiled. "She worked part-time—the morning shift at this little patisserie making croissants. She'd get up at three thirty in the morning to do it. She said she did it because they always let her bring home the day-olds, but she loved it."

"Geez. She ate croissants every day?" Edie asked, sounding a little incredulous. "Was she very fat?"

She surprised him into laughter. Only Edie would ask such a question. And he loved her for it. "Not fat . . . substantial. At least that's what she called it.

I called it womanly. Everything about her was over-sized: her appetite, her bad language—man, she swore like a sailor—her smile."

Edie nodded thoughtfully

"What about you, Edie?" he finally said, finishing his bowl. "Any Mr. Dr. Handelman in your past?"

She did not answer at once, concentrating on her food. Just when he thought she might not answer at all she said, "No. I was engaged for the two years before I joined Global Genetics, but the marriage never made it beyond the theoretical stage. He was a brilliant conceptual engineer I met at a symposium at MIT."

"Am I sorry?" he asked.

"Are you sorry?" she repeated.

"That it didn't work out between you and him?"

"Oh. You mean am I sorry it didn't work out? You're trying to gauge whether to be dismissive of him, or conciliatory."

"Exactly."

Her brow furrowed as she gave his words her usual intent consideration. "Neither. It made no sense for us to enter a marriage. We both understood that."

"Why?" he asked, reading something . . . something lurking in the shadows of her clear amber eyes. "I'm sorry. It's none of my business."

"He wanted children, and I discovered that I couldn't have children," she answered easily enough, but he could see the hurt it caused her by the way she avoided his gaze. She picked up her paper napkin and began shredding it.

He wanted to take her in his arms and comfort her, but he couldn't. "What about adoption?"

"He wouldn't. He felt that with his genius and physique—and he did have a nice physique, though not as nice as yours—the world ought to be able to benefit from his donation to the genetic pool." She'd finished fringing one edge of the napkin and began on the other.

Jim stared, incredulous. "He didn't want to deprive the world of his *genes*?"

"Yes." She nodded. Shred, shred, shred. "It makes sense. Although with the world population exploding beyond terra firma's capacity to sustain it, a case could be made for childless unions—"

"Edie," he interrupted, "he left you because you couldn't have his baby?"

"It was a mutual leaving," she replied primly. She turned the napkin, moving on to side three.

"I'm sorry."

"I wish you wouldn't be. That's one of the things I like most about you. You don't feel sorry for me."

"I'm not sorry for you," he said in surprise. "I'm sorry for the guy who thought his swimmers were so important that he let you go."

For a minute she just stared at him, and he could read her thoughts as clearly as a screaming headline on a gas station tabloid: *You are kidding*.

But he wasn't. "Done with that?" he asked, nodding at her empty bowl.

"Yes."

"Then let's get out of here."

They drove to a small park near Edie's condo and took a long walk in the soft summer night. Crickets and the occasional cicada serenaded them. They spoke eagerly, filling in the gaps left during their conversations at the shelter. Edie liked to cycle to work; Jim swam five mornings a week. She'd been raised in Seattle; he'd been raised here. They talked about everything and nothing, and Jim could have kept her walking the two-mile loop around the park until dawn, but he was afraid she'd drop in her tracks if they kept up much longer.

So, finally, reluctantly, he walked her to her front door and stood looking down into her eyes, tongue-tied and uncertain. She brought out an old-fashioned chivalry in him, though frankly he suspected chivalry was simply a whitewashed version of fear: fear of rejection, fear of overstepping boundaries, fear he didn't know what those boundaries were, fear if he did step over these undefined boundaries, she'd never go out with him again. He didn't know what she wanted of him, and what she wanted was important to him, more important than what he wanted, which was to take her in his arms and kiss her breathless.

"So, ah, thanks for having dinner with me."

"You're welcome." She half turned from him and inserted her key into the lock.

"I guess I'll see you tomorrow."

"No. I have a seven a.m. flight to Seattle. It's work related."

"Oh. Will you be gone long?"

"I'll be back Saturday morning." She turned the key and pushed the door open.

He bit back his disappointment. Three days was too long. "Oh. Well, then, I'll bring Chloe over to the shelter on the weekend." It was a question.

"Sure." She turned back toward him, grabbed his face between her hands, and kissed him full on the lips.

He forgot all about chivalry and boundaries and fear. He clamped her to him, lifting her up and walking her backward through the open door, his lips never leaving hers. Once inside, he kicked the door shut behind them, slanting his mouth sideways so he could see where he was going. The room was a blur of bright colors and textures, and he couldn't focus because she was raking her hands through his hair, her tongue was playing tease with his, and her breasts were lush and soft against his chest.

"Couch?" he managed to growl against her mouth.

"Bed," she croaked hoarsely, gesturing wildly to their side. "Bed."

He looked around, spotted an open door, and swung her up into his arms, moving swiftly into the next room. He spied a bed, not the narrow single he half expected, but a nice roomy queen with a plump, aqua-blue silk duvet. He strode to the side and dropped her down in the middle of it, following her down, a knee by her hip.

She clasped handfuls of his shirt and jerked it out of his waistband, running her hands up underneath, coursing over his belly and chest. He groaned, his eyelids sliding closed with the pleasure of it, kissing her while his fingers worked frantically to undo the damnably small buttons holding her blouse together.

She lifted her shoulders, wiggling out of the blouse and shoving it off the bed. Seconds later her cotton bra followed. Her body was svelte and toned, her breasts full and high. His whole body shuddered, and he felt his cock jerk against his pants crotch.

They were going fast, too fast.

He grabbed both her hands, pulling her into a sitting position. Then he stood up in front of her, raking his hair back with one hand. "Look, I'm getting a little carried away here."

"Good," she said. "Me, too. Let's keep going." She spoke in a rough staccato, her breasts rising and falling, the sound of her breathy assurance and the sight of her body nearly bringing him to his knees.

"You sure?"

In answer, she rose to her feet, stepped between his legs, and began clumsily unzipping his fly. His erection sprang free, and she delved her hand into his boxers, finding him. She made a soft sound, half hiss, half moan, as her fist closed around him. His head snapped back as he gritted his teeth, seeking control. She let him go, wrapping her arms around his neck and pulling his head down to hers. "Yes, I'm sure."

He didn't need any further invitation. He hooked his foot behind her ankle and tumbled her gently onto her back on the bed. She went down with a startled gasp, her eyes wide and dark with excitement. Reaching up, he grabbed her slacks' waistband and stripped them off her in one long stroke. Her panties, white cotton, God love her, followed. He took hold of her knees and pulled her to the edge of the bed, pushing them open and moving in between them.

He slid his hands up the backs of her silky thighs to beneath her bottom, positioning himself at the entry of her body. He moved his hips forward. She was tight and slick, like a heated steel fist gripping him as he entered. She gasped and he looked down into her eyes. They were wide and smoky, but there wasn't a trace of apprehension there; just a trembling eagerness.

He rocked forward, moving over her, covering her. She felt small beneath him, light, and he wanted to absorb her into his flesh, to feel every inch of her pressing into every inch of himself. He moved and her knees came up, clamping his hips. Her back arched, exposing her throat in an exquisite curve. Her fingers dug into his shoulders as he moved, slowly, with measured, controlled . . .

She bucked beneath him, seating him deeper inside, and all bets were off. He thrust deeply, her legs climbing higher up his flanks, clasping him tightly to her. She moved with him in breathless rhythm, meeting him thrust for thrust. Her eyes were half closed, her lips half open, and a sheen of sweat glazed her perfect, creamy skin. The sight of her like that, the severe, stiff Dr. Handelman caught on the very point of sexual gratification, almost sent him over the edge.

Grimly, he hung on, waiting to feel the clutch of her climax, to see the telltale flush of fulfillment that would spread over her breasts and throat and lips. . . . He dipped his head and stole a kiss across her mouth. She lifted her face, her mouth clinging hungrily to his. He rocked into her, faster, harder, deeper.

Abruptly, her head dropped back on the bed and her body bowed up as her beautiful mouth opened in a soundless cry, and he felt the muscles inside her contract to hold him in a delicious vise of completion. For long seconds, they held like that until a tiny sob broke from her throat and she collapsed beneath him.

Her eyes fluttered open. Her breath was ragged, but no more so than his. "Oh. Oh. Oh, my. That was intense."

"Yeah."

She shifted beneath him, and his body screamed at him to take up the rhythm again. Her eyes went wide as she felt him inside. "You haven't . . . ?"

"Not yet."

"Oh? Oh!" A smile blossomed on her face, untutored in guile or coquetry. "Then we can do it again?"

"Oh, yeah," he breathed.

And they did.

And again after that for good measure.

Chapter 8

"*I* strongly maintain that unexpectedly introducing a stranger into a clan ritual is an idea bound to make all participants unnecessarily uncomfortable," Edie said, casting a sidelong glance at Jim from the passenger seat of his car.

It had been ten days since their date and in the days that followed, Jim's attentions had only grown more romantic and more . . . She blushed, thinking of how lovely it was to move in Jim's arms, to feel him inside her, to wake up with his tender gaze on her, or to find him snoring beside her, his arms still around her. A man's snore shouldn't fill a woman with such profound contentment, but it did her.

Of course, she had known they would suit each other. He smelled good. When she'd told him this, he'd seemed to think it uproariously funny and then he'd kissed her some more. He took her to dinner and lunch, often with Chloe joining them. He stopped at her office each morning, bringing her a croissant and coffee. They talked about things she never would have believed could interest her and things she never would have suspected could have ever interested a man like Jim.

"I'm surprised you find me so interesting," she'd told him a few days earlier. "Oh, I completely understand the sexual compatibility. You smell good." He didn't even blink. "But, well . . . it's like the high school quarterback going out with the math team captain."

"I wasn't the quarterback; I was a wide receiver. But I was also the math team captain. 'Nuff said?" Then he kissed her again, right in front of Chloe, who, despite going very still and her eyes going very large, remained uncharacteristically mute.

"Your coming to Chloe's birthday party is a great idea, and you're not unexpected," he told her now, turning the car off the main thoroughfare. "I told Susie you were coming. And besides, you were invited by the birthday girl herself." He glanced into the rearview mirror at his daughter. "Right, Chloe?"

"Roger that, Daddy!" Chloe said snappily. "Invited and accepted!" Chloe had clearly been coached by her father.

"And finally, you *promised*," Jim finished.

"I was under duress at the time," she replied. Actually, she'd been under Jim, but she could hardly say that in front of Chloe. He had exercised not inconsiderable persuasive skills, and other skills she was learning to appreciate even more, in securing her promise to attend Chloe's sixth birthday party with his family. It hadn't seemed a matter for much concern at the time.

But now Edie was petrified.

Edie hadn't been so scared since her first day at Princeton when she was twelve. Just like then, all she could think about was how different she was from those she'd be joining. Jim's family represented a huge congregate of interrelated people—Jim had tossed off a casual estimate of fifty attendees—with mutual histories and shared experiences, familial affections and tribal loyalties.

She was an outsider.

Not only was she a stranger, but she was strange even by "stranger" standards. She didn't fit into normal situations easily. She was shy, and the shier she felt, the stiffer her expression became until her face felt like a mask from which she was looking out from behind. Then, if she followed her usual pattern, she'd begin throwing out huge words and building walls between her and other people with her vocabulary.

She didn't mean to. Where other people became tongue-tied and resorted to simple grunts when they were uncomfortable, she had the opposite response; she'd open her mouth and multisyllabic magniloquent words would pour out. She could feel them even now, crowding behind her teeth, waiting to escape.

She should just keep quiet.

"Just 'member to smile, Edie. Sometimes you forget to smile," Chloe said.

Edie glanced up, startled, and found Chloe's gaze meeting hers in the rearview mirror. Her small face was sympathetic.

"Okay. Thank you." Smiling. Yes. That was good. Sometimes she forgot to smile. . . . Dear heavens, she was taking comportment lessons from a five-year-old. And she was grateful for them, too.

Too soon, they entered a tree-shaded neighborhood of 1940s ramblers and ranchers. Jim pulled alongside a curb behind a long line of cars on the side of the street.

He got out and came around to her side to open the back door. Chloe popped out, reaching back inside to snag her DivaZ doll. Jim opened Edie's door and held out his hand, one dark eyebrow cocked challengingly. "It's just for an hour or so."

"Why is this so important to you?" she blurted out unhappily.

"Because I want my family to meet you. I want you to meet them. That's what you do when you are going out with someone."

"I think that's a very old-fashioned attitude," she said, stalling.

"I'm an old-fashioned guy."

He wasn't going to relent. She set her hand ungraciously in his and he helped her out. "You look very nice," he said reassuringly.

"Chloe picked it out," she said, somewhat mollified, smoothing her hands down over the lilac-patterned cotton sundress. She and Chloe had gone shopping yesterday because she hadn't had anything suitable for an outdoor picnic. She didn't own any shorts, except bike shorts, and it was too hot for slacks. Jim had already seen her one pair of capris, and she was discovering she was just enough of a girl to want to dress up for her beau. Besides, she wanted to see the admiration in his gaze. And she had. He looked quite impressed as he took in the dipped neckline, the spaghetti straps, and cinched waist. Then his gaze fell to her feet and he became amused.

She frowned self-consciously. "I shouldn't have worn tennis shoes, should I?" she asked. "But the only other shoes I have are dark brown or black."

"They're fine. Come on."

He pulled her hand through his arm, took Chloe's hand in the other, and led them down the sidewalk to a cream-colored rambler with a driveway stacked with cars. "Everyone'll be out back," he said, bypassing the front walk and escorting her along the side of the house.

A few feet from the corner, Chloe broke rank and ran ahead. "I'm here!" she hollered, rounding the corner of the house, her arms flung wide.

What sounded like a hundred people burst into laughter, clapping and hooting just as Edie and Jim rounded the corner.

It was worse than she imagined. The backyard was filled with people, crowded with people, stuffed with people: young, old, male, female, seated around tables, standing around open coolers filled with ice and canned drinks, playing lawn games or tending a series of Weber grills that were sending up shimmering waves of heat. And all sixty or seventy pairs of eyes turned toward them as everyone there fell silent, leaving her in a vacuum, the air sucked from her lungs, her face rigid with immobility, her body frozen in place. It seemed to go on forever, though in reality it was probably less than a couple of seconds.

Then a tall woman with brightly dyed short red hair and Jim's blue eyes came hurrying across the lawn and waving a long-handled spatula.

"I see the birthday girl is handling things with her usual modesty," she said, her interested gaze latching onto Edie. "This is your friend?"

"Yup, this is Edie. Edie, this is my sister Susie."

"How do you do?" Edie said, forgetting to smile.

"Fine, hon. Thanks for coming. I've heard a lot about you. Not from Jim"—she jabbed him in the side with her elbow—"but from Chloe. She thinks you hang the moon."

Oh God. Jargon. She knew what "hang the moon" meant but only because it was a relatively archaic term. As soon as anyone used more modern idioms, she'd be lost. She foresaw an afternoon filled with oblique references that would leave her even more ignorant of what was going on than usual. "I think she hangs the moon, too," she answered weakly.

Sue smiled, apparently reading some of her discomfort in her expression. "Don't worry, Edie. The Curran clan can be a bit overwhelming. Even to us Currans. Let me introduce you to the key players."

Without a glance at Jim, Susie linked her arm through Edie's and guided her from group to group, stopping every now and then to raise her voice at any one of a dozen teenage girls and boys who had Chloe on a blanket stretched between them and were tossing her into the air on it. "Not that high!"

Chloe was shrieking and giggling with pleasure. Edie couldn't watch. Jim, she noticed, though seeming to be in a casual conversation with a group near where his daughter was being used as a human popcorn kernel, was keeping a close eye on the proceedings. He had one hand in his pocket and the other held a bottle of beer.

He looked so good—so male and healthy and adult. And handsome. And athletic. And relaxed. She loved how he held himself, his easygoing charm, his competence and warmth. She loved . . . him.

"You gotta love Jim, don't you?" Susie said, echoing Edie's thoughts so closely that it startled her.

"Yes," she said eagerly and without thinking. "I do."

Susie's eyes widened for an instant, and a spot of red appeared high on her cheeks. "Wow. Jim said you didn't have any filters, but you really *don't* have any filters, do you?"

"I'm not sure what you mean by filters," Edie replied uncomfortably.

"You think something, so you say it."

"Oh no," she said. "Not at all. I keep quite a bit of what I think to myself. I just . . . I thought . . . I thought you meant it," she finished lamely. Now she was embarrassed. She could feel the heat surging up her neck.

"Hey. It's okay. Just don't say it to Melissa. She's not your biggest fan."

"I know." She wasn't thinking of Melissa. She was thinking about Jim and her love for him. It wasn't something she could back up with detailed evidence, but she didn't need to. As she'd said to Jim, whether or not she understood how something happened didn't affect its efficacy. She loved Jim. It was just that simple.

"She'll come around," Susie was saying. "In fact, let's go beard the lion in her den, shall we?"

Now Susie had Edie's full attention.

"You don't want to spend the afternoon avoiding her," Susie said, reading Edie's reluctance. "It would be awkward."

"I'm used to awkward."

"I'm not. Come on. Grow a spine. That means—"

"I understand. And you're correct. If I am able to make the day more felicitous for you and others by interacting with a woman who not only demonstrates a lack of judgment in her opinions but also a certain puerile mentality in her unwillingness to change those opinions when confronted with substantial evidence that negates it, I will do so."

"Yeah." Susie patted her arm. "We'll just keep that to ourselves, okay?"

"Okay."

She steered Edie toward a circle of people sitting in plastic lawn chairs, idly poking at the embers in a fire ring. "Hey-ho. This is Jim's friend, Edith Handelman. Edie, I'd like you to meet Tom and Mary Rayburn, Chloe's grandparents, and her uncle, Todd Rayburn. His sixteen-year-old twins are part of the Chloe-toss you just witnessed. And you know Melissa."

The grandparents, a robust, rawboned couple in their early seventies, were from Chloe's mother's side of the family, Edie realized. The husband was a tall, thickset bald man with Chloe's wide mouth and snub nose. The group returned her interest, definitely curious but not unfriendly—except for one. Melissa's flat regard clearly found her wanting.

She wasn't wanting. She was . . .

"*Dr*. Handelman," she heard herself murmur. She was building her protective walls, brick by brick, word by word. She felt her cheeks and lips stiffening into a rigorlike facade.

"Yeah. Don't forget she's a doctor," Melissa said.

"May we call you Edith?" the bald man, Todd Rayburn, asked.

"Yes." *Smile, Edith.* She smiled. Her face felt as if it might crack.

"Edie." Chloe appeared beside her, tucking her small hand into hers and saying, "Her name is *Edie.* No one calls her Edith." She sounded disgusted.

Melissa's cold expression thawed. "Hey, it's the birthday girl! How's it feel to be six years old?"

"A lot older," Chloe said seriously. "Did you get me a present?"

"Of course I got you a present. But you're going to have to wait to open it with the rest of that tower over there." She nodded toward a card table stacked high with brightly wrapped gifts.

The sight of it nonplussed Edie—so much for one small girl.

"Edie didn't get me a present," Chloe said matter-of-factly. "She says she thinks the mom oughta get all the presents on a kid's birthday on accounta she was the one who had all the calk-ee-um sucked from her bones when the baby was inside her."

"Calcium," Edie corrected faintly. Everyone regarded her in faint shock. "I only meant that since a child has no say in whether or not he's conceived, let alone born, and the mother's decision to bear children in spite of the myriad and overwhelming challenges presented to the individual, the society, and the planet at large could be seen as either an act of supreme courage or rampant lunacy, in my opinion it is the mother—not the child—who should be celebrated or condemned, depending on ethical beliefs."

No one spoke. They just stared at her. Finally, Melissa wriggled straighter in her chair and announced, "Well, *we're* all very glad Chloe is here."

"Oh, I am, too," Edie said. "I lo . . ." She recalled Susie's discomfort with her earlier disclosure. She wasn't going to make the same mistake twice. "I am, too."

"Her mother wanted Chloe above all things," Melissa continued. "Even life itself. You do know about Stephanie, don't you?"

"Oh, yes. Jim has told me quite a bit about her."

Melissa affected not to have heard. "She was an amazing woman. A free spirit. A bon vivant. Everyone loved her. *Everyone*," Melissa said, and gave Jim's in-laws a damp-eyed look of solicitude. They smiled back, looking none too comfortable to Edie's admittedly untutored eye. "She was Jim's soul mate."

"Oh." She couldn't think of anything to say that she could be certain would be appropriate. Chloe sidled closer to her.

"Come and sit on Aunt Melissa's lap, Chlo-Schmo" Melissa said, holding her arms open.

Chloe looked around at her cousins hooting and hollering, dodging a boy of about fifteen who was darting at them with outstretched arms. Every time he touched one of them, they froze in place.

"I wanna play freeze tag!" Chloe declared, and disappeared.

Susie smiled after her as her cousins welcomed her into the game. "You can see why she's a little spoiled," she told Chloe. "Her cousins treat her like a pet."

"It's because she's the youngest," Chloe's grandmother said. "Steph was the youngest, too."

"Did Steph have issues with temper tantrums, too?" Edie asked curiously.

"Temper tantrums?" Melissa echoed in an odd voice.

"Yes," Edie replied, frowning in confusion as Susie laid a hand lightly on her wrist. "Chloe has temper tantrums sometimes. They are quite spectacular. So I was wondering if it was the result of being overindulged or a genetic predisposition or perhaps a combination of both."

Melissa flushed. Todd looked away uncomfortably, and the grandparents stared at her, as if seeing her for the first time.

"Steph was a saint," Melissa declared. "Everyone loved her. She never—"

"Stephanie," Chloe's grandfather interrupted, "had a temper like a spanked cat."

All eyes in their little group swung toward Stephanie's father, who was staring off in the distance, a soft expression on his face. He began to chuckle. "Oh, she had it under control most times, and I suspect Chloe'll learn to dunk the fuse, but man, when it got away from her . . . watch out!"

Todd, Jim's brother-in-law, nodded, grinning broadly. "And you didn't even see the half of it. The things that girl subjected me to, it's amazing I lived to tell the tale. I remember once when she was about fifteen and I was twelve. She came home from a date with some kid, and I was hiding on the front porch. When the guy leaned over to kiss her good night, I jumped out in a Halloween mask. The poor guy fainted dead away, and Steph chased me through the neighborhood with a broom for a half hour. By the time she gave up and went home, the kid was long gone. I kept my bedroom door locked for a month after that."

"She was a firebrand," Chloe's grandmother admitted ruefully.

"But she outgrew it?" Edie asked.

"Ha!" Susie said. "She and Jim had only been married a short while when she decided she wanted to become a blonde. A really blond blonde. And off she headed to the drugstore, got a bottle of peroxide, and spent the afternoon bleaching her hair. Only it didn't turn blond; it turned this hideous shade of orange. Well, Jim came home, took one look at her, and burst out laughing. Man, was she mad! So she stomped into the bathroom and whacked off every bit of hair on her head. She looked like something out of a zombie movie."

"When she got really mad, she'd jump up and down like Rumpelstiltskin," her mother confided, shaking her head.

"Was she on medication?" Edie asked, shocked by the idea of a grown woman jumping up and down in a temper tantrum.

Melissa bristled.

"No, honey." Mary Rayburn shook her head, laughing. "Steph was just a little spoiled and a little volatile. Her temper was like a summer tornado, a lot of wind that blew itself out quick. If she were here now, she'd be laughing right along with us." She glanced at Melissa.

"Folks tend to turn those they've lost into saints and talk only about the good. Trouble is, that would rob most of us of half the memories folks would have of us, and Steph's no different. Thanks for reminding me of that, Edith," Chloe's grandfather said.

"Edie," she said.

"Edie."

"Come on, Edie." Chloe reappeared beside her, grabbing her hand and tugging. "You gotta play freeze tag. You gotta. It's my birthday."

"All right," she said, relieved. No matter how nice the Rayburns seemed, no matter how pleasant and accepting Jim's sister Susie appeared to be, Edie was navigating a minefield on unfamiliar terrain and had the distinct impression she had almost set off an explosion more than once.

"It was nice to have met you," she said.

"Smile," Chloe whispered.

She smiled.

Two hours later, Edie's head was swimming. She had learned to play freeze tag and had won several games, discovering to her surprise that she was rather adept at feinting and dodging. She had eaten several hamburgers at Jim and Chloe's urging and been introduced to a dizzying array of family members whose names she was using all her mnemonic skills to learn. She hadn't spent this much time amongst this many strangers since the Genome Convention of 2007. As interesting and unique an experience as it was, it was also exhausting.

Jim was attentive, but he did not hover, though often she would catch him watching her from across the lawn, a slight smile on his well-formed lips and unreserved warmth in his startlingly blue eyes. For this she was grateful. She was already self-conscious enough without worrying that he was grading her performance. Indeed, he acted as if her presence here were the most natural thing in the world, an attitude Chloe apparently shared if evidenced by the way she kept dodging in and out of her periphery. Edie wished she could feel the same. But she could not quite lose the feeling that she was an odd fish amongst fowl.

She decided to take a few minutes to herself to regroup and was headed toward the house in search of a glass of water when she heard Melissa's voice coming from the open kitchen window. "*Dr*. Handelman. Full of herself much?"

She stopped. She didn't think she could have moved if she'd tried; the ridicule in Melissa's voice froze her. A woman she could not identify murmured a reply.

"Ha! You're not serious. Of course not. She's just another one of Jim's little projects."

Despite loathing herself for it, she strained to hear the reply. "Chloe likes her."

"I know, and that's what really pisses me off," Melissa said. "She might come across as harmless, but she's not above using Chloe to get Jim—as if that hasn't been tried before. Jim's wise to that game, but poor little Chloe doesn't realize 'Edie' is just playing mommy so Jim will play daddy. It's downright vile."

"Don't you think . . ." The other woman must have turned as she spoke, for the rest of her words grew muffled.

"No. No and no. Trust me. It's a flash in the pan. Come on. Can you think of any way that woman could be more different from Steph? She's the *anti-Steph*, scrawny, mousy, and stuck-up."

The other speaker made an unintelligible reply. "Did you catch the sundress?" Melissa's voice had risen. "Yegads. With Jim's looks and personality, he should be dating supermodels, not Ugly Betty. She doesn't belong with him—or here."

"Enough, Melissa," the other female replied. "You're Jim's older sister, not his Jewish mother."

Edith hid—there was no other word for it—for half an hour, the wounding words playing again and again in her mind.

She doesn't belong.

But she'd known that, hadn't she? She'd told herself that exact same thing on the way over. She'd always known that suburban backyard barbecues were not part of her future. Nor big families. Nor children. Nor a man like Jim. So then why did hearing it from someone else hurt so very, very badly? It didn't matter. All that mattered now was to try to end this with as much dignity as possible.

She needed to leave.

She found Jim in the backyard.

"There you are!" he said, his face lighting up. "Where'd you go to? I've been looking everywhere. The gift opening is about to commence, and I thought we'd better fortify ourselves for the marathon event."

"I've called a taxi. It'll be here in a few minutes," Edie said.

"*What?* Why?" Jim asked, raking his hair back from his forehead.

"I have a migraine. I am prone to them."

"Geez," he said, concern filling his voice. "I'm sorry, but you don't need a taxi. I'll take you home."

"No," she said. "It's Chloe's birthday party and you can't leave."

"I'll come back." His brows were drawn together, lowering over his brilliant blue eyes. He scanned her face, trying to read her expression. She wouldn't let him. She did not want to ruin any part of this day for Chloe.

"No. You said they were about to start opening presents, and you know how incapable Chloe is of delaying gratification. She'd be disappointed if you weren't here. That's why I called a taxi. You stay here with your daughter."

"She'll be disappointed if you're not here. You know she will. She loves you."

She flinched at the reminder of Melissa's accusation that she had embroiled herself in Chloe's affections. "I've already spoken with her. Her excitement over her presents has served to mitigate a great deal of her disappointment over my early departure."

"What's wrong, Edie?" he asked, taking both her hands in his. They felt strong and warm and certain, and she didn't want to let them go. She wanted to tell him that she hadn't fallen in love with him and then gone on to use his daughter to attempt to secure his affection but that it had been the reverse; she had fallen in love with Chloe and then him. But she didn't. Because . . . she didn't belong here.

"Nothing."

"Something's up. Something's wrong."

"My head hurts and conversation is painful. I really would like to go home and lie down."

At once he was all solicitude, wrapping his arm loosely around her shoulder and guiding her toward the house. "I'm sorry, Edie. I didn't mean to be insensitive." As if he ever could be. "I'm just disappointed. Everything was going . . . beautifully."

"I'm disappointed, too," she murmured.

A horn beeped sharply from the front of the house. She broke free of his half embrace and hurried away, pausing at the corner to turn and look back. His brows were furrowed again, the sun glinting off his black Irish curls and slanting a shadow beneath his hard jawline.

"Good-bye, Jim."

Chapter 9

"You still have a fever, Chloe, you didn't sleep well last night, and you've been up since five. You have to take a nap."

"I don't want to!" Chloe insisted for the third time.

On one hand, Jim welcomed the defiance; it meant she was definitely on the mend after being down with a cold for the past few days. On the other hand, she was really testing him.

"You promised we could go see Edie!" she shouted, then added, "And Ishy-Pixie." She paused. "And Divaz." Divaz was the name she'd given the albino kitten, the contender for her heart against Ishy-Pixie's elusive but undeniable magic "And *Edie*!" she finished, just in case Jim hadn't understood the real heart of her grievance.

He did: Chloe wanted to see Edie. And that was the problem. Edie had gone missing in action. He hadn't seen her since Chloe's birthday party last weekend. She hadn't answered his calls on Sunday, and on Monday she'd been away at staff meetings all day. Monday after work he and Chloe had walked down the street to Cupid Cats, but when they'd entered, they'd been informed by a bewildered-looking Carol that Edie had just taken off on some mysterious errand. She hadn't returned while they'd been there, even though he'd dawdled at the place for more than an hour and still had the cat hair on his slacks to prove it.

Tuesday he'd been out of the office on business, and that evening had been a repeat of the previous one. And she still wasn't picking up her phone. He'd even gone so far as to drive past her apartment, but when he'd rung through on the security phone, she hadn't answered. Then on Wednesday, Chloe had woken with sniffles and a low-grade fever, and he'd taken the last three days off work to care for her.

"You saw Ishy-Pixie and Divaz on Tuesday, toots." Tuesday was an eternity ago to a six-year-old. Ishy-Pixie hadn't been looking too good then, either. Jim hoped the cat would last until Chloe had been won over by Divaz's pink-eyed charms.

"But not Edie," Chloe said, glaring at him accusingly. "I haven't seen her in forever! Where is she?"

"I don't know." And he would dearly love to. Had he been too inattentive at Chloe's birthday party? He hadn't wanted to make her self-conscious with his attention, so he'd purposefully hung back, even though he'd want to take her hand, wrap his arm around her slender waist, keep her close just because he liked being near her so much. He loved being near her. And he missed her. God, how he missed her.

Maybe she'd been overwhelmed by his family. She was a shy woman and the Currans were loud, raucous, and pushy enough to intimidate even the most outgoing person. But she had seemed to be enjoying herself. Her eyes had been sparkling, her face tanned by the sun, her smile open and frequent. He would have staked his life on it—or his heart.

In fact, he had.

"Please, Daddy?"

He looked down. Chloe had secured his hand and was tugging at it insistently. He knelt down beside her. "Chloe, you were coughing all last night. There are circles under your eyes that would make a raccoon green with envy, and you still have a fever. I'm sorry but no. You have to take a nap. Maybe tomorrow."

"I hate naps," Chloe said, her lower lip quivering. "Only babies take naps, and you made me take one yesterday."

"Sick people take naps, too."

"I'm not sick anymore," she insisted, and then, to put lie to the statement, wiped the back of her hand across a gooey nose and sniffed.

"Chloe . . ."

"If we can't go see Edie, can I go outside and play with Barnaby B?"

Chloe had discovered the neighbor's boy, Barnaby B. Bigg, last week. He lived three houses down and had one blue eye and one brown eye. His daughter had a thing for strange eyes. Jim half expected an engagement announcement any day now. "Not this morning. This afternoon you're taking a nap."

"Uh-uh." Chloe shook her head violently.

"If you keep this up, you won't be seeing anyone either today or tomorrow. I mean it, Chloe. The discussion's over. Now let's get you into bed."

"You're mean! I hate you!" With an angry stomp Chloe tore her hand free of Jim's and wheeled around, stomping angrily down the hall, each small boom of her foot announcing her displeasure until she reached her room. Without looking back, she slammed the door shut.

An angry little roar issued from behind the closed door, replete with frustration and exhaustion, followed by wet-sounding snuffles and sobs. Jim listened. The sobs grew muffled, as if she'd turned her face to her pillow. At least she was lying down. Jim relaxed and headed into the kitchen, dropping onto the stool by the breakfast bar and pouring himself a cup of coffee from the Thermos carafe he'd filled that morning.

He eyed the cordless phone in its cradle. He could try calling Edie at the shelter. He assumed she would be there, as it was Saturday; however, Carol always answered, and she'd just return with the message that Edie would call back. And then she wouldn't. He could go to her apartment again. *Damn.* He wasn't going to start stalking her—start? He braced his forehead in his hand. He had to talk to her. He had to know what had gone wrong so he could make it right.

Chloe Curran stood at the street corner feeling very brave and a little frightened. This was the farthest she'd ever gone from her new house by herself. She looked both ways even though she didn't have to cross against the traffic. Her path took her across the residential street and then past the older five houses that stood between her and Cupid Cats.

The child had never done anything so bold before, and had she understood the fear her act would inspire in her father, she might not have done so now. Then

again, she may well have continued on her course. Her
sense of justice was acute and to her, because a promise
had been broken, any acts of rebellion were justified.
Still, she hesitated, considering returning to her house
before her father discovered her absence, but just as she
was about to turn back, a form in the size and shape of
an old and tiny ginger-colored cat flashed around the
corner of the house in front of which she stood and
disappeared into the nearby rosebushes.

Chloe started forward, all thoughts of returning
gone because the cat looked exactly like the one that
had inspired this perhaps ill-considered journey.

She reached the rosebushes and leaned over, peering beneath the thicket of cool, brambly shadows. Far
back, just out of reach, she made out a pair of glittering
eyes.

"Ishy Pixie?" she called softly.

In answer, the figure darted from beneath the bushes
and dashed across the lawn between the houses, heading in the direction of the shelter. Chloe snapped
upright, going a little light-headed with the abrupt
motion. Squinting against the sun, she tried to see if
the cat was indeed Ishy-Pixie. All she saw was a feline shape standing by the front porch steps of the next
house down. The cat seemed to Chloe to be looking at
her—waiting for her.

She wiped her runny nose with the back of her
hand and followed the cat across the lawn, moving
slowly, because in her experience Ishy-Pixie did not
like abrupt movements. But every time she drew
within a dozen feet of the animal, it moved on, disappearing beneath shrubs or stairs, around a tree or

behind a fence, leading her on, always in the shadow or in the direct line of the sun so that Chloe never got a good look to see whether or not the cat was indeed her old, old friend.

If it was Ishy-Pixie, she had never been so light and quick. And why would she be out here when Edie had said she never left the building? It was too much of a mystery for Chloe to resist, and she didn't try. The cat disappeared into the backyard of the house next door to Cupid Cats, and Chloe followed her into the alley behind the shelter. The cat was gone; yet the fire door that Edie always kept locked was slightly, ever so slightly ajar, although not widely enough for a cat, even one as small and finely built as Ishy-Pixie, to enter.

Chloe pushed the door open and slipped inside, looking around. After all, this had been her intended destination from the beginning. Inside, it was silent. The door to the Meet and Greet room stood open, but all the other doors were shut.

She started forward, intending to find Edie . . . but as she moved, the enormity of her transgression dawned on her. Her daddy would be very, very angry. *Edie* might even be angry. The righteous indignation that had bolstered the spirit of her rebellion had faded by now, and the walk in the hot sun had left her feeling tired and a little dizzy and sticky.

She wavered uncertainly, and her glance chanced to fall inside the Meet and Greet room, or what little of it she could see, where she saw a little shadow flitting across the wall. She edged forward and looked inside. Ishy-Pixie lay in the very center of the old battered couch, her paws all neatly tucked beneath her,

her head up. As soon as she saw Chloe, she stood up and trilled a greeting.

Charmed, Chloe went to her and sat down beside her. She petted the little animal. Her fur was cool and silky, not even the least bit warm, and while consciously Chloe did not recognize the importance of that, at some level she understood that this cat had not been the one she'd followed or she would have been sun-warmed. Besides, the crack that the door had been opened hadn't been big enough for a cat to pass through.

The cat climbed into her lap and settled right in, and Chloe eased herself down beside her, carefully curling her body around that of the ginger-colored cat in a little nest. It was quiet here, and the gentle hum of the air conditioner couldn't quite dispel the soft warmth pouring in from the window. Chloe's eyelids drifted half closed, fluttered shut, opened briefly, then drifted closed again as she finally heeded her father's direction and took a nap.

A woman's voice nudged her toward wakefulness. "Hello, my old sweetheart. It's time to come home to me." It was a light voice, unfamiliar to Chloe but attractive. She felt Ishy-Pixie get up and leap lightly off the couch.

Drowsily, she opened her eyes. A woman, backlit by the door, stood next to the couch. She was tall, but other than the shimmer of light on blond hair, Chloe couldn't see much of her features. In her arms, Chloe could just make out Ishy-Pixie, her legs moving up on the woman's shoulder. She bumped her head against the woman's chin, purring loudly.

Chloe was so tired, she could barely keep her eyes open. Still, she started to push herself up, but the woman forestalled her. "No, don't get up, my darling. You look very sleepy. Rest. I've just come to collect my cat."

The woman was right. She was sleepy—*so* sleepy.

"What cat? Who're you?" Chloe muttered, already half asleep again.

"I'm the owner of that cat you're so kindly providing a mattress for," the woman answered, sounding vastly amused.

In her semi-sleeping state, Chloe didn't question this assertion. She'd always known deep within that Ishy-Pixie was waiting for someone, and though she never could quite bring herself to admit it, she'd long since recognized that she wasn't the one. In her half-conscious state, her lips turned down at the corners. "Are you taking her now?"

"Soon. But not this exact minute. Just relax."

Chloe sighed and her eyes slipped shut again. She felt cushions sink next to her head and a hand lightly brush the hair from her brow. She heard a murmur but could only pick out the words "love" and "forever." A tear slipped out of the corner of her eye.

"Don't cry, darling. I know you loved her," the woman said. "Thank you for that."

Chloe gave a slight nod, her lower lip trembling.

"She loves you, too. But she's been waiting for me to come for a long time."

Reluctantly, Chloe nodded again.

"Besides, I have here a little girl who needs your love even more," the woman said, and Chloe felt her shift. "And when someone needs your love, you have to give it."

She opened her eyes as the woman rose and from seemingly nowhere produced a white kitten with pink eyes. Carefully she set the kitten down in the same place Ishy-Pixie had just vacated.

The kitten stared at Chloe for a long unblinking moment and then, as though liking what she saw, she nestled in closer against Chloe's heart.

"We have to go," the woman whispered. Once again she brushed the hair from Chloe's temples. A frisson of warmth rippled through Chloe. "You go back to sleep. Dream lovely dreams."

Chloe's arm crept up and curled around the sleeping kitten as through half-closed eyes she watched the woman disappear through the door, Ishy-Pixie curled contentedly over her shoulder. Her last waking thought was that the woman really must have been Ishy-Pixie's owner.

Chloe must have been more tired than he realized, Jim thought. She hadn't stirred in half an hour. Not so much as a cough . . . He frowned, rose from the kitchen table, and headed into the adjoining short hallway and down to her bedroom. He knocked lightly, calling her name. "Chloe? Chloo-Schmoo?"

No reply. He turned the knob and eased the door open, peering inside before pushing it all the way. The room was empty. Alarm raced through him. He stepped into the room, quickly scanning across the bed, barely mussed; the windows, still shut and locked against the heat outside; the floor—the floor. Her favorite shoes, the pink zebra-stripe sandals, were missing. She'd been barefoot when she stomped into her bedroom, but now her shoes were missing. A thin, potent ray of relief swept through him. She'd put them on herself, then.

Damn it! If she was outside or had snuck over to Barnaby B.'s house—

He strode quickly out of her room and down the hall, back through the kitchen to the door that led to the backyard. He shoved it open and stepped out, standing at the top of the stairs leading down to the lawn. She wasn't there. He peered across the back lawns to Barnaby's house. No one was in sight. Maybe she was inside.

He turned, swiftly reentering the house, grabbing the cordless, and jabbing out the Bigg family's phone number.

"Hello?"

"Hi, Nadine. This is Jim Curran. Is Chloe down there by any chance?"

"Chloe?" Nadine echoed. "No. Barnaby is with his dad this week. I haven't seen Chloe. Is she missing?" Her voice filled with concern.

"I think she's lit out on me. Thanks—"

"Listen, Jim. If you need me to help look—"

"I'll call. Thanks." He hung up, raking his hair back with his hand and staring outside, his face tense with worry. Jesus. Where could she have—

A small butterscotch-colored cat dashed out from beneath the privet hedge that marked the border between his yard and the next-door neighbor's and raced off, disappearing into the alley.

Of course. She'd gone to see Edie.

He stabbed out the number on the phone still clutched in his hand. It was picked up on the third ring.

"Cupid Cats, feline shelter and rescue." It was Edie. Even through his alarm he noticed how tired she sounded.

"Edie, it's Jim. I can't find Chloe. Is she down there?"

"What do you mean you can't find her?" Edie's voice rose on a note of alarm.

"She got mad at me when I sent her to her room to take a nap. I thought she might have gone down there."

"I just got in. Carol's in the back. Maybe Chloe's with her. Hold on."

The sound of the phone clattered to some hard surface, and he heard her footsteps quickly fading in the background. Anxiety made the next ninety seconds seem an eternity. *Please God. Please, let her be there.*

Edie picked up the phone. "She's here. She's asleep on the couch. I don't know how she got in. Carol swears she was at the front desk until I arrived, and the rest of the doors are locked."

"I don't give a damn," Jim said, his voice cracking gruffly under the profundity of his relief. "I'll be right down."

Chapter 10

*T*wo minutes later, the shelter's front door swung open and Jim Curran came through. He was breathing heavily, his white T-shirt sticking to his broad shoulders and chest, his dark curls shimmering with perspiration. He had clearly sprinted down here, barefoot on the cast iron–hot pavement. His expression was stark, angry. Edie had never seen him wearing such an expression.

"Where is she?" he demanded.

He didn't bother waiting for an answer but strode toward the door leading into the hallway. Edie dashed in front of him, turning to face him and bracing her arms on either side of the door frame. "I don't believe in corporal punishment!" she said a little wildly.

Jim blinked, startled.

Behind them, Carol, who'd been watching open-mouthed, picked up her handbag. "Ah. Lookee there. Time for lunch," she said, and without glancing at the clock hanging on the wall behind her, she bustled around the counter and out the front door.

Edie ignored her. Her worried gaze was fixed on Jim, whose lips had curled in a manner more exasperated

than angry. Without a word of warning, he grabbed
her around the waist, picked her up, and moved her
three feet to the left of the door. Then he strode down
the corridor. She trotted after him.

"I didn't wake her. She looks tired even in her sleep,
and her nose is running," she said worriedly. It wasn't
her business. She had spent the last week convincing
herself that nothing about Jim or Chloe Curran was or
would be her concern. So much for that failed effort.
One runny nose and all resolve to maintain emotional
distance dissolved like sugar icing in the rain. "I think
she has a cold."

He didn't answer.

"Did you know she has a cold?" She should stop.
He wouldn't like her interference. She didn't care. This
was Chloe, whom she loved. She had to know for her
own peace of mind. "I felt her forehead and I think she
has a fever, too. Did you know that?"

His head snapped around, and he glared wordlessly
at her. And then they were at the Meet and Greet room
and he was in the door. He stopped abruptly and just
stared at his daughter. All the anger flowed from his
face, leaving nothing behind but intense relief and
love.

He'd just needed to see her, Edie realized, and to
see for himself that she was safe and well. The tension
released from his shoulders and the set of his back. His
eyes squeezed shut for a brief instant.

Then, taking a deep breath, he turned around and
grabbed hold of Edie's upper arm, spinning her around
to half pull, half steer her back down the corridor and
into the lobby. Abruptly, he released her and with ex-

aggerated care shut the door leading into the corridor. Only then did he speak.

"Do I know that my daughter has a runny nose and a fever and a cold?" he asked. "Of course I know!" he answered his own question in a low, thunderous voice. "I've spent the last three days taking care of her."

So that was why he hadn't been at work. She'd thought maybe he'd been avoiding her, that he'd realized how out of place she was in a family like his, and that all the phone calls she'd been too cowardly to answer or return were to be his polite explanation of why he wouldn't be taking her out to dinner, or coming to the shelter, or kissing her, or making love to her anymore. It had seemed a cowardly sort of way for a man like Jim to end a relationship, even one as brief as theirs, but what did she know of men like Jim and how they ended their relationships?

She should have, though. Because she *did* know Jim, and he wouldn't—what was the popular parlance? Oh yes, "dump her"—he wouldn't dump her with a phone call. The thought made her flush with shame, unable to meet his gaze.

"And, just for the record, I don't believe in corporal punishment, either."

Of course he didn't. Her cheeks grew even hotter.

"The real question, though," he continued in that strained, angry tone, "the real question is why *you* didn't know."

Her gaze flew up to meet his, her eyes encountering sapphire fire. Tension snapped and cackled between them. He took a step forward. She took a step back and bumped into the closed door behind her.

He didn't stop. He took another step, right past the boundaries of propriety, invading her personal space, making her acutely, uncomfortably aware of him not only as a personality but as a very physical, very male presence. It didn't matter that she understood the principle behind her racing heart and quickened breath; it was damned effective.

He reached up and she braced herself against his touch, but he didn't grab her chin; he didn't give physical voice to the roughness of his tone. His touch was far more devastating. His fingertips brushed lightly along her cheekbones, a warm, feathering stroke that made her go weak in the knees.

"Why is that, Edie?" he whispered roughly. "Why didn't you know Chloe was sick?"

"Because I haven't seen her. Or you. Or spoken to either of you," she answered breathlessly.

He stared at her, shaking his head, his expression segueing from smoldering to bemused in a space of seconds. "You don't have a bit of guile to you, do you?"

"No," she answered, uncertain if he considered this a good or a bad thing. His fingertips continued their seductive dance down her cheekbones, to the corner of her lip. His gaze scoured her face.

"You've been crying," he said slowly.

"Yes."

"Edie, what's wrong? Why?"

Why? *Why?* Because everything she loved was going or gone; because it wasn't fair she'd fallen in love with him; because it wasn't fair she'd fallen in love with Chloe; because it wasn't fair she wasn't a supermodel and because it wasn't fair that all those things a person loved always ended up leaving them. All the emotions of the last week—avoiding his phone calls and running out the opposite door when she saw him coming at work, the loneliness, the worry over Ishy-Pixie's declining health, the sudden jolt of panic she'd endured when he told her Chloe was missing, the pain of seeing him again and realizing that not a millimeter of her broken heart had been mended—rushed in, swamping her, destroying every shred of self-containment she owned. "Because I have had a *really shitty* week!" she howled.

He blinked at her, stunned. The tears that should have been long spent sprang anew, overflowing her eyelids and streaming down her face.

"Oh," he said, and without waiting for permission, he swung her easily into his arms and strode over to one of the two vinyl-covered chairs in the lobby and sat down, holding her tightly against him on his lap. Much to her chagrin she couldn't produce even a thin thread of indignation and instead, just gave in, accepting the comfort of his strong, warm embrace. He tucked her head beneath his chin and began rubbing her shoulders and back. "Tell me about it." His breath stirred the hair by her temple.

She didn't even try to hold back. "I came home from the picnic and I threw up, and then I went to work and I had to avoid you, and all week I was so distracted that my entire team called a meeting just to ask me"—she sobbed at the memory—"what was wrong! And I couldn't tell them! And I jumped every time the phone rang because I was afraid it was you, but I didn't have the nerve to pick it up. And then I spent so much time on my bike riding so I could work off some angst that I got a blister on my behind."

A breath on her hair stirred it in a little puff and she thought maybe he'd laughed, but she didn't care. The words kept tumbling out. "And then this morning I came in and found Ishy-Pixie had died, and I was just about to call you and I didn't want to, but I was going to when you called and said Chloe was missing and I was so scared, and then she wasn't missing, but I thought you were angry and I made that stupid, stupid remark about corporal punishment and I knew better. And I knew you'd know she had a cold, but I couldn't stop myself because I still needed to know you knew because . . . because I *love* her and . . . oh!" She buried her head against his shoulder.

He stroked her head for a long moment before saying in a rough, controlled voice, "And me? Do you love me, too?"

Her head snapped up, and she found herself looking into intense blue eyes, candidly, nakedly worried. "Yes," she said, astounded he didn't know. "Yes. Of course, I do."

His arms tightened around her. "Then why wouldn't you talk to me?"

Didn't he know? Hadn't Melissa told him what she'd been telling the unknown woman at Chloe's birthday party? "Because I didn't want to say good-bye."

"Good-bye," he repeated in an odd, flat voice. "Why? You said you loved me, but I must have done something to make you avoid me. What did I do wrong?"

Edie stared, shocked. In all the scenes she had composed trying to imagine what he was thinking, none of them had included one where Jim Curran—gorgeous, successful, kind, funny, athletic—blamed himself for the end of their misfit relationship. She shook her head. "Nothing. You didn't do anything wrong."

"It was my family, then, wasn't it?"

"Yes."

A sound like a growl issued from his throat, and he raked his hair back with one hand. "Look, we don't have to see them often. And then we'll stick to taking them on just a few at a time. I promise. They're my family, Edie, and I love them, but I know how over-powering they can be in numbers. I never should have dragged you there."

We don't have to see them often? We'll stick to taking them on just a few at a time? Something within her, something new and hopeful, took root. She shook her head, refusing to acknowledge it.

"You misunderstand me. I like your family, Jim." Honesty compelled an addendum. "Most of them. I—I really enjoyed myself, but that doesn't negate the fact that I was definitely a fish out of a fry pan."

"Fish out of water," he corrected. "And so what?"

"I'm never going to fit in."

"You already do," he said, taking hold of her shoulders and turning her to face him. "Families aren't made of identical parts, Edie. There's not a preprogrammed position, one role for every person. It's a mess. The roles change; the people change, grow. Believe me, the Currans need a reticent, guileless, blunt woman. *I* need a reticent, guileless, blunt woman."

Hope sprouted, new and vibrant, but she mistrusted

such an ephemeral thing, doubted whether it was enough on which to turn a dream into reality. "But . . . you could be dating a supermodel," she said.

He stared at her in open bewilderment. "Why would I want to do that? The only way I'd want to date a supermodel is if she were you, and you're not, so I guess I'll just have to settle for a genetic research genius. Besides, I don't want to date anyone. I want to marry you."

Her heart thundered in her chest. Hope refused to be beaten down; it sprang forth, sending waves of joy coursing through her. But she had one more misgiving to voice—*the* misgiving.

She swallowed hard. "I'm nothing like your wife. Nothing. I'm like . . ." How had Melissa put it? "I'm like the anti-Stephanie. I can never belong in your family like she did. I can never replace her."

He'd gone very still, and now he looked at her hard. "Anti-Stephanie? Where did you hear that? Who said that to you?"

"No one. I—I was eavesdropping. Inadvertently."

"And whom were you eavesdropping on?"

She didn't answer, but he seemed to already know.

"Melissa," he said. "Geez. Don't put any credence in anything Melissa says. Melissa doesn't know jack."

"Jack? Who's he?"

"It's not a 'he'; it's a—" Jim shook his head. "Never mind. The bottom line is that Melissa is overcontrolling and overinvolved in her siblings' lives."

"It doesn't matter. What she said is true," Edie insisted sadly.

"No." He gave her shoulders a little shake. "It's not.

Listen to me, Edie. I loved Stephanie. We had a wonderful relationship and a great marriage. She wasn't
perfect, but neither am I. I'm incapable of holding a
civil conversation before my first cup of coffee in the
morning. I eat way too many spicy foods and the re-
sults can be . . . offensive. Wait. It gets worse. I own all
the *Three Stooges* DVDs. *And* I watch them. You'll see."

He sounded so confident. She wanted to see. She
did. But . . .

He smiled at her. "I loved Stephanie, and I wouldn't
trade a day of the life we had together. And you're
right, Edie; you never could replace her."

Her heart plummeted and her gaze fell to the floor.

"Just as she could never replace you."

She looked up.

"I don't want to spend my life with a replica of
Steph. I don't want a replica of anything. I want the
genuine Edith Handelman, one of a kind. Entirely herself. Incomparable to anyone. I love you, Edie. I want
to spend my life with you. Please. Please marry me."

Dr. Edith Handelman was a genius, but it didn't take
a genius to realize there was only one possible answer.
"Yes," she said. And as Jim's mouth descended toward
hers, "Yes, and yes, and yes and y—"

A long time later, breathless and amazed and filled
with joy, Edie lifted her head.

"What is it?" Jim asked, nuzzling her neck.

She looked into his eyes, shining as they were with
love, and her every doubt was erased by his ardor and
his tenderness. "Nothing," she said, pulling his head
to hers. "I just thought I heard a cat purring."

A Cat's Game

by Vicki Lewis Thompson

Chapter 1

Kate Archer considered herself a brave woman. She'd skinny-dipped in a river full of piranhas and peed in the jungle while staring at a cockroach the size of a football; yet as she stood on the porch of her sister Maggie's bed-and-breakfast in the little town of Bisbee, Arizona, her tummy churned.

Maggie was leaving her in charge of the B and B, and Hollywood superstar Jon Ramsey would arrive in less than two hours. She would've rather faced a hungry boa constrictor than spend a week with Jon, aka her old high school sweetheart.

"I really appreciate this favor." Maggie lifted her suitcase and carried it down the steps to the sidewalk. A cool breeze from the recent afternoon rain ruffled her brown hair, cut short for the trip.

"You deserve a vacation, Mags." Kate liked the short haircut on Maggie, but not for herself. In college, a psych major had told her that she used her dark shoulder-length hair as a shield against intrusive people. It could have been true.

As Kate picked up Maggie's carry-on, she took a deep breath of Bisbee air, savoring the aroma of cedar and creosote. She loved the summer monsoons, loved watching the storm clouds march in and out from this vantage point on top of one of Bisbee's many hills.

The Hummingbird Inn was a lovely spot, but Maggie had spent far too much time there since she'd bought it. Her workaholic lifestyle had been Kate's motivation for saying yes to taking over for a week, and she'd convinced herself that spending that week with Jon wouldn't be a big deal.

"I deserve a vacation with a *man*." Maggie sounded giddy as she walked over to the parking lot adjacent to the inn. "When Ted surprised me with cruise tickets for the same week the Hummingbird Inn will be empty except for Jon, it seemed like fate."

"Could be." Kate hoped to hell fate wasn't involved in bringing Jon back into her life.

Maggie unlocked her truck, which was parked next to Kate's hybrid. "Looks like somebody's been out with flyers today."

Sure enough, a pink sheet of paper flapped from under the wipers of both Maggie's pickup and Kate's sedan. They were the only two vehicles in the lot because Jon had booked the entire Hummingbird Inn, as he had for the past two years. So far, he'd managed to keep this hideaway a secret from the paparazzi.

Lowering the carry-on to the pavement, Kate removed the flyer from under her car's wiper, folded it, and stuck it in her pocket. She'd deliberately dressed down for this reunion with Jon, choosing old shorts and a University of Arizona T-shirt that had faded from red to pink.

She helped Maggie wrestle the heavy suitcase into

the passenger seat of the truck and then put the carry-on satchel on the floor.

"Thanks." Maggie closed the door. "Good thing I'll be on a cruise and won't have to lug that suitcase around. I packed my whole damned closet. I wish I'd had time to get a bikini wax, but everything happened so fast."

"You could probably get one during the cruise." Focusing on Maggie's trip helped calm Kate's butterflies.

"I hope to be way too busy for that." Maggie grinned and headed for the driver's side. "In fact, I'm not sure why I packed so many clothes, because I hope not to be wearing clothes all that much."

"You sexy wench." Kate wrapped an arm around her sister and gave her a squeeze. "Don't spend the whole cruise in the cabin, okay?"

"You think we could get away with doing it out on deck?"

Kate laughed, knowing Maggie would never consider sex in a public place. Neither would she or their sister Jess. A childhood spent dealing with their parents' tumultuous Hollywood marriage and very public divorce had made them all private people. Kate estimated she was the most private of them all.

Gun-shy about men and marriage, the sisters hadn't dated much, choosing to concentrate on their careers, instead. They'd all received an unexpected boost in that direction last year when their mostly absentee father had died in a boating accident and left them money. Maggie had paid off the B and B mortgage, Jessica had opened a gym in Phoenix, and Kate had financed her research trip to Brazil.

272 Vicki Lewis Thompson

Maggie pulled her flyer off the windshield and handed it to Kate. "Recycle this for me, okay?"

"Sure."

Putting her hands on Kate's shoulders, Maggie looked into her eyes. "You're okay with staying here for the week, right?"

Kate broke out her trusty "I'm okay" smile. She was almost two years older than Maggie, but sometimes Maggie acted like a big sister. "I'm perfectly okay with staying here."

"So you're not still hung up on him."

"God, no!"

"Well, I didn't think so. Mom does, but I told her that was wishful thinking on her part."

Kate rolled her eyes. "Oh, yeah. She'd love me to hook up with a big-deal actor like Jon. Did she tell you she invited him to lunch one time when I was over there?"

"No, but it doesn't surprise me. We're all a disappointment to her, I guess. We were supposed to have our names in lights by now, or at least marry somebody famous."

Kate made a face.

"Backatcha, sister. Anyway, I just wanted to double-check that you're cool with the plan, 'cause you've been a little twitchy today. I hope this wasn't a bad idea, but Jess wasn't available and I really don't know whom else I could have—"

"Maggie, it's *fine*. Good grief, it's been ten years. Jon and I are completely different people from who we were in high school. And it's not as if he'll be up here promoting his next movie or anything."

"God forbid! This is where he comes to decompress from all that. As I said, he might want you to pick up some groceries so he can cook. And he'll hike a lot. You probably won't see much of him."

Kate shrugged. "Doesn't matter one way or the other. I'll be typing up my notes from my research trip." She really did have work to do; three months' worth of notes that needed to be transcribed while they were still fresh in her mind. That should keep her very involved.

"Well, good." Maggie looked relieved. "He seemed fine with it when I e-mailed him that you'd be filling in for me."

Kate resisted the urge to ask what Jon had said when presented with that news. Asking would only create more questions in Maggie's mind. "You'd better go. You don't want to be late."

"No, I sure don't." Maggie gave her a tight hug. "Thanks again." She climbed into the truck. "Tell Jon hi for me, and tell him I loved him in *Synchronicity*. He should've won the Oscar."

"Will do. Have fun!" Kate waved as Maggie pulled out of the parking lot. Then she tried not to panic at her sense of abandonment when the truck headed down the hill toward town. Maggie *would* have to mention Jon's last movie, which Kate had avoided at the box office because she avoided all Jon's movies. But, as always, her mother had sent her the DVD in her not-so-subtle campaign.

Kate wished her mom wouldn't do that, but asking her to stop sending the movies would look like an overreaction, and her mom already suspected that

Kate had a love/hate thing going when it came to Jon. Once the movies were in her house, she couldn't resist watching them.

One particular scene from *Synchronicity* haunted her, no matter how hard she'd tried to forget it. Jon's character had just walked away from the woman he loved, for noble reasons of course. He stood on a cliff gazing out at the ocean, his jaw set and his body language communicating loss. He'd never looked more appealing.

The setting sun—or lights designed to mimic the setting sun—had burnished his hair, picking out the natural blond streaks woven into the brown. Anyone who didn't know his grandfather, Hollywood leading man Trevor Ramsey, would think Jon had spent time in a salon to get that effect. But those who remembered Trevor at thirty said Jon closely resembled him right down to his strong jaw and aristocratic nose.

Wire-rimmed designer shades perched on the bridge of that famous nose, which meant the camera couldn't lovingly detail his famous green eyes. No matter. Kate knew exactly what those eyes looked like and the sensual power they wielded. So did most of the female population of the country and a good part of the world.

Kate hadn't yet accepted the surreal concept that after all these years of not seeing him in the flesh, she would be spending a whole week at the Hummingbird Inn with him.

She tried calming herself by taking a deep breath of the rain-scented air as she returned to the porch. Monsoon season brought rain nearly every afternoon in the summer, and the Hummingbird Inn, perched at the top of one of Bisbee's many hills, had a ringside seat for storm watching. Gazing out from the porch over the valley, Kate caught a glimpse of Maggie's truck on the road as it curved down into Brewery Gulch.

Some people called Bisbee a miniature version of San Francisco—minus the bay and the Golden Gate Bridge. The former mining town lay nestled in the hills, a jumble of crooked narrow streets, steep concrete stairs that linked those streets, and weathered brick storefronts transformed into art galleries and antiques shops. The venerable Copper Queen Hotel served as a focal point for the community, and renovated mining cabins clung to the steep hillsides.

Seeing Maggie's truck on the road that eventually climbed out of the canyon and led to the highway set Maggie's tummy to churning again. That was the same road Jon would use to drive into Bisbee. According to Maggie, he'd be at the wheel of an inconspicuous sedan that he'd picked up at the Executive Terminal in Tucson after landing in his private jet. Maggie said Jon usually let his beard grow a little to make himself less recognizable.

Kate shuddered. What a way to live. She couldn't imagine how Jon stood the pressure of that constant spotlight, but then again, he'd chosen that path a long time ago. He'd been marked for stardom from the moment he'd taken his first film role, which he'd landed during the six-month period when they'd dated their senior year.

That role had signaled the beginning of the end for them. He'd wanted fame; she'd wanted obscurity.

They'd fought about it, each trying to convince the other to change.

But that hadn't been the worst part. Even at eighteen, Jon had already attracted the attention of the paparazzi, and pictures of their angry split, which took place rather publicly at the prom, had shown up in a tabloid. Kate could have died of humiliation. She'd vowed never to let that happen to her; yet because of Jon, it had.

At least his fame wouldn't be an issue this week. But now came the tough part—suffering through the hour or more of waiting until he showed up. Kate headed back toward Maggie's lovingly renovated Victorian. Maybe she could lose herself in her work.

Once inside, she pulled the folded flyer from her pocket and added it to the one in her other hand. Then she walked into the kitchen where Maggie kept her recycling bins. She'd started to toss the flyers inside when she saw that the border was made up of cats and hearts. She loved cats and paused to look at the flyer.

Scanning the page, Kate quickly figured out it advertised a shelter less than a block away. The text of the flyer intrigued her.

Cupid Cats Shelter:
Bring a little magic and love into your life
Adopt a Cat

As far as Kate was concerned, all cats were magical. She'd grieved mightily when her tabby, Cheeta, had died at the age of fourteen. She'd intended to adopt

another cat, but she'd started dating a guy who was allergic. When they'd broken up, she hadn't been terrifi-
cally sorry to see him go, because she wanted to have
a cat again.

She would have adopted immediately, except the
research trip to Brazil had become a reality. The trip
had been great and she hoped to return, but she had
no idea when she'd be able to do that. Grant money
seemed to be drying up these days.

She really did want a cat. And Jon wouldn't arrive
for at least another hour.

She couldn't take a cat today, of course. The Hummingbird Inn was filled with all sorts of breakable and
scratchable antiques; yet she had an irresistible com-
pulsion to walk down to Cupid Cats and take a look,
anyway. What could it hurt? And it sure beat hanging
around the B and B waiting for Jon to show up.

Grabbing her purse and the Hummingbird Inn key
ring, she locked up the house and started down the
street. The cat shelter was easy to spot once she knew
what to look for. She'd noticed the pink house with
white trim on her way to the Hummingbird Inn two
days ago.

The paint job made it stand out, but it was cheerful
rather than garish, with pots of petunias hanging from
the front porch rafters and a neat green lawn divided
by a brick sidewalk. Until now, Kate hadn't taken
a close look at the sign out front. She'd assumed the
place was a gift shop or another B and B.

The pink and white heart dangling from a post in
the front yard said CUPID CATS in large letters. Underneath that lettering was a white kitten sporting angel

wings and brandishing a tiny bow and arrow. Below the logo was a slogan—FALL IN LOVE WITH A CAT.

She might just do that, but even if she found the cat of her dreams, she wouldn't be able to take it with her until after her week at the Hummingbird. Hoisting her purse more firmly onto her shoulder, she climbed the porch steps and rang the doorbell. It played the opening bars of "Love Is in the Air."

A plump blonde in a purple caftan opened the door. Kate didn't recognize her from other visits to Bisbee, and she would have remembered this woman with her sparkling purple eye shadow and bright red lipstick.

New Age music drifted from inside, along with the scent of incense.

"I saw your flyer," Kate said. "I'm Kate Archer, Maggie's sister."

"Ah, yes. From the Hummingbird Inn. Are you looking for love, Kate?"

For a moment Kate wondered if she'd stumbled upon another business entirely. Then she remembered the marketing angle from the flyer. "Yes," she said. "And I have a special fondness for cats. But I'm not ready to adopt one today. I'd just like to look."

"Of course, of course. Come in. I'm Esmeralda Fitch. I run the shelter."

"By yourself?"

"Yes."

"That's very ambitious." Kate walked into a living room filled with rainbows. Sunlight streamed through a west-facing window, and at least ten crystals hung from the curtain rod. She glanced to the other side of the room and noticed the east window treatment was

the same. Yep, she was in Bisbee, all right. Crystals, incense, and flutes in the background were part of the
local flavor.

"So you're not from Bisbee, then?" Esmeralda
asked.

"No. I'm on a six-month sabbatical from the U of
A in Tucson." The dancing rainbows swirled over the
furniture, which was upholstered in a variety of fab-
rics. Kate searched for a sign of cats but didn't see any.
Maybe they were in another room.

"And your area of expertise is?"

Kate turned to her with a smile. "Monkeys. I'm a
primatologist."

"How fascinating!"

"I happen to think so. So where are the cats?"

"Right here."

"I don't . . . Oh, wait." Temporarily ignoring the
rainbows, Kate finally saw them. A black Manx jumped
down from a black suede easy chair and strolled to a
window ledge. A black and white spotted cat stood
and stretched before settling back onto a black and
white spotted ottoman.

When Kate peered more closely at a tiger-striped
sofa, she found three tiger-striped cats lying there
watching her. It was like playing a game of *Where's
Waldo*.

She glanced at Esmeralda. "Did you teach them to
lie on the appropriately colored furniture?"

"Not exactly. I just encouraged their natural instinct
toward camouflage. Makes cleanup easier."

"And they all do this?"

"All except Darwin."

She had Kate at the name Darwin. Surely a cat with that name would be perfect for a woman who studied monkeys for a living. "And where is this Darwin character?"

"Back here." Esmeralda led the way through a small dining room and turned down a hallway. "He likes my bed." She stood aside so Kate could peek through the bedroom door.

Esmeralda obviously enjoyed sleeping in splendor. She'd draped her canopy bed in dark purple velvet, with a lighter purple duvet and cushions in various shades of violet. Darwin, a silver and black tabby, reclined amongst the pillows like a king.

Kate felt an immediate connection and then tried to rationalize it as simply admiration for a striking animal. Darwin's black swirls and stripes looked fingerpainted on, and one spot on his right haunch was heart-shaped. How appropriate to find a cat like this at a place called Cupid Cats.

As if sensing an admiring stare, Darwin opened his eyes, and Kate fell in love. His eyes were an amazing shade of turquoise.

"He's leash trained," Esmeralda said.

"You're kidding."

"Nope." Esmeralda walked to the bedside table, opened a drawer, and took out a black harness and leash decorated with silver stars and bits of turquoise. Darwin's ears perked up.

"Nice accessory. The stones match his eyes." Kate hoped they were plastic stones. She'd like to buy the leash, too, but real turquoise would be pricey and sort of ridiculous for a cat.

"They're from the local mine."

"The turquoise is Bisbee Blue?" That particular type was legendary and definitely not cheap.

"Yep. I had a local jeweler embed the stones. Turquoise balances the chakras. Some say it also unites the male and female energies and stimulates romantic love."

Kate sensed Esmeralda was dead-on serious, so she restrained herself from making any sarcastic comments, although she couldn't help having skeptical thoughts. She was a scientist after all. "He's neutered, right?"

Esmeralda looked offended. "Of course."

"Then I'm afraid romantic love is pretty much out for this guy."

"Well, that's true." Esmeralda reached over and rubbed a finger along Darwin's jaw. "But he still needs to stay balanced. The leash is part of the deal."

A cash register rang in Kate's head, but she supposed, at the end of the week, she'd shell out for both cat and leash. "I can see why he'd want the leash he's become used to. But the thing is I'm not ready to . . ." She forgot what she meant to say as she looked into Darwin's eyes. "Can I pet him?"

"Absolutely."

Crossing to the bed, Kate slowly reached out a hand toward the cat, who was regarding her with an unblinking gaze. Crooking her finger, she scratched along the side of his jaw the same way Esmeralda had. His fur felt soft as a mink's. Closing his eyes, he began to purr.

"Looks like you've found the one," Esmeralda said.

"Yes . . . I mean, no, I can't take him. Not yet. Maybe at the end of the week." Kate rubbed a spot behind Darwin's ear, and he purred louder.

"Might not be here at the end of the week. A cat like that attracts a lot of attention."

"Could you hold him?"

"That's against our policy."

Kate tried to think of all the reasons she shouldn't do this, but she couldn't remember a single one. "Then I'll take him now."

Chapter 2

*A*s Jon drove the winding canyon road approaching Bisbee, he felt a sense of homecoming. He'd tried tropical getaways and glamorous ski lodges, but they hadn't worked for him. This homey B and B, tucked into a small town only a short plane ride from LA, hit the spot, partly because nobody expected him to spend time at such a glitz-free establishment.

He'd stumbled on it by accident while researching quiet retreats on the Internet. The name Maggie Archer had caught his attention, and with a little detective work he'd discovered that she was indeed one of the Archer sisters. That meant she'd completely understand his need to drop out for a week.

That also meant he had a tenuous connection with Kate, not that he'd expected anything to come of that. She'd seemed distant during that lunch at her mom's house a couple of years ago, and he'd concluded there was nothing to pursue. He wondered why she'd agreed to watch the inn for her sister this week. Given that amount of time in the same house with her, he'd probably find out.

His anticipation grew, but he told himself it was only because he looked forward to chilling out for seven days in a hideaway where he could catch up on his reading, cook, hike, and listen to the rain on the B and B's tin roof. It had nothing to do with Kate.

And yet . . . He smiled as he neared the Time Tunnel through the Mule Mountains. The locals had dubbed it that, and when Jon had first come to Bisbee, he'd been charmed by this gateway into town. The residents insisted that passing through it took a visitor back to the way life used to be before BlackBerries, Twitter, and TiVo.

If he could truly go back in time and start all over with Kate, would he do anything differently? He'd liked her a lot in high school—maybe even loved her, he realized now. But he didn't think he would do anything differently. Nothing he could have tried short of abandoning his acting dreams would have satisfied her. He hadn't been ready to do that then, and he sure as hell wasn't ready to do that now, after almost winning the damned Oscar.

On the other side of the tunnel lay the quirky little town. He wished he could explore it, but even a scruffy beard wouldn't disguise him enough to patronize one of the restaurants or have a beer in a tavern on Brewery Gulch Road.

He wound his way up that road toward the Hummingbird Inn. Man, he was looking forward to this. He couldn't remember feeling so excited since Oscar night. Sure, he'd lost, but being nominated had been a huge thrill. Next time he planned to take home that gold statue.

But this week he was putting ambition on the back burner. He'd learned that if he didn't get away for at least a full week every year and plan activities that had nothing to do with his job, his work suffered. He credited his first year at the Hummingbird Inn for giving him the necessary focus for his role in *Synchronicity.* When he returned to LA, he'd start work on a new project. He planned to be rested and energized.

As he crested the hill, he got his first good view of the B and B. Maggie had restored the old house with style and grace. She'd had it painted a rich cream accented by dark green gingerbread trim and a green tin roof. Hummingbird feeders hung from tree branches and porch rafters. Last year he'd counted seventeen feeders.

A blue hybrid was the only car in the parking lot. He figured Kate would drive something like that. Casual questions to Maggie had revealed that Kate's interest in monkey habitats extended to conservation efforts in general. Seeing the hybrid made Jon feel a little guilty about his Lamborghini and his newest indulgence, a Bugatti.

So he was a car snob. So what? But today he'd accepted the silver-gray sedan with no complaints. This week he would blend in.

After parking the car, he got out and took a deep breath of the Bisbee air, which smelled incredibly sweet after a recent rain. The reddish earth under his feet was still damp. It was quite a change from freeways and smog.

He might have missed the monsoon today, but more would come along this week. Once he'd heard about the tin roof, he'd deliberately scheduled his visits to coincide with the summer rainy season.

About this time Maggie usually came out to greet him, but that might not be Kate's style. He didn't care. Opening the back door of the sedan, he pulled out his suitcase and headed for the house.

Moments later, after repeatedly shoving his thumb against the doorbell, he concluded nobody was around. Okay, that sucked. He might not expect a red carpet, but he'd like to have somebody answer the door. He should have a key made that he could keep from year to year. Maggie would probably be okay with that.

Damn it. He was hungry and tired. But he couldn't go into town for food and risk blowing his cover. He couldn't call anybody, either. Maggie was on her way to LA for her cruise, and Kate was . . . Where the hell was Kate, anyway?

Feeling cranky, he sat on the porch swing to wait. A mellow guy would be happy to watch the humming-birds zipping around the feeders, but he wasn't mel-low. He hoped to be mellow in a few days, but for now he was still in LA mode, wound tight.

It would serve Kate right if he jimmied a window and climbed through it, but his dignity wouldn't allow that. He wasn't about to let her find him with his ass sticking out of a window he'd pried open with his Swiss Army knife.

It seemed like forever, but five minutes hadn't passed when he saw her coming up the street carry-ing something in her arms. The sight of her striding to-ward him with her long tanned legs and her shiny fall of dark hair swinging with each step made him forget his hunger pangs and his travel fatigue.

He'd had a weakness for Kate Archer ever since they

were six years old attending the same private school in Beverly Hills. She'd had a long braided ponytail then and a sweet smile. The smile had grown more wistful and sad during middle school and had almost disappeared during high school. He'd ached for her misery through the years of scandal. Her parents, both famous Hollywood stars, had indulged in public fights about her dad's affairs and had eventually divorced amidst much acrimony.

Meanwhile he'd enjoyed a stable life, probably because his tycoon father had been killed in a plane crash when Jon was only two and his movie-star mother had retired from the film business to raise him. Together they'd moved into his grandfather Trevor's mansion. For the most part he'd been protected from the paparazzi and he'd definitely been encouraged to develop his talents. The Archer girls had been thrown to the wolves.

He doubted any of them had suffered as much as Kate, the shiest of the three. He'd been fascinated with her big dark eyes and her long black hair. She'd worn it longer as a young girl, like some tragic heroine out of a Shakespearean play.

Now he saw she wore it loose and shoulder length, and it still had that luxurious sheen of a shampoo commercial. Her big eyes remained temptingly mysterious, although she wore less makeup now than she did in high school, so she didn't look quite so much like a poster child for *Les Misérables*.

She spotted him and called out. "Jon, I'm sorry! I went down the street to"—she glanced at the silver and black animal in her arms—"to adopt a cat."

"Okay. No problem." She what? He wasn't sure how that would work out with Maggie's antiques and her flower arrangements in cut-glass vases, but that was an issue to be settled between Maggie and Kate.

Kate mounted the steps, bringing with her the aroma of a new perfume. He'd associated her with a flowery scent, but that sensory memory was obviously out-dated. These days she evidently preferred something headier. It reminded him of ripe peaches. He levered himself out of the porch swing.

"This is Darwin." Her color was high, her breathing uneven, but that could be explained by the climb up the hill.

"Good-looking cat." His uneven breathing couldn't be explained by anything, unless he was willing to admit that Kate still turned him on. He hesitated to admit that right off the bat. He was supposed to be over her just as she was over him. "Shouldn't he be in a carrier or something?"

"Esmeralda, the lady who runs the shelter, thought the harness and leash would do the trick, but I don't want to put him down until he's officially inside the house. I was wondering if you'd be able to get the key out of my purse so we can go in. It's in the front pocket."

"I can do that." He stepped closer so he could fish around in her purse, which she'd slung over her shoulder. God, she smelled good. He was getting a definite sexual buzz. Embarrassing though it might be, the chemistry he'd always felt with Kate seemed to be alive and well and making its way to his groin.

Locating the key ring with the hummingbird on it,

he pulled it out of her purse and walked over to the door. Maggie was proud of this door, he remembered. She'd insisted he admire the leaded glass inserts and the brass door knocker in the shape of a hummingbird.

He shoved the key into the lock and opened the door. "We're in." Then he stood back to let Kate go ahead of him.

"Thanks, Jon." She walked into the house, clutching the cat to her chest. "I'm not being a very good hostess, am I? First you had to wait, and now you have to unlock the door yourself."

"I don't mind." He wondered if he was imagining the nervous tremor in her voice. "Let me get my suitcase before you let go of him." Back out on the porch, he grabbed it in one hand and lifted it into the entryway. Once he had the door closed, he turned back to Kate. "That's it. You can put him down. He looks more than ready to be free."

"I know, but—"

"Wow, his eyes are the exact color of the turquoise in the harness. That whole presentation would be a big hit on Rodeo Drive." He probably shouldn't have mentioned Rodeo Drive, knowing how she used to hate anything to do with Hollywood. He wouldn't be surprised if she made some snarky comment.

She didn't. Instead she glanced up at him uneasily, a plea in her dark eyes. "I just realized I have another issue."

She was definitely nervous. Either the cat was throwing her off her game or she was jumpy about being here with him. But he decided to keep it low-key. "What's that?"

"I should probably unfasten his harness before I put him down. If he takes off, the leash will go flying behind him and could catch on something. That wouldn't be good."

"You're right. It wouldn't." He had an idea where this discussion was leading.

"But I don't think I can get it off and maintain my hold on him."

Bingo. "So you'd like some help." Jon could see the wisdom in unharnessing the cat, but he was afraid getting close enough to do it would add jet fuel to his already potent reaction. He wasn't prepared to deal with that, at least not yet.

"If you wouldn't mind. I promise it's the last favor I'll ask this week."

He gazed at her. She was acting freaked-out, almost as if he intimidated her. That was not good. If they were going to inhabit the same house all week, she'd need to loosen up, for both their sakes.

So he gave her a Chesire cat grin. "I certainly hope you won't keep asking me to do stuff. I am, after all, a VIP, an Oscar nominee, even."

She stared at him for so long he wondered if she actually believed he was pulling rank. Then her shoulders visibly relaxed and a hint of laughter sparkled in her dark eyes. "My apologies, Your Oscar Nomineeness. Once the harness is off the cat, I'll commence with the flag waving and rose petal scattering."

"Much better." Jon winked at her before he stepped forward and studied the harness. The way she was cradling Darwin against her chest, a guy would have to be careful or he might accidentally grope her in the process of unhooking the clasp. Not a good move. "Maybe I should just unfasten the leash and leave the harness on. That way you can grab him more easily if you need to."

"I'd rather take it all off." The cat wiggled at that, and she worked hard to hold him. "There's an adjustable loop around his neck, and I sure don't want him to hang himself."

"Well, yeah, that would be bad." Jon leaned closer. If he could see the clasp before he started this procedure, he'd have less chance of committing a social blunder. But his concentration was broken as he inhaled her ripe-peaches scent. He'd always been a sucker for ripe peaches.

He could also hear her breathe, and it seemed to him she was breathing faster the longer they stood there fooling with the cat.

"The clasp is on the part that goes around his body," she said.

He didn't dare look into her eyes in case she was also rediscovering their long-lost lust for each other. If he saw awareness in her gaze, he'd want to kiss her, which was a bad idea on many levels, the principle one being the cat that would be squeezed between them.

"I can't see where it unhooks," he said. "Can you turn him a little?"

"I'll try." She dipped her head and whacked it painfully into his. Immediately she moved back, still clutching the cat. "I'm so sorry!"

"Hey, it's nothing." He resisted the urge to rub the spot. He couldn't avoid looking at her now, though. Her color was high, but he wasn't sure whether that

was agitation over smashing her head against his or
sexual excitement. "Are you okay?"

She swallowed. "I'm fine. I promise to keep my head
away from yours so you can do this. He's been moving
so much, the clasp could be tucked under him by now.
You'll just have to feel around for it."

Good Lord. He'd just been invited to feel around for
a hook on a harness that was plastered between the cat
and her breasts.

"Please hurry. I don't think I can hold on to him
much longer."

"Okay, I'm going in." Taking a deep breath, he
grasped the harness and tried to ignore her ripe-peaches
scent while he worked his fingers along the length of
the nylon strap. The cat's fur was incredibly soft, which
only added to the erotic nature of this project.

Darwin meowed in protest and tried to break free,
which meant Jon had to move faster, less deliberately,
and sure enough, his knuckles made contact with her
left breast.

She gasped.

"Sorry. I just—"

"I know. You couldn't help it."

"Nope." He also couldn't help the sensations wash-
ing over him as he fumbled around searching for the
damned clasp. He wanted Kate Archer. He told himself he was over it, that she just haunted his memories
because she was the last girl he'd dated before becoming famous, but he couldn't lie to himself anymore. It
wasn't the timing; it was Kate.

Maybe it was a case of unfulfilled fantasies. During
their dating days she'd been so paranoid about getting

caught by the paparazzi that they'd never found the right time and place to have sex. They'd planned to remedy that on prom night, but they'd split up before the night was over.

He didn't know if she had unfulfilled fantasies about him, but he'd love to find out. Usually he could control his urges better than this, but this hot yearning was so fierce it made his mouth water.

Maybe casual conversation was the answer. "So, how've you been, Kate?" he asked as he continued to fumble with the strap.

"Fine."

He found the clasp but had to use both hands to unfasten it, which meant his hands were sandwiched between her breasts. "Last year Maggie said you might be headed to Brazil." The clasp refused to open.

"Just got back from there."

"Have fun?" He gritted his teeth and fought with the clasp as thoughts of making love to Kate right here in the hallway absorbed most of his brainpower.

"Loved it. Listen, are you—"

"Seeing anyone? No."

"I was going to ask if you're making any progress on the clasp."

"It's stuck." He glanced up, and ten years fell away in an instant. He could taste her kisses as if they'd been in the back row of a movie theater last night. He'd been so green then, so untutored. Many times he'd regretted they'd never made love, but now he was glad. At eighteen he hadn't been very accomplished.

Her eyes darkened the way they used to when she wanted him to kiss her. "Jon . . ."

Insane as it seemed, he thought she'd let him kiss her now, except the damned cat was growling and twisting in her arms.

He returned his attention to the clasp. "Are you seeing anyone?"

"No, but that doesn't—"

"You're right. It doesn't have anything to do with anything. I just . . ." The clasp gave way. "There." He pulled the harness off the cat. "You can let him go."

She loosened her grip. Darwin leaped from her arms, landed with a thump on the hardwood floor, and scampered down the hall.

She half turned as if to follow. "I should keep track of him."

"Wait."

Slowly she faced him again, her gaze wary. "What? Oh, sorry. You still have the leash." She held out her hand.

"This isn't about the leash, but here." He gave it to her. He was the kind of guy who focused on a woman's face when he talked to her. But he'd still managed to quickly check the front of her old worn T-shirt. Her nipples made a dent in the cotton.

He took satisfaction in that. It made him feel a little less foolish for the surge of lust he felt whenever he looked at her. He cleared his throat. "Am I the only one who feels as if we're right where we were in high school?"

"In what way?"

"In a sexual way."

"Nope. Nothing sexual going on over here."

He was surprised—and disappointed. He could

challenge her on that, but he wouldn't. He'd be here for seven days and seven nights. He was in no rush. His body might be in a hell of a rush, but he wasn't a kid anymore. He could wait.

He shrugged. "Okay. Just checking. Guess I'll go up to my room, then."

"You'll need to delay that trip a couple of minutes."

"Why?"

"I need time to locate my basket of rose petals."

He laughed. "You know, Kate, I have a feeling this is going to be a very interesting week."

Chapter 3

What had just happened? Kate had managed to keep her cool, sort of, long enough to end that crazy scene in the hallway with a joke about the rose petals, but as she headed toward the back of the house to locate Darwin, adrenaline rushed through her system, leaving her shaky.

She'd been uptight about seeing Jon, but she'd expected awkwardness between them, not enough heat to burn a hole in the hardwood floor. It was really his fault for looking so damned sexy in his casual shorts and T-shirt. He must have known dressing like that made women want to rip his clothes off and do him. Then that deal with the harness had turned into unexpected foreplay. *Yikes.*

The instant chemistry put things in a whole new light. Jon had come here to escape, which meant he'd taken great pains to keep this location secret. Though she felt ambushed by her strong reaction to him, she couldn't help but smile as she thought of a twist on the old Vegas line—whatever happens in Bisbee stays in Bisbee.

Was she seriously thinking of getting involved with Jon this week? Surely not. But he had made that remark about feeling as if they were back in high school, which was sort of an invitation to explore further. She couldn't deny fantasizing about what he'd be like as a lover. With his security precautions, she wouldn't have to worry about some paparazzo leaping out of the bushes with a camera.

But for the moment, she needed to put thoughts of Jon out of her mind and concentrate on this new responsibility—her cat. Going through the kitchen she glanced at a peg by the back door. It was perfect for the leash and harness. She hung them on it, looping the strap so it was out of Darwin's reach.

Maggie had designed an owner's suite that opened off the kitchen, and those rooms were Kate's for the duration of her stay. First she entered a small sitting room with a rolltop desk, a wingback chair, and a television. French doors led to the bedroom with its king-sized bed created to look like an antique four-poster. Beyond that was a bathroom also designed to look antique, complete with a deep claw-foot tub and a pedestal sink.

Darwin was relaxing on the bed. On his back, he lay up against the mound of snowy pillows with his front and back legs stretched as far as they would go. His posture said plainly, "This is all mine."

Kate chuckled. "Please make yourself at home, cat."

He opened those turquoise eyes and gave her an upside-down stare, as if annoyed that she'd disturbed his nap. Then he stretched with a little quiver of pleasure, closed his eyes, and went back to sleep. The silver hair on his belly rose and fell softly with each breath.

Kate leaned in the open doorway and gazed at her new cat, who obviously was satisfied with his new digs. She was glad she'd gone ahead with the adoption, although it had been the strangest pet adoption Kate had ever been through.

Esmeralda had refused to take any money, not even as a donation for the shelter. Even the leash had been free. Kate had given up arguing with her and had concluded that Esmeralda must have inherited millions that she'd chosen to spend on stray cats.

Whatever Esmeralda's situation, Kate had lucked out finding Darwin. She was already starting to love him, partly because of his sense of entitlement. Darwin was a cat who would get his due, and she admired that. She also admired his ability to go with the flow and make himself so perfectly comfortable so quickly in his new home.

She hadn't been very good at that in the past. Usually she had to orchestrate everything to death. Maybe now that she had a cat with such a gift for enjoying life, she'd be able to use him as a role model.

Sounds coming from the upstairs indicated that Jon was settling in. She could hear his footsteps as he moved back and forth. Maggie had made up the back bedroom for him because he liked returning to the same one each year. On the second floor he could hear the rain on the tin roof, which was apparently something he cherished.

Kate had a sudden image of making love to the music of rain on a tin roof. She'd never done that before. She probably had no business thinking about it now. And yet, what woman in her right mind wouldn't think about it with a hottie like Jon in the house? If Darwin could talk, no doubt he'd advise her to go for it.

Water ran in the upstairs bathroom, so Jon was probably freshening up. Normally that bathroom was shared with whoever had one of the other two upstairs rooms, but Jon would have it all to himself this week.

The intimacy of their situation gradually settled over her like a fragrant set of satin sheets. For seven days the only occupants of this house would be her, Jon, and the cat. She'd thought that would feel strange and unnerving. She hadn't expected it to feel exciting and just the slightest bit illicit.

A few minutes later she heard him on the stairs, which jacked up her pulse rate. He came into the kitchen calling her name, which jacked up her pulse rate a little more.

"I'm here." Her body humming with awareness, she walked back through the sitting room and out into Maggie's comfortable kitchen with the yellow tile counters and the cherry-patterned curtains. Then she paused, trying to decide what was different about him. He wore the same khaki shorts and leather sandals, the same white Tommy Hilfiger T-shirt.

And he'd shaved.

Maybe he did that every time he arrived, but why would he bother? Why not let his beard grow out during the week to make his disguise even more convincing? She could text Maggie to find out if he normally shaved first thing after unpacking, but that would reveal that Kate was interested in such info.

For a perceptive person like Maggie, a question like that would be enough on which to base a whole theory. Kate didn't want Maggie constructing theories. If something happened here this week, Kate would rather nobody ever knew, including her sister.

She decided not to comment on the shaving because she was still debating whether to follow through on this attraction they had going. But the longer they stood gazing at each other, the more the air between them heated up.

He'd finished off his shave with some brand of yummy-smelling cologne. That didn't seem like the act of a man ready to kick back and abandon his usual routine. That seemed like the act of a man interested in getting it on.

Shoving her hands in her pockets, she rocked back on her heels. "All settled in?"

"Yep. And I'm starving."

The way he was looking at her, she wondered what he was starving for. Could be food; could be something else. A slight tremor moved through her as she remembered how intense his kisses had been at eighteen. "Maggie said you like to cook while you're here."

"Yeah, it relaxes me."

She didn't remember moving toward him, and she didn't think he'd stepped closer, but somehow they'd managed to draw close enough to touch, although they didn't. "I guess you'll need me to go to the store for groceries." Obviously her mind was operating on a single track, because she wondered if she should pick up condoms while she was out.

"It's probably not necessary for tonight," he said. "You must have food in the house. I can use whatever's here."

Then again, maybe condom shopping was a presumption on her part. He might want a good meal and an early night . . . alone. Flirting might be such a habit for him that he couldn't help doing it.

She battened down her hormones. "To tell you the truth, I have no idea what's in the pantry and very little idea of what's in the refrigerator. I'm not much of a cook, and the restaurants are terrific in Bisbee. I'd planned to eat all my meals out."

His highly photogenic mouth tipped into a smile. "And what were you planning to do about providing the breakfast part of this B and B?"

She blinked. "You know, that's an excellent question. Maggie said you liked to cook and I—I suppose I thought you'd make yourself some coffee and toast."

"Good thing I can fend for myself, then."

"Guess so." Kate realized that her usual eating plan might not work out, after all. She had a cat now, and she couldn't very well leave all the time. This first night might be especially critical, no matter how at home Darwin might look stretched out on her bed. Besides, that wasn't fair to Jon. He was a guest and shouldn't be expected to cat-sit.

She glanced at him. "Would you be willing to fend for me, too? At least until I have a better idea of what to expect from Darwin? I mean, if it's not too much trouble."

He wore that teasing expression that made women all over the world flock to his movies. "I'll be happy to feed you, but you'll have to be willing to eat whatever I cook. As I recall, you were a picky eater."

Although she hadn't noticed him move before, she

did this time. He was definitely moving into her intimate space with a sureness born of sexual confidence.

Determined not to come across as less than confident herself, she stood her ground and lifted her chin. "Define picky."

"Unwilling to experiment. When I'm on vacation I like to try new things."

They were almost touching, and she was having a real problem getting her breath. "Are we still talking about food?"

He held her gaze. "I don't know. Are we?"

Oh, what the hell? I'm going for it. "Because if we are, I've heard you can do some very interesting things with a can of whipped cream and a handful of chocolate-covered strawberries."

Heat flashed in his green eyes. "Don't say anything you're not ready to back up."

"I'm not a vulnerable teenager anymore, Jon." Her heart thumped so fast she grew dizzy.

He leaned down, his lips a breath away. "You're making that perfectly clear, Kate."

She hoped she didn't pass out from the flush of pleasure that rushed through her. This was the most thrilling moment she'd ever known, including when the black crocodile had almost sunk her canoe. "So, why did you shave?"

"Why do you think?"

The doorbell rang. Kate swore.

"Just don't answer."

"I have to." With a sigh she stepped back and walked around him. "This is a place of business."

"Not this week," he called after her.

As she went through the living room to answer the door, she had to admit he was right. This week the entire B and B belonged to him, and he was the kind of client Maggie wouldn't want to tick off.

If Jon asked her to hang a sign on the front door saying the Hummingbird Inn was closed for a private party, she should probably do that. Come to think of it, such a sign sounded like a great idea. So did the private party.

She also needed to remember that Jon was a celebrity, and answering the door without seeing who it was might not be very smart. What if a reporter stood on the other side?

She took the time to peek out the front window and was surprised to see neither a reporter nor snooping fans, but Esmeralda holding what looked like a litter box with the lid upside down and two bags inside the lid.

Kate opened the door. "You are so sweet, but you didn't have to do that, especially after giving me the cat and the leash."

"I had a feeling you might not want to leave Darwin this first night to go out to the store. He likes this kind of food, and this is the litter he's used to. I had an extra box." She held out her offering.

"Thank you *so* much." Kate took the blue plastic litter box. With the food and litter inside, it was surprisingly heavy; yet there was no car parked out front. "Did you walk up the hill with this?"

"Sure did." Esmeralda didn't sound the least bit winded.

"You must be in excellent shape." Good manners meant inviting Esmeralda in after her trek, but Kate was now aware that she'd trap Jon back in the kitchen by doing that. Or maybe he was so involved in his cooking that he wouldn't care. She heard him banging pots and pans around and opening and closing the refrigerator door.

"I keep in pretty good shape," Esmeralda said. "Surprisingly, a broom is great exercise."

Kate would have thought Esmeralda would use a vacuum cleaner, but maybe a broom didn't frighten the animals. "I suppose there is a lot of cleaning involved in running a cat shelter."

"Oh, it's not so bad." Esmeralda glanced toward the parking lot. "Looks like you have only one guest."

Kate wasn't about to confirm or deny. "Mm."

"How's Darwin?" Esmeralda looked eager, as if she'd love to come in and take a look at the cat's new lodgings.

"He's fine. Esmeralda, I'd love to ask you in, but my guest is . . . Well, my guest has developed this terrible rash, and I need to . . . I need to go check on him. I mean *her*. She's embarrassed about anyone seeing her, and I don't blame her because this rash is nasty. It would make you hurl if you saw it, truly."

Esmeralda smiled. "I wouldn't want to intrude."

"No, that's not it. He just . . . I mean *she* just—"

"I understand. Enjoy yourselves!" She turned, gave a brief wave, and descended the steps.

"Thank you!" Kate called after her. "I'll come by to say good-bye before I leave." After closing the door and locking it, she smacked her forehead and groaned. Talk about lame excuses. Muttering to herself, she carried the litter box and its contents back to the kitchen.

Jon was at the counter slicing veggies. He turned to her with a grin that could have melted the polar ice cap. "It's a damned good thing you didn't go into acting."

"Yes, it is, for numerous reasons." She was embarrassed by how easily he turned her on and how ready she was to drag him out of the kitchen and back to her bed. Except Darwin was there. She set the litter box on the floor and went to a cupboard in search of a bowl for his food.

Jon returned to his chopping. "You know, the rash was pretty gross, but did you have to give me a sex change?"

"I was afraid if I said you were a guy, she'd think I was shacked up with somebody." She opened the bag of food and poured some into a bowl. The sound must have tripped Darwin's trigger, because he came running into the kitchen.

"She still thinks that."

"I know. I'm sorry."

"I'm not. This way she'll leave us alone. Listen, I found some chicken breasts in the freezer. Is it okay if I use a couple of them?"

"Sure, go ahead." She moved the litter box into the laundry room and set that up. By the time she walked back into the kitchen, Darwin had hopped to the top of the refrigerator where he could survey the action. His blue gaze followed Jon's every movement.

Kate understood the impulse, although Darwin was probably interested in the chicken, whereas Kate was interested in the man. The muscles in Jon's arms put on quite the show as he diced veggies on the cutting board. Not being a cook, Kate hadn't caught more than brief snatches of cooking shows when she was changing channels, but she couldn't remember a single chef who'd looked as sexy as Jon.

The action also invited her to focus on his hands, which moved with practiced ease as he deftly wielded the knife. She was reminded that he was left-handed.

Left-handed people were supposed to be more hooked into their creative impulses. She'd read that somewhere, and considering Jon's success in film, it was probably true of him. Cooking was a creative outlet, too. So was sex.

She couldn't seem to derail that train of thought as she admired his long, flexible fingers working with the knife and the veggies. Manual dexterity, she realized in that instant, could turn a girl on. She'd never thought of a kitchen as being particularly erotic, but for some reason, this one was.

He stopped slicing and glanced at her. "Want to help?"

She backed away, palms out. "Trust me, you don't want my help. When I said I don't cook, I meant I *really* don't cook. I can ruin a microwave dinner—and have."

"I'll bet you could find us a bottle of wine."

Oh, my. He was turning on the charm, and now he'd suggested wine. She didn't have to be a genius to know how this could end up.

He laughed. "Don't look like that. I'm not planning to get you drunk and have my way with you."

Little did he know that was her plan.

Chapter 4

Jon prided himself on his sense of timing. The way Kate was looking at him right now, he'd be wise to put down the knife and cross the room to where she was standing. And he was no fool.

She drew in a quick breath as he approached. "I wonder if this is—"

"It is. It's a very good idea." Cradling her face in both hands, he leaned in. "I've missed you, Kate." Then he closed his eyes and allowed himself the pleasure of kissing her.

Even better, she kissed him back. Silken skin brushed against his neck as she wound both arms around him. Her mouth flowered under his, inviting him inside. The innocence of a young girl had been replaced by the knowledge of a woman.

And yet there was something achingly familiar about kissing Kate, as if his lips had instant recall of her velvet softness and her unique taste, a combination of sweet and tart that had driven him crazy at eighteen. With great effort he'd resisted making love to her then. He could see no reason to resist now.

He tunneled his fingers through her hair so he could tilt back her head and deepen the kiss. Her body called to him, and in a moment he'd give in to the temptation to pull her close. His groin tightened as lust heated his blood and pumped it all south. Soon his brain would surrender all control to his cock.

A crash coming from the floor above them was only a small blip on his sensual radar.

But Kate pulled away and glanced to the top of the refrigerator, which was now catless. "Darwin." She was out of Jon's arms and leaving the kitchen before he'd regained mental functioning. Eventually he realized he should probably go see what the problem was. Luckily, he hadn't started cooking his chopped ingredients yet and the stove was still off. He walked out of the kitchen.

Kate's footsteps thumped rapidly overhead. "Darwin, come back here! Bad kitty! Give me that!"

A silver and black streak raced down the stairs and turned the corner, headed for the kitchen. The cat had something in his mouth, but Jon couldn't tell what it was.

Kate clamored down after him. "I'm sorry, Jon." She spun around on the newel post at the foot of the stairs and dashed after the cat. "He dumped your shaving kit on the floor."

Jon followed her. "So what's he got in his mouth?"

"I'm not sure," she called over her shoulder. "But I'll get it back."

By the time Jon arrived in the kitchen, Darwin had leaped back onto the top of the refrigerator. His paws closed protectively over whatever treasure he'd snatched from Jon's shaving kit. The cat gazed down at them, sphinxlike. Jon could swear those blue eyes glowed with devilment.

Kate pulled a wooden step stool over to the refrigerator and hopped on it so she could reach the cat. "That was not nice, Darwin." She reached under his paws and pulled out a shiny packet.

The cat tried to grab it back, but she held it out of reach as she climbed down from the stool. Then she turned around and offered the packet to Jon, her expression giving nothing away. "Here it is. You'll have to check it over to make sure he hasn't bitten through the package and compromised the contents."

From the moment Jon had glimpsed the packet, he'd been scrambling for a graceful way to handle the situation. He always kept condoms in his shaving kit because . . . well, a guy could never predict the future. But he hadn't purposely brought them on this trip. In point of fact, this was the one trip during the year when he had no intention of using them.

Kate shook the condom packet so it made a crinkly, flapping sound. "Do you want it back?"

"Yeah, okay." He took the package and looked it over. No holes. He shoved it in his pocket. "Look, I know what you must be thinking."

She crossed her arms over her breasts. "I doubt it, but I'll be happy to tell you. I'm thinking that Darwin shouldn't have dumped your shaving kit, but now that he has, I'm looking upon it as the cat's doing us both a favor."

If she'd been laughing as she said that, he would have taken heart. She could be thankful the cat had

saved them a trip upstairs for birth control. But he
didn't think that was her take on the situation.

He cleared his throat. "And that would be because?"

"Because it reminds me that in your world a person
carries condoms the way in my world a person carries
antiseptic cream and bandages. I just spent months ca-
noeing down the Amazon, and I didn't pack a single
condom. But I stocked up on antiseptics and bandages
because I was much more likely to get a cut or scrape
than to have sex. Obviously for you the situation is
reversed."

Sometime soon he'd love to ask her about her Amazon trip, but now wasn't optimal. First he had to do
some damage control. "I didn't come here expecting
to have sex."

"I'm relieved to hear it since Maggie never mentioned that as part of the hostessing duties."

If only she'd uncross her arms and stop looking
so . . . so . . . adorably miffed. Damn, he still wanted
her. The cat had thrown a spanner into the works, but
as far as he was concerned that only meant a delay, not
a complete derailment.

He took a deep breath. "As I said, I had no plans to
have sex on this trip."

"Which begs the question as to why you arrived
armed with—how many condoms do you have?"

"I don't know. I don't keep an exact count. But before you start thinking that I—"

"Have designs on the women of Bisbee?" She un-
crossed her arms and began waving them in the air.
"That makes no sense, either. You're supposed to be

avoiding the locals, not trying to lure them into your bed."

"For the last time, I don't come to Bisbee looking for sex, okay? It's not part of the program."

"Then why bring a boatload of condoms?"

"Apparently you know exactly how many condoms I have—a boatload. Actually, it's a shipload if you count the extra five hundred tucked into a secret compartment of my specially designed condom-carrying suitcase. A guy can never have too many of those little raincoats."

"You're hysterical, Ramsey. Okay, forget the exact tally. The mere presence of *any* condoms on this trip has me wondering if you just assumed I would—"

"Hold it right there, Archer." Out of patience with this dumb situation, he pointed a finger at her. "You were not the reason I came to Bisbee packing condoms. For your information, they are a permanent part of my shaving kit."

She stared at him. "I'm not sure I want to contemplate why that's the case."

"Look, I travel a lot. A *lot*. And I can't predict how my romantic life will go, or where I'll be, and if the local *pharmacia* will even be open when I need it to be."

"I see."

He had the distinct feeling he hadn't helped his cause any with that little speech. "But it's not as if I jet around the world seducing women."

She shrugged. "Couldn't prove it by me. You've been here about"—she paused to glance at the kitchen clock—"an hour, give or take, and you've already kissed me. Oh, and earlier you touched my breasts."

"Because you asked me to!"

"I *asked* you to help with the harness. I didn't—"

"I couldn't help touching your breasts, and you know it."

"Okay, forget about the breast nudge and get back to the condom issue. Let's face it: You are a big star, an Oscar nominee, and I'm sure you could have just about any woman you want by crooking your . . . whatever part of your anatomy you care to crook."

He blew out a breath. "You are not just any woman, damn it. We didn't meet each other for the first time today. We have history. And we're still attracted to each other. If you take that all into consideration, we could be in bed by now."

"Not bloody likely!"

"Oh, it's extremely likely, if I'd followed my first instinct after that whole harness incident. I decided not to push, but if I had, we'd be upstairs right now and you'd be thanking me for having the foresight to pack condoms, because obviously *you* would only be able to come up with bandages and antiseptic salve, which makes for lousy birth control!"

"You arrogant, egotistical son of a . . . of a movie star! How *dare* you assume that if you, the great Oscar nominee, had decided we'd have sex right away, we'd have sex right away? I'll have you know that you are *not* in charge of that decision."

"You're right." He gazed at her eyes flashing with dark fire, her cheeks pink with indignation, her mouth slightly open as she gasped for breath. She'd been beautiful as a teenager, but she was stunning now. "So, Kate, want to have sex with me?"

"*No!* I can't believe you even asked!"

That made him laugh. "You said you wanted to be part of the decision, but if you'd rather be thrown over my shoulder and hauled upstairs without asking, that works, too." He stepped toward her. She'd reject his advance, but only a wuss would threaten caveman tactics without making a token effort to follow through.

"You touch me and I'll sic my cat on you."

"Whoa." He held up both hands in surrender. "Not the cat. Anything but the cat. I guess I'll have to settle for a meal instead." With a wink, he turned back to the counter to continue his preparations. "Care to open some wine?"

When she didn't answer, he glanced over to find her studying him like a bug under a microscope. "What?"

"I'm thinking."

Typical. He seemed to remember that Kate was always thinking, and he'd like to point out that it wasn't always a good thing, but she was already mad at him, so he didn't want to add to her list of gripes.

He went back to cutting up a carrot. "Hey, if you don't want to indulge, that's fine, but this chicken and veggie stir-fry cries out for a good white wine. And somebody, not saying who, has tucked a nice bottle of chardonnay in the refrigerator."

"It was me. I brought it with me from Tucson, in case I decided to get an order to go some night."

"Want to save it for some other time?"

"No, of course not. I'll open it." Moments later she'd poured the chardonnay into two goblets and handed him one.

"Thanks." He touched his glass to hers and looked into her eyes. "To renewing old friendships."

She met his gaze. "To honesty."

"I'll drink to that." He took a sip of his wine and set down the glass. "Kate, I swear I didn't bring those condoms because I thought we'd end up in bed together."

"Sad to say, I believe you." She tipped her glass and drank. "It was sort of arrogant on my part to assume you'd still be interested in me."

"Oh, I don't know about that." He turned toward the stove and warmed some olive oil in a skillet. "After all, you're the one who got away."

"Ah." She leaned against the counter. "So you're curious about what you might have missed out on."

"Since we just toasted honesty, yes, I'm curious. Aren't you?" He added some minced garlic to the oil, and the kitchen began to smell really good.

"That would be only natural, wouldn't it?"

He nudged a piece of garlic into the oil with a wooden spoon and turned down the heat. "So you're saying you're curious, too?" He liked the way this conversation was going. It had legs, as they said in Hollywood.

"Well, yeah, I'll admit to wondering what it would be like."

He took his time adding chopped onions to the pan, blending them in as if the fate of the world depended on how evenly they cooked. The next few moments he'd be picking his way through a minefield. "Looks like we have a golden opportunity to find out." He glanced up from the skillet to gauge her reaction.

She was giving him that under-the-microscope look again. "Are you *sure* you didn't plan this?"

"Scout's honor."

"You were never a Scout, Ramsey."

"I'm pretty sure my grandfather was." Picking up a bowl of diced chicken, he scooped it into the skillet. "I think that makes me an honorary Scout. I'll bet they'd take me if I asked."

"Oh, I'm sure they would. I'll bet the Girl Scouts would take you, too. You could probably get an honorary membership in the DAR if you asked. You're a hot commodity on the market."

He stirred the chicken in with the garlic and onion. "Not this week. This week I'm your average Joe on vacation. And by coincidence, I meet up with the girl I dated in high school, the girl I've fantasized about having sex with but never did."

"Poor you. Surely you've found solace in the arms of some A-List beauties. It's hard to believe you've been pining for me all these years."

He scooped the veggies into the skillet. "Granted, I haven't been saving myself for you, but I doubt you've been saving yourself for me, either."

"Can't say I have."

He felt a prick of irritation, which was totally unreasonable. Of course she'd had lovers. So had he. That meant they could approach this as two experienced adults, which increased their chances of having a really good time.

Picking up his goblet, he took a fortifying swallow of the wine. "Anyway, now that I've had sex with other people, I—like you, I might add—have entertained a stray thought or two about being in bed with you."

"That doesn't mean we have to act on those thoughts."

"No, but it could be fun." He'd never discussed having sex with this amount of restraint, as if they were debating a change in weather. But his blood pumped a hell of a lot faster than it would have if he'd been talking about the chances of rain.

"What if we're disappointed?"

"That's the chance we'd take." He unscrewed the cap on a bottle of tamari sauce and poured a little of that into his stir-fry. "And if it doesn't turn out, oh, well. We're both grown-ups. We can handle a little disappointment."

"Jon Ramsey, are you propositioning me?"

"Yes, I do believe I am." He put the lid on the skillet and moved it off the burner.

"But you just got here!"

Despite his jacked-up pulse, he chuckled at that. He turned to her. Thank God the desire flooding through him was mirrored in her dark eyes. This would all sort itself out, and very soon.

"Seriously, Jon, this is too fast."

He shrugged. "Your cat brought me a condom. It seems a shame to waste that kind of effort."

"What if he'd brought you dental floss? Would you—"

"Have felt a strong urge to start flossing? I doubt it. Doesn't have quite the same appeal."

She cleared her throat. "You'll have to let me think about it."

"I don't think so, Archer." He took her glass and set it on the counter before she quite realized what he intended. "It's time to fish or cut bait."

She backed up a step. "You're supposed to be cooking."

"It's simmering."

"How long will it do that?"

He came closer, much closer. "Long enough."

Chapter 5

*K*ate's heart beat like a Brazilian jungle drum as she looked at Jon. He was dead serious. Unless she told him no, he would take her to bed. If she told him no, she might regret it for the rest of her life. But the thought of telling him yes was about to give her a heart attack.

His gaze searched hers. "If we don't do this, we'll always wonder."

"At least you're not quoting movie lines. No scriptwriter would come up with anything that un-romantic."

"Do you want me to quote movie lines?"

"No, thanks. First of all, that would be cheesy, and second of all, I'm trying to forget you're a big star who memorizes love scenes for a living."

"Then what do you want?"

She took a deep breath. "You."

"Ditto." A subtle change in his breathing was the only indication that he wasn't quite as composed as he appeared.

"Then follow me." Eagerness made her blood sing as she led him through her sitting room and into her bedroom. She took the time to close the French doors to keep Darwin on the other side of them. She might be a little scared, a little nervous, but she was a lot aroused. And she was at least as curious as he was.

He stopped next to the king-sized four-poster and faced her. "Listen, if you want a more romantic approach, I can do that."

"Too late. You've already ruined that possibility with the 'fish or cut bait' line." She might sound like a smart-ass, but inside she was quivering with anticipation.

His glance traveled from her feet to the top of her head. "Nothing's ruined, especially if you let me undress you."

"Shorts, a T-shirt, and flip-flops? Where's the challenge in that?"

His lazy smile curled her bare toes. "The challenge is to make the ordinary erotic."

"Ha." Her pulse jumped wildly as she sat on the bed and leaned back on her elbows. "This outfit is serviceable, but there ain't no way it's erotic." *Prove me wrong.*

"We'll see about that." Keeping his gaze locked with hers, he sank to his knees, lifted her foot, and slowly slid off her flip-flop.

That one gesture drenched her panties. By the time he'd eased off the second flip-flop and leaned down to kiss her toes, she was reconsidering her challenge. When he spread her knees and licked the inside of each one, she was truly lost. She appeared to be in the hands of a master of seduction.

And she'd never last through this assault. She pictured the embarrassment of having an orgasm while he was caressing her thighs, before he'd even arrived at the main event.

She sat up and reached for the hem of her T-shirt. "You win. This outfit is freaking erotic, and I want it off."

He circled her wrists with strong fingers and looked into her eyes. "Not yet. This moment has been years in the making. We're not rushing it."

"What if I want to rush it?" She glared back at him.

"Reconsider." Rising to his feet, he urged her backward until she was lying on the bed, her legs dangling over the edge. Then he followed her down, pinning her there, stretching her arms over her head. "Reconsider, Kate."

Then he kissed her, plundering her mouth with a confidence that hadn't existed before they'd made this decision to finally have each other. That confident kiss ignited a frenzy of wanting that stunned her with its intensity.

They were both fully clothed except that he'd taken off her flip-flops, and their unnecessary clothes drove her crazy. She felt him—aroused and covered with way too much material—as he pressed between her thighs. What were they waiting for? She wanted him now, *now*, but he seemed to have other ideas.

Grasping both of her wrists in one hand, he used the other to slide beneath her back and unhook her bra. She arched upward, wanting that item gone perhaps even more than he did. Once he'd unfastened it, he shifted so he could stroke her breasts. Once again, she was sure that would make her come. She would have told him so, but he was keeping her mouth very busy.

As the spiraling tension threatened to overwhelm her, he slowed his practiced caress and eased his mouth from hers. Gratifyingly, he was struggling for breath as much as she was. "I wanted to take longer, but I can't."

"Thank God. I'm dying here."

His chuckle was low and dark with sensuality. "Allow me."

He was deft; she'd give him that. He had his hand inside her panties before she'd drawn another ragged breath. And then . . . oh, sweetness. He knew exactly what she needed and how she needed it.

"Jon, I'm going to . . ."

"That's the idea." His voice was thick with passion. "Then you'll get to do it again in a minute." His clever fingers brought her to the gates of Nirvana and flung them wide-open.

She cried out as waves of release rolled through her with enough impact to leave her gasping in their wake. She was still vibrating with pleasure as he stripped off her clothes. She was vaguely aware that he'd done away with his, too. She heard the snap of latex that meant he'd rolled on a condom.

Standing next to the bed, his knees braced against the side of the mattress, he cradled her hips in his hands and lifted her up. She wrapped her legs around his waist and abandoned herself completely to his control. His green eyes filled with intensity as he thrust deep.

He groaned softly. "That's a good start."

"Mm." She was too blissed out to form actual words. Nothing in her sexual past had prepared her for this incredible feeling of connection. Through eyes glazed with passion she looked up. There, poised above her, was the kind of man most women only dreamed of having.

His biceps bulged as he held her in midair, open to his every whim. His chest muscles flexed and his abs contracted as he began a steady rhythm. His sun-bleached hair fell carelessly over his forehead and quivered with each stroke.

All the while he watched her with those hot green eyes. "Ah, Kate," he murmured. "You're so beautiful."

His words flowed over her, making her feel like the most desired woman in the universe. Perhaps he made all women feel that way. Perhaps that was his gift, his talent.

She could believe it. He knew exactly what to do with that potent equipment of his. As he unerringly found her G-spot, her climax drew near once again.

His jaw clenched. "Kate?"

Her response was a gasp that sounded a little bit like yes. He must have understood, because he drove home as she erupted in a fiery orgasm that burned away everything but the wonder of this moment.

With a shudder, he came, his eyes closing at last, his groan of completion vibrating in the air. Slowly, keeping the connection between them, he lowered himself to the mattress.

Resting his cheek against her shoulder, he sighed. "Incredible."

Kate drew a shaky breath. "You can say that again."

"Incredible." There was a definite smile in his voice. Slowly he relaxed against her as they lay together in silence. "Give me a minute. I really am going to feed you."

"All this and food, too?"

He kissed her shoulder. "You'd better believe it. Great sex works up an appetite."

Great sex. She'd take that compliment. After all, he'd been to bed with famous movie stars, so he might have a different yardstick from hers. She'd call this the best sex she'd ever had in her life, but that was just her. No matter what happened between them this week, she'd try to keep some kind of perspective on it.

In a sensual daze, Jon pulled on his shorts and walked into the kitchen to make good on his promise to provide food for them. If he'd been curious about whether sex with Kate would be any good, that question had been well and truly answered. Her response was off the charts, and he was a lucky dog to have the next week with her.

He turned the burner on low and set the skillet on it. The veggies would be a little overcooked, but if he and Kate had plenty of wine, it wouldn't matter. Hell, it wouldn't matter anyway, if she felt as terrific as he did right now.

"Smells wonderful." She padded into the kitchen barefoot, although she'd put on her shorts and shirt.

"So do you." Turning away from the stove, he drew her into his arms, which was when he determined that she'd decided against a bra. He liked the way she thought. "What's the perfume you're wearing these days?"

"It's called *Peaches and Cream*. One of those new natural scents made with essential oils."

"Nice." He leaned down to get a good whiff, which of course ended up with him kissing her. As his lips met hers, he promised himself that after one kiss, he'd keep his hands off her until after they'd eaten a decent meal.

Yeah, right. Once she arched into him, that promise disappeared along with every ounce of his willpower. She tasted good, smelled good, felt good. He wondered how he'd survived this long without her.

While he used his tongue to suggest how they might employ themselves later on, he pulled her in so tight that a thief wielding a credit card wouldn't have been able to slide it between them. He moaned at the sweet crush of her breasts and the way her bottom fit his cupped hands.

Judging from her whimpers and the way she squirmed against him, she was having at least as good a time as he was. With dinner on the stove, kissing her was such a mistake, such a—ah, when she rubbed against him right *there*, and stuck her hands in the back pockets of his shorts so they could wiggle even closer together, then—

"Smthin's brnin."

He couldn't understand her because she was muttering between kisses, and those kisses were driving him insane.

"Smthin's brnin."

He lifted his mouth a fraction from hers and tried to catch his breath. "What?"

"Something's burning."

At last the acrid odor of scorched food penetrated her fresh-peach scent. "Shit!" Abandoning what was fast becoming one of his top ten kisses of all time, he whirled toward the stove, where smoke crept out from under the lid of the skillet. "Damn it!"

Amazingly, he remembered to grab a pot holder before seizing the skillet handle. Moving the skillet to an unheated burner, he cursed under his breath as he took off the lid. "So much for my cooking skills."

She laughed softly. "You were busy demonstrating one of your other skills."

"A more talented man would be able to handle both at once." He picked up a wooden spoon and poked at the food. "I might be able to salvage something from this mess." He glanced over at her and couldn't believe how beautiful she looked with her hair mussed, her eyes dark with passion, and her lips parted as if she wanted to start it all again. But if they did, this food would be beyond redemption.

Turning back to the skillet, he used the spoon to assess the damage. "There's a scorched layer on the bottom, but I can probably dish out the rest. Let's eat before we grow weak from lack of food."

"I'll get plates."

They worked well together and were soon seated in the Hummingbird Inn's modest dining room, each with a plate of food, a fork and napkin, and more wine.

He set his plate at the end of the rectangular table, and after joking about taking the chair at the opposite end, she put her plate down on his right.

He had to ask. "Did you do that because you remembered I'm left-handed?"

"To be honest, I'd forgotten, but when I watched you cook, I remembered."

"Thanks for sitting there." He walked around and pulled out her chair. "It means we won't bang into each other all the time."

She smiled over her shoulder as she slid gracefully into her seat. "That sounds kind of fun."

"Yeah, it does." He leaned down and nuzzled her neck. "You know what? Food's overrated. Let's forget dinner."

"No." Laughing, she shoved him gently away. "You worked hard to fix this meal, and we really should eat."

"Spoilsport." He returned to his seat.

"I'm just thinking of your health. Thanks for holding my chair, by the way. I see your grandfather's deportment lessons stuck."

"I couldn't forget them if I tried. He was anal about manners. Still is." As if to prove the point, he unfolded his napkin and put it on his lap.

"How's your grandfather doing?"

Jon pictured his very proper, very British grandfather and smiled. "Slowing down a little, but gets up and dresses in a three-piece suit every day of the year. Mom's deeply involved with all her charities. They both seem happy."

"Good."

He hesitated, not sure how to continue the conversational tennis match, but the manners his grandfather had drilled into him dictated that he mention her parents. "I was . . . sorry to hear about your dad."

She nodded without looking at him. "It was sad, but my sisters and I hardly ever saw him. He spent all his time carousing down in Puerta Vallarta and every so often a tabloid would do another story on his antics, so it was . . kind of a reprieve from all that. I think for Mom, too. She seems more settled."

"Makes sense." He was glad to leave that charged topic as he gestured toward her plate. "Might as well dig in. I'd say this meal peaked a long time ago, but if you drink enough wine, it'll probably taste okay."

"Hey, if this doesn't work out, there's always PB and J. That's what I mostly ate in Brazil." Kate picked up her fork and took a bite.

He waited with far too much anticipation for her verdict.

She swallowed. "Not bad, Ramsey. Under the challenging circumstances, not bad at all."

"Thanks." Being pleased that she liked his cooking was dumb on his part. It shouldn't make any difference to him, but . . . it did. He refilled their glasses. "So what were you doing in the jungles of Brazil?"

"I found a new monkey."

"Hey! We need to toast that." He lifted his glass.

Her laugh had a happy, carefree lilt to it. "You know, you're absolutely right. I don't think I ever did properly celebrate, but finding a new species of capuchin definitely deserves a toast. To increasing our knowledge of the natural world." She touched her glass to his before taking a long swallow.

He watched her slender throat move as she drank the wine and wanted to put his lips there. Now that he'd discovered the wonder of a naked Kate, he wanted to put his lips everywhere. He needed to pace himself, though, and he was interested in this part of her life, something he knew nothing about. "So tell me about your new monkey. Is it cute? Is it ugly?"

"Very cute. Looks kind of like an organ-grinder's monkey. And smart. Capuchins are the smartest monkeys in the New World. It took us a while to track down the colony, which means they're good at concealment, and—" She glanced at him with an apologetic smile. "Sorry. I tend to get carried away."

"Don't apologize. I want to hear about your discovery."

She sipped her wine and studied him. "I think you're humoring me, but I love talking about this stuff."

"So talk to me." He poured the last of the wine into her glass.

"All right. You asked for it." She launched into a narrative of her adventures leading up to the moment when she'd first suspected she'd found something no one else had discovered.

She had a gift for vivid description, but he was also mesmerized by her obvious love of the subject. With her animated presentation and her knowledge of primates she could hit the talk-show circuit, but with her aversion to celebrity of any kind he could imagine how she'd react to that suggestion.

"So now I have to write up my findings and see what money I can get for a return trip. I'm sure I won't be able to stay as long, but that's okay, because now I have Darwin to think about."

"Where is he, anyway?"

"Curled up on the chair to your left."

Jon peered over the table to find Darwin asleep on

the cushioned chair. "Now that I've heard this story, I'm surprised you wanted a cat for a pet," he said. "Why not a monkey?"

She stared at him in horror. "For a pet? God, no. They belong in their native habitat. I'm not the least in favor of domesticating them."

"There goes my idea for a Christmas present. Now I have no idea what to get you. I suppose a boa constrictor is out, too."

She smiled at him. "You're a good guy, Jon."

"I am not. Don't you dare pin that label on me. Go with your first instinct and stick with the arrogant and conceited evaluation."

"Sometimes you are that, too, but you get credit for sitting here for a good thirty minutes while I blathered on. You didn't yawn once."

"Trust me, I wasn't bored. I'm impressed that you put up with the snakes and the bugs and the big scary crocodiles. But you forgot to mention the natives with the poisoned darts. When did they attack?"

"You've watched too many movies."

"Or been on the Jungle Cruise one too many times as a kid. That's about the level of realism I can handle. I'm not a huge fan of giant snakes, Chihuahua-sized bugs, and crocs that can swallow a canoe whole."

She laughed. "I'll take them over the paparazzi any day."

He twirled his wineglass by the stem, unsure whether to bring up what might still be a sore subject. But he'd always wanted a private moment to apologize, and this appeared to be it. "I felt horrible about what happened at the prom."

"It was a long time ago"—she shrugged—"and it taught me to be more careful about attracting unwanted attention."

"Speaking of that, with this kind of discovery, what if you accidentally get famous like Jane Goodall or Dian Fossey?"

"Nah." She shook her head and picked up her wineglass. "I'd have to write a book or become a spokesperson for saving the monkeys. I'd help with such a project, but I'd stay in the background." Draining the last of her wine, she set the glass down and pushed back her chair. "You cooked the meal, plus you listened to me talk about my new monkey, so I'm going to wash the dishes."

"I hope not. I hope you're planning to stack them in the dishwasher."

"Well, yeah." She picked up his plate and piled it on top of hers before taking them into the kitchen. "But somebody has to tackle that skillet."

He picked up both wineglasses and followed her. "My suggestion? Toss it and buy another one. I'll gladly pay not to have to scrub that mess."

She turned to stare at him. "Throw out a perfectly good skillet because there's some food baked on the bottom?"

"It's not just baked on. It's welded on. You'd have to sandblast that crud off there. Pitch it."

"No."

"I mean it, Kate. I feel responsible for that disaster. I plan to take that responsibility seriously."

"By throwing it in the Dumpster?" She put the plates

beside the sink. Then she picked up the skillet. "That's wasteful. I can . . ." She glanced down and wrinkled her nose. "It is disgusting, isn't it?"

"Told you."

"But I'm still going to clean it."

He grabbed hold of it. "No, you're not. Give it to me. I'll make it disappear."

She clutched the handle and wrestled it back. "You will not. I'll bet Maggie loves this skillet. I'll bet she'd be horrified to come home and find it gone."

He managed to get his hands on it again. "I'll buy her one twice as good." He tried to tug it free, but he didn't want to be so rough that he hurt her. "Give me the damned thing, Kate."

She gave him a mutinous glare. "No."

"I won't have you wasting your time." He pulled harder.

"I won't have you wasting precious resources." She dragged it back toward her.

Naturally, because he was still holding tight to the skillet, he ended up very close to her, too—within kissing distance, in fact. Their faces were inches apart and their arms were tangled up together as they wrestled over the skillet.

He met her angry gaze. "You are a stubborn woman."

"Look who's talking."

"I may be a lot of things, but I'm not a stubborn woman."

Her lips twitched. "You know what I meant."

"But I'm going to make you laugh."

"No, you're not."

"I am. You're picturing me in drag right this minute, aren't you?"

"No, I'm not! I'm . . ." She gave up and dissolved into giggles. "Oh, Jon. No fair."

"I know." He took the skillet from her unresisting grip and slid it onto the counter. Then he pulled her into his arms. "Just so you know, I recycle."

She was still laughing when he kissed her, which made access so much easier. He should make a new kissing rule—always catch a woman when she's laughing. She'll be in a good mood and her mouth will be open.

Chapter 6

With Jon kissing her like that, Kate couldn't concentrate very well on saving Maggie's skillet.

"Leave everything," Jon murmured between kisses. "Come upstairs with me."

Kate had a tough time getting a word in edgewise, but eventually she managed. "The plates will be harder to clean in the morning."

"We can throw them—"

She clapped a hand over his mouth. "You are so wasteful!"

"Mm-mm." He shook his head and ran his tongue over her palm, which reminded her of where else she'd like to feel that tongue. His voice was muffled by her hand pressing against his mouth, but she was able to understand the single word of explanation he offered—*priorities*. After uttering that single word, he commenced licking her hand again.

She was melting fast and needed a quick compromise. "We'll let everything soak." And speaking of soaked, that described her underwear, which meant for the second time in one night she'd have to put on a fresh pair.

She removed her damp hand, which tingled where

he'd been circling it with his tongue. "Do we have a deal?"

"You bet." Releasing her, he turned and ran water in the sink. "Feel free to go upstairs and rummage around in my shaving kit. Not that I'm impatient or anything."

Laughing, she hurried out of the kitchen and up the stairs. She hadn't felt this carefree with a man since . . . Come to think of it, she'd never felt this carefree. There was something to be said for hiding away from the world for a week.

The contents of Jon's shaving kit lay scattered over the bathroom floor, evidence of Darwin's little stunt. The scent of aftershave hung in the air, but she found the bottle—an expensive label, of course—lying on the floor unbroken. Scooping everything back into the zippered case, she set it on the counter, plucked out a condom, and turned to find Jon leaning in the bathroom doorway.

He arched an eyebrow. "Only one? Is that your opinion of my sexual stamina?"

Oh, baby. She tried to sound as nonchalant as he did, but still her words came out sounding breathy and excited. "I thought you'd be tired. It's been a long day."

"Yes, but we have a long night ahead of us. Bring a handful."

"*A handful?* Are you serious?"

"No, but at least bring two." He winked at her. "Just in case."

She grabbed another foil packet. When she looked up, Jon was holding out his hand.

"Come play," he murmured. When she put her hand

in his, he interlaced their fingers and paused to gaze into her eyes. "Thank you."

"For what?"

"For putting aside whatever plans you had for this week so that we could . . . be together like this."

She smiled. "You're welcome. So far it's been pure torture."

"Then come into my bedroom." He tugged on her hand. "I want to torture you some more."

"Not so fast." She put up a token resistance.

He frowned. "Is something wrong?"

"Only that you're a bossy sort of guy who likes to be in charge all the time. I realize you're an Oscar nominee and all, but your reign is over. It's my turn to torture you."

His gaze heated. "Yeah?"

She drew close enough to stroke him through his shorts. "Yeah."

"Mm." He ran a finger down her cheek. "I suppose you're going to make me beg for mercy."

She cupped his family jewels. "That's the idea."

"Then let's get this party started."

As they walked into his darkened bedroom, she wondered if he'd had lovers who were more accomplished at this than she was. But within moments she had him where she wanted him, naked and lying on his back on the bed. At that point she forgot to worry about other women. This was one hell of a man, and she planned to relish every minute of making him squirm with desire.

She stripped off her own clothes so she could use her breasts and thighs to tease him even more. But mostly she used her mouth, and she measured her success by the volume of his moans and his increasingly rapid breathing.

Touching him was like running her hands over a living sculpture. No body double for this guy. He was pure sensual delight from head to toe and in the middle— especially in the middle. When she availed herself of the wonders centered there, his muscles tensed.

He spoke through clenched teeth. "If you keep that up, we won't need any of those little raincoats."

She eased up on her ministrations. "Your choice, big boy."

"Much as I love this . . ." He took a shaky breath. "I love it even more when I'm . . . when we're . . ."

Leaning forward, she whispered a very graphic Anglo-Saxon word in his ear.

"Uh-huh. That."

Talking dirty was a new adventure for her, and she discovered it packed a wallop. One explicit suggestion, and she was ready to mount up and ride. "Give me a sec."

She'd left the condoms strategically placed on the bedside table, and she grabbed a crinkly packet. Although she'd never tackled this chore, necessity proved to be the mother of invention. She was amazingly quick, and Jon seemed touchingly grateful.

As she straddled him and braced her arms against his impressive shoulders, he bracketed her waist with both hands.

"I want you so much it hurts. Come to me, Kate." Urging her down, he groaned with pleasure. "That's . . . perfect."

"Well said." A moonbeam spilling through the window was all the light they had, but it was enough for her to see the glitter of desire in his eyes. He might have bedded countless women more polished than she, but at this very moment, she was the one he wanted.

As for her, this ultimate connection felt like coming home. She didn't plan to analyze that sensation too closely, but she'd be hard-pressed to remember a time when sex had felt this good, this right.

Being in charge meant she could set the pace, so she started out slow, savoring every motion as she lifted her hips and eased them back down.

He cradled her breasts in both hands. "Lean over," he murmured.

She complied, and he drew her nipple into his mouth. Oh, this was good. This was very, very . . . Her orgasm took her completely by surprise. One moment she was riding him gently, and the next she was flying off into space, propelled by a climax that whirled through her.

Jon urged her on until a second climax hovered near. She reached it at the same instant Jon arched upward, his body quivering in reaction. She hung on for dear life, gripping his shoulders as their combined tremors shook her to the core of her being. Every cell in her body seemed to be vibrating with joy.

At last she slumped forward, boneless with pleasure. "Oh, Jon."

"I'm here." He held her close. "I'm here, Kate."

The thought warmed her for many long minutes, but as her euphoria faded, a thought she didn't want to have nudged its way in and shoved aside her bubble of happiness. He was here now, but a week from now he'd be gone.

Even though the second condom never came into play, Jon woke up in a fantastic mood. He was a little disappointed that Kate wasn't still in bed with him, but he couldn't blame her. He'd slept in, exhausted from weeks of hard work topped off with amazing sex.

Once his feet hit the floor, he was wide-awake and ready to spend the day with Kate. He smelled coffee brewing, so she might not be quite as helpless in the kitchen as she pretended. He could hardly wait to see her, to share a cup of coffee with her, to coax her back to bed.

He took the shortest shower in history and was lucky he didn't nick himself shaving because he was more interested in speed than accuracy. The week that had once seemed like a big chunk of time was shrinking rapidly in his mind. He didn't want to waste a minute on routine chores when he could be with Kate instead.

Wearing shorts and a T-shirt but dispensing with shoes, he headed downstairs toward the kitchen. He heard water running, so he could guess what she was up to. He'd bet good money she was scrubbing the damned skillet.

Her back was to him, giving him an enticing view of soft gray exercise shorts that hugged her rear and a midriff-skimming T-shirt in baby blue. Her hair was loose and slightly damp, as if she'd just washed it, and she was also barefoot.

Darwin crouched at his food bowl, munching away,

but Jon didn't waste time focusing on the cat. He was all about Kate. The scrubbing motion made her bottom wiggle, which was not a motion designed to help him keep his cool. He wanted her desperately, but the skillet, if it was to be scrubbed, was his job.

He most definitely didn't want to squander potential Kate time cleaning a skillet. "You do *not* have to do that." Marching into the kitchen, he pulled the skillet out of her hands so fast that water slopped onto the counter and the kitchen floor.

"Jon, wait!"

He wasn't about to wait. Storming out of the kitchen door, he galloped down the steps, dripping soapy water the whole way. The Hummingbird Inn had its own private Dumpster in the back of the lot, and he made for it. His feet slid on the dew-slick grass Maggie had carefully cultivated in the backyard.

"You agreed we'd put it in to soak!" She charged after him. "That meant you were willing to try and save it!"

"I had a moment of insanity brought on by raging lust." Lifting the black lid of the Dumpster, he threw the offending skillet inside where it clattered against the metal interior.

"I can't believe you did that."

He turned to find her standing in the grass of the backyard, her arms crossed under her breasts, her expression stormy.

He waggled a finger at her. "Don't you dare go Dumpster diving to get it when I'm not looking. Don't you dare."

"You are not the boss of me, Jon Ramsey. You may

have women everywhere falling at your feet, but you are not the boss of me."

"Women don't fall at my feet. They grab at my clothes"—he grinned—"which you must admit you have done."

She lifted her chin. "Maybe I have, but that doesn't give you dominion over me or over Maggie's skillet."

He didn't think she'd be flattered if he told her she looked exactly like her six-year-old self taking a stand against taunts on the playground. The other kids had heard their parents talking about the Archers making scenes in public and they were only parroting what they'd heard, but Kate had obviously been wounded by it.

She hadn't cowered, though. She'd met their jeers with the same defiance he saw now. He'd waded in to help her, which was when he'd decided that someday they would get married. It had made sense to his first-grade self.

"All right," he said. "Then let me, as a valued guest of the Hummingbird Inn, ask you to leave that skillet where it belongs in the Dumpster."

"I almost had it cleaned up."

"I saw plenty of black goop when I sent it to its final reward. Don't turn this into a battle of wills, Kate. It's a skillet."

"Maggie's favorite skillet."

He wondered how such a stubborn female could look so appealing, but as she stood in the dew-soaked grass of the backyard, she reminded him of a nymph out of some fairy tale. "You don't know it was her favorite."

"I'm sure she told me so."

"I'm sure she didn't. You're pulling that tidbit of information right out of your cute little—by the way, did you mean to let Darwin out?" He saw the cat poised on the back stoop, observing the proceedings.

She spun around. "He's out? Omigod, he's out."

"Don't panic. Stay calm."

"But I promised Esmeralda he wouldn't ever get out unless he was wearing his leash, and now he's out. It's not safe for a cat outside, especially here where there are coyotes and snakes. That back screen doesn't shut tight. He must have nudged it open."

"He's only on the back stoop." Jon crept forward. "He's . . . Whoops, now he's headed down the steps."

"I'll get him." Her bare feet slipped on the wet grass and she went down. "Don't let him get past you!"

Easier said than done. Jon had never tried to out-guess a cat. Jon went left; the cat went right, bounding through the grass in obvious delight. Jon circled warily, keeping Darwin in sight as the cat discovered a grasshopper and went leaping after it.

Kate got to her feet, her gaze fixed on the cat as she wiped bits of grass from her shirt. "Okay, Jon, if you can keep him from going off into the woods, I'll make sure he doesn't head out front."

"Right." Jon went into a baseball player's crouch. "We can do this."

"He's only one little cat." Kate edged slowly up behind Darwin as Jon moved in closer.

The grasshopper did its part. Darwin seemed fascinated by the hopping insect and hunkered down in the grass, ready to pounce.

"We have to decide who's going to get him," Jon said.

"I will." Kate flexed her fingers.

"Then I'll be backup in case you miss."

"Good plan. Okay, on three. One, two, *three.*" Kate made a grab for the cat, but Darwin slipped easily out of her grasp.

Jon had one second to make a dive for him. He got a handful of cat and held on. "Kate!"

A second later Kate wrapped both hands around the squirming body. "Got him."

"You're sure?" Jon had either a leg or the tail. Tail. It wasn't the most humane place to hold on, but he wasn't letting go until he knew for certain Kate had control of the cat.

"I'm sure. Thanks, Jon." She sat back on her haunches and held Darwin in her arms. The cat squirmed and protested, but she started scratching under his chin and eventually he settled down.

Jon watched her caress the cat and was jealous as hell. He wanted to be petted like that, although he'd prefer she use that caress on a different area of his body.

He plopped down on the grass, not caring if it soaked his shorts, just content to look at her. "You're welcome."

"I probably shouldn't have adopted this cat right now."

"So why did you?"

"Esmeralda's one hell of a saleswoman. She made me think if I didn't take Darwin immediately, I might never see him again."

"Look, I'm not saying he isn't appealing with his blue eyes, and his fur is really soft, but . . ." He shrugged. "I mean, there are a lot of cats out there. You wouldn't have had any trouble finding another one."

She continued to rub behind Darwin's ears, and his purr grew louder. "That's totally logical, but something besides logic was going on yesterday. I can't explain it, but I had the feeling if I didn't adopt this very cat, I would be making a huge mistake."

"A huge mistake for him, obviously. He's in heaven."

"Yeah, but I'll bet he's not used to being inside so much. Esmeralda said she used to walk him all the time. I should take him out this morning."

"I'll go with you." The words were out before Jon gave himself time to think it through.

"Are you sure that's a good idea? We could stay away from the main part of town, but I can't guarantee that someone wouldn't notice us, or rather, you. Especially if we're walking a cat."

He'd offered to go with her, and it suddenly seemed important that he prove he could do something simple and ordinary this week. Taking a stroll with Kate would be fun. He didn't like the idea of her going out by herself while he stayed behind on the slight chance he'd be spotted.

"Nobody expects to see me here," he said. "You know how it is—you catch a glimpse of somebody you think might be famous, but if it's not where you'd expect them, you doubt yourself. I'll wear a baseball cap and shades. It'll be fine."

Chapter 7

Kate wasn't so sure it would be fine. But Jon seemed determined to take this walk with her and Darwin, so after he made them a breakfast of omelets, coffee, and toast, she harnessed up the cat and led the way out the door.

Jon followed her down the steps. "This is great. Not too hot yet, a few clouds gathering to make the sky look more interesting. Maybe it'll rain this afternoon."

"Maybe." While Darwin found a small patch of wild grass to munch on, Kate checked the area for any suspicious people or vehicles. She didn't notice anything unusual. Cars seldom came up this far unless they were looking specifically for the Hummingbird Inn, and not many people walked up this way, either. The sidewalk ended right past the B and B.

"I want to make love to you under that tin roof while it's raining."

That suggestion pushed the threat of paparazzi straight out of Kate's head. She glanced at Jon and enjoyed the delicious sizzle as they smiled at each other.

He'd done his best to look inconspicuous, but she thought it was a lost cause. Or maybe she was predisposed to see the hot movie star hiding behind shades and a Dodgers baseball cap. His white T-shirt had no logo on it, but Jon didn't need designer clothes to stand out. He never had.

He leaned over and gave her a quick kiss on the mouth. "Come on. We need to start walking before I change my mind and haul you back inside."

"Okeydoke." Life didn't get any better than standing in the morning sunshine listening to Jon make sexy promises that would become reality in the hours and days ahead. Kate felt like dancing, and she might have except that she had Darwin on a leash, and she didn't think he'd appreciate having her cavort around.

"Let's go this way." Jon started down the hill.

"That's toward town. If we go the other way, then you'll have less chance of being recognized."

Jon glanced in the other direction. "But there's no sidewalk in that direction, and the edge of the pavement's eroded from the rain. This way will be fine." He motioned her forward. "I'll prove to you that nobody will take a second look. I've done this before and gotten away with it."

"Yes, but I doubt you were with a woman walking a cat."

"Ah, I'll bet that's nothing in Bisbee. Maggie's told me all sorts of strange stories about the people here, both living and dead. You have ghosts in this town, for God's sake. Nobody will pay attention to a cat on a leash."

"I hope you're right." Kate reluctantly joined him on his trek down the hill. Their progress was slow because Darwin wanted to stop and smell everything. He also tried to walk up the sidewalk of each house they passed, as if he had every intention of visiting all the neighbors.

At first Kate imagined those same neighbors would surely be peering out their windows and spot the famous Jon Ramsey going down the sidewalk. But she was being paranoid. And after they passed a few people who barely glanced at them, she realized Jon had described the situation accurately. People didn't expect to see him here, so they didn't give him a second glance.

"It's kind of nice taking an animal for a walk," Jon said. "I haven't had much opportunity to do that."

"Not even as a kid?"

"You remember, Mom's allergic. Now I could get a dog, I guess. I'd have to buy a bigger place with lots of acreage to let it run around. But I'm gone so much, and taking a dog on location doesn't always work out well."

"It'd be easier to take a cat."

He nodded. "Could be. Although when I go out of the country, there's no pet I could take. In the end, I'm afraid my dog, or my cat, or my hamster would bond more with whomever I hired as a pet-sitter than with me. That's not right."

"You'd want a hamster?"

He flashed that famous grin. "Probably not."

"Because a manly Oscar nominee couldn't have a cute little hamster as a pet?"

His grin widened. "No, because the squeak of the exercise wheel would drive me batshit crazy."

"Better stop smiling like that."

"Why?"

"Because a teenage girl just turned onto this street and is walking toward us. Your smile is one of a kind."

"You're paranoid, you know that?"

"Sometimes paranoia is a good thing. I'm telling you, wipe that grin off your face before she gets close enough to see it. Oh, by the way, we're passing the shelter where I got Darwin."

Jon glanced at the house. "That's a very pink paint job. I guess it goes with the Cupid Cats theme, huh?"

"That's my guess."

"Have you noticed Darwin has this spot on his right haunch that looks exactly like a heart?"

"I have. And I've wondered if it's natural or if Esmeralda gave him a dye job. She's just strange enough that she might have. Listen, maybe we should turn around before we pass that girl."

Jon laughed. "Take it easy. It will attract more attention if we hang a U-turn and hotfoot it in the other direction. Just act normal."

Kate took a slow breath and let it out. She probably was overreacting. One skinny teenager with dark curly hair did not equate to a mob of camera-wielding fans and media types.

The teenager—dressed in shorts, a halter top, and sandals—was only about ten yards away now. Kate noticed that she was talking on her cell phone, so maybe they could pass by her without being noticed.

Except the girl stopped and pointed to Darwin. "That is adorable," she said into her phone. "Megan, you should see this. A lady is walking a cat on a leash! Wait—I'll show you."

Before Kate could react, the girl had pointed her camera phone at Darwin and snapped a picture. Fortunately, all her attention was focused on the cat.

The girl smiled as she was about to pass them. "That's so cute. I had to show my friend. You don't mind, do you?"

"It's fine," Kate said. She hoped Jon would have the good sense to keep his mouth shut. So far, so good.

Darwin, however, wasn't nearly so savvy. The darned cat stopped in the middle of the sidewalk, gazed up at the girl, and meowed as if making his bid to be fawned over.

"And he has blue eyes!" The girl crouched down to pet a loudly purring and happily prancing Darwin. "Megan, his eyes are the same blue as that turquoise necklace Jared gave you for your birthday. And there's turquoise in the harness, too."

Kate's jaw clenched. "You know what? We really should be going. Come along, Darwin."

The girl stood. "Thanks for letting me pet him. He's really soft." Then she glanced at Kate and Jon. "Nice to meet you. I'm . . ." Her jaw dropped. "No way. No *way*."

Kate's stomach pitched as she anticipated what was coming.

"You're Jon Ramsey!" The girl practically screamed it. "You're freakin' Jon Ramsey! I own all your movies! I can't freakin' believe this!"

Kate glanced at Jon. He shrugged as if to say there was no help for it. Kate decided he was right. This girl was a loyal fan, and trying to lie his way out wouldn't be right.

Jon stepped forward. "What's your name?"

"Courtney." She began jumping up and down. "Courtney Spinelli! Omigod, omigod, omigod. I need you to autograph something, but I don't even have a pen. I didn't bring my purse. I just decided to come up and see the cats. Omigod, omigod! Can I take your picture?"

"Sure." Jon sounded cool as a blended margarita. "Listen, Courtney, could I ask you a big favor?"

"*Anything!* I'd do anything for you!"

"I'm here on vacation for a few days just to get away from everything, so if you could keep it to yourself about seeing me, I'd appreciate it."

Courtney winced. "I won't tell anyone, except . . ." She held up the cell phone. Wild screeching noises could be heard coming from it. "Except for Megan."

"You could tell Megan to keep it to herself, too," Jon said.

"I will. Right now." She held the phone to her ear. "Megan, you can't tell anybody about this. You . . . Oh no . . . you didn't . . . Oh, Megan, that's bad. That's very bad." Courtney glanced at Jon. "She just sent an e-mail blast to everyone in her address book. And she—she knows a lot of people."

"Then we need to leave now." Kate scooped Darwin into her arms and started back toward the B and B. Jon followed.

"I'm sorry!" Courtney called after them. "I got so excited! I love you, Jon!"

"That shout-out didn't help." Kate walked faster as she heard a front door opening. Then the motor of a car sounded behind them.

"She's probably fifteen, if that. It's not her fault. It's mine, for thinking I could walk around unrecognized."

"Oh my goodness! Megan was right!" Ahead of them, a woman hurried down her porch steps with her camera in her hand. She was breathing fast. "This is probably an imposition, but can I take your picture? Better yet, could she take a picture of me with you?"

"I'd love to," Jon said, "but I'm a little concerned that we'll have a mob scene in a minute if I stop."

Behind them, the car engine cut off and doors slammed. "Jon! Jon Ramsey!"

Jon turned. "Listen, I—"

Cameras clicked as at least five people emerged from the car.

"This is so cool," said a guy who looked to be a little older than Courtney. "Can we take a picture with you, man?"

"Not right this minute," Jon said. "But contact my Facebook page, okay? And I'm on Twitter. We can hook up that way." He grabbed Kate's elbow and propelled her down the street.

Panic wrapped icy fingers around her throat, cutting off her breath. She had flashbacks of being at the senior prom with Jon and the resulting media feeding frenzy.

"I'm sorry," he said. "I know how you hate this."

"No, you don't! You have no idea how much I hate this. Oh, Jon, they're coming from the other direction, too. We're trapped."

"Maybe not, dearies." Esmeralda appeared on the sidewalk in front of her pink house. "When the dust devil comes into my yard, duck into my place."

"Esmeralda?" Kate was surprised to see the woman appear so suddenly, and even more surprised by what she'd said. She scanned the area. I don't see a dust devil."

"It's right there." Esmeralda pointed to her neighbor's yard where a mini-tornado filled with dust and debris rose up as if by magic and headed toward them.

Jon grabbed Kate's arm. "Let's go."

As the dust devil obscured their retreat, Kate held tight to Darwin and ran up Esmeralda's walk. Jon wrenched open the front door and Kate dashed inside. Quickly following after her, Jon closed the door.

Darwin clung to Kate, his whole body rigid. She forced herself to relax. Leaning down, she rubbed the top of his head with her chin. "It's okay," she murmured. "Everything's okay."

Jon moved to a front window and peered out. "That's the most peculiar dust devil I've ever seen. It's just hovering around the front yard, except sometimes it moves toward the crowd. Usually dust devils sweep through and are gone."

Kate joined him at the window. "That is strange. Maybe it's a Bisbee dust devil, so therefore it's different."

"Maybe. But look at Esmeralda. She's standing there as if she's . . . No, that's stupid."

"What?"

"If I didn't know better, I'd say she's spinning her finger the same way the dust devil is turning, as if . . ."

"But that's impossible."

"Yeah, I know. My mind's playing tricks on me." He turned from the window and looked at Kate. "I'm so sorry. Going on the walk with you was dumb on my part."

"Or maybe it was for the best."

He looked into her eyes. "Kate, I—"

"Dust devils can come in very handy!" A slightly windblown Esmeralda came through the door. "Can I make you two a cup of tea?"

"Not for me, thanks." Jon glanced at her. "It's uncanny how that thing came out of nowhere and then hung around your yard."

"Nature is amazing." Esmeralda smiled. "Rash all cleared up?"

Kate felt the need to explain. "I was trying to protect Jon's identity," she said. "I hated making up stories, but he—"

"Is a famous movie star." Esmeralda looked him up and down. "I saw *Synchronicity* three times. You should have won the Oscar."

"Thank you. Maybe next time."

"I predict you will win one for your next film." Esmeralda walked toward her tiger-striped sofa. "Did Kate point out my camouflaged kitties?" She plucked a nearly invisible cat from the sofa and cuddled it against her ample breasts.

Jon surveyed the room. "Good God, they match the upholstery. Lucky I didn't try to sit down."

"Oh, they would have moved," Esmeralda said. "They're smart cats. And now I suppose you two would like to sneak out the back way and go home."

"Yes," Kate said. "Yes, please. But I've never walked

along the back side of the properties. Is there an obvious path?"

"Of course there is." Esmeralda chuckled. "Wherever you have kids there's a path behind the houses. Some of them like to come up the back way to see the crazy lady with all the cats. I do magic tricks for them, you see. Well, come along. I'll take you to the back door and point you in the right direction."

Esmeralda led them through her house, which was filled with the scent of incense and New Age music. Then she ushered them through the back door and into the yard, which contained a fire pit with a circle of stones around it.

"Nice fire pit," Jon said. "Do you cook over it?"

"Sometimes." At the back gate, Esmeralda scratched under Darwin's chin. "He's working out for you?"

"He's terrific," Kate said. "I wish he hadn't stopped to be petted by that young girl, because that's what started the ruckus, but I can't blame him for loving the attention."

Esmeralda gave Darwin a last scratch behind his ears. "Just remember that everything happens as it should."

"Thanks for everything, Esmeralda. And I will remember that." As Kate walked with Jon along a dirt path to the back of the B and B, she thought about what Esmeralda had said in parting—*everything happens as it should.*

Kate had been living in a dream world, thinking that she could have a temporary relationship with Jon and emerge in one piece. Darwin had helped wake her up.

Once they were back in the kitchen and she'd removed Darwin's harness, she turned to Jon. "We need to talk."

"I'll make coffee."

"That would be nice." She didn't want coffee, but she supposed it would give them something to focus on while they had what she perceived as a difficult discussion.

She could feel a storm coming outside, too, as if to mirror the tension inside. But the air was still and hot. She left the back door open so they could catch any breeze coming through the screen.

As Jon set the coffee mugs on the walnut kitchen table, Darwin claimed his perch on top of the refrigerator.

Kate sat across from Jon at the round table and cradled her coffee mug in both hands. "You probably think I overreacted out there."

"No. Well, maybe a little." Jon wrapped his hands around his warm mug. "It's never nice to be taken by surprise. But Kate, it doesn't have to be like that. I usually manage my public appearances so they don't get out of hand. I had the bad judgment to be spontaneous. That was a mistake, and I apologize."

Kate left her coffee untouched as she gazed at him across the small table. "Now that you've been spotted here, you'll have to leave, won't you?"

"I'm afraid so. The word will make its way to the media pretty quick." He hesitated. "Come with me."

"Jon, I can't."

"Sure, you can. Close up the B and B for the rest of the week. It's not as if you'd be losing business for Maggie. And you can bring Darwin. We'll buy him a soft-sided carrier and take him on the plane. I can call now and my jet will be waiting for us at Tucson International."

Dear God, he was serious. "It's not the B and B or Darwin I'm worried about. It's me. I can't go with you. Or maybe I should say I *won't*."

He reached for her hand and sandwiched it between both of his. "Kate, please don't freak out on me because of this incident today. I think we have something special between us. I'd like to explore that and see where it leads."

His hands felt so warm and reassuring. She wanted to weep. "Being here together was great, but it's not the way you live. What just happened is more normal for you, and it's—it's not the way I want to live. I had enough of it as a child, and you know that."

"Hey, I'm hardly ever forced to duck into a cat shelter under cover of a dust devil." He smiled as he caressed her warm palm with his thumb.

She braced herself, unwilling to be charmed into a decision that would be so wrong for her. "Maybe not, but you'll have to admit that crowd control is a constant problem."

"It's an issue, but don't judge my situation based on what happened this morning. My team is amazing. With the right precautions, you'd hardly ever have that kind of situation. I was stupid, and I take all the blame for that mismanaged fustercluck."

"You don't get it. I don't want my life to be managed by a team of experts." Kate swallowed a lump of sorrow and soldiered on. "Esmeralda told me to remember that everything happens as it should. She's right.

I needed something like this to happen before"—she looked into his eyes—"before it's too late."

His grip tightened. "I think it's already too late. It was probably too late the minute I walked into this B and B and realized . . ." His green eyes glowed with purpose. "Please come to LA with me. Let me show you that fame doesn't have to be the monster you imagine. Look at stars such as Paul Newman and Joanne Woodward. For that matter, look at my grandfather."

"Those are the exceptions. You were lucky to have a grandfather like Trevor Ramsey. My sisters and I weren't so lucky." She shivered. "You can't imagine the hell of walking past a magazine rack and seeing a picture of your haggard-looking father staring back at you with the headline 'Ben Back in Rehab.'"

Jon's voice was soothing. "You're right. I don't know how that feels. I'm the living proof that it doesn't have to be that way. And you're not eighteen anymore. You can deal with a little public attention, especially if it's not negative. I know you can."

She pulled her hand away. "But I don't want to, Jon! I escaped from that life, and I never want to go back. Never."

He gazed at her for several long seconds. "Not even to be with me?"

She couldn't make herself say the word, but her silence was answer enough.

"Okay, then. I guess that's it." He shoved back his chair and stood. "I might as well pack up and get out of here if you won't even . . . Damn it, Kate! Couldn't you just try? Couldn't you at least give us a chance?"

"And have my picture show up in the tabloids

every other week? It'll probably be there after what happened this morning, won't it?"

He opened his mouth as if to deny it, then closed it again. "Maybe," he said at last. "Yeah, maybe. But so what? Who cares about the tabloids? Are you going to let that keep us from being together, when what we have is so amazing?"

Her throat was tight with unshed tears. She hated hearing the agony in his voice, hated seeing the pain in his eyes. But she had no words of comfort for him. "I'm sorry, Jon. I shudder every time I think of being in a fishbowl again. It won't work between us."

"Because you won't let it." Blowing out a breath, he turned and left the kitchen.

Numb with sorrow, Kate sat at the table listening to him slam and bang around upstairs. This moment would have come eventually, she realized—if not now, then at the end of the week. Yes, they were falling back into love with each other. They both knew that, but nothing had changed since high school. They still wanted completely different lives.

When she heard him coming down the stairs, she walked out of the kitchen and down the hall. She'd dig deep and find the courage to say good-bye with grace and dignity.

Jon stared at her, his hands shoved into the pockets of his shorts.

"I'm sorry your vacation didn't work out the way you'd hoped," she said.

"It had its good points."

"Take care of yourself, Jon."

"I will. Say good-bye to Darwin."

"Do you want me to go get him?"

Jon shook his head. "Don't disturb him." He picked up his suitcase. "Good-bye, Kate." As he opened the front door, the wind caught it, slamming it against the stopper with a loud thump.

"I guess the storm's finally coming," she said.

"I guess." Another gust blew in and barreled through the house.

"Listen, you'd better head out before—" The back screen door banged once, twice. A second later Kate realized what that could mean. "Omigod. Darwin." She raced back toward the kitchen.

The top of the refrigerator was empty. "Darwin?" She spun around. "Darwin, where are you?"

Running to the door, she saw a black and silver blur streaking across the yard. "He's out!" As she bounded down the steps, lightning crackled overhead followed by a boom as it hit somewhere nearby. Rain pelted her with fat, heavy drops.

"Where is he?" Jon joined her at the foot of the steps.

Kate scanned the backyard. "I don't know. But you can leave. I'll handle this."

"No, *we'll* handle this."

"But the paparazzi—"

"Sure as hell aren't coming out in weather like this. Come on. Let's find that cat."

Chapter 8

"Thanks, Jon." Kate appreciated his presence more than he probably realized. Knowing he was there helped ease the dread that had settled in the pit of her stomach.

She stood still and forced herself not to run frantically around the yard yelling Darwin's name. That sort of tactic wouldn't work for a cat. "Keep looking and calling softly," she said. "I'm going to see if Maggie has a can of tuna."

"She does. Middle shelf of the pantry."

"Then maybe you should get it. You know that kitchen way better than I do."

"Okay. Be right back." He sprinted up the steps.

"Darwin," Kate called. "Here, kitty, kitty, kitty." She walked slowly around the yard and tried to think like a cat. Thunder rolled through the clouds and lightning streaked across the horizon. She supposed this wasn't the brightest idea in the world, to be out during a lightning storm, but she had no choice.

She was the genius who'd decided to leave the back door open to invite a breeze into the kitchen. In her angst-ridden state over Jon, she'd forgotten that the screen didn't latch unless given an extra tug. Now Darwin was out and hiding somewhere, probably terrified by the thunder, but she would by God find him if it took all night.

The yard was unfenced because Maggie liked it that way. A fence wouldn't have been a deterrent, anyway, with an athletic cat like Darwin.

The boundary of the yard was marked by a series of reddish lava boulders. Beyond that, the scrub brush and junipers were interspersed with areas of prickly pear and yucca. It was wild out there, home to jackrabbits, rattlesnakes, and coyotes. No place for a house cat.

Kate prayed that Darwin hadn't run beyond the boulders. The rain was falling more heavily, which might keep him in the yard. Most cats didn't like to venture out in the rain. They sought shelter such as— such as in a tree! There was only one tree nearby, a large oak that grew close to the house, so close that one branch arched over the building's roof.

As Kate walked toward the tree, her flip-flops squished through the grass. Her T-shirt and shorts were soaked, and rain dripped from her hair and her eyelashes. It didn't matter.

Peering up into the branches of the tree, she thought she saw something. She scooped her wet hair back from her face and looked again. "Darwin?"

He stared down at her from a branch at least fifteen feet from the ground. He looked more regal than scared, but she knew appearances could be deceiving.

Jon arrived with an open can of tuna.

"He's up there." Kate pointed to the branch where Darwin rested like a miniature white tiger. "I'll take the tuna if you'll go into Maggie's storage shed and get her extension ladder."

Jon handed her the tuna without argument, which she found fairly remarkable. Most men she'd known would have attempted to take charge of the rescue.

Holding the tuna, she tried to coax Darwin down from the tree. His nose twitched, which meant he could smell it. He crept back along the branch and peered down, but the descent seemed to intimidate him. He returned to his branch.

"I have the ladder." Jon propped it against the tree trunk with a clang of metal parts. He was soaked, too, and his T-shirt was almost transparent. But he didn't utter a word of complaint. "I'll go up."

"I can."

"I know you can, but I work out all the time back in LA. Muscles are required for my job. Let me do this."

She acknowledged he was probably right, that he'd have a better chance of making it down with the cat than she would. "Take the tuna, then." She handed him the can.

As he climbed, tuna in his right hand, she thought about his relaxing vacation. She'd certainly done her part to make a hash of it. If she'd adopted Darwin at the end of the week as any sane person would have, they wouldn't have had the incident with his fans. Instead of planning to leave, he would have been making love to her while rain fell on the tin roof.

Her decision to adopt Darwin had resulted in Jon's being exposed to the elements and getting drenched while he tried to entice the cat back into the house. He could rightly have refused to be part of this rescue.

But that wasn't Jon. She still had a vivid memory of the day on the playground when a group of kids had been making fun of her parents. Jon had stepped in and helped her face them down.

In order to check out Jon's progress, she had to keep wiping the rain out of her eyes. He made it to the branch, held out the can of tuna . . . and dropped it, dumping the contents all over the ground. That was when she learned the full extent of his vocabulary. It was more colorful than she would have imagined.

"Don't worry." She sank to her knees on the muddy ground. "I'll pick it up and bring it to you." She wasn't sure how much tuna she could retrieve or how muddy it would be, but even a little bit should do the trick.

"Never mind. I think I can get a hold on him, and . . . *Shit*. Come back here, cat!"

She looked up in time to watch Darwin scampering toward the end of the branch and leaping onto the roof. It was wet and he slipped a little, but then he crouched there, in the pelting rain, and glared at Jon.

Jon climbed from the ladder into the tree and moved carefully along the branch Darwin had used. "I guess we'll have to do this the hard way, cat."

Kate gulped back hysterical laughter. So far the rescue hadn't been what she'd call easy. "I really think tuna will help," she said.

"Don't worry about it," he called down.

But she was worried, and she saw no choice but to climb the ladder and bring it to him. She didn't feel secure climbing the slippery ladder one-handed with the tuna as he had, but her exercise shorts had no pockets.

Finally she pulled up her shirt and wedged the can in her cleavage before pulling the shirt down over her bra again.

"What was it Esmeralda said?" Jon paused on the branch and surveyed the situation. "That her cats are smart?"

Kate kicked off her flip-flops and mounted the ladder. "She said something like that, yes."

"I beg to differ. This cat doesn't have enough sense to come in out of the rain." With that, Jon dropped to the roof.

Kate held her breath as he slipped around a bit before grabbing a ridged section and hanging on. She really didn't want to add a fall from the roof and broken body parts to her sins against him.

He inched toward Darwin as Kate climbed from the ladder to the tree. Following Jon's lead, she edged out on the branch and inched along it toward the roof.

"I'm here," she said as she sat poised above the roof. "I have tuna."

Jon was still a good six feet away from Darwin, but at least Darwin hadn't moved. Jon glanced at Kate in startled surprise. "I thought you were still on the ground. What the hell are you doing in the tree?"

"Bringing you the tuna!"

"Where is it?"

"Stuck between my boobs. Where else?"

His answering snort could have been laughter or disbelief. She wasn't sure which, and she'd rather not know. They were equally distasteful after she'd made the supreme effort to get up here.

"Whatever you do," he said, "don't drop onto the roof. It's extremely slippery."

"But how can I transfer the tuna?"

"Forget the tuna!"

Something about that comment hit her wrong, and she decided to deliver the tuna whether he thought it was a good idea or not. As she'd said earlier today, he wasn't the boss of her. "I'm coming down."

"Damn it all, Kate! This day has been bad enough. Don't top it off by breaking something vital."

She tested the branch and determined the best spot to land. "Hey, it hasn't been all bad. You got your rain on the roof."

"This is not exactly the way I had planned to enjoy it."

"Yeah, I know. Me, either." She wondered if she'd ever make love to the music of rain on galvanized tin—probably not because it would remind her of an aborted fantasy with Jon. She let go of the branch and slid onto the roof, which was still surprisingly warm, even after the rain. Unfortunately, she kept sliding.

Muttering a pithy swear word, Jon grabbed the back of her T-shirt. It ripped at first, but then it held.

With her downward slide halted and his grip tight, she managed to creep slowly up to where he lay panting, his eyes closed.

"You could have killed yourself," he said.

"I doubt it. I've paddled a canoe down the—"

"*I know about the stupid canoe, God damn it*, but I wasn't there to see you and hyperventilate while you risked your life." Opening his eyes, he turned his head to look at her. "Hearing about something over a glass of wine and actually witnessing someone's reckless behavior are two different things."

"I'm not any more reckless than you are." Rain pattered on her face. "You did it."

"Because I'm a trained professional! I do lots of my own stunts!"

"Well, I'm a trained . . . primatologist."

"God help us."

"I really do have the tuna."

"In your cleavage."

"Yeah."

With a sigh of resignation, he carefully turned on his side. "As long as you brought it, we might as well see if it helps."

"Right." She pulled up her shirt and extracted the tuna. "I'm going to need a shower after this."

"You know what? I must be deranged. Your lifting up that wet T-shirt and pulling a tuna can out of your bra is one of the sexiest moves I've ever seen, either on-screen or off."

She gazed at him through the drips coming off her hair and eyelashes. His hair was plastered to his head, which might not be her favorite style on him, but the rain had molded his clothes to his body so that every muscle was lovingly defined. "Now that you mention it, wet looks mighty fine on you, too."

"Look, you can't kick me to the curb and then say stuff like that. It's not nice."

"Sorry. And I didn't kick you to the curb. I just—"

"Forget it. Let's finish this cat job." He turned toward Darwin. "Hey, sport, want some tuna?"

Darwin sniffed the air and eased forward, obviously

tempted, but it was a tedious process—a very wet process. Darwin looked skinny and miserable with his coat plastered to his body by the rain.

"How do you like our odds of being struck by lightning while lying on a tin roof in a thunderstorm?" Jon asked conversationally.

"Oh, I think the odds are excellent."

"Yeah, me, too. Hey, Darwin, could you move a little faster over here, buddy?"

Darwin eased closer, and closer yet. Kate sighed with relief when the cat finally put his dripping nose in the tuna can.

Jon closed his hand over the scruff of Darwin's neck. "Gotcha."

"Now you have to let go of me."

"Not until you can promise you won't slide down the roof."

"I won't. My shorts are all bunched up under me. They'll slow me down, I think."

Jon glanced at her. "That's good, because the shirt isn't much use anymore. Every time you move, it rips again. It's about to come off you."

She discovered he was right—the shirt no longer covered much.

He chuckled. Gradually his chuckle turned to laughter until finally he was gasping from the effort to stop.

"What's so damned funny, Ramsey?"

He gulped for air. "Do you realize this is a classic good news/bad news situation?"

"No."

"The good news is we're lying together listening to rain on a tin roof. The bad news is we're lying on the tin roof instead of under it. It suddenly struck me as hysterically funny."

"You are just strange, Jon." *Strange and wonderful. And I am so in love with you, which bites.* But she couldn't spend time agonizing about that now. "I have an idea. I'll climb down by using the tree limb, and then I'll get the ladder and lean it against the side of the house."

"Brilliant. If only I'd thought of that when he made a run for it."

"If only I'd thought of that when you followed him. But I thought of it now. Stay here and I'll be right back."

Moving carefully along the roof and using her soggy shorts as a brake against any sliding, she made it to the tree branch. Thanks to good conditioning and a dare-devil nature, she was able to swing up to the branch and then work her way back to the trunk and the ladder. Her shirt caught on the branches, and when necessary, she ripped it free. It was in tatters by the time she reached the ladder, and her palms were skinned, but she didn't care about any of that.

She descended the ladder as fast as she dared, hoisted it with both hands, and positioned it at the point of the eaves below Jon and Darwin. "Your ladder awaits, m'lord!"

"I see it! Just hold it steady. We're coming down."

Tinny, scraping sounds followed, and then the soles of his shoes appeared at the top of the ladder. Kate kept waiting for Darwin's yowl of protest, but Jon's grip on his neck must have put the cat into kitten mode. Darwin hung like a wet rag from Jon's outstretched fist as the two of them came slowly down.

"Here." Jon handed Darwin to her.

Instead of cradling him, she took the same hold on the scruff of his neck.

"Got him?"

"Yes."

"Go ahead and take him in. I'll put away the ladder."

She didn't argue. Darwin was shivering, probably from fear as well as from being wet and cold. She hurried into the house and went straight to her bathroom, where she grabbed a fluffy bath towel and wrapped the wet cat in it. Then she sat on the closed toilet lid and began drying him off.

"You are almost more trouble than you're worth, cat," she murmured.

Darwin began to purr.

As she listened to his contented sounds, she was filled with gratitude toward Jon for helping keep her cat safe. "We owe Jon a lot, Darwin. We have to find some way to thank him."

Chapter 9

Jon made it to Kate's bathroom doorway in time to hear her last comment. "I can imagine several ways you could thank me."

She glanced up, and the warmth in her eyes was promising. "Is that right?"

"Uh-huh." He really did like the way she was gazing at him. Her expression was extremely friendly. He might be down, but he sure as hell wasn't out. And she'd said he looked good wet. Well, he had all sorts of wet going on now. He was dripping like a sprinkler system. "How is Darwin?"

"He's purring. I'd say that's a good sign."

"A very good sign. By the way, the ladder's in the shed and the back door is closed and locked."

She took a deep breath. "You've been wonderful."

He'd take that. "Just so you know, it's still raining."

She picked right up on that. "I know, and those winding roads can be slippery. You might want to wait until it stops before you leave."

"I was thinking that, myself. Also if it's a bad time to drive out, it's a bad time to drive in. I'm not expecting any media types until after the storm lets up."

Her eyebrows lifted. "So . . ."

He surveyed her tattered shirt and her wet bra, which was completely transparent. "So . . ."

"I guess we need a plan." Apparently she'd been rubbing Darwin too vigorously, because he growled in protest and scrambled out of her lap. Once on the bathroom floor, he began grooming himself.

"Actually, I have a plan." Jon's groin stirred in anticipation. "Stay right there. I'll be back." As he hurried out to the hallway and unzipped his suitcase, he wondered if she'd resent his telling her to stay there. She didn't like being ordered around, and he'd be wise to remember that. She needed to be wooed.

Condoms tucked in his shorts pocket, he went back to the bathroom and discovered the door was closed. *Damn.*

"Kate?" He rapped softly. "You in there?"

"Yep."

"Are you coming out?"

"Yep." When she opened the door, she was wearing a white terry robe and a smile.

If there was a God, the robe and the smile would be the only two things she was wearing. Jon's body reacted instantly to that possibility.

She lifted her gaze to his. "Now, if you'd care to tell me how best to thank you for helping me save Darwin . . ." She let the sentence dangle suggestively.

Hallelujah. He hadn't ruined everything by giving her a direct order. "I'd much rather show you." He'd always been grateful for the abilities he'd gained through acting, but never more so than now.

Not every guy was capable of scooping a woman into his arms and carrying her up a flight of stairs, but he was. She screeched when he first picked her up, though.

"Jon!" She wiggled as if to get away. "You don't have to carry me!"

"Sure I do. Stop struggling."

"Is this some sort of macho thing?"

"Absolutely." He carried her through the kitchen and down the hall. "In monkey terms, it's the equivalent of beating my chest and roaring."

"You're insane."

"No, I'm trying to impress the hell out of you."

"I'm already impressed. You can put me down."

"You're not impressed enough." He climbed the stairs. "If you were, you'd come to LA with me."

"Oh, Jon." She rested her head against his shoulder. "You don't know what you're asking."

"You don't know what you're rejecting. But I plan to stage a demonstration."

Striding down the hall and into his room, he held her over the mattress. After carrying her all the way there without dropping her or banging any part of her against a door frame, he miscalculated the distance down to the bed and let her go a little early. She bounced on the quilt, which made her laugh.

"I love kissing you when you laugh." Following her down, he pulled open her robe and discovered a very naked Kate underneath. *Jackpot*.

As he worked her completely out of the robe, he kissed her thoroughly, letting his tongue convey in no uncertain terms what he had in mind as the grand finale. Then he quickly tore off his wet clothes and started kissing the rest of her.

She sighed with pleasure. "That's . . . That's lovely."

"Here?"

"Yes, oh, yes."

"How about here?"

She moaned and shifted to give him greater access.

"Listen to the rain," he murmured against her skin.

"I hear it."

"It's like a steel drum band."

"Mmm."

He wasn't sure if that was a comment on the rain or on his tongue circling her nipple. "Come home with me. I'll take you to Jamaica and we'll make love on the beach."

"Ahhh." She lifted her hips as he moved slowly down her body.

Now the rain tinkled like the tiny finger cymbals played by a belly dancer. "I'll take you to India, wrap you in silk, and then peel it away."

Her moans of pleasure blended with the rain as he settled between her thighs and used his tongue to drive her slightly crazy, but not too crazy. He wanted to be deep inside her when she came. He wanted to be looking into her eyes.

Dreams of a lifetime of loving her swirled in his head as he licked and nibbled his way back to her mouth. "I could show you the world, Kate."

"You're . . ." She gulped for air. "You're a devil, Jon Ramsey. Tempting me with a . . . devil's bargain."

"Ah, but we make love like angels." Reaching for a condom, he eased back on his heels and held her gaze as he rolled it on. He moved deliberately, keeping eye contact as he braced his hands on either side of her and knelt between her thighs.

She reached up and cupped his face in both hands. "I do love making love to you."

"That's a start." And he thrust deep.

Her eyes darkened. "You feel . . . perfect there."

"That's what I'm saying." He eased back and pushed in tight again. "We belong together. Like this."

"But we can't—"

"Expand your mind. You might be surprised what we can do." He began a slow, steady rhythm. "Something this great . . . doesn't come along every day." He shifted his angle slightly and zeroed in on her G-spot.

She gasped with pleasure.

"Good?"

"You know it is. You know exactly what you're doing."

"I do," he murmured. "I'm loving you." And he gave it everything he had.

Her climax lifted her inches off the bed, and she cried out his name. He followed soon after, his body shuddering in the grip of an orgasm that obliterated any memory of other women. He needed Kate and only Kate.

As the world slowly stopped spinning, he drew a shaky breath and combed her damp hair back from her face. "Here's the thing. I'm in love with you."

Moisture glistened in her dark eyes. "I'm in love with you, too."

Joy filled his heart.

"But—"

His joy began to leak away. "I've learned that the real truth comes after that nasty little word."

"I love you, but it's not enough."

He closed his eyes so she wouldn't see how deeply she'd wounded him. "Okay." He drew another steadying breath. "Okay. I gave it my best shot."

He rolled away from her and climbed from the bed. "The rain seems to have stopped. I'll be on my way."

In the misery-laden hours and days that followed, Kate would have loved to pack up her cat and take the road out of Bisbee, too. Everything about the place was a reminder of Jon, and each memory twisted the knife in her heart.

But it turned out she was a prisoner in the B and B. Jon had left just in time. He'd been gone about two hours when the first phone call came from a reporter in Hollywood.

Thinking it might be something to do with Jon, she'd picked up. But she'd quickly realized the person wanted a story about Jon and his new girlfriend, who was reportedly Kate Archer, daughter of Benjamin Archer, the late Hollywood star. Was Kate there? Was the Hummingbird Inn their love nest? She'd hung up.

Eventually she'd unplugged the phone to end its constant ringing. Then she'd had to turn off her cell phone. By the next morning the reporters had begun ringing the doorbell, and she'd finally called the Cochise County sheriff's office for some help.

The deputy had warned away the media folks, but Kate still didn't feel comfortable leaving the B and B. Fortunately, Esmeralda came by with a couple of casseroles, so she had enough food to last her until Maggie came home. Esmeralda also tried to explain to Kate that Darwin's magical presence had created situations that would ultimately bring Kate and Jon together. Kate listened politely, but privately she concluded that poor Esmeralda was delusional.

Prior to Maggie's arrival, Kate turned on her phone long enough to send her sister a text with the basic information in it. She wanted Maggie to be prepared in case she was waylaid on her way in. By a stroke of luck, on the afternoon Maggie parked her truck next to Kate's hybrid, no one was watching the B and B. Kate chanced running out to help Maggie in with her bags.

Maggie looked more tanned but not much happier than Kate. She waved a tabloid as she climbed out of the truck. "After your text message, I looked for this in the grocery store when I stopped for coffee. Have you seen it?"

"Nope." Grabbing the newspaper without looking at it, Kate took Maggie's carry-on. "Let's get inside before somebody shows up with a camera or a microphone." She hustled Maggie up the steps and into the parlor. Then she closed and locked the front door.

"Whew." Maggie put down her suitcase. "That'll teach me to leave for a week."

"Maggie, I'm sorry." Kate gazed at her sister. "I know Jon was a valuable customer, and I don't think he'll ever be able to stay here again."

"Are you kidding? Who cares? You and Jon have put the Hummingbird Inn on the map. I'll bet you've been swamped with calls requesting reservations."

Kate groaned. "I don't know. The reporters were

driving me nuts, so I turned off the phone. I probably lost you a bunch of business, but I—"

"I'm sure you didn't. Not being able to get in touch by phone will confirm that the Hummingbird Inn is one exclusive destination. I'll guarantee that when I check the Web site, we'll have people clamoring to stay here."

Kate felt marginally better. "I hope you're right."

"I am. Business will boom, so don't worry about that. But I'm sure this has been traumatic for you, and I feel responsible."

"Maggie, it's not your fault."

"It's sort of my fault, and it would ease my guilt if we shared a bottle of wine. Let's leave my suitcase right here and open the special red I tucked away for emergencies. I think this qualifies."

"Sounds like a fabulous idea." Still holding the tabloid, Kate headed for the kitchen. "What about your trip? Was it good?"

"No. Ted is cheap and he flirts with other women constantly. Who knew?" Maggie paused in the kitchen doorway as Darwin leaped down from the top of the refrigerator and strolled over to greet her. "This must be the famous kitty."

"That's Darwin. He came from the shelter down the street, the one that put the flyers on our windshields." It seemed years ago that Kate had looked at that flyer and decided to pay Cupid Cats a visit.

"Hello, Darwin. You have the perfect name, did you know that?" Maggie crouched down and gave Darwin a good scratch down his spine. He arched his back in obvious delight.

"According to the woman who runs the shelter, this cat is magical."

"Oh?" Maggie glanced up. "How so?"

"She says he's somehow influenced the chain of events, and it will ultimately turn out well for Jon and me."

"Sounds as if a Bisbee flake runs the shelter."

"I'm afraid so. I don't see how any of this could be a good thing, except for my adopting Darwin."

"He is gorgeous." Rising to her feet, Maggie walked over to a deep cupboard and pulled out a bottle of red wine from the very back. Then she handed it to Kate and reached for a couple of glasses. "Those eyes are amazing. I don't blame you for bringing him home."

"I'm not sorry I did." Kate twisted the corkscrew in and levered the cork out of the bottle. "But regardless of what the shelter lady thinks, he's caused me a fair amount of trouble."

Maggie put the glasses on the counter. "Pour the wine, and then we'll talk."

In moments they were seated at the kitchen table, their glasses in front of them and the bottle between them. The moment for looking at the tabloid spread had come. But before Kate faced it, she raised her glass to Maggie's. "To the Archer sisters."

"To the Archer sisters. Three tough broads." Maggie clicked her glass to Kate's and drank.

"Amen to that." Once Kate had taken a hefty swallow of her wine, she flipped the tabloid over.

"It could've been worse," Maggie said.

"Yes, it certainly could have." Kate gazed at a grainy picture of Jon standing on the sidewalk, gazing at her with obvious interest. She was looking right back at him with similar absorption. Darwin's head was down, so he'd probably been munching on a tuft of grass at the time.

The three-inch headline read CAT GOT THEIR TONGUES? A line in smaller type announced HIGH SCHOOL SWEET-HEART MONKEYING AROUND WITH JON. Kate scanned the story, which identified her as a primatologist working at the U of A in Tucson. Her parents were both mentioned, and on the inside pages were pictures of her and Jon during their infamous fight at the prom.

"So what happened?" Maggie asked gently.

Tears threatened, and Kate blinked them back. She thought of a million ways to explain, but in the end it all came down to one thing. "Bottom line, I still love him."

"And he took advantage of that, didn't he? That slimeball! I'll boycott his movies. I'll find a picture of him at fourteen when he had zits, and I'll put it on the Internet. I'll—"

"No, Maggie." Kate took a gulp of wine. "He didn't take advantage of me. He still loves me, too."

"He does?" Maggie stared at her across the table. "So why is he back in LA and you're here drinking wine with me?"

"Because I don't want to be shoved into the spotlight again!"

Maggie held up the tabloid. "Too late, babe."

"Right! One brush with Jon Ramsey and I'm plastered all over the gossip rags. Reporters have pestered me for days trying to get a story. It's my worst nightmare."

"Is it?" Maggie turned the newspaper around to look at the front cover. "Forgive me for saying so, but this is a sweet picture of you two. You look happy. You have a cute little cat on a leash. Neither of you is half naked or shockingly overweight or high on some illegal substance. As tabloid pictures go, this one is fairly innocent."

"Innocent or not, that picture is everywhere. All over the country, probably all over the world by now. I really, really hate that."

"Yeah, I see your point." Maggie tossed the paper down on the table. "Sure, Jon Ramsey is one of the hottest men on the planet and richer than God. He's also—and I know this because he's stayed here twice—fun to be around and a terrific cook. He's a little full of himself sometimes, but considering his level of success, he's actually quite modest."

Kate remembered his macho trick of carrying her up the stairs to bed. "Sometimes he's a show-off."

"Well, duh. He's an *entertainer*. Showing off is how he makes all that lovely money."

"Exactly, Maggie, which means he enjoys being in the public eye. I, on the other hand—"

"Oh, you're so right to reject him. Rich, handsome, and fun mean nothing if you have to put up with people taking your picture all the time. What a drag. Besides, I'll bet he's lousy in bed. Those pretty boys often are." Maggie paused and gazed at Kate expectantly.

"Maggie, that's beside the point."

"Beside the point? What have you been smokin'? Good sex is never beside the point. Sometimes it's the whole point!"

Kate sighed. "He's great in bed, okay?"

"Great in bed? Damn, girl!" Maggie flung the tabloid into the air. "I just got off the boat with the biggest loser known to womankind, so if you don't want Jon, maybe I can interest him in a substitute Archer sister."

Kate stared at her in disbelief.

"Don't look like that. I'm kidding. There's no chemistry between Jon and me, more's the pity. Apparently he's always had a thing for you, though, and I would hate to see you pass up the love of your life."

"But—but I thought all three of us took an oath never to get involved with anyone from Hollywood. I thought—"

"Number one, we took that oath at least ten years ago, and number two, I've had the privilege of getting reacquainted with Jon, and I think he's terrific. If he loves you and you love him, and you don't grab him and hang on for dear life, then you're one taco short of a combo plate."

Kate received that message in stunned silence.

"Look, you said you love him."

Her chest felt tight and her pulse rate kicked up a notch. "I do."

"And he loves you."

"That's what he said."

"From what I know of Jon, he wouldn't say that unless he meant it." Maggie gazed at the top of the refrigerator where Darwin had taken up residence. "I'm not admitting your cat has magical powers, but taking him for a walk did bring this issue to a head."

"I suppose."

"Are you really going to let an old fear keep you from the man you love? The man who loves you?"

Kate's heart thudded painfully in her chest. "Sounds pretty stupid, doesn't it?"

"Your words, not mine, but . . . yeah."

"So what—what do you think I should do?"

"Get to LA as fast as you can and apologize for being an idiot. And if a bunch of people take your picture, smile."

Chapter 10

Wearing a tux shirt and slacks, Jon dragged himself out of the surf for what seemed like the hundredth time. The scene called for him to leap from a yacht and swim to shore. The leaping and swimming part were in the can, but the director wasn't satisfied with the shot as Jon came out of the water.

Jon figured it shouldn't matter as long as he looked wet.

And he was definitely that. He hadn't felt this soggy since the rescue mission to fetch Darwin off the roof. The minute he started thinking about his time in Bisbee, he brought his thoughts to a screeching halt and made an abrupt mental U-turn. He'd get nothing from sorting through that wreckage, especially when he was working and needed every creative instinct to be fully operative.

Thank God he was a pro who could compartmentalize or he wouldn't be able to function. Off the set, when he didn't have a script to follow and another persona to inhabit, he wasn't in very good shape. But here he did well, and he was thrilled to finally be back at work today. The tail end of his "vacation" had been hell. He'd rather shoot this scene twenty more times than go home to face his empty house.

The director's voice boomed out over the sand. "Cut! Nice job, Jon. That's a wrap."

With a sigh, Jon started back toward his trailer to get rid of his wet costume. Now that he was out of the water and in the sun, he was starting to steam—not quite the same as being in a thunderstorm with a cold wind blowing.

He had the rest of the day free, so he needed to schedule things to do. Stay busy; that was his motto. He might be wrecked inside, but he wasn't letting anyone know that. Maybe he'd work out, see if any of his friends were available for a game of racquetball. Tonight he'd watch a movie. He was on a Paul Newman kick this week.

Or he could drop by his grandfather's house for dinner. His mom and grandfather were always glad to see him—except he'd done that twice since coming home from Bisbee, and they were starting to get suspicious that something was wrong.

Something was, but Jon didn't want to talk about it. They'd asked him, very gently, about Kate, and he'd said that incident had been blown out of proportion. He and Kate were just friends. Fortunately, the media were losing interest in the story now that the two of them hadn't made any more appearances together.

Tracy, his assistant, hurried to meet him, a baseball cap on her short curls. As usual, her elfin face was animated. She was the perfect assistant—bright, enthusiastic, cute, and not his type at all.

She handed him a pair of flip-flops, and after he'd put them on she walked with him to the trailer. "Kate Archer's waiting for you inside."

He stopped walking. "What did you say?"

"Kate Archer. I guess you forgot to tell me she'd be visiting the set today."

Jon peered at Tracy, his brain stalled on "Kate Archer is waiting for you." "I didn't authorize it."

"Oh. Well, somebody did. She had a pass. It's okay, isn't it? I mean, you said you were friends."

"Yeah, it's okay." Jon walked faster. Kate was here. It made no sense unless . . . No, he wouldn't set himself up for getting kicked in the teeth again.

Tracy churned along beside him, kicking up little rooster tails of sand. "I offered her snacks and stuff, but she didn't want anything. I hope she brought a book, because she's been here for almost two hours. Everyone expected the shoot to be over sooner."

"Right." Jon tried to make his mind a blank. He would approach this meeting with no expectations. But what was she doing here? It was the last thing he'd expected of her.

"Are you going to want me to make lunch reservations? Or maybe for dinner?"

"Huh?"

"For you and Kate."

Jon almost laughed. Kate would go ballistic if he suggested the two of them patronize a hot spot for lunch or dinner. "Kate doesn't like being on display, so I don't think we'll need reservations anywhere."

"Let me know if that changes. I'm heading out."

"Thanks, Tracy. See you tomorrow." He'd started

up the trailer steps when he heard the familiar staccato sound of rapid-fire questions being directed at someone. For once he wasn't that someone.

He glanced off to his right where barricades cordoned off the set. During filming, fans often gathered beyond the barricades to catch a glimpse of the cast.

And there stood Kate, wearing a white halter dress and wedge sandals. With her oversized sunglasses and the trendy purse on her shoulder, she looked like the star she never wanted to be. On the other side of the barricade, fans brandished cameras and cell phones as they called out questions. A few waved autograph books.

Jon called to his assistant. When Tracy turned around, he jerked a thumb in Kate's direction. "Can you tell me what she's doing over there?"

Tracy followed the direction of his gaze. "Oh, wow. Maybe she got bored in the trailer. Go ahead and change your clothes. I'll handle it."

"No, let me handle it."

Tracy frowned. "Are you sure?"

"Yep."

"I thought you said she didn't like being on display?"

"She doesn't. She's just being nice." He went back down the steps and turned toward the barricade. Kate must have decided to wander and then been caught by the fans who often hung around the outskirts of a set. Paparazzi didn't frequent sets because security was tight and there were seldom any juicy stories to be had, but if word got out that Kate was here to see him, the pros would show up soon enough.

In his wet tux shirt and pants he felt like a walking sauna as he approached. He hadn't planned on seeing Kate again, but any fantasies he'd had on that score wouldn't have played out like this.

Once the fans noticed he was headed in their direction, they started calling out his name, which caused Kate to turn around. She shoved her sunglasses to the top of her head and faced him, squinting a little in the midday sun.

He told himself not to get his hopes up. She might have some reason for being here that had nothing to do with their relationship or their lack of a relationship. Maybe she wanted him to do a public service spot focused on saving the monkeys of the Amazon.

But he couldn't help noticing how gorgeous she looked in the halter dress. And he couldn't help loving her. He hadn't been able to stop doing that when she wasn't even present, so not loving her when she was standing right in front of him would be impossible.

He waved to the fans. "You'll have to excuse me for a minute. I need to talk to this lady."

A few people stopped asking questions, but others continued to shout them out.

He turned his back on the crowd. "Hi, Kate."

"Hi, Jon." She seemed a little breathless, but otherwise calm. "Wet seems to be your new look."

"Yeah, it does."

She smiled, although the smile trembled slightly at the corners. "I like it."

He had the feeling she was being brave under trying circumstances. He stepped closer and lowered his voice. "Look, I don't know why you're here, but we should go back to my trailer. All it takes is one phone call from somebody in this crowd and the media will be all over you."

"I'm sure you're right." She squared her shoulders and glanced around.

"You don't seem to understand. You're in LA now. It'll be way worse than what happened in Bisbee. You and I being seen together will start a feeding frenzy."

She took a deep breath. "Actually, I do understand perfectly well, which is why I need to ask you something before we leave these folks."

"You can ask me in the trailer." He took her arm.

She resisted his attempt to steer her away. "For demonstration purposes, I need to ask you now. And you're not—"

"The boss of you. I know that, but—"

"Jon, do you still want to be with me?"

He stared at her in total incomprehension. "What?"

"You. Me. Us. Are you still interested?"

"This is really the sort of conversation best held in the privacy of my trailer."

"Is it because you don't want to embarrass me by rejecting me in front of these people?"

He ran a hand over his face. "Kate, are you okay? Because this isn't sounding like you at all." He realized the fans had gone completely silent as if they didn't want to miss a word.

"Yes, I know." Her voice grew stronger. "That's on purpose. I'm trying to show you something."

"That's fine, but could we take this party somewhere else? Please?"

"After you give me an answer. Do you want me or not?"

He kept his voice low. "Yes, I want you. But you don't want me, so what's this all about?"

"It's about my changing my mind and going public with it."

It took him a moment to absorb what she'd just said. Even then, he was afraid to believe, afraid he'd misunderstood. "You want to try living in my world after all?"

"Jon, if you remember your Yoda quotes, there is no *try*. There's only do or do not. I want to do." Then she leaned close and murmured in his ear. "You."

Blood pumped through his veins so fast he could swear he heard it rushing. He didn't know what had brought on this change of heart, but he wanted to take her somewhere private and find out. He tightened his grip on her arm. "Let's get out of here."

"So is that a yes?"

"Of course it's a yes. Let's go."

"Just a minute." She turned to the fans. "It's official. We're together. Okay, Jon. We can go now."

The fans cheered, but Jon didn't stop to acknowledge that as he propelled her back to the trailer as fast as her wedge-heeled sandals would allow. "Am I dreaming, or did you just make a public announcement about our relationship?"

"I told you I wanted to go public as part of my demonstration. Would you rather we issued a joint press release? I didn't mean to screw up any potential PR plan."

Tracy stood by the trailer steps looking concerned. "Anything I can do, Jon?"

"I'll let you know. Go on home, and I'll be in touch."

"Okay. The trailer's unlocked. Call me if you need anything."

"Thanks, Tracy."

"She's very nice," Kate said as they went up the trailer steps.

"She feels the same about you." Jon ushered Kate into the trailer before closing and locking the door. "Now, what in hell is happening here?"

She set her purse on a nearby counter. "I should think it would be obvious."

"Well, it's not. You'll have to spell it out for me."

"I can do that. I-L-O-V-E-Y-O-U."

"And loving me has sent you around the bend? Because the Kate I know wouldn't have been looking for a public forum where she could make announcements about her personal life. The Kate I know would be doing everything in her power to keep any and all personal info private."

"Then it's time for you to meet the new Kate." She stepped toward him and cupped his face in both hands. "You are the best thing that's ever happened to me, and I want to prove I can handle the spotlight."

He searched her expression and found nothing but sincerity there. "I'm still having a little trouble comprehending that you—"

"I knew you would. That's why I decided to talk to those fans, because I wanted to show you I'm working on my paranoia. It was a small step, but I'll get better at it. As you said, who cares about a few stupid tabloid pictures if it means you and I can be together?"

"I must be going around the bend, too, because this is starting to make sense. Wonderful, crazy sense."

"Then could you please give me a hug? In fact, I'd go for more than a hug."

He looked down at his clothes. "I'm sopping wet."

"As if I haven't dealt with that before." She slipped her arms around his waist and nestled against him as she tilted her face up to his. "I believe I've mentioned before that wet looks good on you."

He gave in and wrapped her in his arms. "Soon it'll be looking good on you, too." His clothes squished as he pulled her close, but holding her made his body happier than it had been since leaving Bisbee. "Where'd you stash your cat?"

"At my mom's. Incidentally, Esmeralda insists Darwin's a magical cat who helped orchestrate the whole chain of events leading up to this moment."

"I'm in the mood to believe in magic." How he'd craved the scent of her and the feel of her body tucked against his. "In any event, Darwin's been a significant player, and for that reason, I'm a big fan of your cat."

"I was hoping you'd start thinking of Darwin as *our* cat."

He realized that was a significant detail, and joy flooded through him. "You'd really share Darwin with me?"

"My cat's only the beginning of what I'll share with you, Jon Ramsey. Now kiss me."

"I intend to do a lot more than that." His lips hovered over hers. He'd waited years for this moment, and he wanted to savor it. "I hope you're not in a hurry."

"Take your time."

"A lifetime?"

She brushed her lips against his. "I think that can be arranged."

"It'll be a very private ceremony."

"Yeah, right, Ramsey." Then she kissed him with so much confidence that all his remaining doubts faded away. They would face whatever the future might hold . . . together.